THE DEVIL'S ELIXIRS

THE DEVIL'S ELIXIRS

E. T. A. HOFFMANN
Translated by Ronald Taylor

JOHN CALDER · LONDON

FIRST PUBLISHED IN GREAT BRITAIN IN 1963
BY JOHN CALDER (PUBLISHERS) LTD.
17 SACKVILLE STREET, LONDON, W.1.
© THIS TRANSLATION JOHN CALDER (PUBLISHERS) LTD. 1963

The line drawings are by Hellmuth Weissenborn

MADE AND PRINTED IN THE REPUBLIC OF IRELAND BY
ALEX THOM & CO. LTD., DUBLIN.

CONTENTS

INTRODUCTION

Among the intense, often contradictory passions released
by the Romantic movement in European literature at the
turn of the eighteenth century, was an obsession with the
hidden, apparently uncontrollable forces acting upon the
human mind, above all in moments of powerful mental
stress. It is with the portrayal of the grotesque, bizarre
forms of experience produced by such moments that the
name of E. T. A. Hoffmann has come to be primarily
associated. Hypnotism, somnambulism and telepathy are
the phenomena which fascinated him; delirium, persecution mania and schizophrenia are the mental states with
which he invested his characters; fright, fear and terror are
the emotions released by these forces and experiences. From
such elements his influence spread to writers as diverse as
Gérard de Nerval and Gogol, Dostoevsky and Edgar Allan
Poe; on such sources the librettists of Offenbach's best-
known opera drew; and chiefly for the literary progeny of
such interests he is remembered today.

But this is not the only, nor perhaps even the most important Hoffmann. For the last eight years of his life he was a much-respected judge at the *Kammergericht* in Berlin; he had been artistic director and producer at the Bamberg theatre and music-director to an operatic company in Leipzig and Dresden; he was a composer with nine operas, two masses, a symphony and a considerable quantity of choral, vocal and instrumental music to his name; above all he was a theorist and critic who has left a body of perceptive and stimulating writing, both in the form of music-reviews and of literary essays, on the aesthetics of music, its relationship to the other arts, and its focal significance as the centre of a Romantic metaphysic. Many of these writings are of considerable importance in the history of musical aesthetics, while composers of opera in particular, such as Wagner and Busoni, have acknowledged their indebtedness to him in matters of both principle and practice.

When his first story, *Ritter Gluck,* appeared in 1809, Hoffmann was thirty-three. In the thirteen years that were left to him he wrote over seventy literary works—novels, short stories, allegorical fantasies, essays—apart from a great deal of music and numerous music-reviews. This fecundity is the more striking in that at hardly any period of his life did he devote more than a fraction of his energy to creative artistic activity or preparation for it. The tardy emergence of his literary powers and the almost incidental nature of his literary success are due mainly to a stubborn and rather desperate belief, which stayed with him until within a few years of his death, that it was as a composer that he would make his mark on the world. Not until his final return to Berlin and to the service of the Prussian law-courts did he embark on his long series of popular spine-chilling stories.

Apart from works such as *Über alte und neue Kirchenmusik* (*On Church Music, Past and Present*) and *Der Dichter und der Komponist* (*The Poet and the Composer*), which are in reality critical essays set in a fictional narrative context, it is through his portraits of the artist in society that Hoffmann gave expression to that domination which music held over his mind. And with the very first of these portraits, *Johannes Kreislers, des Kapellmeisters musikalische Leiden* (*The Musical Agony of Kapellmeister Johannes Kreisler*) we make the acquaintance of that most complete creature of his fantastic imagination, that eccentric, disturbing, yet somehow pathetic spokesman for the artist in society—Kapellmeister Johannes Kreisler, the lone, unhappy figure who lurks behind the lines of so many of Hoffmann's stories, even those in which he does not appear by name, and who finally, in the unfinished masterpiece *Kater Murr* (*Murr the Tom-Cat*), stalks into the centre of the now completed scene and openly establishes himself as the supreme, all-absorbing symbol of his creator's thoughts and attitudes.

Part One of *Die Elixiere des Teufels* (*The Devil's Elixirs*) was written in 1814, Part Two the following year, and the whole work published in Berlin in 1816. With a characteristically fanciful gesture—he also employs it in *Kater Murr*—Hoffmann presents himself to the reader as merely the editor of an unpublished manuscript upon which he has chanced and to which he is therefore free to add his own glosses. Its aim, he wrote to a friend, was 'to reveal, through the strange, perverted life of a man who from his birth had been tossed to and fro by the forces of Heaven and Hell, those mysterious relationships between the human mind and the higher values enshrined in Nature, values whose meaning we glimpse in those rare moments of insight which we choose to call the products of Chance.' The work thus exists on two planes: the one carries the sequence of lurid adventures with which the story makes its initial impact, the 'strange, perverted life' of the monk Medardus, who renounces the monastery for the sinful pleasures of the

world and is led by the Devil into the depths of treachery
and lasciviousness, into incest and murder; the other bears
the complex of moral, psychological and mystical principles
which constituted for Hoffman the *raison d'être* of the whole
book, the 'mysterious relationships' which designate the
course of man's actions but of which he is at the time
unaware, and the 'higher values' from which derives, and
on which rests the central truths of human existence.

Many of the external trappings upon which Hoffmann
relies in the exposition of his story are the common property
of nineteenth-century German writers: the employment of
a fateful dagger, for instance, and strange chronological
coincidences between the lives of certain characters, recall
works such as Grillparzer's play *Die Ahnfrau* and the fate-
dramas of Zacharias Werner and Adolf Müllner. The
device of the *Doppelgänger* itself—the eerie wraith evoked
here by the schizophrenic mind under the stress of guilt
and persecution—had already been exploited, albeit in
terms almost trivial in comparison, by Jean Paul, and re-
appears in various forms in the work of Heine, Wilhelm
Hauff and others who had found stimulation in the discoveries of Mesmer and the pseudo-metaphysical specula-
tions of G. H. Schubert.

But Hoffmann's concern went far beyond the spectacular
presentation of a series of sensational events and coincidences. The course of Medardus' life is determined by the sins
of his forbears. Ironically, he thinks that by ridding himself
of the irksome restrictions of monastic life, he will find the
freedom in which to indulge to the full the earthly desires
welling up within him. Fate, however, has decreed otherwise: to him has fallen the charge of redeeming the sins
of his degenerate line, and after the vicious temptations and
wanton brutalities have run their course, salvation finally
comes with the transfiguration of his love for Aurelia in the
moment of her death. This is the deepest meaning of

Hoffmann's novel: Redemption through pure, transcendental Love—the Romantic doctrine proclaimed by German artists and philosophers from Schelling to Richard Wagner.

In the year 1824 a quaint and much shortened version of the story took its place among the many English translations from the German which were appearing at that period. It made little lasting impression, however, and not until now, so far as I am aware, has there been any further attempt to present it to English readers. The astonishing intricacies of the plot, and above all of the personal relationships within it, are the inevitable accompaniment to Hoffmann's insistence on identifying every overtone in the motivation of action, and the primary meaning is sometimes hidden in a flurry of subsidiary themes. In this translation, however, there has been no abridgment of the original text, and Hoffmann's novel is presented in its entirety as one of the most complex, most fascinating and most grotesque manifestations of the Romantic spirit.

RONALD TAYLOR

EDITOR'S PREFACE

(From the posthumous papers of Brother Medardus, a Capuchin Friar)

DEARLY would I take you, gentle reader, beneath those dark plane-trees where I first read the strange story of Brother Medardus. You would sit with me on the same stone bench half-hidden in fragrant bushes and bright flowers, and would gaze in deep yearning at the blue mountains whose mysterious forms tower up behind the sunlit valley which stretches out before us.

Then you would turn and see scarcely twenty paces behind us a Gothic building, its porch richly ornamented with statues. Through the dark branches of the plane-trees, paintings of the saints—the new frescoes in all their glory on the long wall—look straight at you with bright, living eyes. The sun glows on the mountain tops, the evening breeze rises, everywhere there is life and movement; strange voices whisper through the rustling trees and shrubs, swelling like the sound of chant and organ as they reach us from afar; solemn figures in broadly-folded robes walk silently through the embowered garden, their pious gaze fixed on the heavens: have the figures of the saints come to life and descended from their lofty cornices? The air throbs with the mystic thrill of the wonderful legends which the paintings portray, and willingly you believe that everything is really happening before your eyes. It is in such surroundings that you would read the story of Medardus, and you might come to consider the monk's strange visions to be more than just the caprice of an inflamed imagination.

Since, gentle reader, you have now seen the monks, their monastery, and paintings of the saints, I need hardly add that it is the glorious garden of the Capuchin monastery in B.* to which I have brought you.

* Bamberg (Transl.)

1

Once when I was staying at the monastery for a few days, the venerable prior showed me Brother Medardus' posthumous papers, which were preserved in the library as a curio. Only with difficulty did I overcome his objections to letting me see them; in fact, he considered that they should have been burned.

And so, gentle reader, it is not without fear that you may share the prior's opinion, that I place in your hands the book that has been fashioned from those papers. But if you decide to accompany Medardus through gloomy cloisters and cells, through the lurid episodes of his passage through the world, and to bear the horror, the fear, the madness, the ludicrous perversity of his life as if you were his faithful companion—then, maybe, you will derive some pleasure from those glimpses of a *camera obscura* which have been vouchsafed to you. It may even be that, as you look more closely, what seemed formless will become clear and precise; you will come to recognise the hidden seed which, born of a secret union, grows into a luxuriant plant and spreads forth in a thousand tendrils, until a single blossom, swelling to maturity, absorbs all the life-sap and kills the seed itself.

After I had with great diligence read through the papers of Medardus the Capuchin—which was extremely difficult because of his minute and barely legible monastic handwriting I came to feel that what we call simply dream and imagination might represent the secret thread that runs through our lives and links its varied facets; and that the man who thinks that, because he has perceived this, he has acquired the power to break the thread and challenge that mysterious force which rules us, is to be given up as lost.

Perhaps your experience, gentle reader, will be the same as mine. For the profoundest of reasons I sincerely hope that it may be so.

2

PART ONE

I—CHILDHOOD YEARS AND LIFE IN THE
MONASTERY

My mother never told me of the circumstances in which
my father lived, but when I call to mind the stories she
told about him in my childhood years, I cannot help
thinking that he must have been a man of great experience
and profound knowledge. From these stories, and from
various remarks which my mother made about her earlier
life and which I only later came to understand, I know
that my parents sank from a life of plenty to a state of the
most abject poverty. I learned too that my father had been
led by Satan to commit a heinous crime, a deadly sin.
When, in his old age, the grace of God shone upon him, it
became his desire to do penance by making a pilgrimage
to the shrine of the Holy Linden in cold, far distant Prussia.

During the wearisome journey my mother felt for the
first time in the many years of her marriage that she would
not remain childless, as my father had always feared. In
spite of his poverty he was overjoyed, for now the vision
would be fulfilled in which Saint Bernard had promised
him comfort and redemption through the birth of a son.

In the monastery of the Holy Linden he fell sick, but in
spite of his weakness he would not relax the rigorous
devotional discipline imposed upon him, and his condition
became more and more serious. He died, at peace in the
knowledge of his salvation, at the moment I was born.

The first conscious impressions that dawn in my mind

3

are of the monastery and the wonderful chapel of the
Holy Linden. The dark woods still rustle around me; the
rich flowering grass and bright flowers, which were my
cradle, still shed their fragrance about me. No hostile beast,
no harmful insect lives in the sanctuary of the blessed;
neither the buzzing of flies nor the chirruping of crickets
disturbs the holy silence. The stillness is broken only by the
devout chanting of the priests who, together with the
pilgrims, file past in long lines, swinging golden censers
from which ascends the odour of sacrificial incense. I still
see in the centre of the church the silver-covered trunk of
the linden on which the angels set the healing image of
the Holy Virgin. The shining figures of saints and angels
still smile down upon me. The stories which my mother
told me of the wonderful monastery where she received
grace and comfort for her deepest suffering, have so entered
into my mind that I seem to have seen and experienced
everything myself. Yet my memory cannot possibly reach
back so far, for my mother left that holy place after a year
and a half.

Thus I feel as if I had seen in the deserted chapel that
strange, solemn figure, the mysterious painter whose
language nobody could understand, who came there in
those distant days when the church was being built, and
with skilled hand decorated it with remarkable speed in
the most glorious colours, only to vanish again without
trace.

I also recall an old, oddly-dressed pilgrim with a long
grey beard who used to play with me and carry me about
on his arm, searching for coloured mosses and stones in
the woods. Yet I am sure that the vivid impression I have
of him only springs from my mother's description.

Once he brought with him a handsome young boy the
same age as myself. I gave him my coloured stones, and
he laid them out on the ground in all sorts of shapes, but

in the end they always came together in the form of a cross.
My mother sat beside us on a stone bench, and the old
pilgrim, standing behind her, watched our game with a
grave yet gentle expression. Then a group of youths
sprang out from behind the bushes; to judge from their
clothes and their general attitude they had only come to
the Holy Linden out of curiosity. One of them noticed
us and cried laughingly:

"Look over there! A holy family! That's something for
my book!"

And he actually took out paper and pencil and prepared
to sketch us. The old pilgrim raised his head and cried
in wrath:

"Miserable scoffer! You call yourself an artist, but the
flame of faith and love has never burned in your heart.
Your works, like you yourself, will remain dead and lifeless.
You will despair like an outcast in the wilderness, and
perish in your own wretchedness."

The boys hurried away in confusion. Turning to my
mother, the pilgrim said:

"Today I brought with me a marvellous child in order
that he might kindle the flame of love in your son, but I
must now take him from you, and you will probably never
see either him or me again. Your son is richly gifted, but
the sin of his father still festers within him. Yet despite
this he can rise to become a soldier of Christ. Let him
enter the service of the Church."

My mother never tired of telling what a profound impression the pilgrim's words had made upon her. In spite of
my natural inclination, however, she decided to bring no
kind of persuasion to bear on me, but to await quietly
what providence held in store.

My clear recollection of personal experience begins with
the occasion when, on the journey home, my mother came
to a Cistercian convent where the abbess—by birth a

2

princess—who had known my father, received her kindly. From the time of that encounter with the old pilgrim, to the moment when my mother first took me to the abbess, I have not the slightest memory.

I remember that one day my mother had brushed and cleaned my suit as best she could in preparation for my first visit to the abbess. She had bought new ribbons in the town, and trimming my tousled hair, she made me as smart as possible and enjoined me to behave to the abbess with the utmost courtesy. At last, holding my mother's hand, I mounted the wide stone steps and entered the high, arched chamber adorned with paintings of the saints, where we found the abbess. She was a majestic, handsome woman whose religious habit gave her an awe-inspiring dignity. She turned her grave, penetrating gaze upon me and asked:

"Is this your son?"

Her voice, her whole aspect, even the strange surroundings, had such an effect on me that I felt frightened and began to weep. The abbess, regarding me more kindly and gently, said:

"What is the matter, little boy? Are you afraid of me? What is your son's name, good lady?"

"Franz," replied my mother.

The abbess cried in tones of deep emotion:

"Franciscus!"

And she lifted me up and pressed me tightly to herself. At that moment I felt a sudden pain in my neck and gave a loud cry, so that the abbess became frightened, and let me go. My mother, in great consternation at my behaviour, jumped up at once to take me away. But the abbess would not allow her to. The diamond crucifix she wore on her breast had so hurt my neck when she clasped me to her, that the place was red and bruised.

"Poor Franz," said the abbess, "I have hurt you, but

we shall still become good friends."

One of the sisters fetched biscuits and sweet wine. My shyness was leaving me, and without further ado I began to nibble the delicacies which the noble lady, who had drawn me on to her knee, put into my mouth. After I had tasted a few drops of the new drink, I regained the cheerfulness and vivacity which my mother said had always been characteristic of me since my earliest childhood. By my chatter and laughter I greatly delighted the abbess and the other nuns who had stayed in the room.

I still cannot explain how it was that my mother urged me to tell the abbess about the beautiful place where I had been born, nor do I recollect how it came about that, as though inspired by a divine power, and as though I had understood their deepest meaning, I was able to describe to her the glorious pictures which the mysterious artist had painted; for I recounted in detail the wonderful legends of the saints as though I were already fully conversant with the writings of the Church. The abbess, and even my mother, stared at me in amazement as my enthusiasm grew and grew. Finally the abbess asked me:

"Tell me, child, how do you come to know all this?"

Without reflecting for an instant, I replied that a handsome boy whom a poor pilgrim had brought with him to the monastery had once interpreted the meaning of all the paintings in the chapel; he had even made mosaics with coloured stones, explaining to me what they signified and relating many other holy legends besides.

The bell sounded for vespers. The abbess rose and said to my mother:

"Good lady, I regard your son as my protégé, and from now on I will provide for him."

My mother was unable to speak for emotion. Sobbing violently, she kissed the abbess' hands.

Just as we were about to go out of the door, the abbess

came after us, lifted me up again and, carefully moving the crucifix to one side, embraced me. As her burning tears fell on my brow, she cried:

"Franciscus!—Be kind and good!"

I was moved to the depths of my heart and could not help weeping myself, without really knowing why.

*   *   *   *   *

With the abbess' support my mother's little household, on a small farm not far from the convent, began to take on a better aspect. The period of hardship was over. I now had better clothes to wear and took lessons from the priest, for whom I acted as cantor when he celebrated mass in the convent chapel.

The memories of that happy childhood linger like a faery dream. My home lies far, far behind me—a distant land where abide the unclouded joy and happiness of an innocent, childlike mind. But when I look back, I face the yawning gulf that has for ever separated me from this land. More and more I am seized with an ardent desire to know the dear ones whose voices I seem to hear, and whose forms I see beyond that gulf, walking as in the purple shimmer of early dawn. Yet is there any gulf which love, with its strong wings, cannot bridge? Do time and place mean anything to love? Does not love live in the mind, and is not the mind boundless?

But dark figures rise up, crowd closer and closer together and advance menacingly upon me, cutting off my view and entangling my thoughts in the afflictions of the present, so that even the yearning which used to fill me with indescribable rapture now turns to cruel, paralysing torment.

The priest was kindness itself. He knew how to control my lively mind and adapt his instruction to my temperament, with the result that I enjoyed my lessons and made rapid progress. More dearly than anyone else I loved my mother, but I revered the abbess like a saint, and the days on which I was allowed to see her were solemn occasions for me; each time I was resolved to show off my newly-acquired knowledge, but whenever she came up to me, addressing me in kindly tones, I could scarcely stammer a single word—I had eyes and ears only for her. Her every word struck deep into my soul. I remained in a strangely exalted mood throughout such days, and her vision went before me wherever I walked. As I stood before the high altar, swinging the censer while the deep, moving tones of the organ rolled through the chapel in a gradual crescendo, I heard her voice raised in a hymn of praise, and my heart was filled with intimations of a divine providence.

The most glorious of days, however, an occasion to which I looked forward for weeks and which sent a tremor of excitement through me whenever the thought of it entered my mind, was the feast of Saint Bernard, father of the Cistercian order, which was solemnly celebrated with a general dispensation. On the day beforehand people were already streaming to the convent from the nearby town and the surrounding countryside, and camping in the flower-covered field which adjoined the convent building, making it a hive of activity day and night. Saint Bernard's Day falls in August, and I cannot recall the weather ever proving unfavourable in that most favoured of seasons; devout pilgrims walked to and fro, chanting hymns, village lads made merry with their pretty maidens, priests gazed heavenwards in silent contemplation, their hands folded in reverence, families sat on the grass and ate the food which they had unpacked from their well-filled baskets. Cheerful songs, hymns, the deep sighs of the penitent, the laughter of the well-content, lamentation, rejoicing, jubilation, jesting, prayer—such were the sounds borne through the air in strange, confused concert.

Then the convent-bell began to toll. The tumult suddenly died away, and the congregation fell on their knees; row upon row, as far as the eye could see, they knelt close to each other, the reverent silence broken only by the murmur of prayer. As the sound of the final stroke died away, the crowd began to mingle with each other again, and the rejoicing which had been interrupted only for a matter of minutes broke out afresh.

On Saint Bernard's Day itself the Bishop came from the nearby town, attended by the lesser clergy, to celebrate High Mass in the convent chapel, and the episcopalian choir, for whom a platform draped with rich tapestry had been erected at the side of the high altar, performed the music. I can still re-live the emotions which filled me on these occasions, and they return to me whenever I call to mind that blissful time which passed all too soon. Vividly I recall a Gloria which was performed several times because the abbess found it so moving; the Bishop intoned the opening phrase, and when the majestic voices of the choir rang out—'*Gloria in excelsis deo*'—it was as though the heavens above the high altar opened, as though the paintings of the cherubim and seraphim came to life, beating their wings and hovering above the congregation, praising God in song and in the music of instruments. In silent amazement at the devotional intensity of the celebrations, I felt myself transported across the shining clouds to the familiar, yet distant land of my childhood; soft, angelic voices were wafted towards me from the fragrant woods, and the wonderful boy stepped out from behind the tall lilies and said: 'Where have you been all this time, Franciscus? I have many beautiful flowers which I shall give all to you if you will but stay with me and love me for ever.'

After mass the nuns, led by the abbess, who was wearing

the infula and carrying her silver crook, walked in reverent procession through the corridors of the convent and through the chapel. What godliness, what dignity, what supernal majesty shone from her every glance, emanated from her every movement! It was the Church triumphant itself which pronounced the benediction over the congregation of pious believers. Whenever her eyes lighted on me, I wanted to throw myself in the dust at her feet.

When the service was over, the clergy, together with the choir, were entertained in a large hall in the convent. Benefactors, minor dignitaries and merchants from the town also came, and I too was allowed to be present, since the choirmaster had developed an affection for me and liked to have me with him. As my mind, inspired with holy devotion, had earlier been filled with celestial thoughts, so now the joys of life, in a pageant of glorious colour, took hold of me. Merry tales, anecdotes and jests evoked hearty laughter, and wine was drunk with great gusto. When evening came, the carriages arrived to take the guests home.

When I was sixteen years old, the priest declared that I was now qualified to begin higher theological studies at the seminary in the neighbouring town. I was quite resolved to enter the priesthood, a decision which filled my mother with the greatest joy, as she saw in it the fulfilment of my father's mysterious vision. As a result of my decision she was able to believe for the first time that my father's soul would be redeemed from the tortures of eternal damnation. The abbess, too, warmly approved of my intention and repeated her promise to help me in any way necessary until I attained the status of priest.

Although the town was so near that its spires were visible from the monastery, I found it very hard to bid farewell to my good mother, to that wonderful lady I so deeply revered, and to my teacher. It is indeed true that a single step outside one's family circle seems to bring the same sorrow at departure as does a journey to the ends of the earth.

The abbess was particularly moved, and her voice trembled as she spoke comforting words of exhortation. She gave me a finely-worked rosary and a little prayer-book with wonderful illuminated pictures. Then she handed me a letter of introduction to the prior of the Capuchin monastery in the town and advised me to seek him out at once, as he would readily offer me whatever advice and assistance I required.

It would certainly not be easy to find a more attractive district than that in which the Capuchin monastery lies, just outside the town. The lovely garden, with its views up into the mountains, seemed to shine in fresh splendour each time I walked down the long avenues, stopping now here, now there among the luxurious trees.

It was in this very garden that I met Prior Leonardus when I first visited the monastery to present my letter of introduction. His natural kindness grew even greater as he read the letter, and he had so many delightful tales to relate about that wonderful lady, whom he had met in Rome in his young days, that on this account alone I was attracted to him from the start. He was surrounded by the brethren, and it was not hard to appreciate the nature of the relationship between him and them, and of the whole mode of life in the monastery. The peace and serenity of spirit which so plainly characterised the prior's features had spread to all the brethren. Nowhere was there a trace of discontent or of that consuming self-centredness so often seen on monks' faces. For all the strictness of the rules of the order, devotional duties were for Prior Leonardus more a need felt by the religious spirit than an ascetic atonement for the inborn frailties of human nature, and he had been able to stimulate this attitude towards devotion in the brethren to such an extent that everything they had to perform in satisfaction of the rule became imbued with a serenity and a natural geniality which had virtually brought about a higher mode of existence within those earthly confines.

Prior Leonardus even knew how to maintain a discreet contact with the outside world which could not but be beneficial to the brethren. Generous bequests to the monastery, which was held in universal esteem, made it possible to entertain the many friends and patrons in the refectory. On these occasions a long table was set in the middle of the room and Leonardus took his place at its head. Whereas this table was neatly laid out with china and glass, the monks remained at their own narrow board by the wall and used the simple utensils which the rule pre-scribed. The cook was skilled in the art of preparing dainty maigre dishes which the guests found extremely tasty. The guests themselves provided the wine, and these feasts thus became a pleasant meeting-ground where the sacred and the profane came together in convivial intercourse to their mutual benefit and to the benefit of life itself. For by penetrating the walls of the monastery, in which everything reflected the totally different life of the monks, those whose lives were governed solely by earthly concerns were moved to confess that peace and happiness were also to be found in ways other than those which they themselves had followed; and that the mind, by lifting itself above earthly things, might even be able to create for man a higher form of existence here on earth. The monks, for their part, gained wisdom and breadth of experience, for what they learned of the dealings of the outside world stimulated in them reflections of the most varied kinds; without ascribing any false value to the things of earth, they yet came to perceive that the various modes of human existence, the product of an inner determinism, represented a kind of refraction of the spiritual principle, without which everything would be without colour and without sparkle.

The prior had always far outshone the other brethren both in spiritual and in worldly wisdom, for besides being an acknowledged master of theology, in that he elucidated the most complex subjects with ease and was often asked by the professors of the seminary for advice and assistance, he had a greater experience of worldly affairs than one would expect of a priest. He spoke Italian and French with fluency and elegance, and his ability had led to his being sent, in his younger days, on many important missions. At the time I came to know him he was already advanced in years, but despite his white hair, which testified to his age, the fire of youth still burned in his eyes, and the gentle smile which played on his lips added to his expression of contentment and peace of soul. The elegance which marked his speech also characterised his movements, and even the shapeless habit of his order moulded itself to his well-built frame. There was not a single brother who had not taken the cowl from free choice, in response to an inner calling, but if some unhappy man had ever sought refuge in the monastery from angry pursuers, Leonardus would have comforted him; his penance would have been the brief transition to a state of harmony, he would have made his peace with the world, heedless of its trivialities, and his life would have taken on a higher significance. Leonardus had penetrated these unusual aspects of monastic life in Italy, where the rite, and with it the whole attitude towards the spiritual life, is less grave and sombre than in Germany. Just as Classical forms of architecture have been preserved in the churches, so a ray of light from the joyful age of Antiquity seems to have shone into the dark mysticism of Christianity, bringing with it something of the radiant glory which surrounded the ancient gods and heroes.

Leonardus became very fond of me. He taught me

Italian and French, but my mind developed chiefly through the many books he gave me and through his conversations. Almost the whole of the spare time that my studies in the seminary allowed was spent in the monastery, and all the while I felt a growing inclination to take the cowl. I revealed my wish to the prior, but without actually dissuading me he advised me to wait a few years longer, and to use this time to look about me in the world more than I had done hitherto. Although I had no lack of friends, most of whom I had met through the choirmaster, who gave me music lessons, I felt an unpleasant embarrassment in the company of other people, particularly when women were present, and it was this, together with my natural tendency towards a life of contemplation, that seemed to determine my vocation as a monk.

The prior told me many remarkable things about the life of the world. He delved into matters of a most equivocal nature, but treated them with his accustomed lightness of touch and thus never gave the slightest offence. Finally he took me by the hand, looked me straight in the face and asked me whether I was still innocent.

I felt my face go red, for as Leonardus asked this embarrassing question there sprang to my mind a vivid picture which had not entered my mind for a long time.

The choirmaster had a sister, who, though not quite meriting the description of beautiful, was a most attractive young woman, in the full glory of her sex. She displayed above all a well-developed body of the purest contours, with the most beautiful arms and the most beautiful breasts, both in form and complexion, that one could imagine.

One morning when I was going to the choirmaster for my music lesson, I caught his sister by surprise in a light negligé, her breast almost completely bare. She swiftly covered it up, but my prying eyes had already seen too much. Words failed me. New, unknown feelings welled up within me and drove the red-hot blood through my veins so that my pulse beat out loud for all to hear. My heart was held in a convulsive grip and nearly bursting, until I eased my torment with a gentle sigh.

The girl approached me innocently, took my hand and asked what was agitating me. This only made things worse, and it was my good fortune that the choirmaster happened to enter the room at that moment and release me from my anguish.

Never had I played so many wrong chords or sung so out-of-tune as on that occasion. I was pious enough to see the whole affair later as a vicious attack by the Devil, and I counted myself fortunate to have defeated the enemy through the ascetic discipline which I undertook.

As the prior put this awkward question I saw the girl standing before me with her bare breast; I felt her warm breath and the pressure of her hand, and my anguish grew with every moment.

Leonardus regarded me with an ironic smile which made me tremble. I could not bear his gaze and lowered my eyes.

Touching my burning cheeks, he said:

"I can see, my son, that you have grasped my meaning and are still pure. May the Lord preserve you from the temptations of the world. The pleasures it offers are short-lived; it is even as though a curse rests upon them, for they produce an indescribable disgust, a complete enervation, an insensibility to higher values, which spells the frustration of man's spiritual life."

Try as I might, I could not forget the prior's question and the vision that it recalled, and although I had previously been able to appear innocent in the presence of that girl, I now avoided her more than ever. At the very thought of her a feeling of confusion, an inner unrest, came over me, which seemed the more dangerous because with it I felt within me a strange new longing, a sinful lasciviousness.

This equivocal situation was soon to be settled. The choirmaster had invited me, as he often did, to a musical evening which he had arranged with a few friends. There were several other women present besides his sister, and this aggravated the embarrassment which made me unable to speak even in her presence alone.

She was charmingly dressed and seemed more attractive than ever. I felt drawn to her by an invisible, irresistible force.

Without knowing how, I always found myself near her, seizing avidly on her every look, her every word, and pressing close towards her so that at least her dress would touch me as she passed by. She seemed to notice it and take pleasure in it. Sometimes I felt as if I would have to clasp her to my heart in a mad fit of love.

For a long time she had been sitting near the harpsichord. At last she got up, leaving one of her gloves lying on the chair. I took it and pressed it madly to my lips. One of the ladies noticed it, and going over to the choirmaster's sister, whispered something in her ear. Then they looked at me and giggled.

I was utterly crushed. An icy tremor pierced my heart, and blindly I rushed over to the monastery and into my cell. I threw myself on the ground in a fit of frantic despair, and burning tears poured from my eyes. I uttered curses on myself and on the girl, now praying to Heaven, now laughing like a madman. Derisive voices sounded all around me; I would have thrown myself through the window had it not been for the iron bars. Not until dawn did I become quieter. By then I was firmly resolved never to see her again and to renounce the world altogether. My calling to a secluded monastic life, from which no temptation would again make me swerve, confronted me more clearly than ever.

As soon as I could free myself from my lessons, I hurried to the monastery to see the prior and revealed to him that I was now determined to start my novitiate and had already informed my mother and the abbess of my intention.

Leonardus seemed surprised at my sudden enthusiasm, and without pressing me he tried in various ways to discover what had led me to insist so urgently on entering a monastery, for he apparently suspected that some particular incident must have provoked my decision. A deep feeling of shame, which I could not overcome, prevented me from confessing the truth. Instead I told him, with the fire of exaltation that still glowed within me, of the wonderful events of my childhood years, all of which pointed to my being destined for monastic life.

Leonardus listened to me quietly, and without exactly questioning my visions, he did not appear to take much notice of them. On the contrary, he showed that all this gave little support to the genuineness of my calling, since it might very well be a delusion. In point of fact, Leonardus was not fond of talking about the miracles performed by the early Christians, and there were moments when I was tempted to take him for a secret sceptic.

On one occasion, in order to compel him to express a definite opinion, I made bold to speak of those who despised the Catholic faith, and above all to rail at those who in puerile presumptousness disposed of everything supernatural by branding it as mere superstition.

Leonardus said with a gentle smile:

"My son, the worst superstition is doubt!"

And he embarked on a discussion of quite different and unimportant matters.

Not until later was I allowed to penetrate his sublime thoughts on the mystical aspect of our religion, which enshrines the mysterious union of our own spiritual purpose with the essence of things divine, and I then had to admit that Leonardus was right in saving for the supreme ordination of his pupils the revelation of all the inspired thoughts which abounded in his mind.

My mother wrote that she had long known that I would not be satisfied with the status of lay brother and would choose the life of a monk, as on St Medardus' Day she had dreamt that the old pilgrim from the Holy Linden had dressed me in the habit of the Capuchin order and taken me by the hand.

The abbess, too, was in complete agreement with my intention. I saw both her and my mother again before taking the cowl, which followed very soon afterwards—since half my novitiate had been remitted in deference to my urgent request—and I adopted the name of Medardus.

The atmosphere among the brethren, the ethos of the devotions and the whole manner of life in the monastery remained just as they had appeared to me when I first arrived. The serenity which prevailed in everything filled my soul with heavenly peace, such as had surrounded my happy childhood years in the Holy Linden.

During the solemn ceremony of my investiture I caught sight of the choirmaster's sister, who was in the congregation; she looked sad, and I thought I saw tears in her eyes. But the time of temptation was over, and maybe it was guilty pride at my easily-won victory that caused me to smile. Brother Cyrillus, who was walking at my side, noticed it.

"What are you so happy about, Brother?" he asked.

"Should I not be happy, when I am in the act of renouncing the world and its vanities?" I answered.

But I cannot deny that, as I spoke these words, a feeling of uneasiness passed over me, punishing me for the lie I had uttered. This was, however, the last attack of earthly egotism before I gained my peace of mind. Would that it had never left me! But the might of the enemy is great,

Who can trust his vigilance or the strength of his weapons when the powers of darkness are lying in wait for him?

*   *   *   *

I had been in the monastery five years when the prior instructed Brother Cyrillus, who had grown old and feeble, to hand over to me the supervision of the chamber where the valuable relics were kept. There were bones of the saints, fragments from the cross of the Redeemer, and other holy remains, which were preserved in neat glass cases and displayed on certain days for the edification of the people. Brother Cyrillus made me familiar with every item as well as with the documents that testified to their genuineness and to the miracles that they had worked.

In breadth of mind Cyrillus was the equal of our prior, and all the less did I therefore hesitate to give expression to the ideas that were surging up inside me.

"Good Brother Cyrillus", I said, "are all these things really and truly what they are made out to be? May it not be that through deceitful covetousness many spurious objects have been surreptitiously included among the genuine relics of this or that saint? A certain monastery, for example, possesses the whole of the Saviour's cross, yet so many pieces of it are displayed in various places that, as one of us said in wanton jest, they would provide our monastery with firewood for a whole year.

"I doubt whether it is meet for us to subject these matters to such an examination", replied Cyrillus, "but, to be frank, I must admit that in my opinion only a few of these objects are likely to be what they are claimed to be, in spite of the documents that describe them. Yet to me this does not seem to matter. Pay good heed to the views which our prior and I hold on these subjects, and you will see the Christian faith in a new splendour.

"Is it not a wonderful thought, good Brother Medardus, that our Church is striving to grasp the mysterious threads which link the real with the supernatural; so to inspire the material aspect of our existence that its origin in the supreme spiritual principle, yea, its vital relatedness to that celestial existence whose burning power pervades the whole of nature, shall be revealed for all to see, and so that the premonition of a higher life whose seed we bear within us shall hover before our eyes as though on the wings of the seraph? What is that bit of wood, that old bone, that rag? People say that it was hewn from the cross of Christ, taken from the body or the robe of this or that saint. But the believer does not brood over these things: he is absorbed with the thought of that supernatural power which will open to him a realm of bliss which he only dreamed of here below. In this way the spiritual influence of the saint is aroused, even if the relic, though spurious, gives the first impulse and the faith of man is strengthened by the higher spirit whose aid and comfort he has invoked. Moreover, this spiritual strength will of itself be able to overcome the sufferings of the body, and that is why the relics work those miracles which happen so often before the eyes of the assembled multitude that they can scarcely be denied."

I recalled at that moment certain of the prior's remarks which coincided exactly with Brother Cyrillus' words, and the relics which had formerly seemed just religious trivialities I now regarded with a real awe and devotion. Cyrillus did not fail to notice the effect of his words, and proceeded to explain the collection to me piece by piece with touching conviction and enthusiasm.

Last of all he took a little chest out of a securely-locked cupboard and said:

"This, dear Brother Medardus, is the most marvellous, most mysterious relic that our monastery possesses. For as long as I have been here nobody has handled it but the

3

prior and me. Not even the other brethren, let alone
strangers, know of its existence. I cannot touch the chest
without shuddering, for it is as if it contained a demon
which, if it succeeded in bursting the bonds which now
render it powerless, would bring irrevocable disaster upon
everyone it overtook. The contents of the chest were
prepared by Satan himself at the time when he was still
fighting to prevent man's salvation."

I looked at him in astonishment. Without allowing me
time to reply, he went on:

"I will refrain, dear Brother, from expressing any
personal opinion on this most mysterious affair and from
putting out this or that hypothesis which has passed through
my mind. Rather I will tell you faithfully what the
relevant documents say about the relic; you will find these
documents in that cupboard and can read them afterwards
for yourself.

"You are well acquainted with the life of Saint Anthony,
and will therefore recall that, in order to free himself from
all earthly ties and devote himself utterly to the things of
the spirit, he went into the wilderness and submitted to
the most rigorous discipline of penance and devotion. Satan
pursued him and often came into his presence with the
intention of disturbing his pious meditations.

"On one occasion Saint Anthony noticed a dark figure
creeping up on him in the twilight. As the figure came
closer he saw to his surprise that bottles were sticking out
of the holes in the tattered cloak that the figure was wearing. It was Satan. He leered mockingly at the saint and
asked him whether he would like to taste the elixirs that
were in the bottles he was carrying. Saint Anthony was
not even irritated by this insolence, for Satan, now weak
and powerless, was no longer in a position to engage in
combat and had to confine himself to derisive taunts. He
asked Satan why he carried so many bottles about with

him in this strange manner. Satan replied:

'Well, when someone meets me, he looks at me in surprise and cannot resist inquiring about my potions and indulging his desire to taste them. Among so many elixirs he will always find one that suits his palate. He drains the bottle, and surrenders himself to me and my kingdom.'

"This much is found in all the legends, but according to the particular document that we possess concerning this vision of Saint Anthony's, when Satan went away he left a few of his bottles behind on the grass. Saint Anthony took them quickly to his cave and hid them, for fear lest even in the wilderness someone who had lost his way—perhaps even one of his own disciples—might taste the terrible drink and fall into eternal damnation.

"The document goes on to record that Saint Anthony once happened to open one of the bottles. A stupefying cloud of smoke shot out, surrounding him with all manner of hideous, diabolical figures which sought to lead him astray by seductive trickery, until he finally drove them off by strict fasting and incessant prayer.

"This chest contains a bottle with one of those elixirs of the Devil which Saint Anthony left when he died, and the documents are so authentic and precise that there can be little doubt but that the bottle really was found among Saint Anthony's effects. And I must confess that whenever I touch the bottle, or even this chest in which it is locked, an uncanny fear comes over me, and I seem to detect a queer aroma which dazes me and at the same time produces an inner restlessness which disturbs my devotions. By constant prayer, however, I can overcome this evil feeling, which I realise must spring from the influence of some malevolent demon, even though I do not actually believe in the direct agency of Satan. My advice to you, good Brother Medardus, who are still so young, who still see in bright, shining colours everything that your vivid

imagination presents to you, and who, like a bold but inex-
perienced warrior, alert but over-eager, trust too much
in your own strength and essay the impossible—my advice
to you, good Brother, is never to open the chest, or at least
only after many years, and to put it away far out of sight
lest curiosity lead you into temptation."

He locked the mysterious chest up again in the cupboard
and handed me the bunch of keys. The whole story had
made a strange impression on me, but the more I felt a
greedy desire to look at the wonderful relic, the more I
strove, remembering Brother Cyrillus' warning, to suppress
it. When he had gone I looked again through the holy
possessions now entrusted to me, then took the little key
of the dangerous cupboard off the bunch and hid it deep
among the papers in my desk.

Among the professors in the seminary there was one who
was an outstanding orator. Every time he preached the
chapel was crowded. His stream of fiery words carried
everyone away and inspired the most fervent devotion. I,
too, was deeply moved by his magnificent sermons, but
at the same time as I realised how fortunate this highly-
gifted man was, I felt a powerful urge to emulate him.
After I had listened to him I used to preach to my empty
cell, surrendering myself completely to the inspiration of
the moment, until I succeeded in capturing and writing
down my words and ideas.

The brother whose duty it was to preach in the monastery
was getting weaker and weaker. His sermons dragged
laboriously and monotonously on, like a half dried-up
stream. The extraordinarily inflated language which
resulted from his paucity of ideas—he spoke without notes—
made his sermons so intolerably long that the majority of
the congregation fell quietly asleep well before the amen,
and were only woken up again by the sound of the organ.
Prior Leonardus himself was also an excellent speaker,

but he was loath to preach because it was too much of a strain on him in his already advanced years. Apart from him there was nobody in the monastery who could replace the ailing brother.

Leonardus spoke to me about this unfortunate situation, which was causing the chapel to lose the patronage of many pious people. I plucked up courage and told him how even in the seminary I had felt an urge to preach and had written a number of sermons. He asked to see them and was so pleased with what he read that he insisted I should now undertake to preach on the next Saint's Day: I was all the more certain to succeed, he said, in that nature had provided me with everything essential to a good preacher— an expressive face, a commanding presence and a powerful, resonant voice. He himself undertook to instruct me in matters of gesture and bearing.

The day arrived. The chapel was fuller than usual, and with trepidation I mounted the pulpit. At the beginning I kept to what I had written, and Leonardus told me afterwards that I had spoken in a faltering voice, but that this had been entirely in keeping with the sombre and devout observations with which my sermon had begun, and had been taken by most people to be a particularly effective piece of oratory. Soon, however, the spark of divine exaltation glowed in my heart. I thought no longer of what I had written but gave myself up to the mood of the moment. I felt the blood coursing through my veins— heard my voice thundering through the arches—imagined the shining halo of inspiration around my proudly-held head and outstretched arms.

I brought my sermon to an end with an aphorism in which I summed up as in the point of a flame all the glorious precepts that I had proclaimed. The effect was unprecedented. Violent weeping, spontaneous cries of rapture, fervent prayers resounded after I had finished

speaking. The brethren expressed their profoundest admiration; Leonardus embraced me and called me the
pride of the monastery.

My fame quickly spread, and the most respected and
cultured inhabitants of the town hurried to the chapel,
which was far from large, an hour before the bell sounded,
in order to listen to Brother Medardus. As this admiration
grew so also did my efforts to bring to my sermons the
greatest possible brilliance and artistry. More and more I
succeeded in gripping my listeners, and more and more
the reverence which was so strikingly evident wherever I
went, came to resemble the worship of a saint. A religious
mania had seized the town, and on the slightest pretext all
the inhabitants flocked to the monastery, even on ordinary
week-days, just to see and speak to Brother Medardus.

The idea then began to grow in me that I was one of the
Lord's elect. The mysterious circumstances of my birth in
a holy place, the consequent forgiveness of my father's sin,
the strange events of my childhood years—everything
suggested that my spirit was in direct contact with the
divine, exalted above the lowly things of earth: I was not of
this world or of mankind, but walked the earth in order to
bring men comfort and salvation. I now realised that the
old pilgrim in the Holy Linden had been Joseph, and the
marvellous boy the Child Jesus himself, who had seen in
me a saint on earth.

But the clearer this became to me, the more oppressive
became my surroundings. The peace and serenity of
spirit that used to be mine had vanished. Even the friendly
remarks of the brethren and the kindness of the prior
aroused my antagonism: they should recognise in me the
saint exalted above them, throw themselves down in the
dust and pray for my intercession before the throne of God,
but as they were, I considered them condemned by their
wicked obduracy. I interpolated allusions in my sermons

to show that a wonderful new era had begun, like the shimmering rays of early dawn, and that one of God's chosen servants was walking the earth, bringing comfort and salvation to all believers. I enshrined my presumptuous message in mystical images whose magic effect on the congregation was the greater the less they were understood.

Leonardus became visibly cooler towards me and avoided speaking to me alone, but at last, when we once happened to be walking together down the path in the monastery garden, he burst out:

"I can no longer conceal from you, good Brother Medardus, that for some time past you have been causing me displeasure by your whole conduct. Something has come into your soul to turn you away from a life of devout simplicity. There is a sinister spirit behind your sermons, and it would not now require much for our friendship to be broken for ever. Let me be frank. At this moment you bear the guilt of our sinful origin. This guilt opens the gates of destruction to every surge of our spiritual strength, and we all too easily wander astray in a moment of careless-ness. The applause, yea, the idolatrous admiration offered by the frivolous world, greedy for any thrill, has dazzled you, and you see yourself in a shape that is not your own but a mirage enticing you into the gulf of perdition. Search your heart, Medardus! Renounce the illusion that has bewitched you—I believe I know what it is. Already you have lost that peace of mind without which there is no salvation here on earth. Heed my warning: avoid the enemy that is lying in wait for you and become again the good-natured youth I used to love with all my heart!"

Tears flowed from the prior's eyes as he said this, and he gripped my hand. Then, releasing it, he went away quickly without waiting for my reply.

But his words had only provoked my anger. He had spoken of the applause and the tremendous admiration which I had earned by my exceptional gifts, and it was obvious to me that the displeasure he so openly expressed was only the product of petty envy. Silent, brooding and with secret bitterness I continued to attend the monks' gatherings, and consumed with the new vision that had been disclosed to me, I pondered day and night how to express and proclaim to the people all that had welled up within me. The more I became estranged from Leonardus and the brethren, the stronger became the bonds with which I drew the multitude towards me.

On Saint Anthony's Day the chapel was crammed so full that the doors had to be thrown open to allow the thronging crowd outside to hear me as well. Never had I spoken with greater power, greater fire, greater penetration. As was the custom, I related various stories from the life of the saint and followed them with profound and pious meditations. I spoke of the temptations of the Devil, to whom the Fall had given power to entice men, and my train of thought led involuntarily to the legend of the elixirs, which I intended to present as a significant allegory.

As I looked round the chapel, my gaze lighted on a tall, gaunt figure who had climbed on to a pew opposite me and was leaning against a pillar. He was wearing a purple cloak over his shoulders in a strange, foreign fashion, his arms folded inside it. His face was deathly pale, but as his great black eyes stared at me, a dagger seemed to pierce my heart. A feeling of horror ran through me, and quickly turning my face away, I summoned all my strength and continued speaking. But as though compelled by some magic force, I could not help looking over towards him again and again. He still stood there, impassive and motionless, his ghostly eyes fixed upon me. Something resembling bitter scorn and hatred lay on his high, furrowed brow and his drawn lips. The whole figure had a horrible, frightening air about it. It was . . . *it was the mysterious painter from the Holy Linden.*

Cruel, icy fingers clutched at my heart. A fearful sweat broke out on my forehead; my phrases stuck in my throat, and my speech became more and more incoherent. But the terrible stranger still leaned silently against the pillar, his glassy eyes set unwaveringly on me.

I cried out in a mad fit of desperation:

"O cursed man! Get away! Get away! For I—I am he! I AM SAINT ANTHONY!"

When I awoke from the state of unconsciousness into which I fell at these words, I found myself lying on my bed with Brother Cyrillus sitting beside me, tending and comforting me. The dreadful vision of the stranger still stood vividly before my eyes, but the more Brother Cyrillus, to whom I told everything, tried to convince me that it was merely a trick of my inflamed imagination, the more profound was the penitence and shame I felt at my conduct. I learned later that the congregation thought that I had been seized with a sudden fit—an opinion which was particularly justified by my final exclamation.

My spirit was torn and crushed. I locked myself in my cell, subjected myself to the strictest penance and fortified myself with fervent prayers to fight the tempter who had appeared to me even on consecrated ground, taking upon himself in brazen scorn the form of the devout painter from the Holy Linden. Nobody, incidentally, had seen any man in a purple cloak, and Prior Leonardus, with his characteristic generosity, at once made it known that a sudden fever had come over me during the sermon and caused my words to become confused.

I was still very sick and weak when I resumed normal monastery life several weeks later. Nevertheless I still undertook to go into the pulpit, but, tortured by fear and persecuted by the dreadful memory of that pale spectre, I was scarcely able to speak coherently, let alone surrender myself to the fire of rhetoric as before. My sermons became commonplace, awkward, disjointed. The congregation lamented the loss of my eloquence and gradually dwindled away, until the old brother who used to preach before and now obviously spoke better than I, took my place again.

Some time later a young count, accompanied on his travels by his tutor, paid a visit to our monastery and asked to see its various interesting possessions. It was my duty to open the chamber which contained the relics, and we had just entered it when the prior, who had accompanied us through the chapel, was called away, leaving me alone with the strangers.   I had shown and explained every item, when the count was struck by the finely-carved antique cupboard which housed the chest with the Devil's elixir. In spite of my initial unwillingness to say what was locked in the cupboard, both the count and the tutor continued to insist, until finally I related the legend of Saint Anthony and the cunning Devil, and gave a full account, faithfully following the words of Brother Cyrillus, of the bottle that was preserved as a holy relic; I even added the warning that he had given me about the danger of opening the chest and displaying the bottle.

Although the count was favourably disposed towards our religion, he seemed to rate the plausibility of the legend as low as did the tutor, and they launched into all kinds of witty comments on the comical Devil who carried the tempting bottles about in his tattered cloak. But at last the tutor assumed an air of seriousness, and said:

"Do not be annoyed at the frivolity of us worldly men, reverend Sir. You may be sure that both I and my count revere the saints as glorious men who were inspired by religion to sacrifice the joys of life, even life itself, for the salvation of their souls and the redemption of mankind. But as for stories such as the one you have just told, I believe them to be simply ingenious allegories invented by the saints, which have mistakenly come to be regarded as events from real life."

While he was speaking, the tutor had quickly slipped the bolt on the chest and brought out the queer-shaped black bottle. A strong aroma really did spread through the room, as Brother Cyrillus had told me, but far from being stupefying, it had a most pleasant and delectable effect.

"Well," cried the count, "I'll wager that the Devil's elixir is nothing more than rich old Syracusan!"

"I'm sure of it," rejoined his tutor. "And if the bottle does in fact belong to Saint Anthony's posthumous possessions, then you are actually better off, reverend Sir, than the King of Naples, who was deprived of the pleasure of tasting old Roman wine by the objectionable Roman habit of preserving the wine, not by corking it, but by allowing oil to drip on to it. For even if this wine is not nearly as old as that was, it is still probably the oldest in existence. You would therefore be well advised to put the relic to your own use and sip it from time to time."

"Quite right," interposed the count. "This Syracusan, of rare maturity, would send fresh vigour into your veins and drive out the infirmity with which you appear to be afflicted."

The tutor took a steel corkscrew from his pocket and in spite of my protestations opened the bottle. As the cork came out, I seemed to see a blue flame shoot up and then vanish. The aroma from the bottle became stronger and filled the room. First the tutor tried the wine and cried enthusiastically:

"O wonderful Syracusan! Saint Anthony's wine-cellar was not at all bad, in faith. And if the Devil was his cellarer, then he was not so ill-disposed towards the holy man as people think. Taste it, Count."

The count did so and confirmed what his tutor had said. They both joked again about the relic: how it was clearly the finest in the entire collection; how they wished that they themselves had a cellar full of such relics; and so on.

With bowed head I listened silently, staring at the ground. Their banter was anguish to me. In vain they insisted that I too should try Saint Anthony's wine; I resolutely refused, and having securely corked the bottle, locked it up again in its resting-place.

*   *   *   *

The strangers had left the monastery, but as I sat in my lonely cell I could not deny feeling a certain warm satisfaction, a liveliness and cheerfulness of spirit. It was evident that the sweet smell of the wine had strengthened me. I felt no trace of the evil effect that Brother Cyrillus had spoken of; on the contrary, its beneficial influence manifested itself in a remarkable way. For the more I reflected on the legend of Saint Anthony, and the more clearly the tutor's words sounded in my mind, the more certain I became that his explanation was the correct one. Only now did the thought strike me, like a flash of lightning, that on that unhappy day when an evil vision had so disastrously interrupted my sermon, I had in fact been on the point of expounding the legend as an ingenious allegory in precisely the same way. With this was connected a further thought which soon absorbed me completely:—what, I thought, if the wonderful potion were to fortify my mind with spiritual power and revive the faded flame so that it would shine forth with new life? Had not a mysterious kinship between my spirit and the forces of nature hidden in that wine already been revealed through the fact that the aroma which caused the feeble Cyrillus to feel dazed had nothing but a favourable effect on me?

Yet although I was firmly resolved to follow the stranger's advice, a strange inner resistance held me back again and again. As I was about to open the cupboard I seemed to see in the carvings the horrible face of the painter with its staring eyes, and seized with fear and terror, I fled from the room to do penance before the altar for my temerity.

More and more I was pursued by the thought that only through the taste of the wonderful wine could my spirit be refreshed and fortified. The behaviour of the prior and the monks, who treated me with well-meant but humiliating care as if I were mentally ill, brought me to desperation, and when Leonardus even granted me a dispensation from the usual devotions so that I might completely regain my strength, I determined, after having spent a sleepless night, racked with pain and terror, to risk everything in order to retrieve the power I had lost—or to perish.

I got up from my bed, lit my lamp at the altar of the Virgin Mary in the passage, and crept like a ghost through the church to the chamber where the relics were. The pictures of the saints, illuminated by the flickering light of the lamp, seemed to be moving and I felt that they were looking down in pity on me. I seemed to hear voices in the dull moaning of the wind which swept into the chapel —voices of lamentation and warning; I even seemed to hear my mother calling to me from a great distance:

"Medardus, my son, what is in your mind? Give up this dangerous plan!"

All was quiet in the chamber. I opened the cupboard, took hold of the chest which contained the bottle, and quickly took a deep draught. My veins glowed and I was filled with a feeling of indescribable satisfaction. I drank again, and there arose in me the desire for a new and glorious life. Swiftly I locked the empty chest away in the cupboard, hurried to my cell with the magic bottle and put it in my desk. Then I came across the little key that I had earlier taken off the bunch lest I should be led into temptation; yet now, as well as on the occasion when the strangers were present, I must have opened the cupboard without it. I examined my bunch of keys, and saw to my surprise that a new key had found its way on to it; with this key I had both then and now opened the cupboard, without noticing it in my distraction.

I shuddered involuntarily, but one vivid impression after another passed through my mind, as if I had suddenly been shaken out of a deep slumber. I found no peace, no rest until the morning dawned brightly and I could hasten down into the garden to bathe myself in the rays of the sun, which was rising from behind the mountains like a ball of fire.

Leonardus and the brethren noticed the change in me. Instead of being taciturn and uncommunicative, I was lively and cheerful and spoke with the fire of my former eloquence, as though in the presence of an assembled congregation.

Once I happened to be left alone with Leonardus. He looked at me for a long time as if trying to read my innermost thoughts, then said, with the trace of an ironical smile on his lips:

"Has Brother Medardus perhaps received in a vision fresh strength and rejuvenation from above?"

I felt my cheeks burning with shame, for at that moment my exaltation, produced by a draught of old wine, appeared miserable and worthless. With downcast eyes and bowed head I stood there. Leonardus left me to my meditations.

Only too greatly did I fear that the stimulation brought about by the wine would not last but would give way to the grief of even greater weakness than before. Yet it was not so. Indeed, having regained my strength, I felt my youthful energy returning, and with it that restless striving after the highest order of activity which the monastery knew. I insisted that I be allowed to preach on the next Saint's Day, and my wish was granted.

Shortly before I entered the pulpit I drank of the magic wine. Never had I spoken with greater passion, greater pathos, greater urgency. The news of my complete rehabilitation quickly spread, and the chapel became full again as before. But the more I gained the applause of the crowd, the graver and more reserved Leonardus became, and I began to hate him with all my might, for I believed that he had been seized by petty jealousy and monkish pride.

Saint Bernard's Day arrived, and I was filled with an ardent desire to let my light shine before the abbess. I therefore asked the prior to arrange for me to preach in the Cistercian convent on that day. Leonardus appeared greatly surprised at my request, and said frankly that he had intended to preach himself on this occasion and that the necessary arrangements had already been made; my wish could, however, easily be granted if he were to excuse himself on grounds of sickness and send me in his place.

And so it came about. I saw my mother and the abbess the evening before, but my mind was so occupied with my sermon, which was to attain a new peak of eloquence, that it only made a trifling impression on me to see them again.

The news had spread around the town that I was to preach in place of the sick Leonardus, and this may have attracted an even greater number of the cultured public. Without writing a single thing down, but only ordering the various parts of the sermon in my mind, I relied on the inspiration that would be aroused in me by the solemnity of High Mass, the devoutness of the congregation, even the magnificence of the lofty vaulted chapel itself. And I had not erred. Like a raging torrent my words swept down, glorifying the memory of Saint Bernard with the most striking metaphors and the most pious meditations, and I read amazement and admiration in all eyes. With joy I anticipated the heartfelt delight with which the abbess would receive me. I felt as though she must now sense more clearly than ever the in-dwelling power of the man, who, even as a child, had filled her with amazement and whom she must needs now receive with instinctive reverence.

When I asked to speak to her I was told that she had been befallen by a sudden indisposition and could not see anyone, not even me. This vexed me the more because my haughty delusion led me to think that in her boundless enthusiasm she should have felt the need to receive words of healing from me. My mother seemed to be nursing some secret grief whose cause I dared not inquire, for the guilt appeared somehow to lie on my own shoulders. She gave me a short letter from the abbess which I was not to open until I was back in the monastery. Scarcely was I in my cell than I read the following:

"By the sermon you delivered in our convent chapel, my dear son—for I will still call you that—you have plunged me into deep sadness. Your words do not spring from a pious heart whose affections are turned towards Heaven. Yours is not the enthusiasm that bears the devout soul aloft on seraph's wings to view with celestial delight the kingdom of the blest. Alas, the proud pomp of your language, your patent striving after originality and brilliance have proved to me that, instead of instructing the congregation and urging them to devout meditation, you seek only the favours and the worthless admiration of the worldly-minded crowd. Hypocritically you have affected emotions that are not in your heart; you have even assumed certain studied expressions and gestures like a vain actor. The demon of deceit has entered you and will destroy you if you do not search your heart and renounce sin. For your deeds are sin, grievous sin, all the more so since you have devoted yourself to heaven and committed yourself in the monastery to the renunciation of earthly folly. May

Saint Bernard, whom you have so vilely offended by your deceitful words, pardon you according to his divine forbearance, and lighten your steps so that you may find again the path from which, enticed by evil, you have strayed. And may he intercede for the salvation of your soul. Farewell.''

The abbess' words pierced me to the quick, and I fumed with rage, for nothing was clearer to me than that Leonardus, whose various references to my sermons pointed in the same direction, had exploited her bigotry and antagonised her against me and my power of oratory. I could hardly look at him without quivering in anger, and thoughts from which even I myself shrank came into my mind as to how to cause his downfall. The reproaches of the abbess and the prior were particularly intolerable to me in that I must have felt them in my heart of hearts to be true, but persisting more and more doggedly in my actions and fortifying myself with sips of wine from the mysterious bottle, I continued to lavish on my sermons all the arts of rhetoric and to study carefully my facial expressions and my gestures. Thus I received greater and greater acclamation, higher and higher esteem.

*   *   *   *

The bright rays of dawn broke through the stained-glass windows of the monastery chapel. Alone, sunk in thought, I sat in the confessional. Only the footsteps of the lay-brother dutifully sweeping the church sounded through the arches.

Suddenly I heard a rustling nearby and saw a tall, slim young woman, who had come in by the side door, approaching me to make confession. She was dressed in an unusual manner, and a veil covered her face. She moved with an indescribable grace and, kneeling down, she uttered a deep sigh. I could feel her burning breath and seemed to be entangled in a spell of enchantment even before she spoke.

How shall I describe the strange, irresistible tone of her voice? Her every word struck at my heart as she confessed that she cherished a forbidden love which she had long tried to resist, and that this love was the more sinful in that he whom she loved was bound by eternal holy vows, vows which she had cursed in moments of frantic despair. She broke off. Then in a flood of tears which almost choked her words, she burst out:

"It is you, Medardus—you for whom I cherish this ineffable love!"

My body shook as though in the convulsive grip of death. I could hardly contain myself. I felt I had to see her and clasp her to my breast. One moment of such bliss for the price of eternal torment in hell!

She faltered, but I could hear her breathing hard. In a kind of savage desperation I forced my senses together. I no longer remember the words I said, but I saw her rise in silence and move away. I drew the curtain shut before my eyes, and remained sitting in the confessional as though paralysed.

Fortunately nobody else came into the chapel, and I was able to creep unnoticed to my cell. Everything now seemed entirely different, all my endeavours so foolish, so trivial. I had not seen the woman's face, yet she was alive in my heart; her gaze was turned upon me, her soft, deep-blue eyes glistening with pearl-like tears which fell like glowing embers into my soul and kindled the flame which no prayer, no penance could quench. I undertook these devotions, chastising myself with the knotted cord till I bled, that I might escape from the eternal damnation which threatened me, for the brand that the unknown woman had cast into my heart aroused sinful desires such as I had never known,

There was an altar in our chapel dedicated to Saint Rosalia, above which hung a wonderful painting of her at the moment of her martyrdom. *It was my beloved—I knew her at once.* Even her dress was the same! As though in the terrible grip of madness, I lay prostrate for hours on the steps of the altar, groaning in despair, so that the monks were afraid and backed away from me nervously. In more tranquil moments I walked up and down in the garden: I saw her wandering in the hazy distance, stepping out from the bushes, rising like a naiad from the springs, hovering over the flowery meadows—everywhere only her, only her! I cursed my vows, my whole existence. I wanted to get out into the world and not rest until I had found her and bought her for the price of my soul's salvation.

At last I managed to control the delirious outbursts which were so mystifying to the brethren and the prior, but although I was able to appear calmer, the flame of perdition consumed me more and more. No sleep, no rest. Pursued by her image, I tossed to and fro on my hard bed and called on the saints—not to save me from the seductive vision that beset me—not to preserve my soul from eternal damnation—no!—but to give me the girl, to loose me from my vow, to set me free to plunge into the abyss of sin.

Finally I resolved to put an end to my agony by fleeing from the monastery. It only seemed necessary to renounce my monastic vows and I would hold my beloved in my arms and gratify the desire that burned within me. I decided to shave my beard, don lay clothes and roam around the town until I found her. It did not occur to me how difficult, indeed, how impossible this would be, nor even that, since I had no money, I would hardly be able to live for a single day outside the walls.

The last day I was to spend in the monastery arrived. By a stroke of fortune I had come into possession of some respectable clothes and intended to leave during the coming night, never to return again. It was already evening when the prior quite unexpectedly summoned me to him. I trembled, for I was convinced that he had sensed something of my secret intent. He received me with unusual gravity, an imposing dignity of demeanour, which overawed me.

"Brother Medardus," he began, "your frenzied behaviour, which I only take to be a more violent manifestation of that mental agitation you have been displaying for some time, perhaps not from the purest motives—your behaviour, as I say, is destroying the peace of our community and having a harmful effect on the serenity and goodwill that I have hitherto tried to maintain among the brethren as the proof of a devout life. But maybe this is the result of some cruel experience that has befallen you. In me, your friend and father, to whom you could have confided everything, you would have found comfort—yet you kept silent. Even less do I desire to press you because your secret might deprive me of that peace of mind which, in my declining years, I treasure above everything. Many times, particularly at the altar of Saint Rosalia, you have wantonly offended not only the brethren but also certain strangers who happened to be in the chapel, by uttering terrible exclamations which seemed to spring from your delirium. In accordance with monastic discipline I could punish you severely, but I will not do so, since some demon whom you have not resisted resolutely enough—perhaps even Satan himself—may bear the blame for your defection. Take it upon yourself to be conscientious in penance and in prayer. I can penetrate deep into your soul. You wish to go out into the world!"

Leonardus looked at me keenly. I could not endure his gaze, and grovelled, sobbing, at his feet, conscious of my evil purpose.

"I understand you," continued Leonardus, "and I even

believe that the world, if you walk it in piety, will turn you from your erring ways better than the seclusion of the monastery. A particular matter requires that one of our brethren be sent to Rome, and I have chosen you. To-morrow you will be able to start your journey, equipped with the necessary powers and directions. You are well-suited to carrying out this commission in that you are young, robust, experienced in business affairs and with a complete command of Italian. Go now to your cell and pray fervently for the salvation of your soul; I will do the same. But cease all chastising, for it will only weaken you and make you unfit for the journey. I shall expect you here in this chamber at dawn."

The words of the venerable Leonardus shone through me like a gleam from Heaven. Burning tears poured from my eyes, and I pressed his hands to my lips. He embraced me, and I felt as if he knew my inmost thoughts and was offering me the freedom to submit to the providence which ruled over me and which might plunge me, after a moment of ecstasy, into everlasting destruction.

My flight had now become unnecessary: I would be able to leave the monastery and pursue her unceasingly, her without whom there was no rest, no salvation for me on earth. The journey to Rome and the various commissions there seemed to me to be simply fabricated by Leonardus as the most convenient way of removing me from the monastery. I spent the night in prayer and in preparation for the journey; the remainder of the mysterious wine I filled into a wicker-bottle, to use as a tried and tested remedy whenever it might be needed, and put back into the chest the bottle in which the elixir had formerly been kept.

It was no small surprise to learn from the complicated instructions which the prior gave me that I really was to be sent to Rome, and that the affair which required the presence of a competent brother was of great importance.

I regretted having thought that with my first step outside the monastery I would surrender myself completely to my freedom, without consideration for anything else, but the vision of her gave me courage, and I resolved to adhere to my plan.

The brethren gathered to take their leave of me, and my parting from them, especially from Father Leonardus, filled me with profound sorrow. Finally the gates of the monastery closed behind me, and I set out on my long journey through the world.

II—INITIATION INTO THE WORLD

Below me in the valley lay the monastery, hidden in a blue haze. The morning zephyrs stirred, wafting up to me the sound of the devout chanting of the brethren, and instinctively I joined in. The glowing sun appeared from behind the town, shedding its lustrous gold upon the trees, and dew-drops fell like glittering diamonds on to the myriad insects which hummed and buzzed below. The birds awoke and flew singing and rejoicing through the forest, caressing each other in happiness and delight.

A group of peasant lads and maidens in festive costume were coming up the mountain.

"Glory be to Jesus Christ!" they cried, as they passed me.

"For ever and ever!" I responded, and visions of a new, free life full of joy and beauty came to me. Never before had I felt like this. I was a different person, and filled with newly-awakened vigour, I strode on through the forest and down the mountainside.

A peasant was coming towards me, and I inquired of him the way to the village where, according to my itinerary, I was to spend the first night. He gave me a detailed description of a path which branched off from the road a little farther on and led straight through the mountains.

I had walked some distance along this lonely track when I thought again of the unknown woman and of my fantastic plan to search for her, but some mysterious influence

43

seemed to blur my image of her so that I could barely distinguish her pale, distorted features. The more I strove to capture the vision, the more it faded into the mist; only my dissolute behaviour in the monastery after that strange incident remained fresh in my mind. It was still inexplicable to me why the prior should have borne everything with such patience and sent me out into the world instead of punishing me as I deserved.

Soon I became convinced that the appearance of the unknown woman had been but an illusion brought about by my overwrought condition, and the fact that she had been dressed like Saint Rosalia seemed to me to prove that the life-like picture of the saint which I could see from the confessional was largely responsible for it. I admired the prior for his wisdom in choosing the right means for my salvation, for had I been shut up inside the monastery walls, perpetually surrounded by the same objects, perpetually brooding and tormenting myself, I would have been driven insane by this vision, to which loneliness had lent starker, more vivid colours. As I came more and more to accept the idea that it had only been a dream, I could scarcely help laughing at myself, and with a frivolity that had never been characteristic of me I made merry at the thought that a saint was in love with me, recalling at the same time that I myself had once been Saint Anthony.

For several days I wandered through the mountains, between terrifying walls of rock which towered up boldly on either side, and across narrow footbridges which spanned hissing mountain streams. The path became more and more desolate, more and more wearisome. It was high noon. The sun scorched down upon my bare head. I was parched with thirst, but there was no spring to be seen, nor was there any sign of the village which I was supposed to come to. Completely exhausted, I sat down on a rock and could not resist taking a draught from the wicker-bottle, although

I wanted to conserve the magic drink as far as possible. New strength surged through my limbs and I pressed on, refreshed and fortified, towards my goal.

The pine forest became denser. I heard a rustling in the thick bushes, and a horse whinnied. A few steps further I found myself standing on the edge of a fearful precipice. A rushing stream, whose thunderous roar I had heard in the distance, plunged between two rocky pinnacles into the gorge below.

Only a few feet from the torrent, on a ledge of rock protruding over the ravine, lay a young man in uniform, his high cocked-hat, sword and dispatch-case on the ground beside him. His body was hanging over the abyss; he seemed to be asleep and gradually falling further and further over the edge.

I moved towards him. As I was about to catch hold of him to stop him from falling, I shouted:

"Wake up, for God's sake! Wake up!"

As soon as I touched him, he awoke from his slumber, but in the same instant he lost his balance and hurtled down into the gorge, his shattered limbs cracking as they were hurled from rock to rock. His piercing scream was lost in the unfathomable depths, and only a muffled groan reached me; then it, too, finally died away.

I stood there petrified with horror. At last I picked up the hat, sword and dispatch-case and was on the point of leaving the scene of the tragedy when a young man dressed as a groom came towards me out of the forest. First he stared at me, and then he began to laugh uproariously, which sent an icy tremor down my spine.

"Well, well, my dear Count," he said eventually, "your disguise is perfect. If your good lady were not informed of it beforehand, she would certainly not recognise you. But what did you do with the uniform?"

"I threw it into the ravine," came the reply from me in

a dull, hollow voice—for it was not I who spoke the words: they escaped involuntarily from my lips.

Dumbfounded I stared into the gorge, wondering whether the bloodstained body of the count would rise up again menacingly. I felt as though I had murdered him, and I still held his hat, sword and dispatch-case in my convulsive grasp. The young man went on:

"I am now going to ride into the town, Sir, and hide in the house on the left just by the gate. I presume you will walk straight down to the castle, where they will be expecting you. I will take the hat and sword with me."

I gave them to him.

"Farewell, Count! The best of luck in the palace!" he cried, and disappeared into the thicket singing and whistling. I heard him release the horse that was tied up there and lead it away.

When I recovered from my daze and thought the whole matter over, I realised that I was the victim of a quirk of fortune which had suddenly thrust me into the most remarkable situation. For it was clear that the strong resemblance between my features and those of the unfortunate count had completely deceived the groom, and that the count must have disguised himself as a Capuchin in order to play some trick in the nearby castle; death had overtaken him, and at that very moment a strange providence had put me in his place. My irresistible urge to continue playing the rôle of the count, as this providence seemed to desire, outweighed any doubts I might have had and drowned the inner voice which accused me of murder and of a shameless outrage. I opened the dispatch-case, which I had kept: it contained letters and valuable bills of exchange. I wanted to look through the papers one by one and read the letters, so as to make myself acquainted with the count's circumstances, but my mental confusion kept me from doing so.

After a few yards I stopped again and sat down on a rock. I wanted to force myself into a calmer state of mind, for I saw the danger of venturing so unpreparedly into a circle of people entirely unknown to me. The merry sound of horns rang through the forest and the noise of cheerful voices came nearer and nearer. My heart beat faster and I caught my breath: I was about to enter a new world, to embark upon a new life! I turned off into a narrow footpath which led down a steep slope, and as I stepped out of the bushes I saw a magnificent palace below me in the valley. This, I thought, must be the place where the count had intended to carry out his escapade. I approached it boldly, and soon found myself among the avenues of the park in which it lay.

*   *   *   *

In a dark avenue on the edge of the park I saw two men walking together, one of them dressed as a lay-priest. They came nearer but passed by deep in conversation without noticing me. The lay-priest was a young man whose handsome face bore the deathly pallor of intense, poignant grief; the other, plainly but respectably dressed, seemed to be a man of some considerable age. They sat down on a stone bench with their backs towards me, and I could hear every word they spoke.

"Hermogenes," began the elder man, "you are bringing your family to desperation by your stubborn silence. Your state of melancholy increases day by day, your strength is broken and the bloom of your youth has withered. Your decision to become a priest has destroyed all your father's hopes and wishes, yet he would willingly abandon them if it were a genuine inner calling, an irresistible urge, discernable since your childhood, to turn aside from the world, that had provoked this decision, for he would not dare to oppose that which providence had decreed against him. But this sudden change in your nature has shown only too clearly that some incident, about which you remain obstinately silent, has profoundly disturbed you and is now wreaking havoc in your mind. You used to be an ingenuous, merry, vivacious youth. What can have so alienated you from humanity that you despair of finding comfort for your ailing spirit in the breast of a fellow-man?

"You say nothing? You stare in front of you? You sigh? Hermogenes! You used to love your father with a rare affection, but even if it is now impossible for you to open your heart to him, at least do not torment him with the sight of your monastic habit, which symbolises the decision which is so terrible to him. Cast off this hateful robe, I entreat you, Hermogenes. Believe me, there is a mysterious power in such external matters. You will not be offended— for I believe you understand me fully—if I think here of an actor who, having donned a costume, feels a strange influence come over him and thus enters the more easily into the rôle he is playing. Let me, according to my nature, speak more lightly about the affair than would normally be proper. Do you not think that, if this long robe did not hamper you, you would stride forth briskly and merrily, yea, even run and jump? The resplendent brightness of the epaulettes which used to shine on your shoulders would bring young blood back into those pallid cheeks, and the jingle of spurs would sound like sweet music to your lively steed, which would whinny and dance for joy at the approach of its beloved master. Up, away, Baron! Off with that black robe that does not suit you! Shall I tell Friedrich to lay out your uniform?"

He stood up and was about to go away, when the young man threw himself into his arms.

"Oh, how you torment me, my good Reinhold!" he cried in despair. "You are causing me unutterable pain!

The greater the effort you make to strike those chords in my heart which used to sound in harmony, the more I feel crushed by the iron hand of fate, so that only discords are left in me, as in a broken lute."

"That is the way it appears to you, my dear Baron," interrupted the other. "You talk of the dreadful fate that has seized you, but you say nothing about what that fate consists of. However, be that as it may, a young man like you, armed with strength of mind and the burning courage of youth, must be able to secure himself against the iron hand of fate—must be able, as if impelled by a divine power, to lift himself above his destiny and soar above the agony of this wretched life. I know of no destiny, Baron, that can destroy this powerful desire."

Hermogenes took a step backwards, looked at his older companion in smouldering anger and cried:

"Learn, then, that I myself am this destiny, and that a monstrous crime lies heavily upon me—a shameful offence for which I must atone in misery and despair! Therefore be merciful and beg the reverend father to admit me within the walls."

"Baron," said the older man, "you are in a mood which one only finds in an utterly distracted mind. It is out of the question for you to go away. Within the next few days the baroness will arrive with Aurelia—and you must see them."

The young man laughed in terrifying scorn and cried in a voice that echoed through my heart:

"Must I? Must I stay?—Yes, indeed I must, old friend; you are right. And my penance will be even more terrible here than within those musty walls."

With this he sprang through the bushes and left the older man standing alone with bowed head, overwhelmed with sorrow.

"Glory be to Jesus Christ!" I cried, approaching him.

He started and looked at me in surprise, yet at the same

time he seemed to find something familiar in my appearance, and said:

"Ah, you are no doubt the priest, reverend Sir, who the Baroness announced some time ago would arrive to console this distressed and unhappy family."

I replied that I was, and Reinhold quickly reverted to the cheerfulness that seemed natural to him. We strolled together through the beautiful park and came at last to a shrubbery close to the palace, from which a splendid view of the mountains unfolded itself. At Reinhold's call the servant who had just come out of the palace hastened over to us, and we were soon served with an excellent breakfast. As we drank a toast Reinhold seemed to be regarding me more and more closely, as if trying hard to revive some faded memory. At last he burst out:

"Wonder of wonders! Unless I am completely mistaken, reverend Sir, you are Father Medardus from the Capuchin monastery in B . . . But how can that be? Yet—it is you! It must be you!"

As if struck by a shaft of lightning, I shuddered at Reinhold's words; I saw myself unmasked, exposed, accused of murder. My life was at stake. Desperation gave me strength.

"I am indeed Father Medardus from the Capuchin monastery in B . . . I am on a mission to Rome on behalf of the monastery," I said, with all the composure I could muster.

"Is it then only by chance that you have arrived here, having perhaps lost your way? Or how did the Baroness come to make your acquaintance and send you here?"

Without reflecting, but blindly repeating what a mysterious voice seemed to whisper to me, I said:

"On my journey I met the Baroness' father-confessor, and he begged me to attend to this charge."

"Ah, yes," rejoined Reinhold, "that is what the Baroness

wrote. Heaven be praised for having guided you here for
the salvation of our house and for having permitted such
a goodly, pious man as yourself to stay his journey for our
sakes. A few years ago I happened to be in B . . . and
heard the inspired words of comfort that you spoke from
the pulpit. I trust in your devoutness, your true vocation
to fight with burning zeal for the redemption of lost souls,
your noble eloquence; for through these you will achieve
that which none of us here has succeeded in achieving.

"I am glad to have met you before you have spoken to
the Baron, reverend Sir, and I will take the opportunity
to acquaint you with the situation of the family in the
straightforward way to which, as a man of God sent from
Heaven itself for our comfort, you are justly entitled. In
order that your efforts may be directed into the proper
channels you will have to hear at least allusions to things
about which I would rather say nothing; for the rest, I
will tell you everything as briefly as I can.

"I grew up together with the Baron. The similarity of
our dispositions made us brothers and broke down the
barrier which the difference between our classes would have
erected. I never left him, and when we finished our
academic studies and he came into possession of his late
father's estates here in the mountains, I became comptroller
of these estates. I remained his brother and closest friend
and was initiated into all the private affairs of the family.
His father wanted him to marry into a certain house with
which they had friendly relations, and he fulfilled this desire
all the more joyfully because in his betrothed he found a
richly-gifted creature who drew him irresistibly towards
her. Rarely, indeed, did the will of two fathers so completely coincide with the decrees of providence, for the
children seemed to have been meant for each other in every
possible respect. Of this happy union Hermogenes and
Aurelia were born,

"We generally spent the winter in the neighbouring town, but when, soon after Aurelia's birth, the Baroness' health began to fail, we stayed in the town for the summer as well. since she was in constant need of the attention of skilled doctors. She died just as the approach of spring had seemed to fill the Baron with joyful hopes of her recovery. We retired to the country, and only time was able to ease his bitter grief.

"Hermogenes grew up a fine boy, and Aurelia became the image of her mother; it was our duty and our pleasure to care for their upbringing. Hermogenes showed a decided inclination towards a military career, and this forced the Baron to send him to the town so that he could start his training under the eye of his father's old friend, the governor. Not until three years ago did the Baron spend the whole winter again in the town with Aurelia and me, as in the old days—partly in order to have his son close at hand, at least for a short time, and partly in order to see his friends again, who had continually been urging him to come.

"There was at this time a considerable stir in the town at the arrival of the governor's niece. She was an orphan and had placed herself in her uncle's protection, although she had her own household in a separate wing of the castle and assembled her own world of beauty around her. Without describing Euphemia in any detail—which is in any case quite unnecessary, reverend Sir, since you will soon see her for yourself—I will content myself with saying that everything she did, everything she said, radiated an indescribable grace which made the charm of her exquisite physical beauty all the more irresistible. Everywhere she went she brought new splendour, and everybody rendered her the most ardent homage; she could inspire the heart of the most insignificant, the most listless man to rise above its own paltriness and revel in the enchanting pleasures of

an existence it had never before known. There was
naturally no dearth of suitors to worship at the shrine of
the goddess, but it was never possible to say with certainty
that she preferred any one of them to the others; rather,
with a roguish irony which stimulated the appetite like a
sharp, pungent herb, she was able to entice them all into
her web, where they moved happily to and fro at her
pleasure.

"This Circe made a remarkable impression on the Baron.
Whenever he appeared, she accorded him a respect that
seemed engendered by childlike awe; in conversation with
him she displayed a culture and an understanding such
as he had scarcely ever found in a woman. With infinite
tenderness she gained Aurelia's friendship, not disdaining
to attend even to her smallest needs and to care for her
in every way like a mother. In high society she encouraged
the coy, innocent girl in such a way that, far from being
observed, her encouragement only served to emphasise
Aurelia's natural understanding and true instincts, so that
she was soon accorded the highest respect. On all occasions
the Baron was loud in his praise of Euphemia, and it was
here, perhaps for the first time in our lives, that we were
of completely different mind.

"In social gatherings I preferred to play the part of the
silent observer rather than engage freely in light gossip and
conversation, and I had studied Euphemia closely; she only
exchanged a few friendly words with me now and again,
however, in accordance with her principle of not over-
looking anybody. I had to admit that she was the most
beautiful, most brilliant of all the women present, and that
intelligence and feeling were reflected in everything she
said. Yet she repelled me in some unaccountable way, and
I could not suppress an uncomfortable sensation whenever
she looked at me or talked to me. Often there was a strange
glow in her eyes from which sudden flashes of light darted

5

out when she thought she was unobserved—a destructive
fire slowly growing until it forced its way out. Moreover
there often played round her mouth, which was normally
so gentle, a malicious irony, a spiteful mockery, which
made my heart shudder. The fact that she often looked
in this way at Hermogenes, who took little or no notice
of her, proved to me that there was much hidden behind
that beautiful mask which nobody knew about.

"To the Baron's boundless praise I could, of course,
oppose nothing but my physiognomical observations, to
which he did not attach the slightest value; in fact, he
found in my deep-seated aversion to Euphemia merely a
remarkable idiosyncrasy. He confided to me that she
would probably become one of the family, as he was going
to do his utmost to unite her with Hermogenes. While we
were engaged in a serious discussion of the matter and I was
producing every conceivable justification for my opinion of
Euphemia, Hermogenes came into the room, and the
Baron, who acted quickly and frankly in everything,
immediately acquainted him with his plans and desires.
Hermogenes listened quietly to all that the Baron said,
including the enthusiastic praise of Euphemia's qualities.
When the panegyric had ended, he replied that he had never
felt in the least attracted to Euphemia, that he could never
love her, and that he would therefore be grateful if the
idea to bring him together with her were dropped. The
Baron was not a little disconcerted at seeing his fondest
plan frustrated at the outset, but he was not anxious to
press Hermogenes, since he did not even know Euphemia's
feelings on the matter. With his characteristic pleasantness
and cheerfulness he made light of his unsuccessful efforts
and thought that maybe Hermogenes shared my idiosyncrasy, though he could not understand how such a dis-
cordant trait could be found in so interesting and beautiful
a woman. His relationship to Euphemia naturally remained

the same. He had grown so used to her that he could not let a day go by without seeing her.

"One day he said jokingly to her that there was only one person in her circle who was not in love with her, namely Hermogenes, and that although he, the Baron, had so sincerely desired a union between her and Hermogenes, it had been flatly rejected. Euphemia said that she would certainly welcome a closer attachment to the Baron, but not through Hermogenes, who was far too serious and moody for her liking. After this conversation Euphemia doubled her attention to the Baron and Aurelia; indeed in various gentle ways she hinted that her own ideal of a happy marriage would be a union with the Baron himself. She firmly refuted any objection such as disparity of ages, and persisted so skilfully and subtly in her attitude towards the whole affair that the Baron could not but believe that all the thoughts and desires which she breathed into his heart had actually been there from the beginning. Strong and vigorous as he was, he soon felt gripped in the glowing passion of youth. I was no longer able to stem the raging tide.

"And so not long afterwards, to the surprise of the town, Euphemia became the Baron's wife. That sinister element which had previously worried me from a distance now seemed to have entered right into my life, and I now had to be on guard for my friend as well as for myself. Hermogenes reacted to his father's marriage with cool indifference; Aurelia, that sweet, sensitive child, wept bitterly.

"Soon after the wedding Euphemia longed for the mountains again. She came here, and I must confess that her demeanour was so consistently kind and good that she compelled my spontaneous admiration. Two years of untroubled happiness went by. We spent both winters in the town, and here too the Baroness showed such unreserved devotion to her consort, such attention to his slightest wish, that all poisonous jealousy was silenced, and none of the young dandies who had dreamt of unlimited scope to display their gallantry before her, could allow himself the slightest liberty. Last winter I was probably the only one who began once again to feel seriously mistrustful, for I was still in the grip of my old prejudice.

"Before Euphemia's marriage to the Baron, Count Victor, a handsome young major in the guard of honour who was only intermittently in the town, had been one of her most ardent admirers, and the only one whom, in the enchantment of the moment, she singled out from the others. Once it was even said that there might well be a closer relationship between them than appearances betrayed, but the rumour died as inauspiciously as it had been born. That winter Count Victor was again in the town and naturally moved in Euphemia's circle, but he did not seem to take the least notice of her—in fact, he rather seemed to avoid her. Yet I often had a feeling that, when they thought they were unobserved, their eyes met, burning with the fire of smouldering passion.

"One evening a brilliant company was assembled at the governor's. I was standing close to a window so that the flowing drapery of the rich curtain almost concealed me. A few yards away from me stood Count Victor. Euphemia, more beautifully dressed than ever and radiant with charm, passed in front of him. He seized her arm violently, so that no-one but me could have noticed it. I saw her tremble and look at him with an indescribable expression of sensual, voluptuous longing. She whispered a few words which I did not catch. She may have seen me, for she turned quickly away, but not before I heard her say hastily:

'We are being watched!'

"O how shall I describe to you, reverend Sir, the mingled feelings of astonishment, fear and sorrow that swept through me? Think of the love, the faithful devotion

I bore the Baron, the forebodings of evil which were now fulfilled! Those few words had revealed to me that there was a secret liaison between the Baroness and the Count. For the present I had to keep silent but I intended to watch the Baroness like a hawk until I was certain of her guilt, and then free my unhappy friend from the shameful ties that bound him. But who can oppose fiendish cunning? My efforts were in vain, utterly in vain, and it would have been ridiculous to tell the Baron what I had seen and heard, since the artful woman would have easily found ways to make me out a stupid fool who was just imagining things.

"The snow lay deep on the mountains when we returned here last spring, but I still went for long walks in the country. As I was passing through the next village I noticed a villager whose gait and bearing had something unusual about them. He turned his head, and I recognised Count Victor, but in the same instant he vanished behind the houses and could not be found. What else could have led him to this disguise but his affair with the Baroness? In fact, I know for certain that he is here again now, because I have seen his groom ride past. Yet I fail to understand why he should not have visited her in the town.

"Three months ago the governor fell seriously ill and wished to see Euphemia. She left immediately with Aurelia, and only a slight indisposition prevented the Baron from accompanying them. Then tragedy descended on our house, for shortly afterwards Euphemia wrote to the Baron that Hermogenes had been stricken with a fit of melancholia which often broke out into raging delirium; that he was wandering about alone, cursing himself and his fate; and that all the efforts of friends and doctors had hitherto been of no avail. You can imagine, reverend Sir, what effect this news had on the Baron. The sight of his son would have disturbed him too violently, so I travelled to the town alone. Through the strong drugs that had been administered, Hermogenes had at least been delivered from his fits of wild madness, but a moroseness had set in which seemed to the doctors to be incurable. When he saw me he was deeply moved, and told me that an evil fate was forcing him to renounce for ever his position in the world, for only as a monk could he save his soul from eternal perdition. I found him dressed as you saw him a moment ago, and in spite of his protests I finally managed to bring him here. He is peaceful but he will not give up his obsession, and every endeavour to probe into the incident which brought him to this condition has remained fruitless, even though the discovery of this mystery might well lead to the most direct and effective means of curing him.

"Some time ago the baroness wrote that, on the advice of her father-confessor, she was going to send a priest here, whose presence might have a better effect on Hermogenes, since his madness had apparently taken a religious turn. It is a source of great pleasure to me, reverend Sir, that the choice has fallen on you, whom a happy chance led to this town. You will restore lost peace to a mourning family if you direct your efforts—which the Lord be pleased to bless—towards a double purpose. Probe into Hermogenes' terrible secret; his heart will be lighter when he has unburdened himself, perhaps even in holy confession, and the Church will return him to the joyful life of the world to which he belongs, instead of imprisoning him within the walls of a monastery. But also approach the Baroness. You are now acquainted with the whole situation, and will agree that my observations are such that, inadequate as they may be for levelling a direct accusation against her, at least there is hardly room for error or unjust suspicion. You will share my opinion entirely when you meet her. She has a religious temperament, and your outstanding gift of rhetoric may so succeed in stirring her

emotions that she will abandon this sinful betrayal of my
friend. Finally, I must add that sometimes the Baron seems
to be bearing in his heart a secret grief whose cause he is
withholding from me, for apart from his anxiety about
Hermogenes he is apparently tormented by some other
thought which he cannot shake off. It has occurred to me
that some cruel chance may have revealed to him, even
more plainly than to me, the course of the Baroness' guilty
association with the accursed count. My bosom friend, the
Baron, I also commend to your care, reverend Sir."

                *   *   *   *

With these words Reinhold concluded his story, which
had released strange, agonising conflicts within me.

I had become the sport of a cruel, mischievous fate and
was now drifting helplessly in a sea of events which were
breaking over me like raging waves, so that I no longer
knew where I was. It was evident that Victor had fallen
into the gorge by an accident brought about by my hand,
but not through my intention; I have taken his place, I
meditated, but Reinhold knows Father Medardus, the
preacher from the Capuchin monastery in B., so to him I
really am what I am. But the affair that Victor is carrying
on with the baroness is also my charge, for I am Victor
as well. I am what I seem to be, yet do not seem to be what
I am; even to myself I am an insoluble riddle, for my
personality has been torn apart.

Despite my agitation I managed to assume the calmness
proper to a priest, and was shortly introduced to the Baron.
He was an ageing man, but in his worn features there were
still signs of a rare strength of mind. It was not age that
had drawn the deep furrows across his broad, high forehead
and turned his hair white—it was sorrow. Nevertheless in
all he said and did there was a cheerfulness and affability

which could not but attract everybody. When Reinhold introduced me as the priest whose arrival the Baroness had announced, he turned on me a keen gaze which became more and more friendly as Reinhold told how he had heard me preach in the Capuchin monastery of B. several years previously, and convinced himself of my exceptional gift of oratory. The Baron stretched out his hand in open friendship towards me and said, turning to Reinhold:

"I cannot tell you, my dear Reinhold, how strangely I was attracted by the reverend gentleman's features immediately I set eyes on him. He stirred a vague memory which is trying in vain to become clear."

I felt as though he would burst out: "It is Count Victor!"

For in some mysterious way I really did believe that I was Victor, and the blood brought a flush to my cheeks. I was relying on Reinhold, who knew me as Father Medardus, although that seemed to be a lie—nothing could resolve the contradictions of my situation.

The baron wanted me to meet Hermogenes at once, but he was nowhere to be found. He had been seen wandering off towards the mountains, and nobody had worried about him because he often stayed away for days on end. I spent the whole day in the company of Reinhold and the Baron. Gradually I took hold of myself, until by evening I felt strong enough to face boldly the strange events that seemed to be in store for me. During the lonely night I opened the dispatch-case and assured myself that it really was Count Victor who lay shattered in the ravine—though the letters written to him were in fact quite unimportant, and not one of them gave me the slightest information about his personal circumstances.

The next morning the Baroness arrived unexpectedly with Aurelia. I saw them alight from the carriage and, having been received by the Baron and Reinhold, pass through the door into the palace. Assailed by unaccountable fears, I paced uneasily up and down in my room.

After a short while I was summoned downstairs. The Baroness, a handsome woman still in her prime, came towards me. As soon as she set eyes on me, her voice faltered and she was hardly able to speak. Her obvious embarrassment gave me courage. I looked her boldly in the face and gave her my blessing according to monastic custom. The blood drained from her cheeks, and she was compelled to kneel before me. Reinhold looked at me, smiling happily and contentedly.

At that moment the door opened and the Baron entered with Aurelia. As I caught sight of her, a firebrand fell into my heart, kindling all the secret emotions, the blissful longing, the ecstasy of passionate love, which had hitherto only felt like intimations from afar. Now for the first time life opened out before me in all its brilliant colours, and the past lay dead in the chill darkness behind me.

For it was she whom I had seen in that wonderful vision in the confessional. The pious, innocent, melancholy expression in her deep blue eyes, her soft lips, her neck gently bowed in prayer and reverence, her tall, slim figure—it was not Aurelia, but Saint Rosalia herself! Even the azure shawl she was wearing over her crimson dress hung in folds exactly like the robe of the saint in that painting. How could the voluptuous beauty of the baroness compare with Aurelia's divine loveliness? I was blind to everything around me and saw only her. My emotion could not escape the notice of those standing by.

"What is the matter, reverend Sir?" asked the Baron. "Something appears to have affected you."

These words brought me to myself, and I felt in that instant a superhuman strength rising within me, a new courage to withstand everything. *She* was to be the reward of victory!

"Be of good cheer, Baron!" I cried, as if seized with

sudden inspiration. "A saint is dwelling among us! Soon the heavens will open in dazzling brightness, and the saint herself, Saint Rosalia, attended by the holy angels, will bring consolation and blessing to the contrite who have prayed to her in reverence and faith. I hear the hymns of the transfigured spirits that yearn for her; I hear her voice as she descends from the shining clouds; I see her head radiant in the glory of divine transfiguration, held aloft towards the choir of the saints. Sancta Rosalia, ora pro nobis!"

Turning my eyes heavenwards, I fell on my knees, and everyone followed my example. Nobody questioned me further. My outburst of exaltation was ascribed to a sudden inspiration from above, and the Baron actually had masses read at the altar of Saint Rosalia in the largest church in the town. I had most effectively covered my confusion, and was more than ever prepared to risk everything since it was now a question of possessing Aurelia, to which end I had already bartered my life. The Baroness now seemed in a particularly happy mood. Her glances followed me everywhere, but whenever I looked her straight in the face she averted her eyes uneasily. The family had gone into another room, and I hurried down into the garden and roamed about the paths, wrestling with a host of ideas, plans and resolutions for my future life in the palace.

It was already evening when Reinhold arrived and told me that the Baroness, profoundly moved by my pious exaltation, wished to speak to me in her room. As I entered, she came a few steps towards me, took hold of both my arms and cried, looking into my eyes:

"Can it be? Can it be? Are you Medardus, the Capuchin friar? But your voice, your form, your eyes, your hair! Speak, or I shall perish in fear and doubt!"

"Victor!" I whispered softly, and she embraced me with the wild impetuosity of unbridled desire. A stream of fire tore through my veins, my blood seethed, an unspeakable rapture overpowered my senses. But my sinful thoughts turned only to Aurelia, and at that moment it was only for her that I was breaking my monastic vows and sacrificing my soul's salvation.

For it was only Aurelia who lived in me. My mind was filled with the thought of her, yet an inner dread took hold of me at the idea of seeing her again, which I would have done that same evening. I felt as if her innocent gaze would acuse me of unpardonable sin, that I would be unmasked and crushed, to sink into ignominy and ruin. For the same reason I could not bring myself to face the Baroness so soon after that first encounter, and all this made me decide, when I was summoned to dinner, to remain in my room under the pretext of devotions.

Nevertheless I only required a few days to overcome my fear and embarrassment. The Baroness was kindness itself, and the more intimate our relationship became, and the richer it grew in guilty pleasures, the more she devoted herself to the Baron. She confessed to me that it was only my tonsure, my untrimmed beard and my genuine monastic gait—which, I must admit, I did not maintain as strictly as at the beginning—that had caused her such untold fears; at my sudden, inspired invocation of Saint Rosalia, indeed, she had almost become convinced that some evil chance had thwarted the cunning plan she had made with Victor, and had put in his place a cursed real Capuchin.

*　　*　　*　　*

From time to time Victor's groom appeared at the edge of the park disguised as a villager, and I took the opportunity to speak secretly to him and warn him to hold himself in readiness to flee with me in case any misfortune were to put my life in danger. The Baron and Reinhold seemed highly pleased with me and urged me to espouse the cause of the melancholy Hermogenes with all the power at my command. But I had still not been able to speak to him, for he clearly shrank from being left alone with me, and if he met me in the company of Reinhold or the Baron he looked at me so queerly that it was an effort for me to avoid showing my uneasiness. His eyes seemed to pierce my soul and spy out my most secret thoughts; whenever he saw me, his pale, drawn face assumed an expression of intense bitterness, suppressed hatred, barely-controlled anger.

Once he crossed my path unexpectedly while I was strolling in the park. I considered this a favourable moment to settle at least the painful relationship between us, and just as he was about to elude me I seized his hand and succeeded in speaking so persuasively and consolingly to him that he appeared genuinely moved. We sat down on a bench at the end of a path that led to the palace. Inspiration took hold of me as I spoke, and I told how it was sinful for a man to allow his heart to be consumed with grief, and to despise the comfort and help which the Church offered to the repentant, for he would thereby stultify the purpose of life as ordained by a higher power; and that the transgressor should not doubt the grace of God, since this very doubt would deprive him of the bliss which, his sins being forgiven through penance and devotion, he could yet receive. Finally I enjoined him to confess to me and to pour out his heart before God, so that I might absolve him from all his misdeeds.

He stood up, frowning darkly. His eyes burned and a flush spread across his deathly-pale face. In a shrill voice he cried:

"Are you then free from sin, that you dare to look in loss to my heart as if you were the purest man alive, yea, as if

you were God Himself, whom you despise; that you dare
to pronounce the remission of my sins—you, who will
struggle in vain for forgiveness, for the blessedness of
Heaven which will always be denied you? Despicable
hypocrite, soon the hour of requital will come, and you
will be ground in the dust like a venomous serpent, writhing
in mortal shame and moaning in vain for release from your
unutterable agony!"

He left me abruptly. I was shattered. My composure
and courage had utterly deserted me. I saw Euphemia
coming out of the palace with her hat and shawl, as though
she were going for a walk. She was the one person with
whom I could find help and comfort, and I ran towards her.
She was frightened by my distraught condition and asked
what had caused it. I described to her faithfully the whole
scene that had just taken place between myself and
Hermogenes, adding that I was afraid lest by some chance
he might have betrayed our secret. Euphemia did not seem
in the least perturbed, and smiling in a strange manner
that made me shiver, she said:

"Let us go further into the park, for here we shall be
too closely watched, and it might attract attention if Father
Medardus were to speak so passionately to me."

When we reached a remote shrubbery, Euphemia
flung her arms round me and her hot kisses burned on my
lips.

"You may set your mind at rest, Victor, about all that
has plunged you into such doubt and anxiety. I am even
glad that this situation has arisen between you and
Hermogenes, for now I can and must talk to you about
certain matters which I have long kept to myself.

"You must admit that I have always had an exceptional
intellectual control over my environment. This, I believe,
is easier for a woman than a man, for it is brought about
by the union of that irresistible physical charm which

nature can confer on a woman and a higher spiritual
principle which rules with complete freedom. One of its
aspects is the power to step outside oneself and view oneself
from without, and this then assumes the rôle of a servant
of the superior will in the task of achieving the highest goals
in life. Is there anything greater than to control life from
within life itself, to dispose over all its manifestations, all
its rich delights with the recklessness permitted to a ruler?
You, Victor, have always been one of the few who completely understand me, and I did not disdain to set you
beside me like a royal consort on the throne of my higher
kingdom. The secrecy accentuated the attraction of this
liaison, and our ostensible parting only served to give scope
to fantasy, which played for our delight with the trivial
affairs of everyday life. Is not this present meeting our
boldest venture, which, conceived in a superior mind, jeers
at the impotence of narrow convention? Even when I
consider your strange appearance—which is not only caused
by your clothes—I feel that strength of mind is subservient
to a dominant principle whose miraculous power shapes
and conditions the physical world. You know how this
deeply-rooted attitude of mine towards life leads me to
despise all conventional restrictions. The Baron has
become for me an automaton for whom I feel nothing but
disgust.

"I have already confessed to you that when I saw
Hermogenes for the first time, he made a remarkable
impression on me. I took him to be capable of entering
that higher life which I wanted to disclose to him. This
was my first mistake. There was something in him that
perpetually rose in opposition to me; indeed, the magic
with which I ensnared the others repelled him. He
remained cold, moody, uncommunicative, and by resisting
me with his own peculiar power, he provoked my resentment
and my desire to embark on the struggle in which he would

ultimately be defeated. I had determined on this struggle at the time when the Baron told me that he had suggested to Hermogenes a union with me but that Hermogenes had rejected it out of hand. In the same instant the thought flashed through my mind that by marrying the Baron himself, I would remove at one fell swoop all the petty considerations of convention which had been so repugnant to me. I have spoken often enough to you about this marriage, Victor, and I took action to allay your suspicions. For after a few days I had succeeded in reducing the old Baron to a fond and foolish lover, and he saw my wishes as the fulfilment of the desires which he himself had hardly dared to express. Yet at the back of my mind lay the thought of revenge on Hermogenes, the achievement of which would now be easier and more gratifying; the blow was to be deferred so that it would eventually fall more surely, more heavily.

"If I did not know your heart so well, and if I did not know that you were able to rise to the eminence of my thoughts, I would hesitate to tell you more. I took pains to understand Hermogenes' real nature. I came to the town melancholy and reflective, in contrast to Hermogenes, who was happily and contentedly involved in the affairs of military life. My uncle's illness prevented any social gatherings, and I was able to avoid even visits from my closest companions. Hermogenes came to see me, probably only in fulfilment of the duty he owed his mother, and found me sunk in sorrowful meditation. Surprised at the striking change that had come over me, he asked what had caused it. Weeping, I confided to him that the Baron's ill health, which he only concealed with difficulty, made me fear that I would soon lose him, and that this was an unbearable thought. As I went on to tell with deep emotion of the happiness of my married life, describing vividly yet delicately the closest details of our life in the country, and presenting the full splendour of the Baron's mind and personality so that it became abundantly clear how boundless was my devotion, how complete my absorption into his life, so his amazement grew. He was obviously struggling with himself, but the power which, as though it were my own self, now penetrated his heart, conquered the force that had formerly resisted me. It was evident that I was victorious when he came again the next evening.

"He found me alone, in greater despair and agitation than the day before. I spoke of the Baron and of my inexpressible longing to see him again. Hermogenes was soon no longer the same person; he was held spellbound by my eyes, and their dangerous fire fell burning into his heart. His hand twitched convulsively as it lay in mine, and deep sighs rent his breast. I had skilfully calculated the climax of his unconscious emotion.

"On the evening planned for his downfall I was not above employing those tricks which are so hackneyed yet always so effectively revived. I succeeded! The consequences were even more terrible than I had imagined; the power with which I had fought the hostile element in him had broken his spirit. He went mad, as you know, although hitherto you did not know the real reason.

"It is a peculiar thing about madmen that, as if in closer contact with a mysterious spiritual force, they often pierce our hidden thoughts and express them in strange ways, so that the dreadful voice of a second self sends an unearthly shudder through us. It may therefore be that, in the particular relationship between you, him and me he has seen through you in some way, but that does not expose us to the slightest danger. For consider: even if he were to launch an open attack against you, shouting: 'Do not trust that hooded priest!'—who would take it for anything but a product of his madness, especially as Reinhold has been kind enough to recognise you as Father Medardus? On the other hand, you will no longer be able to exert any influence over him, as I had thought and hoped. My revenge is accomplished. Hermogenes is now as much use to me as a broken toy, and his presence is all the more tiresome in that he probably considers it an act of penance to be near me and pursue me with his half-dead, half-living stares. He must be made to leave here, and I thought that I could employ you to strengthen him in his intention to go into a monastery, and at the same time to work on the Baron and Reinhold with earnest avowals that the salvation of his soul really does require him to become a priest. He is repugnant to me and the sight of him destroys my composure. The only person who sees him in a different light is Aurelia, that naïve, pious child. Only through her can you influence Hermogenes, and I will see to it that you get to know her better. If a suitable occasion presents itself, you can confide to the Baron or to Reinhold how Hermogenes has confessed a serious crime to you, about which, as your duty demands, you must naturally keep silent. But more of that later. Now you know everything, Victor. Be my own true love, and rule with me over the trivial world of puppets which gyrates around us. Life must give us its most glorious pleasures without forcing us into its cramped confines."

We saw the Baron in the distance, and as if engaged in devout conversation, we went to meet him.

*　　　*　　　*　　　*

It was only this account of Euphemia's mode of life which I needed in order to sense the superior strength which flowed through me. Something superhuman had entered into me, lifting me to an eminence from which everything assumed a different perspective, a different character. That power over life of which she boasted merited nothing but the most bitter scorn, for the moment she set out to play her

reckless, immoral game with the most dangerous relationships in life, she would fall into the clutches of the evil
destiny that I wielded over her. Only I had the power to
delude her into taking for her accomplice and lover him who,
chancing to bear a physical resemblance to that lover,
would seize her and destroy all her hopes of freedom. Her
vain, selfish fancy seemed despicable to me, and my liaison
with her became the more repulsive because it was Aurelia
who was living in my heart, and only she who bore the
guilt of my sins—if I had still considered sinful that which
seemed the summit of all earthly pleasure.

I resolved to make the fullest use of the power within
me and describe as with a magic wand the circles within
which all life around me should dance for my delight.

The Baron and Reinhold vied with each other to make
my life in the palace as pleasant as it could be. They had
not the slightest suspicion of my affair with Euphemia; on
the contrary, the Baron frequently declared that only
through me had she been completely restored to him, which
seemed to confirm Reinhold's conjecture that some ill-
chance had put him on the scent on her forbidden ways.
Only rarely did I see Hermogenes. He avoided me with an
evident uneasiness which the baron and Reinhold attributed
to his dread of my pious, holy nature and to my power of
penetrating his distraught mind. Aurelia, too, seemed
intentionally to avoid my gaze, and when I spoke to her
she was anxious and frightened like Hermogenes. I was
almost certain that he had confided to her his horrible
suspicions, yet I still thought it possible to overcome his
evil influence.

The Baron asked me, probably at the instigation of the
Baroness, to instruct Aurelia in the higher mysteries of
religion. Euphemia herself thus furnished me with the
means of reaching the goal which my glowing imagination
had painted in a myriad colours. For what else was that

vision in the chapel but the promise of a higher power to
surrender to me her whom I had to possess if I were to calm
the tempest that raged in me and tossed me to and fro? Her
presence, her nearness to me, even the touch of her dress
set my heart aflame; the blood surged into the secret
recesses of my mind, and I spoke of the holy mysteries of
religion in vivid images whose ulterior meaning was the
sensual craving of an ardent, insatiable love. The burning
power of my words should pierce Aurelia's heart like shafts
of lightning, and she would seek in vain to protect herself.
Unbeknown to her the images which I had conjured up
would grow in her mind, taking on a deeper meaning and
filling her heart with intimations of unknown rapture, until
at last, distracted with passionate yearning, she threw
herself into my arms.

I prepared my so-called lessons with Aurelia carefully,
and knew when to heighten the intensity of my language.
Demurely, her hands clasped together and her eyes cast
down, the pious child listened to me, but no movement,
no sign betrayed that my words had had any deeper effect.
My efforts proved in vain, and instead of kindling in her
the passion which was to make her surrender herself to her
seduction, they only fanned the flames of my own desire.
Frantic with rage, I hatched plans for her downfall, and as
I feigned my happiness, my ecstasy to Euphemia, so a feeling
of hatred began to smoulder in my heart, giving to my
behaviour a strange and terrible savageness which made
her tremble in my presence. She had no inkling of the
secret which I held in my breast, and more and more she
was forced to give way before the power which I wielded
defiantly over her. Often I thought of putting an end to my
anguish by a calculated act of violence against Aurelia,
but whenever I looked at her it seemed as though an angel
were standing beside her, shielding her from the power of
the enemy. A shudder ran through my body as I saw my

evil purpose frustrated.

Finally it occurred to me to pray with her, for in prayer the fire of devotion burns with greater intensity: secret emotions are aroused, stretching out their tentacles towards that mysterious power which shall gratify the longing by which the heart is gripped; the forces of earth usurp the rights of the forces of Heaven, proclaiming that the Supreme Purpose is fulfilled in the highest delights of earth, and that all aspirations to divine virtue will wither away before the irresistible and hitherto unknown pleasures of physical desire. Even through letting Aurelia repeat my own prayers I thought to further my treacherous intention. And so, kneeling at my side and repeating my prayers with eyes directed heavenwards, she flushed deeper and deeper and her breast rose and fell in agitation. As if in the ardour of reverence I seized her hands and pressed them to my heart. I was so near to her that I felt the warmth of her body, and her flowing tresses fell over my shoulder. I was beside myself with frenzy and embraced her savagely, my kisses burning on her lips, her breast. With a piercing scream she tore herself from my arms and fled. I had not the strength to hold her back, for it was as though I had been paralysed by a shaft of lightning. Suddenly the door opened and Hermogenes appeared. He stopped, glaring at me with the terrifying eyes of a madman. Summoning all my courage, I approached him boldly and cried in a defiant, imperious voice:

"What do you want here? Away with you, you madman!"

Stretching out his right hand and pointing at me, he said in hollow, ghostly tones:

"I was about to engage you in combat, but I have no sword. Murderer! Blood is dripping from your eyes and clotting in your beard!"

He vanished, flinging the door shut behind him and

leaving me alone. I ground my teeth in rage at having allowed myself to be carried away by the impulse of the moment, thus exposing myself to the fatal betrayal of my secret. But nobody else appeared. I was able to collect my senses, and soon my mind lighted on ways of avoiding any evil consequences of my wicked act.

As soon as possible I hurried to Euphemia, and with bold insolence told her of the whole incident with Aurelia. She did not seem to treat the matter as lightly as I had wished, and I could well appreciate that, notwithstanding her vaunted strength of mind and superior attitude towards life, there was a certain petty jealousy in her nature, and that in addition to this she was afraid lest Aurelia might reveal my scandalous conduct, thus destroying the halo of my sanctity and endangering our secret. Out of a reluctance which I could not explain, I said nothing about the appearance of Hermogenes or the terrible words he had uttered.

Euphemia was silent for a few moments and gazed at me in an odd manner, sunk in thought. At last she said:

"Ought you not to be capable of guessing, Victor, what noble thoughts are passing through my mind? But you cannot do so. Yet stir your wings to follow the bold course that I am about to fly. I am astonished that you, who should be able to soar above life with complete control over all its aspects, cannot kneel beside a pretty girl without embracing and kissing her, however little I blame you for such a desire. If I know Aurelia, her shame will force her to keep quiet about the episode, and she will only withdraw herself from your over-passionate lessons under some pretext. I am therefore not worried about any unpleasant consequences to which your wantonness and unbridled lust might have led. I do not hate her, this Aurelia, but I am infuriated by her modesty, her cool piety, behind which there lurks an intolerable pride. Although

I did not disdain to play with her, I never succeeded in gaining her confidence; she remained shy and withdrawn. Her unwillingness to adapt herself to my nature, still more her haughty manner of avoiding me, arouse in me the most unpleasant emotions. It is a sublime vision—a flower broken and withered, which once blossomed in the majesty of its resplendent colours—and I do not grudge you its realisation; there will be no lack of ways to achieve it. The guilt shall fall on Hermogenes' head and bring him to destruction."

Euphemia spoke further about her plan and became more contemptible to me with every word, for I saw in her only a mean, iniquitous woman, and ardently as I longed for Aurelia's downfall, wherein lay my only hope of freedom from the agony which was tearing my heart to pieces, Euphemia's collaboration was repellent to me. To her great astonishment I therefore rejected her proposal outright, since I was determined to achieve by my own strength alone the goal towards which she so importunately wished to drive me.

As the Baroness had expected, Aurelia stayed in her room, excusing herself on grounds of indisposition and thereby avoiding my lessons for the next few days. Hermogenes, contrary to his normal habit, now spent much time in the company of the Baron and Reinhold; he seemed less moody but wilder and angrier. He was frequently heard talking loudly and vehemently, and he looked at me with repressed rage whenever chance led me across his path.

*   *   *   *

In the course of the next few days the attitude of the Baron and Reinhold changed in a remarkable way. Without relaxing in the slightest the ostensible considerateness and respect that they had always shown me, they seemed

weighed down by some misgiving which made them unable
to strike that note of geniality which always used to enliven
our conversation. Everything they said to me sounded so
perfunctory, so forced, that, assailed by all kinds of suspicion, I found it an effort to appear unruffled. Euphemia's
glances, which I could always interpret, told me that
something had happened which had disturbed her, but
there had been no opportunity the whole day for us to
speak to each other unnoticed. In the dead of night,
when everyone in the palace had long gone to bed, a hidden
door opened, and Euphemia rushed into my room in a
state of desperation.

"Victor," she panted, "we are threatened by betrayal.
Through some mysterious premonition Hermogenes, the
mad Hermogenes, has sensed our secret. By means of
manifold allusions, which sound like the pronouncements
of some sinister power, he has instilled in the Baron a
suspicion which, though only vaguely expressed, torments
and persecutes me. Hermogenes seems unaware that it is
Count Victor who is concealed beneath those holy robes,
yet he declares that all the treachery, all the deceit, all
the ruin that will descend upon us, stems from you, and
that the monk came into this house to plot accursed cor-
ruption under the inspiration of Satan himself. Things
cannot go on like this. I am tired of enduring this restraint
which the doddering old Baron has imposed upon me; now,
it seems, he is going to dog my steps with puerile jealousy.
I am going to throw away this useless toy, and you, Victor,
will accommodate yourself to my desire with particular
readiness, since thereby you will at once be free of any
danger of being found out or of seeing the inspired situation
which our minds have contrived deteriorate into a vulgar
masquerade, a hackneyed scandal of married life. The
tiresome old man must be got rid of.

"As you know, every morning, when Reinhold is busy,

the Baron goes out alone into the country to enjoy the view. Steal out earlier and try to meet him at the edge of the park. Not far from there is a wild, awe-inspiring cluster of rocky pinnacles; the wanderer who reaches the summit sees on one side a black, bottomless pit gaping up at him, over which projects the so-called Devil's Seat. According to the legend, poisonous fumes rise from the depths, and whoever is foolhardy enough to look down in order to see what is hidden below, succumbs to the fumes and falls to his death. The Baron scoffs at this fairy-tale and often stands on that projecting rock above the gorge to enjoy the view that it affords. It will be easy to induce him to take you. While he is standing there looking out into the distance, a powerful blow with your fist will relieve us of the impotent fool for ever."

"No, never!" I screamed. "I know the terrible gorge and the Devil's Seat! Away with you—and a curse on the monstrous crime you want to make me commit!"

Euphemia sprang up, her eyes flashing wildly and her face contorted with raging passion.

"Miserable weakling!" she cried. "Do you dare to show such cowardice? Would you rather submit to the shameful yoke than rule with me? You are in my hands and in vain will you strive to escape from the power which holds you enfettered at my feet. You shall carry out my command! By tomorrow the man whose presence torments me shall no longer live!"

As Euphemia spoke, I was seized with profound contempt for her pitiful boasting, and in bitter mockery I laughed shrilly. She trembled, and a deathly pallor came into her face.

"You mad woman!" I cried. "You think that you can rule over life and play with its creatures, but beware—this toy will turn into a sharp weapon in your hand and kill you. Learn, O wretched woman, that I, whom you thought to be in the grip of your impotent delusion, hold you as well as fate itself chained in my power. Your wanton sport is nothing but the convulsive writhing of a captive beast in its cage. Learn, O wretched woman, that your lover lies shattered in that gorge, and that in his stead you have been embracing the spirit of vengeance itself. Go, and grovel in the dust!"

She almost fell to the ground in a paroxysm of fear. I caught her and pushed her through the secret door into the passage. I was tempted to kill her but I must have restrained myself without realising it, for as I shut the door, I felt that I had murdered her. I heard a piercing wail and the sound of doors being slammed.

I had now established myself in a position which lifted me completely above the common run of human affairs; blow must follow on blow, and proclaiming myself as the demon of vengeance, I must complete my monstrous task. I had resolved on Euphemia's destruction. My burning hatred, in company with the supreme passion of love, would grant me a delight worthy of the superhuman spirit within me: in the moment of Euphemia's downfall Aurelia would become mine.

I was amazed at the strength of mind which enabled Euphemia to appear cheerful and unconcerned the next day. She spoke of how she had been walking in her sleep and seized with violent fits. The Baron seemed most sympathetic, whilst Reinhold was sceptical and distrustful. Aurelia stayed in her room, and the more unsuccessful my efforts to see her, the more powerful my wrath became.

Euphemia begged me to steal along to her room when everything in the palace was silent, as I had so often done before. At this I was overjoyed, for the moment had come when her fate would at last be sealed. I hid in my monk's habit a small, pointed knife which I had carried with me since my boyhood, and went to her, intent on murder.

"Yesterday," she began, "we both seem to have had a terrible nightmare. There was a great deal in it about a gorge, but that is now all past." She yielded to my wanton caresses as always, but I was filled with fiendish scorn, and felt only delight at my abuse of her shamefulness. As she lay in my arms, the knife fell from my habit. She shuddered; I picked it up swiftly, delaying the murder which had itself placed another weapon in my hand.

She had left some Italian wine and preserved fruit on the table. "How crude," I thought to myself, adroitly exchanging the glasses, and only pretending to eat the fruit she offered me, dropping it instead into my sleeve. I had drunk two or three glasses of the wine—from the glass that she had placed for herself—when she claimed to hear noises in the castle and urged me to leave her quickly; her intention was that I should die in my room. I crept through the long, dimly-lit passages and came to Aurelia's room. I stopped, spellbound; it was as though she were gliding towards me, her loving eyes turned on me as in my vision, beckoning me to follow her.

I pushed open the door and entered the room. A warm breeze was wafted towards me through the half-open door of the bed-chamber, fanning the flame of love and setting my mind in a whirl. I could hardly breathe. She gave a deep, troubled sigh, as if she were dreaming of treachery and murder, and I heard her praying in her sleep.

"Go to it, go to it! What are you hesitating for? The moment is fleeting!"—thus the force within me urged me on. I took a step towards the bed-chamber, when there was a sudden scream behind me:

"Villain! Murderous monk! Now you are mine!"

I felt myself seized powerfully from behind. It was Hermogenes. Summoning all my strength, I burst loose and was about to rush away when he grasped me again and tore madly at my neck with his teeth. Senseless with pain and rage, I wrestled with him until I finally dealt him a blow which forced him to release his hold. As he fell upon me anew I drew my knife. Two stabs and he fell groaning to the floor, sending dull echoes down the corridor —for our desperate struggle had dragged us right out of the room.

As Hermogenes fell, I rushed down the stairs, blind with fury. Cries rang through the palace: "Murder! Murder!" Lights flickered to and fro and footsteps reverberated through the long corridors. In my panic I took the wrong passage and found myself at the remote back-stairs of the palace. The noise became louder, the lights became brighter, the cries of "Murder! Murder!" came nearer and nearer. I could distinguish the voice of the Baron and Reinhold talking excitedly to the servants. Where could I go? Where could I hide? Only a few moments ago, when I was about to murder Euphemia with the same knife with which I had just killed Hermogenes, I felt as though I could walk out boldly with the blood-soaked weapon in my hand, trusting in my own power, for nobody would dare to stop me, but now I was panic-stricken. At last I reached the main staircase. The noise had shifted to the rooms of the Baroness, and things became quieter. In three mighty leaps I was down the stairs, only a few yards away from the entrance. Then a wail echoed through the passages, like the one I had heard the previous night.

"She is dead, murdered by the poison that she had prepared for me!" I said dully to myself.

The crowd poured out of Euphemia's room. Aurelia cried for help. The horrible shouts of "Murder! Murder!" broke out afresh. They were bringing Hermogenes' corpse.

"After the murderer!" I heard Reinhold shout.

I uttered a raucous laugh which resounded through the corridors, and cried in a terrible voice:

"You mad fools, will you tempt the providence that

passes judgment on guilty sinners?"

The tumult ceased, and the whole crowd stopped still on the staircase, rooted to the spot. I was no longer going to flee from them; I would advance upon them, proclaiming in tones of thunder God's vengeance on all transgressors. But—O horrid sight!—before me stood the bloody figure of Victor. It was he, not I, who had spoken. My hair stood on end with terror, and I rushed out into the park in delirium.

Soon I was in the open. I heard the clatter of horses' hooves behind me, and as I was summoning my last ounce of strength to escape from my pursuers, I tripped over the root of a tree and fell full-length. The horses galloped up to me. It was Victor's groom.

"For Heaven's sake, Sir," he cried, "what has happened in the palace? There are shouts of 'Murder!' and the whole town is in an uproar. Still, whatever it is, it was a happy chance that led me to ride out here. Everything is in the knapsack on your horse, for it seems that we shall have to part company for the time being. Something terrible has happened, has it not?"

I pulled myself together, and swinging myself on to the horse, instructed the groom to ride back to the town and await my orders there. As soon as he had disappeared, I dismounted again and led the horse cautiously into the thick pine forest which stretched out before me.

III—THE ADVENTURES OF THE JOURNEY

As the first rays of the sun broke through the dark pine trees, I found myself lying by a clear, fresh stream which flowed over smooth pebbles. The horse, which I had led with difficulty through the thicket, stood quietly beside me, and I had nothing more pressing to do than examine the knapsack that was strapped to the saddle; in it I found clothes and a purse full of gold. I decided to change my appearance at once, and with the help of a small pair of scissors and a comb, which I had found in a box, I trimmed my beard and tidied my hair as best I could. I threw away the monk's habit, which still contained the fateful knife, Victor's dispatch-case and the wicker-bottle with the remainder of the Devil's elixir, and soon I stood there in lay clothes with a travelling-cap on my head, so that when I saw my image reflected in the stream I scarcely recognised myself.

Soon I came to the end of the forest, and from the smoke rising in the distance and the sound of pealing bells I knew that there must be a village not far away. Hardly had I reached the top of the hill in front of me when a pleasant valley opened up, in which nestled a large village. I walked along the broad path that twined down the side of the valley, and as soon as the slope levelled out, I mounted my horse so as to accustom myself to riding, which was an activity unfamiliar to me. I had hidden my

81

monastic robe in a hollow tree and banished to the gloomy
forest all my gruesome memories of the palace. I was in
high spirits, and I felt as though it had only been my over-
excited imagination that had conjured up the vision of
Victor's horrible, blood-smeared face. The last words, too,
that I had shouted at my pursuers seemed to be but an
involuntary consequence of my agitation, disclosing the
true nature of that destiny which had led me to the palace
and caused me to do what I had done. I had come like
providence itself to chastise evil-doers and to redeem
penitent sinners from perdition. Only the sweet image of
Aurelia still lived in me as before, and I could not think
of her without a dull pain gnawing at my heart. Yet it
seemed as if I would find her again in a distant land; as
if, bound to me by indissoluble ties, she must needs become
mine.

I noticed that the people passing by stopped and looked
at me in astonishment, and that even the landlord of the
village inn could not find words to express his surprise at
my appearance. While I was eating my breakfast and the
horse was being fed, several villagers collected in the parlour,
whispering among themselves and looking at me uneasily
out of the corners of their eyes. More and more people
crowded into the room and gathered round me, gaping in
bewilderment. I did my best to remain calm and unruffled,
and in a loud voice I ordered the landlord to saddle my
horse and secure the knapsack. He gave me a crooked grin
and went out, returning after a few moments with a tall
man who approached me officiously with a comical air
of gravity. He looked at me sternly. I returned his gaze,
standing up and moving closer towards him. This seemed
to disturb his composure, and he looked round anxiously
at the assembled villagers.

"Well, what is it?" I said. "You appear to have something to say to me."

He cleared his throat and with an evident effort to sound as impressive as possible, said:

"Sir, you shall not leave here until you have given us, the village magistrate, a detailed account, in every respect, of who you are, your birth, profession and estate, where you have come from and where you are going, with all details of the location of the place, its name, province and town and any other relevant facts. And to prove all this you must produce identity papers, written, signed and properly sealed, in every respect, as is customary and correct."

It had not occurred to me that it was necessary to adopt a name, still less that my odd appearance, caused by the clothes which were quite unsuited to my monastic bearing, as well as by traces of my badly-trimmed beard, might at any moment expose me to the embarrassment of being interrogated about my activities. The magistrate's question took me so much by surprise that I racked my brains in vain to find a satisfactory reply. I decided to see what determined audacity would do, and said firmly:

"I have good reason to keep secret who I am, and it is no use your demanding to see my papers. Furthermore you had better take care not to delay a person of rank with your long-winded stupidity, whatever the pretext."

"Aha!" cried the magistrate, producing a large box into which, as he took a pinch of snuff, the five bailiffs standing behind him thrust their hands and took huge pinches for themselves. "Not so brusquely, my good Sir! Your Excellency will have to permit us, the magistrate, to seek an explanation and examine your papers. To put the matter bluntly, for some time there have been all sorts of suspicious characters lurking about in this district who peep out of the forest and then vanish again, like Old Nick himself. This cursed rabble rob and steal, waylay and murder travellers and cause great damage by fire-raising. Your remarkable appearance, my good Sir, tallies precisely with

that of the chief robber and villain which the most worship-
ful government of the province has given to us, the
magistrate. So without further ado, your papers—or into
the tower!"

I saw that nothing was to be gained from the man in this
way, and tried another approach.

"Your worship," I said, "if you would be so gracious as
to allow me to speak with you in private, I could easily
allay your suspicions and reveal, with complete confidence
in your wisdom, the secret that brings me here in this guise
which you find so unusual."

"Aha! Secrets to reveal, eh?" cried the magistrate. "I
know what that means. Go outside, the rest of you, guard
the door and the windows and let nobody in or out."

When we were alone, I said:

"You see in me, Sir, a luckless fugitive who has managed
with the aid of friends to escape from being shut up for
ever in a monastery. Spare me the pain of telling the details
of my story; it is a web of intrigue and malice cast by a
vindictive family. My love for a girl of humble birth was
the cause of my suffering. During my long confinement
my beard has grown and I had already been given the
tonsure, as you see; besides this I had to wear a monk's
habit. I could not change my clothes until after my flight
into the forest, for otherwise I would have been caught.
You can now understand the reason for my peculiar appearance, and why you were so suspicious of me. I cannot
produce any papers, but I can give you certain evidence
of the truth of my statements, and I am sure you will
accept it."

With this I took out my purse and laid three shining
ducats on the table. The magistrate's pompous gravity
turned to a smirk.

"Your evidence, Sir," he said, "is plausible enough, but
do not take it amiss if we say that it lacks a certain con-

sistency in all details. If you want us to take the rough with the smooth, your evidence must be thoroughly convincing."

I understood the rogue and laid another ducat on the table.

"Now I see," he said, "that our suspicions did you an injustice. Continue on your journey, but keep well to the byways—as you have been probably accustomed to doing in any case—until you have completely rid yourself of your suspicious appearance."

He then flung open the door and called in a loud voice to the assembled crowd:

"The gentleman here is an honourable gentleman in every respect. He has disclosed to us, the magistrate, in a secret audience that he is travelling *incognito*—that is, in disguise—and none of you louts needs to hear or know anything about it. Well, bon voyage, my good Sir!"

The villagers respectfully doffed their caps as I swung myself on to my horse. I intended to gallop through the gate, but the horse began to rear, and in my ignorance and awkwardness I could find no way of getting it to budge. It turned round and round in a circle and finally, to the accompaniment of resounding peals of laughter from the villagers, threw me into the arms of the magistrate and the landlord, who both happened to be hurrying past.

"That is a devil of a horse," cried the magistrate, suppressing his laughter.

"A devil of a horse," I echoed, brushing the dust off my clothes.

They helped me up again but once more the horse reared, snorting and panting; nothing would induce it to go through the gate. Then an old peasant shouted:

"Look! Liza, the old witch, is sitting by the gate and won't let the noble gentleman pass because he hasn't crossed her palm."

7

Up till now I had not noticed a ragged old beggar woman squatting close to the gate and cackling at me like a madman.

"Will you get out of the way, you old hag?" shouted the magistrate. But the old woman screeched:

"My blood-brother hasn't crossed my palm! Don't you see the dead body lying in front of me? My blood-brother cannot jump over it because it will get up, but I will push it down if my blood-brother crosses my palm!"

The magistrate had taken the horse by the reins and tried to pass through the gate without paying any heed to the old witch, but it was of no avail, and she went on screaming:

"Blood-brother, blood-brother, cross my palm, cross my palm!"

I felt in my pocket and threw some coins into her lap. Shouting for joy, she jumped up and cried:

"Look how my blood-brother has crossed my palm! Just look!"

The magistrate let my horse go. It whinnied and galloped off through the gate.

"Now, Sir, you can ride away happily—in every respect!" cried the magistrate. The villagers, who had run after me as far as the gate, laughed uproariously again when they saw how I bobbed up and down as the horse galloped away, and shouted:

"Look at him! Look at him! He rides like a Capuchin!"

The whole episode in the village, especially the fateful words of the crazy witch, caused me considerable concern. The best steps to take seemed to be to rid my external appearance at the earliest opportunity of everything unusual, and to give myself a name with which I could move unobtrusively among the crowd. Life lay before me like an inscrutable fate; what could I do but allow myself to be caught up in its net? My links with the familiar landmarks of life were broken, and I had nothing to hold on to.

More and more people were astir on the road, and everything pointed, even at this distance, to the prosperous city which I was approaching. A few days later it stood before me. Without any questions being asked of me, and without even being looked at closely, I rode into the outskirts. My eyes lighted on a large house with bright windows, above the door of which hung the sign of a golden lion with wings. People were surging in and out, carriages were coming and going, the sound of laughter and the clink of glasses came from the lower windows. As soon as I stopped at the door a porter jumped out, took my horse by the reins and led it away. Another smartly-dressed porter appeared with a rattling bunch of keys and went up the stairs in front of me. When we reached the second floor he glanced quickly at me again and then led me to the next storey, where he opened a modest room and asked me politely what my immediate requirements were; lunch would be served at two o'clock in Room No. 2, first floor; and so on.

"Bring me a bottle of wine!" These were the first words I spoke to these assiduous and obliging people.

Hardly had the porter left when there was a knock at the door, and a face peeped into the room, looking like one of those comic masks I remembered from my childhood. A red, pointed nose, a pair of small, flashing eyes, a long chin, and a high powdered toupee to match, which, as I learned later, trailed off unexpectedly into a Titus cut,* a large ruff, a fiery red waistcoat below which hung two heavy watch-chains, pantaloons, and a coat which was too small here, too large there—in fact, did not fit at all. This figure, still bent in the bow he made as he entered the room, came

---

*Hair cut short and worn dishevelled, a style cultivated by the Roman emperor of that name. (Transl.)

up to me, holding in his hand his hat, scissors and comb, and said:

"I am the barber of this establishment and offer you my services, my most humble services."

There was something so bizarre about the skinny little figure that I could scarcely refrain from laughing. Yet I was glad to see him and did not hesitate to ask him whether he would undertake to tidy my hair, which had got into a terrible state as a result of the long journey and of my clumsy attempts to trim it. He looked at my head with expert eye and said, crooking his right hand gracefully and laying it with extended fingers on his breast:

"Tidy it? Heavens above! Pietro Belcampo, you whom jealous mockers call simply Peter Schönfeld—just as they call that excellent regimental piper and horn-player Giacomo Punto, Jakob Stich—you are underrated. But do you not yourself hide your light under a bushel, instead of letting it shine through the world? Ought not the shape of this hand, ought not the spark of genius that glitters in these eyes, and, in passing, gives this nose the delicate hue of early dawn, ought not your whole person to reveal at once to the experienced glance that you are possessed by the urge to strive after the Ideal? Tidy it, indeed! A frigid expression, Sir!"

I asked the odd little man not to work himself up so much in making these claims for his skill.

"Skill?" he went on in his enthusiasm. "What is skill? Who is skilful? The man who, having judged the distance, jumps thirty yards into a pit? The man who throws a split pea through the eye of a needle at twenty yards? The man who lifts five hundred weight with his sword and balances it on the end of his nose for six seconds, six minutes, six hours? What is skill? It is foreign to Pietro Belcampo, who is imbued with Art, sacred Art. There is something divine about Art, Sir, for Art is not so much the Art about which people are always talking, as all that actually emerges from what people call Art. I know you will understand me, Sir, for you seem a thoughtful person, as I can see from the curl above your right temple."

I assured him that I understood him perfectly. His quaint eccentricity delighted me, and I decided to put his much-vaunted Art to the test, without interrupting his passionate flow.

"What do you intend to make out of my untidy hair?" I asked.

"Anything you wish," he replied. "But if the advice of Pietro Belcampo the Artist counts for anything, let me first observe the shape of your head, your whole figure, your gait, your expressions, your gestures. Then I shall be able to tell whether you incline more to the Classical or the Romantic, the Heroic, the Great, the Sublime, the Naïve, the Idyllic or the Satirical. I shall conjure up the spirits of Caracalla, Titus, Charlemagne, Henry the Fourth and Gustavus Adolphus, or Vergil, Tasso and Boccaccio. The muscles of my fingers will move under the inspiration of these men and the masterpiece will take shape to the tuneful clipping of the scissors. I shall complete your personality in the way it expresses itself in life. But would you now please walk up and down the room a few times, so that I may study you?"

I had to accommodate the grotesque fellow and walked to and fro as he wished, trying as hard as possible to disguise my monastic gait—which is something nobody can entirely cast off, however long it may be since he left the monastery. The little man observed me closely and then began to skip around behind me, sighing and groaning; he took out his handkerchief and mopped his brow. At last he stopped, and I asked him if he had now satisfied himself as to how to trim my hair. With a sigh he said:

"What can I reply, Sir? You do not behave naturally;

you forced yourself to move like that, and two different natures were in conflict with each other. A few more steps, Sir."

I refused outright to parade myself any further and declared that if he had not decided by now how to cut my hair, I would have to decline to avail myself of his "Art".

"Go and hang yourself, Pietro!" cried the little man in exasperation. "You are utterly misunderstood. There is no more faith, no more honesty in this world. You ought to admire my acumen, Sir; indeed, you ought to revere the genius in me. I have tried in vain to make sense of the contradictions in your nature and your movements. There is something in your bearing which points to a priest: 'Ex profundis clamavi ad te Domine—Oremus— Et in omnia saecula saeculorum. Amen.'"

Belcampo chanted these words in a hoarse, croaking voice, at the same time faithfully imitating the posture and movements of a monk. He turned as if before the altar, knelt, and stood up again; then he assumed a proud, defiant attitude, furrowed his brow, opened his eyes wide and cried:

"Mine is the world! I am richer, wiser, cleverer than you all, for you are as blind as bats. Bow down before me!"

"These, Sir," he went on, "are the main elements in your external bearing, and if you wish, I will produce, having regard to your features, your form and your disposition, a fusion of Caracalla, Abelard and Boccaccio, and thus confer on your ethereal locks a wonderful Classico-Romantic form."

There was so much truth in the man's remarks that I considered it advisable to confess to him that I had in fact been a monk and received the tonsure which, as far as possible, I now wished to conceal. With curious leaps and grimaces, and making queer remarks the whole time, he attended to my hair. Sometimes he looked morose and sullen, sometimes he smiled, sometimes he stood in athletic pose, sometimes he stood on tiptoe—in fact, I could scarcely refrain from laughing even more than I had done already.

At last he had finished, and I asked him, before he could bring out the words that were on the tip of his tongue, to send someone up to perform for my unkempt beard the service that he had just performed for my hair. He grinned impishly, crept on tiptoe to the door and locked it. Then he skipped softly back into the middle of the room and said:

"O for the golden days when beard and hair formed a single growth to adorn the head of man and were the delectable charge of a single Artist! But those days have gone. Man has spurned his noblest pride, and a shameful class of persons has surrendered itself to the destruction of the beard with horrid instruments. O shameful, despicable shavers! Whet your knives on black straps soaked in foul-smelling oil, to the mockery of our Art! Swing your tufted pouches, clatter about with your basins and lather the soap, splashing boiling water around! Ask your patients with wanton insolence whether they would like to be shaved over the thumb or the spoon! There are Pietros who are working against your contemptible trade and, debasing themselves to your activity of exterminating the beard, are still trying to salvage what remains after the flood-tide of fashion has receded. The thousand varieties of side-whiskers with their graceful curls, sometimes softly caressing the side of the face, sometimes drooping sadly over the hollow of the neck, sometimes standing up boldly above the corners of the mouth, sometimes confining themselves modestly to a narrow line, sometimes spreading out in a gallant flourish—what are these but the invention of our Art, in which is revealed our aspiration towards the Beautiful, the Divine? Ah, Pietro! Display your true spirit and show what you are prepared to do on behalf of Art by demeaning yourself to the intolerable job of shaver!"

While he was speaking he had produced a complete set of shaving irons and begun to relieve me of my beard with a light, experienced touch. I left his hands a different person, and only needed some less conspicuous clothes to be completely free of the risk of attracting any unwelcome attention, at any rate by my appearance.

The little man smiled at me with immense satisfaction. I told him that I was a stranger to the city and would be grateful if he could supply me with clothes in the current fashion. In return for his efforts and to encourage him to act as my servant, I pressed a ducat into his hand. He was transfigured with joy.

"O most noble patron of the Arts! My Maecenas!" he cried. "I was not mistaken in you. The spirit directed my hand, and your lofty character is plainly expressed in the magnificent sweep of your side-whiskers. I have a friend, a Damon, an Orestes, who will complete for your body what I have begun for your head, and with the same profound understanding, the same genius. You will observe that he is a Sartorial Artist—for thus I call him, instead of that commonplace expression, tailor. He likes to roam the realms of the Ideal, and from the shapes and forms in his imagination he has arranged a whole display of the most diverse items of clothing. You will see the modern gentleman of fashion in every conceivable refinement—now boldly outshining everyone, now morose and disinterested, now naïvely flirting, now ironic, witty, ill-tempered, melancholic, bizarre, dissolute, graceful, jovial. The youth who for the first time had a coat made without the cramping advice of his mama or his tutor; the gay old man, the scholar, the rich merchant, the prosperous citizen, just as they are found in real life—all these are hanging in my Damon's wardrobe, and in a few moments my friend's masterpieces will be displayed before you."

He skipped nimbly away, reappearing soon afterwards with a tall, strong, well-dressed man, quite the opposite of the barber both in his appearance and in his whole nature, whom he introduced to me as his Damon. Damon studied me for a few seconds, then took out of a parcel, which a boy had carried in after him, some items of apparel which were in complete accordance with the wishes I had expressed. In fact, only later did I come to appreciate the tact of the Sartorial Artist (as the barber preciously called him) in having shown such discernment, for nothing attracted undue attention, yet I was respected whenever I was noticed. It is very difficult to dress oneself so that the general character of one's clothes shall not provoke the thought that one's occupation is this or that. The clothes of the man of the world are characterised by negative features and conform more or less to what is called polite conduct, itself distinguished rather by omission than commission.

The little man launched out into further grotesque opinions, and since few people probably lent him such a willing ear as I, he seemed excessively anxious to impress me. But Damon, a serious and apparently sensible man, suddenly cut him short, and gripping him by the shoulder, said:

"Schönfeld, today you are again in the mood to prattle your stupid rubbish. I'll wager that the gentleman's ears are already aching from all the nonsense you have been pouring out."

Belcampo hung his head sadly, then seized his dusty hat and cried, as he sprang out of the door:

"And that's the way my friends debase me!"

Bidding me good-day, Damon said:

"He is a clown of a most peculiar kind, this Schönfeld! By reading so much he has become half-mad, but for the rest he is a good-humoured fellow and skilled in his trade,

which is why I like him. For if a man can achieve something in one particular direction, I feel that he should be
allowed to kick over the traces in others."

*   *   *   *

As soon as I was left alone I started seriously to practise
my walk in front of the tall mirror that was hanging in
the room. The little barber had made a true observation:
a monk walks with a certain ponderous, ungainly haste,
caused by the long robe that restricts his stride and by his
efforts to move swiftly as his order requires. Similarly there
is something so characteristic about the way his body is
bent back and the way he holds his arms—which must
never hang down, because when his hands are not clasped
together they are tucked into the sleeves of his habit—that
an observant person would not easily overlook it. I tried
to rid myself of all these traits so as to destroy all trace of
my former estate. I consoled myself by thinking of my
former life as worn out, and by imagining that I was now
beginning a new existence. The crowds of people, the
incessant hubbub of activity in the streets—all was new to
me and well suited to the maintenance of the cheerful mood
into which the comical little man had put me. In my new
clothes I ventured downstairs into the well-appointed
restaurant, and all my anxiety disappeared when I saw
that nobody was paying any attention to me, and that my
neighbour did not even trouble to look up as I sat down
beside him. In the guest-book I had entered myself as
Leonard (remembering that it was to the prior that I owed
my freedom), a man of private means, travelling for
pleasure. There were probably many such travellers in the
city, so I was very unlikely to be asked any further questions.

My favourite occupation was to stroll down the streets,
looking at the fine shops and at the paintings and engravings

which were displayed. In the evening I used to join the
promenaders in the park, but the feeling that I was cut off
from the life of the thronging crowds often filled me with
resentment. However useful it was to me in my present
situation, there was something terrifying in the realisation
that I was known to nobody, that no-one could have the
slightest idea who I was, or what singular quirk of fate
had brought me here, or what secrets I was concealing.
I felt like a departed spirit walking an earth in which all
the affection he had once enjoyed had long since perished.
When I called to mind how as preacher I had everywhere
met with cordiality and respect and how everyone crowded
round to exchange a few words with me, a wave of bitterness
swept over me. But that preacher was the monk Medardus,
who now lies buried in a mountain-gorge, so he cannot be
I, for I am alive, enjoying to the full the pleasures which
this new-found life now offers me.

Such were my thoughts whenever my dreams brought
back to me the events in the palace, as though they had
befallen some other person; and this other person was the
Capuchin again, not I. The only link between my former
existence and that which I was now leading was the
thought of Aurelia, but like a deep-seated and ever-
present pain it destroyed the enjoyments of the moment
and estranged me from my new life.

I did not fail to visit the many clubs and casinos in the
city. One particular place had taken my fancy where a
large company gathered every evening on account of the
excellent wine. At a table in a side-room I always found
the same people; their conversation was lively and intelligent, and I succeeded in being accepted into the exclusive
circle by providing an interesting piece of literary information which they were vainly trying to recall. They made
room for me at their table all the more willingly since they
were attracted by my eloquence and erudition, for by

delving every day more deeply into different branches of learning of which I had perforce remained ignorant hitherto, I was constantly increasing the scope of my knowledge. Thus I gained many delightful acquaintances, and as I grew more and more accustomed to life in the world, so my mind became calmer and happier, and I smoothed off all the rough edges left from my former way of life.

For several evenings people had been talking a great deal about a foreign painter who had arrived in the city and was holding an exhibition of his works. Everybody but myself had seen the paintings, and they praised their excellence so warmly that I determined to go and see them for myself.

The painter was not there when I entered the room, but an old man acted as guide and named the other artists whose works the painter was exhibiting together with his own. There were wonderful paintings among them, mostly originals of the great masters, and I was thrilled beyond measure. Some of the paintings which the old man described as sketches made from large frescoes, aroused memories of my childhood. They grew clearer and clearer, brighter and brighter the longer I looked at them. They were copies of pictures in the Holy Linden! In a picture of the Holy Family, for instance, I recognised the features of Joseph as those of that strange pilgrim who had brought the wonderful boy to the convent.

A feeling of profound sorrow came over me, and I could not restrain a loud cry when my gaze lighted on a life-size portrait in which I recognised the abbess, my benefactress. Wearing the magnificent robes in which she used to lead the procession of the nuns on Saint Bernard's Day, she shone with that ideal glory which characterises the portraits of Van Dyck. The artist had caught her at the moment when, having finished her silent prayer, she was about to leave her chamber at the head of the procession for which the congregation, seen in the background, were waiting expectantly. On her noble countenance lay the supreme expression of a spirit utterly devoted to the things of Heaven. It was as if—O agony!—she were seeking forgiveness for a brazen sinner who had torn himself from her heart—and I myself was this sinner. Feelings I had long since forgotten surged through me, and I was again with that kindly priest in the village of the Cistercian convent, a happy, carefree child jumping for joy because it was Saint Bernard's Day. I saw the abbess standing before me. "Have you been kind and good, Franciscus?" she asked in a voice whose solemnity was mellowed by love. What, alas, could I answer? I had broken my vow, I had heaped crime upon crime, I had even committed murder! Torn by grief and contrition I fell on my knees, tears pouring from my eyes. The old man, startled, hastened over to me and asked agitatedly:

"What is the matter, Sir?"

"The portrait of the abbess is very much like my mother, who died a cruel death," I muttered dully, getting to my feet and trying to pull myself together.

"Come, Sir," said the old man, "such memories are too painful and should be avoided. Here is another portrait, which my master considers the best. It is taken from real life and was only recently completed; we removed it from the wall so that the sun should not spoil the paint, which is not yet quite dry."

He made me stand where the light was most suitable and then drew the curtain swiftly aside. *It was Aurelia.* A feeling of horror came over me. I sensed the presence of the fiend who was intent on hurling me back into the roaring torrent from which I had only just escaped, and my courage returned.

Avidly I drank in Aurelia's charms, which shone forth

from the glowing picture. Her meek, innocent eyes seemed
to accuse me of the foul murder of her brother, but all
feeling of penitence perished in the bitter scorn which rose
in my heart and drove me with poisoned darts from a life
of kindness and goodness. The only thought that tantalised
me was that I had not possessed her on that fateful night
in the palace; the appearance of Hermogenes on the scene
had frustrated my plan, but he had paid the penalty with
his life. Aurelia was alive, and that was enough for me
to indulge my hope of making her mine. She was certain
to succumb to me, for an ineluctable fate hung over her—
and was not I myself that fate?

Gazing on the picture I thus emboldened myself for my
crime. The old man seemed surprised at me; he prattled
on about design, tone, colour, but I did not hear him. The
thought of Aurelia and the hope of accomplishing the evil
deed which had only been delayed, absorbed me so completely that I hurried away without inquiring after the
painter or investigating more closely the circumstances
surrounding these pictures, which were like a cycle of
allusions to my whole life. I hatched all manner of plots
for achieving my purpose, and in particular I reckoned on
learning many things from the painter and uncovering
new aspects of the situation which might be useful for the
fulfilment of my aim. For that aim was nothing less than
to return to the palace in my new guise, and this did not
even strike me as a particularly reckless venture.

*   *   *   *

That evening I joined the company in the club, determined to put a curb on the working of my fiery imagination
and to calm the ever-growing agitation in my mind. There
was considerable discussion about the foreign painter's
works, especially about the unusual expressions that he gave

his portraits. I was able to join in the praise, describing the incomparable charms of Aurelia's angelic face in brilliant phrases which were merely the reflection of that mocking irony which burned in my heart like a ravaging fire. One of the company said that he would bring the painter along the following evening; he was staying in the city until he had completed several portraits he had already started, and despite his advanced years he was still an excellent and interesting artist.

Assailed by strange forebodings, I joined the circle later than usual the following evening. The painter was sitting at the table with his back to me. As I sat down and turned my eyes towards him, I found myself looking at the terrible features of that mysterious figure who had leant against the pillar in the chapel on Saint Anthony's Day and filled me with such fear and dread. He studied me gravely for a long time, but the courage and strength that the sight of Aurelia's picture had given me enabled me to meet his gaze. The enemy had entered the field: now was the time for battle to be joined. I decided to wait for the attack and then repulse it with weapons on whose strength I could rely.

The painter did not appear to take any particular notice of me. Turning away, he continued the conversation on art in which he had been engaged when I arrived. The discussion turned to his paintings, and Aurelia's portrait was particularly praised. One person maintained that, although it looked at first sight like a portrait, it might well serve as a study for the picture of a saint. I was asked for my opinion, since I had described the excellencies of the picture in such glowing terms. Instinctively I replied that I could not imagine Saint Rosalia other than in this portrait, The painter hardly seemed to hear my words but went on:

"The woman of whom this is a true likeness is indeed a saint, aspiring to the celestial heights. I painted her at a

time when she was in sore distress and seeking comfort in
religion; it is the expression of this hope, which is only
found in spirits exalted above the lowly affairs of earth,
that I have tried to capture."

The conversation passed to other topics, and the atmosphere was enlivened by the wine, which today, in honour
of the painter, was of better quality and more liberally
dispensed than usual. Everybody had something entertaining to tell, and although the painter only seemed to show
his pleasure by the expression in his eyes, he was able to
keep the party in full swing by interposing spirited comments
now and again. Even though I could not repress a feeling
of uneasiness whenever he looked at me, I gradually over-
came the terror which had seized me when I first set eyes
on him.

I told of the comical Belcampo, whom they all knew, and
so delighted them with my shrewd representation of his
fantastic drolleries that a fat, good-natured merchant sitting
opposite assured me with tears in his eyes that this was the
most delightful evening he had spent for a long while. When
the laughter finally began to subside, the painter asked
suddenly:

"Gentlemen, have you ever seen the Devil?"

All the guests took this question to be the prelude to some
joke or other, and admitted that they had not yet had that
honour. The painter went on:

"Well, I was not far from having that pleasure at
Baron F.'s palace in the mountains."

I trembled in every limb, but the others laughed and
shouted:

"Go on! Go on!"

"When you make the journey through the mountains,"
continued the painter, "you pass, as you probably all
remember, a wild, terrifying spot at which a deep, black
gorge reveals itself to the wanderer as he emerges from the

thick forest on to the high, rocky cliffs. It is the so-called
Devil's Gorge, and overhanging it is a rock called the
Devil's Seat. It is said that Count Victor, with evil thoughts
in his mind, was sitting on this rock, when the Devil
suddenly appeared and hurled him into the abyss because
he was attracted by Victor's foul intentions and had
decided to carry them out himself. The Devil then came
to the Baron's palace in the guise of a Capuchin friar, and
after he had had his pleasure with the Baroness he con-
signed her to eternal damnation. At the same time this
friar strangled the Baron's mad son who would not tolerate
the devil's anonymity and had cried out: 'This monk is
the Devil!'. But through his action a pious soul was saved
from the perdition which the Devil had planned for her.
Afterwards the friar disappeared in a mysterious fashion,
and people say that he fled like a coward from Victor,
whose bloody figure had risen from the grave. However
that may be, I can at least assure you that the Baroness
was poisoned and Hermogenes assassinated; that the Baron
died of a broken heart shortly afterwards; and that
Aurelia—the pious saint whom I portrayed at the time when
these tragic events were happening—fled, a lonely orphan,
to a distant country and sought refuge in a Cistercian
convent where the abbess had been a friend of her father's;
you have seen the picture of this noble woman in my
gallery. But this gentleman here he (pointed to me) will
be able to tell you everything more fully than I, since he
was present in the palace the whole time.

All eyes were turned on me in amazement. I sprang up
indignantly and cried:

"What have I to do with your foolish stories of the Devil
and your tales of murder? You mistake me, Sir, you mistake
me indeed, and I would be glad if you would leave me out
of these affairs."

My emotion made it difficult for me to give my protest

8

even this degree of equanimity, for the effect of the painter's words was only too apparent. My cheerful humour vanished, and the guests, recalling how I had originally been quite unknown to them and only gradually become one of their number, now regarded me with distrust and suspicion.

The painter rose, fixing me with his half-dead, half-living eyes as he had done in the chapel. He said nothing; he stood there still and lifeless, but his ghostly stare made me shudder. A cold sweat broke out on my forehead and my limbs trembled.

"Away with you!" I shouted, beside myself. "You yourself are Satan! You are the evil murderer, but over me you have no power!"

They all jumped up.

"What did he say? What did he say?" they cried. People left their card-tables in the salon and surged into the room, frightened by the fearful tone of my voice. Several of them shouted:

"A drunkard! A madman! Take him away! Take him away!"

But the painter remained impassive. Frantic with rage and desperation, I snatched from my side-pocket the knife which I always carried and with which I had killed Hermogenes, and rushed at the painter, but with a single blow he threw me to the ground with a mocking laugh which rang through the room.

"Brother Medardus! Brother Medardus! You are playing a deceitful game! Go! And humble yourself in shame and sorrow!"

I felt myself gripped from all sides. Summoning my strength, I tore through the crowd like a bull, knocking several of them down as I fought my way to the door. I rushed along the corridor. A small side-door opened, and I was pulled into a dark room; I did not resist, for the mob was close on my heels. When the tumult had passed by, I was led down some steps and into a courtyard, then through the side-buildings and so into the street. By the bright rays of the lanterns I saw that my rescuer was Belcampo, the barber.

"These people," he said, "seem to have had some fateful connection with the painter. I was drinking a modest glass in the next room when the noise started, and I decided, since I know the ins and outs of the house, to rescue you. For it is I who bear the guilt for this ill-starred episode."

"How can that be? I asked in astonishment.

"Who can command the moment? Who can resist the beneficence of the celestial power?" rejoined the little man passionately. "When I was arranging your hair, Sir, the loftiest ideas came to me *comme à l'ordinaire*. I surrendered myself to unbridled fantasy and not only forgot to give the appropriate smooth and graceful form to the temper-curl on the top of your head but also left twenty-seven hairs of fear and terror above your brow. When the painter—who is, incidentally, a ghost—stared at you, these hairs stood up and leaned over in pain towards the temper-curl, which thereupon fell apart with a hissing and crackling. I saw everything. Burning with rage you drew a knife on which, Sir, there were bloodstains. But it is vain to attempt to despatch to Orcus him who already belongs to Orcus, for this painter is Ahasuerus the Wandering Jew, or Bertrand de Born, or Mephistopheles, or Benvenuto Cellini, or Saint Peter—in short, a contemptible ghost who is to be banished either by a red-hot hair-iron that curls the idea which is actually the ghost himself, or by skilfully setting with electric combs the thoughts that he must absorb in order to nourish that idea. As you observe, Sir, to me, an imaginative artist by profession, such matters are nothing but bubbles—a metaphor which, drawn from my own art, becomes more appropriate than one thinks, if the soap from which the bubbles come contains pure oil of cloves."

At last we reached my room. Belcampo helped me pack, and soon everything was ready for my departure. I pressed several ducats into his hand, and he jumped for joy, shouting:

"Hurrah! Now I have some honourable money, pure, shining gold, soaked in life's-blood and flashing its red rays. That is nothing but an idea, Sir, and a merry one at that—nothing more!"

Probably as a result of the disapproval which I showed of this outburst, he begged to be allowed to give the temper-curl its proper form, to trim the hairs of terror, and to take a love-lock as a souvenir. I let him have his way, and he completed these tasks to the accompaniment of the most grotesque grimaces and gestures. Finally, taking hold of the knife which I had laid on the table while changing, he struck a duelling posture and made a lunging movement through the air.

"I am slaying your adversary," he cried, "and since he is a mere thought, it must be possible to kill him with a thought; he will therefore die at the hands of this thought of mine, which, in order that its effect may be the stronger, I am providing with a suitable physical accompaniment. *Apage Satanas, apage, apage, Ahasverus, allez-vous-en!*"

Putting down the knife, he gave a sigh of relief and wiped his brow with the air of one who had strained every fibre in order to accomplish a difficult task. I wanted to hide the knife quickly, and plunged it into my sleeve as though I were still wearing my monk's robe. The little man observed this and gave a cunning grin.

At that moment the post-horn sounded in front of the house. Belcampo's tone and manner suddenly changed. Taking out a small handkerchief and pretending to wipe the tears from his eyes, he bowed respectfully time after time, kissed my hand and the hem of my coat, and said entreatingly:

"Two masses for my grandmother, who died of indigestion, four masses for my father, who died of unavoidable fasting, Sir! But for me, when I am dead, one mass every week. For the time being, remission of many, many sins. O noble Sir, there dwells within me a wicked, sinful fellow who says: 'Peter Schönfeld, do not be such a fool as to believe that you actually exist. It is I who am your real self, I whose name is Belcampo. I am an inspired thought, and if you do not believe it, I will strike you down with one of my sharp, razor-edged ideas.' This evil creature, who calls himself Belcampo, Sir, commits all manner of crimes: amongst other things he often doubts the existence of the present, gets horribly drunk, starts fights and ravishes beautiful virgin thoughts. This Belcampo has driven me, Peter Schönfeld, into a state of utter confusion, causing me to leap about indecorously and disgrace the name of innocence by singing *In dulci jubilo* with white silk stockings on. I crave forgiveness for both of them—Pietro Belcampo and Peter Schönfeld!"

Kneeling at my feet, he pretended to sob. The man's idiotic behaviour began to irritate me.

"Do talk sense!" I cried.

In that instant the servant came in to take my luggage. Belcampo sprang around, and chattering the whole time, helped him to fetch what I needed in my haste.

"That fellow is an out-and-out clown; you must not take too much notice of him," said the servant, as he shut the door of the coach. Belcampo waved his hat and cried, as I laid my finger meaningfully against my lips:

"Till my dying breath!"

When dawn broke, the city lay far behind me, and the haunting vision of that fearful, menacing figure had vanished. The coachman's question: "Where to?" brought home to me how I had forsaken all friendship in life and was roaming the earth at the mercy of the rolling waves of chance. Yet had not an unchallengeable power wrenched me away from everything to which I had been attached, just so that the spirit within me should unfurl and beat its wings with irresistible force? Like a nomad I roved through the countryside, finding no peace. I was driven on and on, further and further southwards. Without realising it, I had up to now hardly deviated from the itinerary laid down for me by Leonardus, and as if impelled by his will, I journeyed onwards.

*   *   *   *

One dark night I was travelling through a thick forest which, the coachman told me, stretched up to and beyond the next stopping-place. He advised me to wait with him till morning, but in my desire to reach my mysterious goal as quickly as possible, I refused. As the coach moved off there were flashes of lightning in the distance and the clouds which the wind had hurled together and was driving across the sky, became blacker and blacker; the thunder rolled in a thousand echoes, and red lightning rent the heavens as far as the eye could see. The tall pines cracked, shattered to their roots, and the rain poured down in torrents. We were in danger of being struck at any moment by falling trees; the horses reared, frightened by the dazzle of the lightning, and soon we were hardly able to move forward at all. At last the coach was flung about so violently that one of the rear wheels broke, and we had to stay in that spot until the storm abated and the moon broke through the clouds.

The coachman now realised that in the darkness he had somehow missed the road and taken a forest track; there was nothing for it but to follow this track as best we could and so perhaps reach the next village by daybreak. He underpinned the coach with the branch of a tree and proceeded step by step. I was walking in front of the coach,

and soon I observed in the distance the twinkle of a light
and thought I heard dogs barking. I was not mistaken, for
a few moments later we came to a large house which stood
in a wide courtyard surrounded by a wall. The coachman
knocked on the gate. The dogs jumped and barked
excitedly but in the house itself everything was deathly
silent. The coachman then sounded his horn. A window
opened upstairs, and a deep, gruff voice shouted down:

"Christian! Christian!"

"Here, Sir!" came the reply from below.

"Somebody is knocking at the gate and blowing a horn,"
continued the voice, "and the dogs are making an infernal
row. Take a lantern and the musket number three and
see what the matter is."

Soon we heard Christian coaxing the dogs away and at
last he appeared with the lantern. The coachman was
certain that, instead of driving straight on at the beginning
of the forest, he had turned off to one side, and that we were
now at the gamekeeper's house which was an hour's ride
to the right of the previous coach-stop. When we told
Christian of our mishap, he immediately opened both the
gates and helped to push the coach in. The dogs, now quiet,
wagged their tails and sniffed around us. The man, who
had not left the window, shouted down repeatedly:

"Who's there? Who's there? What's that procession
down below?"

But neither Christian nor either of us gave any answer.
While Christian was putting the coach and horses away, I
went into the house, and a tall, strong man with a sun-
tanned face came towards me, a green tufted hat on his
head, but still in his nightshirt and with slippers on his feet.
He was holding his hunting-knife in his hand and shouted
harshly at me:

"What's going on? What are you disturbing people for
in the middle of the night? This is not an inn or a coach-

stop. The district gamekeeper lives here—that's me. Christian is a dolt for opening the gate."

Crestfallen I told him of my predicament, saying that only an emergency had led us there. He became more amenable and said:

"That's all very well; I admit that the storm was heavy, but the coachman is a rogue for taking the wrong track and breaking the coach. A fellow like that ought to be able to drive blindfold in the forest and be as much at home there as I am."

He led me upstairs, and putting down the hunting-knife and taking off his hat, he threw his cloak over his shoulders and begged me not to be angry at the brusque way he had received me, for in his remote and lonely house he had to be particularly on his guard against dissolute rabble that often roamed the forest; moreover there was a more-or-less open feud between him and the so-called Devil's marksmen, who had often made attempts on his life.

"But the scoundrels cannot get at me," he went on, "for with God's help I carry out my duty faithfully and defy them in the name of my trust in Him and of my own uprightness."

In accordance with the old habit which I could not break, I involuntarily added a few words of comfort concerning the strength to be derived from a trust in God, and the game-keeper became more and more cheerful. In spite of repeated protestations on my part he awakened his wife, an elderly but merry, active matron, who welcomed me kindly and began, at her husband's behest, to prepare a meal. The gamekeeper had punished the coachman by making him return to the village with the broken coach that same night, whilst he, the gamekeeper, offered to take me to the next coach-stop whenever I wished. I readily accepted his offer, for I felt in need of a short rest, and told him that I would like to stay until the afternoon of the following day so as to recover completely from the weariness caused by travelling uninterruptedly for several days on end.

"If you take my advice," replied the gamekeeper, "you will stay here the whole of tomorrow and wait until the next day; my eldest son, whom I am sending to the town where the Prince's court resides, will be able to take you himself as far as the next coach-stop."

I agreed to his suggestion and spoke in praise of the lonely situation of the house, which greatly attracted me.

"Lonely it certainly is not, Sir," said the gamekeeper, "unless, as the average townsman does, you call every house lonely which is in the forest, even though it depends very much on who lives in it. If, for instance, this old hunting-lodge were still inhabited, as it used to be, by a morose old man who locked himself up in his four walls and took no pleasure in the forest or in hunting, then it probably would be a lonely spot. But after this man's death the Prince turned the building into a gamekeeper's lodge, and it has become a most cheerful place. You, Sir, are probably a townsman who understands nothing of the forest or the joys of hunting, and you cannot imagine what a happy life we huntsmen lead. I and my lads form a single family, and, whether it strikes you as peculiar or not, I include in it my intelligent dogs as well; they understand me and heed my beck and call, and will remain faithful to me until they die. Do you see how intelligently my dachshund looks at me, because he knows I am talking about him?

"There is alway work to do in the forest. In the evening we make our plans; with the first rays of dawn I leave the house, sounding a cheerful call on my horn; the others rouse themselves from their beds and the dogs begin to bark, eagerly waiting for the hunt to start. The lads quickly pull on their clothes, throw their guns and their pouches over their shoulders, and go into the parlour where my wife has prepared breakfast. Then we set out in high spirits.

"When we reach the spot where the game is hiding, we each take our separate positions, while the dogs move softly to and fro, sniffing the ground and watching us with an almost human understanding. We stay motionless and scarcely breathing, our triggers cocked. And when the animals leap from the thicket, and the shots ring out, and the dogs break loose—then Sir, one's heart beats faster and one becomes a different man. It is a new experience every time we go out, for something fresh always happens; even the fact that different animals appear at different times makes the adventure so thrilling that no man could ever tire of it.

"Moreover, the very forest itself, Sir, is so alive and so cheerful that I am never lonely. I know every corner in it, and I feel as though every tree which sways in the wind knows and loves me because I have watched over it and tended it while it grew; I even believe that in its strange murmuring and rustling it is speaking to me in its own tongue, praising God and His almighty power and offering up prayers which cannot be expressed in words. In short, Sir, a devout and honest gamekeeper leads a fine and happy life, for he preserves something of that wonderful freedom which man enjoyed when he lived close to Nature and knew nothing of the contortions and artificialities with which he now torments himself and which have estranged him from all the glories which God provided for his enjoyment and benefit."

The old gamekeeper spoke in a voice which left no doubt how deeply he felt, and I envied him his happy life and the profound serenity of his nature, which was so unlike mine.

In another part of what I now saw to be a rather rambling building the gamekeeper showed me to a small but clean room where my luggage had already been put, and left me alone, assuring me that any early noise in the house would not disturb me since I was quite apart from the other members of the household and could sleep as long as I liked; breakfast would be brought up to me when I called, but I would not see him, the gamekeeper, until lunch-time, because he would be going into the forest with the boys in the early morning and would not return home before midday. I threw myself on to the bed and, exhausted as I was, soon fell into a deep sleep.

But I was tortured by a terrible dream, which in some strange way started with my consciousness of being asleep, for I said to myself: "It is fortunate that I have fallen asleep at once and am slumbering so deeply and peacefully; I shall awake refreshed but I must not open my eyes."

Yet although I could not resist doing so, my sleep was not interrupted. The door opened and a dark figure entered whom I recognised to my horror as my own self in Capuchin robes, with beard and tonsure. The figure came nearer and nearer my bed; I lay motionless, and every sound I tried to utter was stifled in the trance that gripped me. The figure sat down on my bed and leered mockingly at me.

"You must come with me," it said. "Let us climb on to the roof beneath the weathercock, which is playing a merry tune for the owl's wedding. Up there we will fight with each other, and the one who pushes the other over will become king and be able to drink blood."

I felt the figure take hold of me and lift me up. With a strength born of desperation I screamed: "You are not me, you are the Devil!"—and clawed at the face of the menacing spectre. But my fingers went through his eyes as if they were empty cavities, and the figure burst into strident laughter.

At that moment I awoke with a jerk, but the laughter went on. I sprang up; the bright rays of dawn were breaking through the window, and I saw a figure in Capuchin garb standing in front of the table with his back to me. The gruesome dream was coming true.

The monk was rummaging among the things on the table. Then he turned round, and my strength returned when I saw an unknown face with an unkempt black beard and eyes which laughed with the vacant stare of madness; he seemed to bear a faint resemblance to Hermogenes. I decided to await what he would do and only to restrain him if he should become violent. My knife lay beside me, and this, combined with my own physical strength, would be sufficient to overpower him without help from anyone else.

He seemed to be playing with my possessions like a child; his particular pleasure was the red dispatch-case which he swung to and fro towards the window, jumping about in a queer fashion. At last he found the wicker-bottle with the remainder of the mysterious elixir. He opened it and smelled it. Then he shuddered and let out a horrible scream which echoed through the room. A clock in the house struck three. He gave a shriek as if gripped by sudden pain, and broke out afresh into the raucous laughter I had heard in my dream. Leaping around wildly, he drank from the bottle and then, flinging it away, rushed out of the door. I got up swiftly and ran after him but he was already out of sight; I heard him racing down the distant stairs, and there was a dull thud as of a door being slammed. I locked myself in so as to be spared a second visit and got into bed again. I was now too exhausted not to fall asleep immediately, and I awoke, refreshed and strengthened, with the sun streaming into the room.

The gamekeeper, as he had told me he would, had gone into the forest. His younger daughter, a pleasant girl in the bloom of youth, brought me breakfast while the elder daughter was busy in the kitchen with her mother. The girl told me in her charming way how they all lived happily and contentedly together; the only occasions they were disturbed by a crowd of people were when the Prince was hunting in the district and sometimes spent the night in the house.

The hours went by and midday arrived. Sounds of merriment and a fanfare of horns announced the return of the gamekeeper with his four sons, fine, healthy youths, the youngest of whom could have been barely fifteen years old, together with three other boys. He asked how I had slept and whether the noise had woken me too early; but I did not like to tell him of my adventure, since the actual appearance of the terrifying monk had merged so completely with my dream that I could scarcely distinguish where dream passed into reality.

The table was already laid and the soup was steaming. The gamekeeper had taken off his cap to say grace, when the door opened and the Capuchin I had seen in the night entered. The madness had vanished from his face but he looked sullen and peevish.

"Welcome, reverend Sir!" cried the gamekeeper, "Say grace and join us at table!"

The monk looked round, his eyes burning with rage, and screamed:

"The Devil take you and your 'reverend Sir' and your cursed grace! Did you not lure me here to be Number Thirteen, and to have me murdered by the mysterious assassin? Did you not dress me in this habit so that nobody should recognise me as the Count, your lord and master? Beware of my wrath, cursed man!"

With this he seized a heavy jug that was standing on the table, and hurled it at the gamekeeper's head. The gamekeeper ducked adroitly, and the jug, which would have split his skull open, crashed against the wall and broke into a thousand pieces. The boys immediately gripped the madman and held him fast.

"What?" cried the gamekeeper. "Do you dare, you wicked, blasphemous man, to start your insane ravings before pious folk? Do you dare again to make an attempt on my life—I who once rescued you from the condition of an animal and saved you from eternal damnation? Away with you to the tower!"

The monk fell on his knees in tears and pleaded for mercy, but the gamekeeper said:

"You shall be put in the tower and not return here until I know that you have disowned Satan. Otherwise you shall die!"

The monk cried out as if in peril of death, but the boys took him away and reported when they returned that he had become quieter as soon as he had entered the chamber in the tower. They also reported that Christian, who was guarding him, had told them that the monk had been roaming noisily through the house the whole night, shouting, especially just after daybreak: "Give me more of your wine and I will surrender myself to you body and soul! More wine! More wine!" It had, indeed, seemed to Christian as if the monk were tottering about in a drunken state, though he could not understand how he could have come by intoxicating liquor.

When I heard this, I no longer hesitated to tell of my adventure, not forgetting to mention the empty wicker-bottle.

"Ah, that's bad," said the gamekeeper. "But you, Sir, appear to be a devout and courageous man; another might have died of shock."

I asked him to tell me more about this mad monk.

"Oh, it is a long and exciting story," he replied, "quite unsuitable for the table. It is bad enough that the villainous fellow disturbed us with his shameful behaviour just as we were about to receive what God had given to us. But let us now eat without further ado."

He took off his cap and said grace earnestly and rever-ently. Talking cheerfully, we ate the nourishing and tastilyprepared country meal. The gamekeeper had good wine brought up in my honour and drank a toast to me out of a fine goblet, according to patriarchal custom. The table was then cleared, and the boys took some horns from the wall and played a hunting-song. The second time round the girls sang as well, and the gamekeeper's sons joined in the chorus of the last verse. I was strangely moved; for a long time I had not felt as happy as I did now among these simple, honest folk. They sang a few more tuneful songs, then the gamekeeper rose and drained his glass to the toast of "Long live all upright men who honour the noble sport of hunting!" We all drank, and thus ended the meal which with wine and song had been turned into a celebration in my honour.

"I shall now rest for half-an-hour, Sir," said the game-keeper to me, "but afterwards we shall go into the forest, and I will tell you how the monk came into my house and what else I know about him. By that time it will be dusk and we can take up position in our hiding-places to wait for the wild-fowl which Franz tells me are there. You too shall be given a good musket to try your luck."

This was a new experience for me; I had often taken part in target-shooting while I was in the seminary but had never shot fowl or game. I therefore accepted the game-keeper's offer, to his evident pleasure, and even before his rest he good-humouredly tried to teach me in great haste the fundamental principles of shooting.

Equipped with musket and game-bag I sallied out into the wood with the gamekeeper, who then began his story of the strange monk.

*   *   *   *

"It will be two years this coming autumn," he began, "since my boys used to hear a terrible wailing in the forest.

However inhuman the sound seemed to be, Franz, the apprentice I had just taken on, still believed that it might come from a human being. Franz was destined to be plagued by this wailing monster, for when he took up position in his hiding-place, the wailing sound, which sounded close at hand, scared the animals away. At the last moment, just as he was about to take aim, he saw an unrecognisable bristly creature jump out of the bushes and spoil his shot. Franz's head was full of all the weird legends that his father, himself an old hunter, had told him, and was inclined to take the creature for Satan himself. The other boys who had run up against the monster, even my sons, confirmed Franz's story, and I was especially anxious to solve the problem as I took it to be a trick on the part of the Devil's marksmen to scare my hunters away from their vantage-points. I therefore ordered my sons and the boys to challenge the figure if it appeared again and then, if it did not stop or reply, to fire at it without hesitation, as is the huntsman's right.

"Franz was once more the first to meet the monster. He shouted at it and aimed his rifle. The figure sprang into the bushes. Franz pulled the trigger but the gun did not go off, and he ran in fear and terror to the others, who were some distance away from him, for he was convinced that it was Satan who, in defiance, had scared the game away and bewitched his gun. And indeed, after this he did not shoot a single animal, though he had been a fine shot before. The rumour spread that there was a ghost in the forest, and the villagers told wild stories about how Satan had approached Franz and offered him magic bullets, and so on.

"I resolved to put an end to the mystery myself and to lie in wait for the monster, which had never yet crossed my path, in those places where it usually appeared. For a long while I had no luck, but at last, on a foggy November

evening, when I was in the hiding-place from which Franz
had first seen the monster, I heard a rustling in the bushes
nearby. I put the gun softly to my shoulder, expecting to
see an animal, but a dreadful figure with flashing red eyes
and bristling black hair rushed out, dressed in rags. The
monster glared at me, uttering terrible screams. It was a
sight, Sir, that would have made the bravest heart shrink;
I was sweating with fear and felt as though the Devil himself
were standing before me, but I spurred my courage by
praying fervently in a loud voice. As soon as I spoke the
name of Jesus Christ, the monster howled all the more
furiously and burst out into shocking curses and blasphemies.
Then I cried:

'You villain! Stop your blasphemous language and
surrender yourself to me, or I will shoot you on the spot!'

"The man fell whining to the ground and begged for
mercy. My boys came up and, taking hold of him, led him
to the house, where I had him locked in the tower; I
intended to report the matter to the authorities the next
morning. As soon as he was put into the tower he lost
consciousness.

"When I went to him the following day, he was sitting
on a bed of straw that I had had laid down for him, weeping
bitterly. He fell at my feet, and implored me to have pity
on him; he had been living in the forest for weeks and had
eaten nothing but herbs and wild fruits; he was a poor
Capuchin friar from a distant monastery who had escaped
from the prison where he had been kept as insane. He
really was in a pitiful condition. I took compassion on him
and ordered food and wine to be brought. He entreated
me to let him stay in the house for a few days; if I would
obtain a new habit for him he would return to the monastery
by himself. I fulfilled his request, and his insanity appeared
to abate, for his paroxysms became rarer and less violent.
In his fits of delirium he uttered terrible oaths, and I

9

noticed that whenever I addressed him sharply on these occasions and threatened him with death, his spirit broke, and he chastised himself fiercely, calling on God and the saints to free him from the torments of hell. He seemed to imagine that he was Saint Anthony, just as in his frenzy he always raved that he was a Count and a ruler, and that he would have us all shot when his servants came. In his moments of sanity he begged me not to cast him out because he felt that only by staying with me could he be healed.

"Only once did I come to blows with him. The Prince was hunting in the neighbourhood and had spent the night here. After seeing the Prince and his brilliant retinue, he was completely changed. He became silent and peevish; he went away quickly whenever we prayed, and shuddered whenever he heard a pious word; and besides this, he looked at my daughter Anne with such lascivious eyes that I decided to take her away in order to prevent any mischief. But the night before I intended to do this I was awakened by a piercing scream in the passage. I jumped out of bed and ran to the room where my daughters slept. The monk had broken out of the tower and stormed with animal lust to my daughters' room. He had already kicked down the door, but fortunately Franz, who had been unable to sleep for thirst and was about to go into the kitchen to fetch himself some water, heard him rushing down the passage. He ran out and seized him from behind but he was not strong enough to control the madman. The girls screamed as the two men fought by the door, and I arrived just as the monk had hurled the lad to the ground and gripped him by the throat. Unhesitatingly I took hold of him and tore him away from Franz. But suddenly, I still do not know how, a knife gleamed in his hand and he threw himself on me. Franz, who had got up quickly, fell on his arm, and being a strong man, I was soon able to tie him so tightly to the wall that he could hardly breathe. All the boys had woken up and run out of their rooms. We bound the monk hand and foot and flung him into the tower, but I fetched my whip and gave him a few powerful cuts as a warning against any further outrages.

" 'You miserable wretch!' I cried. 'That is far too little for your disgraceful conduct. For trying to ravish my daughter and making an attempt on my life you ought to be shot! '

"He moaned with fear and terror, for the threat of death seemed to crush his spirit completely. The following morning it was impossible to take him away, for he was lying there prostrate, as though dead, and I was touched with pity. I ordered a comfortable bed to be prepared in a better room, and my wife tended him, cooking nourishing soups for him and giving him from our medicine-chest whatever she thought proper. At last he began to get better and often made the sign of the cross according to monastic custom, and prayed. He once started quite unexpectedly to sing Latin hymns, whose wonderful melodies so touched the heart of my wife and daughter—though they could not understand the words—that they were never tired of telling how the sick man had uplifted them.

"The monk had now so far recovered that he was able to get up and walk around the house, but both his appearance and his character were entirely changed. His eyes had a gentle expression instead of the pernicious fire that used to shine in them; he walked up and down softly and devoutly with his hands clasped together, as if he were in the monastery, and all trace of madness had vanished. He ate nothing but vegetables, bread and water, and only rarely could I persuade him to join my table. When he did come he said grace and delighted us with his talk, for he was possessed of a rare eloquence.

"He used to go for lonely walks in the forest, and on one

occasion I happened to meet him. Without any ulterior motive in mind I asked him whether he intended to return soon to his monastery. He appeared greatly disturbed and said, gripping my hand:

" 'My friend, to you I owe the salvation of my soul. You have rescued me from eternal damnation, but I cannot yet leave you. Let me stay here. Have pity on him whom Satan tempted and who would have been irrevocably lost had not the saint to whom he prayed in the hour of terror led him into this forest.'

" 'You found me,' continued the monk after a pause, 'in an utterly degenerate state, and I doubt whether you know even now that I was once a youth rich in nature's blessings, and that I only entered the monastery as the result of a fanciful inclination to solitude and abstruse studies. The brethren were all extremely fond of me, and I experienced a contentedness only to be found in a monastery. I distinguished myself by devoutness and exemplary conduct, and people saw in me a future prior. It so happened that one of the brethren returned to the monastery at that time from far afield, bringing with him a number of relics which he had succeeded in acquiring. One of these was a sealed bottle which Saint Anthony was said to have taken from the Devil, who had kept a captivating elixir in it. This relic was preserved along with the others, although the whole affair seemed to me to be in bad taste and completely opposed to the spirit of devotion which true relics should inspire. I was filled with a desire to learn what the bottle really did contain, and having managed to procure it, I opened it and found a strong drink of wonderful aroma and sweet flavour which I drained to the last drop. I will not tell you how my whole temperament was changed, how I felt a burning urge to taste the pleasures of the world, how the seductive image of vice came to represent the highest in life. My existence became a series of abominable crimes, and when in spite of my cunning I was found out, the prior sentenced me to life-long imprisonment. After I had spent several weeks in a damp, dark cell, I cursed myself and my existence and blasphemed against God and the saints. Then Satan appeared to me in a cloud, promising that if I would turn from Heaven and serve only him, he would release me. Sobbing, I fell on my knees and cried: 'I serve no God. You alone are my master, and from your burning coals of fire shine the joys of life!' There was a mighty rush of air. The walls shuddered as though shaken by an earthquake, a piercing wail filled the dungeon, the iron bars on the window were shattered, and, as if hurled by some invisible force, I found myself in the monastery courtyard. The moon shone brightly through the clouds, and its rays illuminated the statue of Saint Anthony which stood close by a fountain in the middle of the courtyard. An unaccountable fear shot through my heart. I cast myself down in remorse before the saint, abjuring evil and pleading for mercy, but black clouds gathered overhead and the roar of the hurricane was heard again. I lost consciousness and only came to myself in the forest, where I roamed about, frantic with hunger and fear, until you rescued me.' "

"That is the story the monk told me," said the gamekeeper, "and it made such a deep impression on me that in many years' time I shall be able to repeat it word for word just as I can today. Since then he has behaved so piously, so gently that we have all grown fond of him, and it is all the more inexplicable to me how his madness could break out afresh as it did last night."

"Do you not know from what monastery the wretched man escaped?" I asked.

"He never told me," replied the gamekeeper, "and I am unwilling to ask, since it is almost certain that he is the same unhappy person who was recently the talk of the court, though nobody suspected he was in the neighbourhood;

and for his sake I did not want my suspicions to become known at the court, of all places."

"But may I not be allowed to know," I insisted, "since I am a stranger? I will promise not to breathe a word about it."

"First of all, then," the gamekeeper continued, "you must understand that our princess' sister is the abbess of the Cistercian convent in . . . She had adopted and educated the son of a poor woman whose husband is supposed to have had obscure connections with our court. Through his own desire he became a Capuchin, and attained fame far and wide as a preacher. The abbess frequently wrote to her sister about her protégé, and some time ago deeply mourned his loss. He had abused one of the relics and been banished from the monastery whose pride he had been for so long. I learned all this from a conversation I overheard not long ago between the prince's physician and another of the courtiers. They referred also to some highly remarkable circumstances which, because I am not thoroughly familiar with the whole affair, I did not understand and have since forgotten. If, therefore, the monk explains his escape from the monastery prison in some other way, and says that it was due to Satan, then I take it to be pure fantasy, produced by the last remains of his madness. For in my view the monk is none other than that Brother Medardus whom the abbess had brought up to become a priest and whom the Devil tempted into manifold sin, until God punished him by inflicting on him the madness of a beast."

At the mention of the name Medardus a shiver went down my spine. The whole story had felt like a rain of powerful blows on my heart. I was quite convinced that the monk had spoken the truth, for only a Devil's potion such as he had so greedily drunk could have plunged him anew into wicked, blaspheming delirium. But I myself had sunk to the condition of a miserable plaything of that sinister power which held me in its chains, for I who believed myself free could only move about within the cage in which I was helplessly imprisoned. The good teaching of pious Cyrillus which I had not heeded, the visit of the count and his frivolous tutor—everything came back to me.

I was sunk in thought and hardly heard the gamekeeper, who had returned to the subject of hunting, describing to me some of the skirmishes he had had with the Devil's marksmen. It was dusk, and we were standing in front of the bushes where the wild-fowl were said to be; he put me into position and warned me not to speak or move about, and to listen carefully with rifle cocked. The boys crept away softly to their positions, and I stood alone in the gathering darkness. Characters from my life appeared before me in the gloomy forest: I saw my mother and the abbess looking at me reproachfully; Euphemia stole up to me, her face deathly pale and her black eyes fixed on me; she raised her bloody hands menacingly, hands stained with the blood that had gushed from Hermogenes' wound. I let out a scream. There was a beating of wings above my head; I fired blindly into the air and two birds fluttered to the ground.

"Hurrah!" shouted a boy not far from me, as he shot a third. Shots now echoed all around and the huntsmen assembled, each bringing his prize. The boy said, looking askance at me, that I had shouted out when the fowl flew close above my head and then, without even aiming properly, had fired indiscriminately and yet hit two of them; he even said that in the darkness it had looked as though I had pointed the gun in an entirely different direction, but the birds still fell to the ground.

The old gamekeeper laughed at the idea that I had been afraid of the birds and had only fired at them in self-defence.

"Besides, Sir," he continued in jest, "I trust that you are an honest huntsman and not one of the Devil's marksmen, who fire at random yet never fail to hit their target."

His chaff, though meant innocently enough, struck home, and even my lucky shot filled me with terror. My soul was divided within itself, and I was in the grip of a paralysing fear.

When we got back to the house Christian reported that the monk had behaved quietly in the tower: he had not spoken a word, nor had he eaten anything.

"I cannot keep him with me any longer," said the gamekeeper, "for who can guarantee that what appears to be an incurable malady will not break out afresh some time and cause him to wreak havoc in this house? Early tomorrow morning he must go with Christian and Franz to the town; my report on the whole incident has long been finished, and he can be taken to the mental asylum."

When I was left alone in my room I seemed to see Hermogenes standing before me, but whenever I tried to look at him more closely, he turned into the mad monk. I came across the wicker-bottle which was still lying on the floor. The monk had drained it to the last drop, which relieved me of any further temptation to drink from it. But it still gave out a strong smell, and I flung it through the open window and over the courtyard wall so as to destroy any possible effect of the fateful elixir.

I felt drawn irresistibly towards the town. The abbess' sister, who, I now recalled from often having seen her picture, looked very much like the abbess herself, would lead me back to the pious, innocent life I used to lead, for in my present mood I needed only to see her to recapture the memory of those days. I would leave it to providence to bring me into her presence.

Day had hardly dawned when I heard the gamekeeper's voice in the courtyard. I was due to leave early with his son, and dressed hurriedly. When I came down, an open cart with straw seats was standing at the door, ready to leave. The monk was brought out, a hunted look on his pallid features, and allowed himself to be led into the cart. He would not reply to any questions and wanted nothing to eat; he scarcely seemed conscious of the people around him. They lifted him on to the cart and bound him tightly, for his temper was unpredictable and they were by no means safe from a sudden outburst of suppressed rage. As they tied his arms, his face twitched convulsively and he gave a dull groan. His plight touched me deeply: there seemed a kind of kinship between us; indeed, it was perhaps to his very ruin that I owed my salvation. Christian and one of the boys sat on either side of him in the cart. Only as he was driven away did his gaze light on me. Suddenly a look of profound amazement spread over his face; even when the cart was some distance away (we had followed it as far as the gate) his head remained turned, his eyes fixed on me.

"Look how hard he stares at you," said the old game-keeper; "I believe that your presence in the dining-room contributed considerably to his hysterical behaviour, for even in his sane moments he was very timid and always afraid that some stranger would come here to murder him. He lived in perpetual fear of death, and I often countered his frenzied outbursts by threatening to have him shot there and then."

I felt happy and relieved that the monk who was a horrible, distorted reflection of my own self had finally been removed, and I looked forward to my journey to the town, where I felt that the burden of the evil fate that oppressed me would be lifted.

When we had finished breakfast, the gamekeeper's smart coach, pulled by lively horses, drew up at the door, and I scarcely had time to give the good lady of the house some money in return for the hospitality which she had lavished on me, and to press upon the two pretty daughters a few trinkets that I happened to have with me. The whole family said goodbye to me as affectionately as if I had long been a friend of the family, and the old gamekeeper made many more jests about my powers as a marksman. Happy and cheerful, I drove away.

IV—AT THE PRINCE'S COURT

T HE town proved to be precisely the opposite of the city I had left behind. Much smaller in size, it was more uniformly and attractively built, but the streets were almost deserted; some of them in which avenues of trees had been planted seemed more like the grounds of a park than part of a town. The people I saw moved in a quiet and dignified manner, and the rattling of a coach rarely disturbed the stillness. Even in the dress and bearing of the inhabitants, right down to the humblest, there was a certain refinement, an effort to present a cultured appearance.

The Prince's palace was large, though not built in the grand manner, and in respect of elegance and formal proportion one of the finest buildings I had ever seen; adjoining it was a charming park which the Prince had generously thrown open to the townsfolk. At the inn where I was staying I was told that the Prince and his family usually took a stroll through the park in the evening, and that many people took the opportunity to see their noble lord. I hurried into the park at the appropriate hour and the Prince came out of the castle with his lady and a small group of retainers. I soon had eyes for nobody but the Princess—for how she was like the abbess! The same august presence, the same grace of movement, the same intelligent eyes, the same broad forehead, the divine smile; the only difference was that her body seemed fuller and more youthful than her sister's. She was talking kindly to some women who were standing in the avenue, while the Prince seemed absorbed in earnest conversation with a serious-looking man. The way the noble family were dressed, their demeanour, their entourage, everything harmonised with the surroundings. It was clear that the air of peacefulness and unaffected refinement which characterised the town, emanated from the court.

I was standing beside a man, intelligent and of lively disposition, who provided me with information on all kinds of topics, interpolating as he did so many entertaining comments. When the Prince and his family had gone, he suggested that we might take a stroll through the park. I readily consented, and found everything infused with a spirit of elegance and order, except that in a number of pavilions the imitation of Classical forms—which, by their nature, are only successful on a large scale—appeared to have led the architect into trivialities. Greek columns, the capitol of which a tall man can almost reach by stretching out his hand, are somewhat ludicrous. Similarly there were in another part of the park a few Gothic pavilions whose scale was so small as to be absurd. I hold the view that to imitate Gothic forms is almost more dangerous than to strive after Classical ideals, for although small chapels offer considerable opportunities to an architect restricted, both by the size of the building and by the money at his disposal, to build in the Gothic manner, it cannot be done simply by introducing pointed arches, bizarre columns and sundry embellishments copied from this or that church; the only architect who will achieve anything genuine in this style is he who is inspired by its inner spirit, that spirit which filled the old masters who were able to fuse the apparently separate and contradictory elements into a single glorious, meaningful entity. In a word, the Gothic architect must be impelled by a particular awareness of the Romantic, since here there is no question of his keeping to a pattern of rules, as he can with Classical forms.

All this I explained to my companion, who agreed with me completely, merely excusing the presence of these pavilions by saying that in a park it was necessary to have a certain variety, and that such buildings were needed, for example, as shelters in the event of a storm, or simply as resting-places, so that lapses of taste were virtually inevitable. To this I replied that for such purposes I would prefer simple, unassuming chalets—just tree-trunks spanned with a thached roof—shrouded by bushes, to all these finicky little temples and chapels; then if a building of stone and timber ever had to be erected, an architect with only limited scope and means at his disposal would have a style available which, whether tending towards the Classical or the Gothic, would offer the spectator a pleasing prospect, free from affectation and shallow imitation.

"I fully share your opinion," answered my companion, "but all these buildings—in fact, the lay-out of the whole park—are the work of the Prince himself, and this consideration bars any criticism, at least among us inhabitants of the town. The Prince is the noblest man one could imagine; right from the beginning he held to the paternal principle that his subjects were not there for his benefit but he for theirs. There are many things here that will make your stay a pleasant one:—the freedom to express whatever is in one's mind; the low taxes and consequently the low price of all the necessities of life; the virtual absence of police, who are able to check any outbreak of crime quietly and without inconveniencing either inhabitants or visitors with a disagreeable officiousness; the stamping-out of misbehaviour on the part of the soldiers; and above all the relaxed and friendly spirit in which trade and commerce are carried on. I will wager that you have not yet been asked your name and rank: nor, as happens in other towns,

will the hotel-proprietor have come up to you in the first
fifteen minutes, solemnly carrying under his arm a big book
in which he makes you fill in your own death warrant with
a broken pen and pale-coloured ink. In fact, the whole
constitution of our small state, in which a true spirit of
wisdom and tolerance prevails, is the creation of our noble
Prince, for previously, I am told, the people were irritated
by the stupid affectation of the court, which had set itself
up as a small-scale copy of the large court not far away.
The Prince loves the arts and the pursuit of knowledge, and
welcomes any skilled artist, any intelligent thinker; the
extent of his own knowledge is the only test which he applies
to a prospective newcomer to his circle.

"Yet into the learning which the versatile Prince has
acquired has crept something of that affectation which
stunted his education and now shows itself in a slavish
devotion to one style or another. With pedantic thoroughness he gave the architect descriptions and sketches of every
detail of the buildings, and the slightest departure from
these plans, in the preparation of which he had drawn on
all manner of historical works, worried him as greatly as
did the occasions when this or that aspect could not be
adapted to the smaller scale on which the restricted space
compelled him to work. Our theatre also suffers from this.

"The Prince moves from one pet interest to another,
but without offending anybody at all. When the park was
being laid out, he was a passionate architect and gardener;
then he became engrossed in the development of music in
recent years, and it is to this particular enthusiasm that
we owe the existence of our excellent orchestra. He then
turned to painting, in which he himself achieved no small
success. His vacillation even shows itself in court entertain-
ments. There used to be a great deal of dancing; now faro
is played at every party, and although he does not play
himself, he takes delight in witnessing the strange coincid-

ences of fate. However, it only needs a fresh stimulus, and something different will take its place.

"This fickleness has resulted in the Prince being accused of lacking the intellectual capacity to form a picture of life which shall faithfully reflect its many facets, but in my view this is unjust, since it is only an exceptional liveliness of mind which leads him to follow now this, now that impulse, and he never loses sight of the nobility of the interests which he pursues. That is why you find this park so well kept, why our theatre and our orchestra are continually being helped in every conceivable way, and why the art collection is being added to whenever possible. And as for the changes in the order of court entertainment, these are simply quirks which one must permit our hard-working Prince to indulge in when he seeks a rest from his serious and often laborious tasks."

We were just passing a group of shrubs and trees which was particularly tastefully laid out, and I expressed my admiration of the scene.

"All the floral arrangements," said my companion, "are the work of our beloved Princess. She is an accomplished landscape-painter, and besides this, the study of nature is her favourite pursuit. Hence you will find here exotic trees and many rare flowers and plants—not, however, displayed as in an exhibition but sensitively arranged as though they had grown up on their native soil. The Princess expressed a strong dislike of the statues of gods and goddesses, naiads and dryads, all carved from crude sandstone, with which the park was littered, so they were removed. All you will now find are a few good Classical busts which the Prince wanted to keep for sentimental reasons, and these the Princess, with a sympathetic understanding for his feelings, erected in such a way that they made a remarkable impression, even on people unaware of their secret associations."

It was now late evening, and we left the park. My companion accepted my invitation to supper at the inn, and disclosed that he was in fact the curator of the Prince's art gallery. As we grew better acquainted during the course of the meal, I confided in him my desire to get to know the Prince and his family. He replied that this could easily be arranged, since any cultured and intelligent person was welcome at court: I would only need to present myself to the Chamberlain and request him to introduce me to the Prince. Such an official procedure did not appeal to me, for I could scarcely hope to avoid embarrassing questions concerning my background, where I had come from, and so on. I therefore decided to leave everything to chance, in the hope that some easier way would present itself—which it shortly did.

One morning when I happened to be taking a stroll in the park at a time when it was usually deserted, I saw the Prince coming towards me in simple, unassuming dress. I greeted him as though I did not know who he was; he stopped and opened the conversation by asking whether I was a stranger. I admitted that I was, adding that I had arrived a few days ago and had only intended to pass through the town, but that the charm and restfulness of the place, and especially the hospitality I had met with everywhere, had induced me to stay for a while; indeed, being of independent means and living only for the sake of art and learning, I was of a mind to spend a considerable time here, since the whole district greatly attracted me. The Prince seemed pleased at this and offered to act as my guide in a complete tour of the park.

Concealing the fact that I had seen everything already, I allowed myself to be led through all the grottos, chapels, Gothic temples and pavilions, and listened patiently to the long-winded commentaries which he gave on each building. Everywhere he named the originals on which the buildings had been modelled, drew my attention to the precise manner in which the tasks had been carried out, and expatiated on the principles which underlay the arrangement of his park and which ought to underlie the arrangement of every park. He asked my opinion, and I praised the charm of the place and the rich, luxuriant vegetation. He listened attentively and did not seem entirely to reject certain aspects of my judgments, but he cut short any further discussion by saying that, although I might well be right from an idealistic point of view, I seemed to lack knowledge about the practical considerations and the actual manner of execution. The conversation turned to the arts, and I showed myself to be a connoisseur of painting and a practical musician. I ventured at times to oppose his judgments, which expressed accurately and intelligently enough his inner convictions but also revealed that his culture, though far superior to that of most of the nobility, was too superficial to allow him to sense the depths from which the splendours of art spring and kindle in the true artist the spark of aspiration towards truth. He considered my views and contradictions as proof of my dilettantism which was not informed by true practical insight, and he instructed me on the real nature of painting and music, on the requirements of portrait-painting and opera; I learned about colour, drapery, pyramidal groups, serious and comic music, scenes for the prima donna, ensembles, dramatic effect, stage lighting, and so on. I listened to everything without interrupting him, and he seemed well-pleased with himself. At last he broke off his disquisition and asked suddenly:

"Do you play faro?"

I said that I did not.

"It is a wonderful game," he went on; "in its utter simplicity the real game for intelligent men. It takes you out of yourself, or rather, it brings you to a point from which

10

you are able to observe the strange webs and patterns woven by an invisible force we call chance. Win and lose are the twin poles round which revolves the mysterious machine which we have set in motion and which is now driven on inexorably by the spirit dwelling within it. You must learn the game; I will teach you myself."

I confessed that hitherto I had not felt attracted to a game which, I had often been told, was extremely dangerous. The Prince smiled and, looking keenly at me with his bright, twinkling eyes, rejoined:

"Nothing of the kind! Those who maintain such an attitude are childish. But if I go on, you will take me for a gambler who is trying to ensnare you. I am the Prince. If you like it in this town, stay here and join my circle, where we sometimes play faro. I will not admit that it has a disruptive influence, in spite of the fact that the stake must be of some consequence to make the game interesting; for chance is listless if it is offered unimportant tokens."

As he was about to leave me, the Prince turned and asked:

"But with whom have I had the honour?"

I replied that my name was Leonard, a scholar, and not being of noble birth might not be permitted to avail myself of his gracious invitation to mix in court circles.

"Who cares about nobility!" he cried. "I have seen for myself that you are an intelligent and well-informed person. Your knowledge ennobles you and entitles you to move in my circle. Adieu, Herr Leonard!"

My wish was thus to be fulfilled more easily than I had thought. For the first time in my life I was to appear at court—even, in a sense, to live at court—and my head was filled with all the adventurous court intrigues and cabals hatched by writers of romances and comedies. According to the testimony of these gentry the Prince has to be surrounded by villains of all kinds; the seneschal has to be an absurd nincompoop insisting on his ancestral pride, the chief minister a covetous, scheming rogue, the retainers immoral men and seducers; every face is carefully wreathed in smiles, whilst in every heart is trickery and deceit; the courtiers fall over each other with kindness and tenderness, they bow and scrape, but each is the other's deadly enemy, always craftily trying to trip him up and then, when the man behind takes his place, to do the same to him; the ladies-in-waiting are ugly, haughty, intriguing and love-sick, and lay snares which have to be avoided like poison. Such was the picture of court life which I had brought with me from my reading in the seminary; it always seemed as if the Devil had complete freedom to play his tricks there, and although Leonardus had been at many courts and told me much about them which did not tally with my own conception, I still remained rather apprehensive of every-thing courtly, an apprehension which made itself felt in this very moment when I was on the point of actually going to court myself. My desire to become acquainted with the Princess, and an inner voice which kept telling me in strange tones that here my destiny would be revealed, drove me onwards, and at the appointed hour I took my place, not without trepidation, in the Prince's ante-chamber.

My prolonged stay in the city had served to remove from my bearing all the stiffness and awkwardness left from my monastic life. My lithe, well-built body soon accustomed itself to the free, natural movement of the man of the world; the pallor which disfigures the young monk, even if he is handsome, had vanished from my face. I was in my prime, my cheeks flushed and my eyes shining, and my dark-brown hair covered all trace of the tonsure. Add to this my dark, well-cut clothes in the latest fashion, which I had brought with me from the city, and I could not fail to make a favourable impression on the assembled company. This showed itself in their courteous attitude towards me, which always remained within the bounds of refinement and at

no time became obtrusive. According to the theory I had
derived from romances, when the Prince spoke to me in
the park, he ought to have swiftly unbuttoned his coat at
the words 'I am the Prince', and displayed a large, glittering
star. Similarly all the men in his entourage ought to have
stalked about in embroidered cloaks and stiff wigs. So I
was somewhat surprised to observe only simple, if elegant
clothes, and I realised that my picture of life at court had
been nothing but a childish prejudice. I lost my nervousness
and the Prince completely restored my confidence by
coming up to me and saying: "Well, well! Here is Herr
Leonard!" and made merry at the severe critical eye with
which I had assessed the qualities of his park.

The folding-doors opened and the Princess, accompanied
only by two of her ladies-in-waiting, entered the hall. I
trembled at the sight of her. In the light of the lamps she
looked more like the abbess than ever. The ladies in the
hall surrounded her; I was introduced, and she looked at
me in astonishment. She murmured a few words I did not
catch, then turned and said something softly to an old lady
at her side; a look of alarm came over the lady's face, and
she stared at me. All this happened in a moment. The
company now split up into various groups, and lively conversations were started; the atmosphere was relaxed and
natural, yet one still had the feeling that one was in court
circles and in the presence of a Prince, without this causing
the slightest embarrassment. I found scarcely a single figure
that would have fitted into my preconceived picture of a
court. The seneschal was a cheerful, jovial old man, and
the retainers were merry youths who did not look in the
least as if they were harbouring evil designs. The two ladies-
in-waiting seemed to be sisters; both of them were very
youthfully yet unassumingly dressed. The most likely figure
was a little man in black with a turned-up nose and flashing
eyes, with a long sword at his side; he twisted and twined

with incredible speed through the company and was now here, now there, not stopping or replying to anyone, throwing out sarcastic quips like sparks and keeping the atmosphere lively. He was the Prince's physician.

The old lady to whom the princess had spoken moved round so skilfully that, before I knew where I was, I found myself alone with her in a bay-window. She at once started a conversation with me which, despite her artfulness, soon proved to be directed solely at probing the circumstances of my life. I was prepared for these questions, and as I was sure that the simplest story would be the least dangerous, I confined myself to telling her that I had originally studied theology but now, having inherited from my father, was travelling purely for pleasure. I said that I was born in Polish-speaking Prussia, and gave the poor lady such a barbarous name that it hurt her ears and almost split my tongue; this removed any desire she might have had to ask me to repeat it.

"Your face, Sir," she said, "might arouse sorrowful memories in this place, and maybe you are not merely that which you wish to appear, for your bearing certainly does not point to a student of theology."

After refreshments had been passed round, the guests went into the room where the faro-table stood ready. The seneschal was banker, but it was said that he had an understanding with the Prince whereby he kept all his winnings, whilst the Prince redeemed any loss that weakened the bank's funds. The men assembled round the table, except for the physician, who never played; he stayed with the ladies, who took no part in the game. The Prince called me to sit next to him and chose my cards, after having explained in a few words how the game went.

The Prince's cards all lost, and closely as I followed his advice, I, too, found myself perpetually losing—a considerable matter, as the lowest stake was a louis d'or. My purse was fast running out, and I was already wondering what I would do when the last louis d'or had been spent; if the game were suddenly to make me poor, the result could be my downfall.

We cut again, and I asked the Prince to leave me this time entirely to my own resources, as it seemed that, being an indisputably unlucky player, I was causing him to lose as well. The Prince said with a smile that I still might be able to recoup my losses if I were to follow his experienced advice, but nevertheless he would watch how I acted on my own, since I had so much confidence in myself. I drew one of my cards at random. It was the Queen. Ridiculous as it may seem, I thought I detected Aurelia's features in that pale, lifeless picture. I stared at the card and could hardly suppress my emotion; the banker's call for the stakes to be placed brought me to my senses. Unhesitatingly I took the last five louis d'ors from my pocket and staked them on the Queen. It won, and as I continued to stake higher and higher on the same card, so it won again and again. Each time I staked, the players cried:

"No! Impossible! This time the Queen *must* be unfaithful!" But all the other cards lost.

"Incredible! Miraculous!" came the cries from all sides, while I sat still, absorbed in thought, my mind only on Aurelia, scarcely noticing the gold that the banker continued to heap up in front of me. The Queen had won the last four consecutive cuts, and my pockets were full of gold; it amounted to almost two thousand louis d'ors, and although I had now lost all fear of being unmasked, I felt a certain uneasiness. In some strange way I found a secret link between my haphazard shots that had killed the wild-fowl and my present fortune. I realised that it was not I but some mysterious power within me which had brought about these queer happenings, and that I was only a tool which that power was using for purposes unknown to me. Yet the recognition of this destructive conflict within myself afforded consolation in that it betokened the gradual emergence of my own strength, which, as it grew, would resist and overcome the enemy. That I constantly saw reflections of that painting of Aurelia could be nothing but a mischievous temptation, and such a sinful abuse of that sacred picture filled me with horror and loathing.

*   *   *   *

The following morning I was wandering gloomily through the park, when the Prince, who usually took a stroll at this hour, approached me:

"Well, Herr Leonard," he cried, "what do you think of the game of faro? What do you say to the whim of chance which forgave you your recklessness and heaped gold upon you? You were lucky to pick the *carte favorite*, but it is not always to be trusted blindly."

He enlarged on the idea of the *carte favorite*, gave me the most carefully formulated rules how to play into the hands of chance, and concluded by saying that I would now presumably follow up my luck at the game with the utmost vigour. But I assured him candidly that it was my firm intention never to touch a card again. He looked at me in surprise.

"It is precisely my good fortune of yesterday that has produced this decision," I went on, "for all that I have heard about the dangerous and pernicious effects of the game has been confirmed. There is for me something terrible in the fact that by unwittingly drawing a certain card, I awakened a painful memory and was gripped by an unknown power which abandoned me to the luck of the game and brought me despicable success; it is as though this fortune sprang from my own self, and as if, thinking of the creature whose

glowing colours shone from that lifeless card, I understood
the secret machinations of fate and could command their
course."

"I follow you," the Prince interrupted; "you once
cherished an unhappy love, and the card recalled the vision
of your lost beloved. But if you will permit me to say so,
this strikes me as rather laughable when I picture to myself
the broad, pale, comical face of the Queen of Hearts which
you drew. Still, you thought of your loved one, and she
was perhaps more faithful to you in the game than she was
in life, but I cannot see where the frightening effect comes
in; on the contrary, it must be a source of delight to discover
that fortune wishes you well. And in any case, if you find
the ominous association between the luck of the game and
your beloved so disturbing, then the fault lies not with the
game but with your own frame of mind."

"That may be, Sir," I answered, "but I feel acutely
that what makes this game so pernicious is not so much the
danger of drifting into a serious financial position as the
recklessness of embarking on an open feud with a mysterious
power which entices us, like a mirage, into a region where
it can seize us mockingly and crush us. It is this very
struggle that seems to be the most daring act of bravado
that man, with a pathetic faith in his own strength, under-
takes; and once he has started he cannot leave off, for he
constantly hopes for victory, even in the throes of death.
This is the source, in my view, of the passionate enthusiasm
of faro-players and of the mental derangement which
financial loss alone cannot cause and which eventually
destroys them. But in a humbler respect, too, such loss
can bring distress even to the dispassionate player who still
plays as the spirit takes him. I must confess, Sir, that
yesterday I was in danger of seeing my entire wealth float
away."

"I would have noticed it," interrupted the Prince quickly,

"and repaid your loss threefold, for I do not wish anyone to be ruined just for the sake of my entertainment. This, however, could never happen, because I know players and never let them out of my sight."

"But this very control you exercise, Sir," I rejoined, "takes the freedom out of the game and even erects barriers to those fateful associations the observations of which makes the game so interesting to you. And will not this or that man who is in the inescapable grip of the game find, to his peril, means of escaping your supervision and thus cause in his life a state of tension which will bring about his eventual destruction? Forgive my frankness, Sir. I believe that any restriction of freedom, however much this freedom be abused, is oppressive, intolerable, in fact, radically opposed to human nature."

"It seems that you are far from sharing my views, Herr Leonard," said the Prince sharply and left me, throwing over his shoulder a curt "Adieu".

I scarcely knew myself how I had come to express my attitude so bluntly. Although I had frequently stood and watched at large casinos in the city, I had never reflected sufficiently on the game to be able to formulate my beliefs in the way that they had just proceeded involuntarily from my mouth. I regretted having forfeited the Prince's favour and lost the right to appear in court circles and make the closer acquaintance of the Princess. But I was mistaken, for the same evening I received a card inviting me to a concert at the palace, and as the Prince passed by me he said genially:

"Good evening, Herr Leonard! I hope that you will like my music more than you like my park."

The music really was quite pleasant; the players kept well in time, but the choice of pieces seemed to me rather unfortunate, since each destroyed the effect of the others, and above all a *scena,* which seemed to have been composed to some given formula, bored me to tears. I took care not to express my true opinion, and later learned that I had been wiser than I knew, for that long *scena* had been one of the Prince's own compositions.

I was readmitted without hesitation into the most élite circle, and even thought to take part in a game of faro in order to effect my complete reconciliation with the Prince. I was therefore greatly surprised to find not a gaming-table but a number of ordinary card-tables drawn up and the courtiers engrossed in witty conversation. Everyone had some delightful tale to tell, and even spicy anecdotes were not spurned. My eloquence stood me in good stead and I related excerpts from my own life, disguising them as romantic stories. The Prince, however, preferred light, humorous stories, and in this vein nobody could surpass the physician, who had an inexhaustible stock of droll ideas and expressions.

Conversations of this kind often reached the point where one or other of the courtiers wrote something out and read it to the company, so that soon these evenings assumed the character of meetings of a literary society over which the Prince presided and in which each member concerned himself with the subject which appealed to him most. On one occasion a physicist, a well-known savant, astonished us by telling of a number of new discoveries he had made in his field. Great as was the interest of that section of the company which had sufficient scientific knowledge to follow the professor's discourse, those who did not understand the subject became bored. Even the Prince did not appear to be particularly engrossed but rather to be waiting hopefully for the end. At last the savant finished. The physician expressed his praise and admiration of the professor's ideas, adding that after such a learned speech it might be appropriate to introduce something light and entertaining. Those whose feeble wits had been crushed by the power of science recovered their strength; a smile even crossed the lips of the Prince himself, showing how much he welcomed a return to everyday matters.

"As you know, Sir," the physician began, turning to the Prince, "I never omit to record in my diary the strange experiences which befall me on my travels, especially those of a grotesque nature, and it is from this diary that I am about to relate a story which, without being particularly significant, yet strikes me as rather amusing.

"In the course of my journey last year I arrived late one night at a large village some four hours' ride from B., and decided to spend the night in the excellent inn, where the friendly landlord welcomed me cheerfully. So tired was I from the long journey that as soon as I was shown to my room, I threw myself on to the bed and fell asleep. Just as one o'clock was striking, however, I was awakened by the sound of a flute being played close by. Never in my life had I heard such a row. The man must have had tremendous lungs, for in a shrill, piercing tone which completely destroyed the character of the instrument he was playing the same passage over and over again. One could hardly imagine anything more infuriating or more senseless. I cursed and shouted at the mad fellow who had ruined my sleep and was shattering my ear-drums, but the passage went on and on like clockwork until I finally heard a dull thud, as though something had been hurled against the wall, and all was quiet again, so that I was able to continue my sleep in peace.

"The next morning I heard a violent quarrel going on below. I detected the voice of the landlord and also that of another man who was shouting: 'A curse on your house! Would that I had never crossed its threshold! It must have been the Devil who led me to this place, where there's nothing to drink and nothing decent to eat. Everything is unspeakably bad, and damned expensive as well. There's

your money. And you won't see me in this wretched hole
again! ' With this a small, skinny figure, wearing a coffee-
coloured coat and an auburn wig, on top of which he had
stuck a crooked grey hat at a defiant angle, ran out of the
house and across to the stable, from which I watched him
fetch a somewhat stiff-jointed nag and ride out of the yard
at a lumbering gallop.

"I naturally took him to be a stranger who had had an
argument with the landlord and left in a rage, so when I
was later sitting at lunch in the inn, I was extremely
surprised to see the same comical figure return and sit down
at the table without comment. It was at once the ugliest
and drollest face that I had ever come across, and there
was in the man's whole bearing an air of quaint gravity
which made it difficult not to laugh when one looked at him.
As we ate together, I carried on a laconic conversation
with the landlord, but the stranger, who had an enormous
appetite, showed no wish to take part in it.

"As I later realised, it was obviously malice on the landlord's part to turn the conversation into a discussion on
national characteristics and to ask me outright whether I
had met any Irishmen or knew any of their practical jokes.
I replied that I did, and told the story of the Irishman who,
on being asked why he was wearing one of his socks inside-
out, retorted: 'The other side has got a hole in it!' I also
recalled the excellent joke about the Irishman who was
sharing a bed with a quick-tempered Scotsman, and had
fallen asleep with his bare foot protruding from beneath the
bedclothes. An Englishman in the same room noticed this
and quickly clipped on to the Irishman's foot a spur which
he had taken from one of the Irishman's boots. When the
Irishman drew his foot in under the bedclothes again during
the night, the spur scratched the Scotsman, who woke up
and gave the Irishman a sound cuff on the head. Then
the following sharp-witted exchanges took place: 'What

the devil did you hit me for?'—'Because you scratched me with your spur!'—'How could I have done, when I am lying in bed barefoot like you?'—'You did—just look at this!'—'You're right, damn it! That knave of a servant must have taken off my boot and left my spur on!'

"The landlord broke into hearty guffaws, but the stranger, who had just finished his meal and swilled it down with a large tankard of beer, looked gravely at me and said: 'You are quite right, Irishmen often do play such pranks, yet this is by no means due to the nature of the people themselves, who are lively and intelligent, but rather to the confounded atmosphere of the country, which infects one with such lunacies just like the germs of a cold. I, Sir, am an Englishman but I was born and bred in Ireland, and that is the only reason why I have become contaminated with these damned pranks.'

"At this the landlord laughed even more uproariously, and I could not refrain from joining in, for it was a delightful situation that an Irishman who was only talking about jokes should also play an excellent one on us himself.

"Far from being offended by our hilarity, the stranger regarded us wide-eyed, placed his finger at the side of his nose and said: 'In England the Irish are the leavening which is added in order to make society palatable. In one respect I am like Falstaff, in that I am not only witty in myself but also the cause that wit is in other men, and in these sober times that is no small merit. Can you imagine such wit stirring in the unresponsive soul of this publican just because of my presence? But this landlord is a good landlord, for far from living on his own meagre intellectual capital, he just borrows a single idea from some well-stocked source at a high rate of interest; if, as now, he cannot pay this interest, he will only show you the cover of his ledger, namely his uncontrollable laughter, for into this laughter he has put his wit. Farewell, gentlemen!'

"With this the strange fellow went out, and I at once asked the landlord about him. 'He is an Irishman called Ewson,' he answered, 'who wants to be considered an Englishman because his family originally came from England; he has been living here now for twenty-two years. I bought this inn when I was a young man, and during my wedding celebrations this Mr Ewson, at that time a mere youth but already wearing an auburn wig, a grey hat and a coffee-coloured coat of the same cut as he was wearing today, happened to be passing by on his way back to his homeland and was tempted to come inside, having been attracted by the merry sound of music and dancing. He avowed that it was only on ships, where he himself had learned, that people really knew how to dance, and to prove it he danced a hornpipe, whistling the tune through his teeth at the same time and making a terrible din. Unfortunately, however, he sprained his foot while executing a particularly high leap and was forced to stay with me until he recovered. Since that time he has never left. His eccentricities cause me considerable vexation; he quarrels with me every single day, criticises the service, accuses me of overcharging him, claims that he can no longer live without roast beef and porter, packs his saddle-bag, puts his three wigs on, one on top of the other, takes his leave of me and rides off on his old hack. But he only goes for a canter, and returns at midday by the other gate, sits down quietly at the table, as you saw today, and eats enough of the unpalatable food for three men.

" 'Every year he receives a substantial cheque. On these occasions he bids me a particularly touching farewell, calls me his best friend and begins to weep; the tears run down my cheeks as well, but they are tears of laughter. Having made his will and left his estate, as he tells me, to my eldest daughter, he rides off slowly and disconsolately towards the town. On the third or, at the most, the fourth day afterwards, however, he is back again, bringing with him two coffee-coloured coats, three auburn wigs, each more sleek than the next, six shirts, a new grey hat and other items of clothing. For my eldest daughter, his favourite, he brings a little bag of sweets, as though she were a child, whereas she is now eighteen. He entirely forgets about his stay in the town and about his journey home. Every evening he pays his bill, and every morning he throws down the money for his breakfast in rage before he rides out, never to return. Apart from this he is the most amiable man you could wish to meet; he is always giving presents to my children and he helps the poor in the village. The only person he does not like is the pastor, a man who, as Mr. Ewson learned from the schoolmaster, once took out a gold coin that he, Ewson, had put in the poor box, and changed it into a lot of copper pfennigs. Since that time Ewson has never been to church and has avoided the preacher, who, for his part, has therefore branded him as an atheist.

" 'As I say, I have a great deal of trouble with him because he is so irascible and has such crazy ideas. Only yesterday, when I was coming home, I heard loud shouting long before I reached the house, and recognised Ewson's voice. When I went in I found him in a violent quarrel with the housemaid. As he always did when in a rage, he had thrown his wig on to the floor and was standing there bareheaded and in his shirt-sleeves in front of the maid, holding up a book in front of her face and pointing to something written in it, shouting and cursing the whole time. The maid stood with arms akimbo and cried: "Take your tricks somewhere else! You are an evil man and have no faith!" With difficulty I managed to separate them and find out the source of the trouble. It appears that Mr Ewson told the maid to bring him some wafers in order to seal his letters; at first the maid did not understand what he meant, but then she remembered that wafers were what were taken at communion, and knowing that the pastor had said that Ewson was an atheist, she thought he wanted to perform some heinous blasphemy. She therefore refused to do his bidding, whereupon, assuming that he had not pronounced the word properly, he at once fetched his English-German dictionary and showed the girl, who could not read a word, what he meant. To make matters worse, he was now speaking entirely in English, which the maid took to be some diabolical trick intended to add to her confusion. It was only my arrival that prevented a fight, in which Mr Ewson would probably have come off second best.'

"I interrupted the landlord to ask whether it might have been this Mr Ewson who had ruined my night's sleep with his terrible flute-playing. 'Indeed it was,' he replied, 'and this is one of his habits which almost scare my guests away. Three years ago my son came here from the town; he is an excellent flautist and practises here a great deal. Mr Ewson then recalled that he, too, had used to play the flute, and he did not rest until Fritz had sold him his, together with a concerto which he had brought with him, paying him a considerable sum of money.

" 'And so Mr Ewson, who has no ear for music and no sense of rhythm, began laboriously to play the concerto. But when he had only got as far as the second solo in the first Allegro, he came to a passage which he could not get through, and for the last three years he has played this one passage a hundred times in succession almost every day, until he flings first the flute, then his wig at the wall in his fury. Since there are not many flutes which will stand this treatment for long, he frequently needs new ones, and usually keeps three or four going at one time. Even if a little screw breaks or just one of the keys is faulty, he hurls the flute out of the window and cries: "Damn the thing! The only instruments that are any good are made in England!"

" 'Particularly disastrous is the fact that this passion for flute-playing often comes over him at night, causing him to wake my guests with his wailing row. And, incredible as you may find it, there lives in the bailiff's house here an English doctor called Green, who has been staying there almost as long as Mr Ewson has been staying with me, and who sympathises with him in his activities to such an extent that he has become almost as eccentric and full of drollery as Ewson himself. The two are continually quarelling but they cannot live without each other.—I have just remembered that Mr Ewson has ordered a bowl of punch for this evening and has invited the bailiff and Dr Green. If you are prepared to stay here until tomorrow morning Sir, you will be able to watch the most comical trio the world has ever seen.'

"As you can imagine, I willingly put off my departure in order to meet this Mr Ewson in all his splendour. When evening fell, he entered the room and was courteous enough to invite me to join him in drinking the punch, adding how much he regretted only being able to offer me the miserable brew which passed there as punch: real punch, he said, was only drunk in England, and as he would be returning there shortly, he hoped that, if ever I came to England, he would be allowed to prove it to me.

"Soon afterwards the other guests arrived. The bailiff was a short, tubby, extremely affable little man with friendly, twinkling eyes and a red nose; Dr. Green was a robust, middle-aged man with a typically English face, stylishly but carelessly dressed, spectacles on his nose, hat on his head. 'Bring me champagne,' he shouted excitedly, 'so that my eyes will get red!' Going up to the landlord, he seized him by the lapels and shook him violently. 'You villainous Cambyses!' he cried. 'Where are the princesses? I smell coffee, not the nectar of the gods!' 'Take your hands off me!' gasped the landlord. 'You're breaking my ribs!

11

Let me go!' 'Not before the steam from the sweet-smelling punch swirls round my head and tickles my nose, you cowardly weakling, you inhospitable host!' retorted the doctor. At this Ewson rushed across to the doctor and cried: 'Ungrateful Green! If you do not desist from this undignified behaviour, everything will turn green in front of your eyes, and you will sit down and weep.'

"I expected a noisy quarrel to break out, but the doctor said: 'Very well, then. Permitting myself merely to express my scorn of such faint-heartedness, I will be quiet and await the divine potion which you are preparing, my dear Ewson.' He released the landlord, who hurriedly jumped away from him, sat down with a Catonian expression on his face and, taking hold of his pipe, blew out great clouds of smoke. 'It's just like being at the theatre, is it not?' said the friendly bailiff to me. 'The doctor, who normally never looks at German books, once happened to find Schlegel's translation of Shakespeare in my house, and since then, to use his own expression, he has been playing old and familiar tunes on a strange instrument. You may have observed that even the landlord speaks rhythmically; the doctor has, as it were, iambicised him.'

"The landlord brought the steaming bowl of punch, and although both Ewson and Green avowed that it was hardly drinkable, they quaffed one glass after another. The conversation was tolerably entertaining. Green remained laconic, opposing with an occasional droll comment the opinions expressed by the others. The bailiff, for instance, was speaking about the local theatre, and I gave it as my opinion that the leading role in the present production was excellently played. 'I cannot agree with that,' the doctor broke in at once. 'Do you not think that if the man had acted six times better he would have been far worthier of the applause he received?' I had to admit that this was so, adding only that the need to act six times better was more urgent for some poverty-stricken actor of tragic roles. 'I cannot agree with that either,' said Green again. 'A man expresses what is in him. Can he help it if his tendency is towards the bad? If he has achieved perfection in his badness, he deserves our praise.'

"The bailiff, who had the gift of kindling in the two men all kinds of bizarre ideas and opinions, sat between them as a kind of agitator, and so things went on until the punch began to have its effect. Then Ewson became exceedingly merry, started to sing folk-songs in his croaking voice, threw his wig and his coat out of the window into the yard and proceeded to dance, pulling such grotesque faces as he did so that we almost collapsed with laughter. The doctor, on the other hand, remained solemn but had the strangest visions: he took the punch-bowl to be a violoncello and wanted to accompany Ewson on it with a spoon, and was only restrained from doing so by the landlord's vigorous protests. The bailiff became quieter and quieter until finally, stumbling over to a corner of the room, he sat down and began to weep. The landlord made a gesture to me, and I asked the bailiff why he was so sad. 'Alas!' he sobbed. 'Prince Eugène was a great general, yet, hero that he was, he had to die!' And he wept even more bitterly, the tears running down his cheeks. I tried as best I could to ease his grief over the passing of this noble prince in the previous century, but in vain.

"In the meantime Dr Green had got hold of a large candle-snuffer and was poking it out of the open window, trying to snuff the moon which was shining in. Ewson jumped about and screamed as though possessed by a thousand devils, until at last the servant came in, carrying a large lantern in spite of the bright moonlight, and cried: 'Here I am, gentlemen! Now we can go!' Going up to him, the doctor said, breathing punch-fumes into his face: 'Welcome, friend! Are you Peter Quince, the bearer of

moonshine, with dog and bush of thorn? It is because I
have polished you off*, you rogue, that you shine so
brightly! Good night to you all—I have drunk a great
deal of this vulgar brew—so good night, good landlord—
good night, my faithful Pylades!' Ewson declared that
neither of them would get home without breaking his neck,
but they paid no heed to him. The servant took hold of
the doctor with one arm and the bailiff, who was still
mourning the death of Prince Eugène, with the other, and
together they tottered down the street towards the bailiff's
house. After some difficulty we got Ewson to his room,
where he spent half the night rampaging about with his
flute. He kept me awake the whole time, and only when I
was driving away in my coach next day was I able to get
some sleep and recover from the fantastic night."

The physician's tale had been frequently interrupted by
laughter, and the Prince appeared greatly amused.

"There is just one character," he said to the physician,
"whom you have kept too much in the background, and
that is yourself. For I will wager that in your mischievous
moments you actually encouraged Ewson and the doctor
in their drolleries, and that in reality you yourself were the
agitator which you made the pathetic bailiff out to be."

"I assure you, Sir," replied the physician, "that this
private circle of *farceurs* was already so complete that the
entry of any outsider would only have struck a dissonant
note. To continue the musical metaphor, the three men
formed a perfect triad, each element different but in harmony with the others; and the landlord was as a seventh
to this triad."

The conversation swung backwards and forwards in this
way until, as was customary, the Prince and his family

*A play on two meanings of the word *putzen*: to snuff (a candle), and
to polish (Transl).

retired to their rooms, and the company dispersed in the
most cordial atmosphere. I was moving happily and
contentedly in a new world; the more I mingled in the
peaceful life of the town and the court, and the more I
succeeded in gaining a place of respect and approval,
the less I thought of the past and of the possibility that my
situation here could ever change. The Prince seemed to
have a special liking for me, and I could glean from various
passing allusions that he wanted to keep me in his entourage
at all costs. It was undeniable that a uniformity of accomplishment, a certain similarity of manner in all artistic
activities, had spread from the court over the whole town
and would have soon caused an intelligent man, accustomed
to unrestricted freedom, to take a dislike to the place, but,
frequently as I was irritated by the restricting monotony
of the court, I was well served by my former adherence
to a fixed pattern of life which controlled at least external
conduct; for I still felt the influence of my monastic life
in such matters, though nobody could have noticed it.

However much the Prince showed his respect for me,
and however hard I tried to gain the Princess' attention,
she remained cold and reserved; sometimes my presence
even seemed to disturb her, and only with difficulty did she
bring herself to exchange a few words with me as she did
with the others. I was more fortunate with her ladies-in-
waiting; my appearance had evidently made a favourable
impression, and as I was often in their company, I soon
succeeded in acquiring that remarkable accomplishment
the world calls gallantry, which consists simply in trans-
ferring to one's conversation the physical attractiveness that
is a sure passport to any society; it is the singular gift
of talking in weighty words about nothing and thus arousing
in women a certain satisfaction which even they cannot
account for. That this superior gallantry is not content with
crude flatteries goes without saying, for in that fascinating

chatter which sounds like a hymn of adoration lies the way
to their hearts; their real being seems to become clear to
them and they delight to see themselves in the reflection
of what they regard as their true selves. But who could have
recognised me as a monk? Perhaps the only dangerous
place was the chapel, where I found it hard to avoid those
monastic devotions which are characterised by a particular
rhythm and regularity.

The only man not stamped with the die that had been
impressed on the courtiers as on so many identical coins, was
the physician, and this attracted me to him; he in his turn
attached himself to me because, as he knew, I had been
the first to show any opposition at court, and my frank
remarks which had stung the Prince, sensitive as he was
to naked truths, had outlawed at a blow the detested game
of faro.

We were often in each other's company and spoke about
the sciences and the arts, about life as it lay spread out
before us. The physician had as high an opinion of the
Princess as I and told me that it was only she who prevented
many lapses of taste on the part of the Prince and dispelled
that peculiar boredom which drove him to and fro on the
surface of things. I did not let the opportunity slip by to
complain that my presence seemed to cause the Princess
displeasure, and that I could not discover the reason. The
physician immediately got up, fetched a small portrait from
the writing-desk (we were in his room) and handed it to me,
telling me to study it carefully. I did so and was amazed to
recognise my own features; it only needed a change in the
hair-style, different clothes, and the addition of my long
side-whiskers—Belcampo's masterpiece—for it to become a
picture of myself. I expressed my astonishment to the
physician.

"It is precisely this resemblance," he said, "which
frightens the Princess whenever you approach her, for your

face revives the memory of a terrible incident which befell
the court several years back. My predecessor here, who died
two or three years ago and who was my master in the
science of medicine, told me about it in confidence and
gave me that picture, which portrays the Prince's former
favourite, Francesco, and is, as you see, a real masterpiece
from the technical point of view. It is the work of a mysterious painter who was at court in those days, and he it is who
plays the main part in this tragedy."

As I looked at the picture, strange, confused impressions
stirred in my heart which I tried in vain to grasp. That
event seemed as if it would reveal a mystery in which I
myself was involved, and I urged the physician to confide
to me what, in view of my remarkable resemblance to
Francesco, I seemed entitled to know.

"This most unusual circumstance must cause you no
little curiosity," said the physician, "and unwilling as I
am to talk about that episode over which, for me at least,
there still hangs a veil which I do not want to lift, you shall
nevertheless learn everything that I know. Many years have
passed by, and the main characters have now left the stage;
it is only the memory that has this malignant effect. I
must ask you not to tell anyone about what you hear."

I promised, and the physician started his story.

*   *   *   *

"At the time when our Prince's wedding had just taken
place, his brother arrived back from journeyings abroad,
accompanied by a man he called Francesco—though he
was known to be a German—and also by a painter. The
Duke was one of the handsomest men I have ever seen, and
for that reason alone he would have outshone our Prince,
even if he had not also surpassed him in vitality and
strength of mind. On the young Princess, who was at that

time vivacious to the point of wantonness, and found the
Prince far too formal, far too frigid, he made a particular
impression, while he in his turn was fascinated by his
brother's young and beautiful wife. As the Duke drew his
brother's wife towards him, so Francesco exerted an
attraction on the Princess' elder sister. Francesco soon
became aware of his fortune and exploited it with such
premeditated cunning that the Duchess' attraction turned
into passionate love. The Prince was too convinced of his
wife's virtue not to scorn any mischievous scandal-monger-
ing, although the strained relationship between him and his
brother worried him; Francesco, for whom he had developed a liking on account of his rare intellect and
shrewdness, was the only one able to maintain a certain
equanimity in him. The Prince wanted to put him among
the leading courtiers but Francesco contented himself with
the secret privileges of the foremost favourite and with the
love of the Duchess.

"Such was the situation in which, for better or for worse,
the court lived, and the only happy persons were the four
who were linked together in their own exclusive Eldorado
by the invisible ties of love. It may well have been the
Prince who arranged, without the knowledge of the others,
for an Italian Princess to appear at court with great pomp;
she was formerly to have been betrothed to the Duke, who
had developed an obvious attachment to her when he
stayed at her father's court during his travels. She was said
to be exceptionally beautiful and the image of grace and
charm, and this is clearly expressed in the wonderful
portrait of her that you can still see in the gallery. Her
presence enlivened the court, which had sunk into gloomy
boredom, and she outshone everybody, not excepting even
the Princess and her sister. After she had arrived,
Francesco's behaviour changed in a remarkable way; a
secret grief seemed to be gnawing at the roots of his

vivacity, he became morose and sulky and neglected his lover. The Duke had also become pensive and felt gripped by emotions which he could not withstand. The arrival of the Italian noblewoman was like a dagger in the Princess' heart, while the happiness of her sister, a woman of passionate nature, had departed with Francesco's love. The four happy, enviable people were plunged into sorrow and dejection.

"The Duke was the first to recover, for the unshakable virtue of his sister-in-law made him unable to resist the allurements of the beautiful newcomer. His simple, sincere attachment to the Princess perished in the inexpressible delights which the Italian lady seemed to promise him, and soon he found himself once more in the grip of the chains from which he had not long ago escaped. The more he surrendered to this love, the more remarkable became Francesco's behaviour; he was now scarcely ever seen at court, but roamed about alone, often staying away from the town for weeks. The mysterious painter, on the other hand, was more in evidence than ever, working mainly in the studio which the Italian Princess had installed for him in her house; he painted several portraits of her of incomparable beauty. He seemed unfavourably disposed towards the Princess, and would not paint her at all, yet he completed a wonderful likeness of the Duchess without a single sitting. The Italian beauty was so attracted to the painter, and he for his part displayed so many intimate courtesies towards her that the Duke became jealous. Once, when he found the painter at work in the studio on a wonderful portrait of his lady, he asked him outright to do him the favour of not working there any longer, but to find himself another studio. The painter gently flicked the paint from his brush and, without a word, took the portrait from the easel. In a fit of temper the Duke tore the picture from his hand, and said that, as it was such an excellent likeness, it ought to belong to him. The painter, still calm and unruffled, asked to be allowed to make a few final strokes; the Duke put it back on the easel, and a few minutes later the painter returned it to him, laughing out loud as the Duke recoiled at the sight of the horrible, disfigured face into which the portrait had turned. The painter then went slowly out of the room, but turning at the door and regarding the duke steadily and gravely, he said:

'For this you shall perish!'

"These events took place at a time when the Italian Princess was already betrothed to the Duke, a few days before the wedding ceremony, but the Duke took little notice of this incident, particularly as the painter was generally held to be afflicted with periodical fits of madness. It was said that he sat in his little room staring for days at a large, empty canvas stretched out before him and telling people that he was at the moment working on a wonderful picture; in this way he forgot the court, and was in turn forgotten by it.

"The wedding of the Duke and the Italian lady was solemnly celebrated in the palace. The Princess had resigned herself to her fate, and renounced the purposeless affection which would never be returned; the Duchess was as if transfigured, for her beloved Francesco had returned, more radiant and joyful than ever. The Duke and his bride were to occupy a wing of the castle which the Prince had had specially laid out; during this work of construction he was in his element, and people only saw him when he was surrounded by architects, painters and paper-hangers, looking through big books and spreading out plans, sections and sketches in front of him, some of them his own more-or-less unfortunate efforts. Neither the Duke nor his lady was allowed to see any of the decorations until, late on the evening of their wedding-day, the Prince led them in a long, majestic procession through the rooms, which were indeed richly and tastefully decorated. The festivities ended with a ball.

"During the night a deep rumbling was heard in the Duke's wing, which became louder and louder until it woke the Prince himself. Fearing some misfortune, he jumped up and hastened to the distant wing, accompanied by the guard. He entered the broad corridor just as they were bringing out the Duke's body; he had been found lying in front of the door to the bridal chamber, murdered by a stab in the throat.

"You can imagine the Prince's horror, the bride's despair, the Princess' deep lamentation. When the Prince became calmer, he began to investigate how the murder could have been committed and how the murderer had been able to escape through the passages that were everywhere guarded by sentries; every nook and cranny was searched, but all in vain. The page who attended the Duke said that his master had been very restless and had paced up and down his room for a long time; finally he had allowed himself to be disrobed, and the page had taken the candelabrum and accompanied him as far as the ante-room of the bridal chamber; the Duke had then taken the candelabrum from him and sent him back, but hardly had he left the room when he heard a muffled scream, a blow, and the clatter of the falling candelabrum; rushing back to the room he saw, by the light of one of the candles still burning on the floor, the Duke's body lying in front of the door to the bridal chamber, and beside it a small, blood-smeared knife, whereupon he had at once raised a hue and cry. According to the bride of the unfortunate Duke, he had hastily entered her room as soon as she had sent her maid away; he had quickly extinguished all the lights, stayed with her about half-an-hour and then left again; a few moments later the murder took place.

"When all the possible avenues of investigation had been exhausted, one of the Duchess' chambermaids came forward who had overheard the embarrassing scene between the Duke and the painter, and she related in detail all that had taken place. Nobody doubted that the painter had somehow managed to creep into the palace and murder the Duke. A warrant was sent out for his immediate arrest, but he had been missing for two days; nobody knew where he had gone, and all enquiries proved fruitless. Court and town alike were plunged into deep mourning, and Francesco, now constantly at court again, was the only one able to coax a little sunshine from the dark clouds that hung over the family circle.

"The Duchess was pregnant, and since it appeared obvious that the murderer had taken advantage of his resemblance to her consort to commit this foul outrage, she went away to a distant castle of the Prince's so that her confinement should remain secret and the fruit of the diabolical crime not disgrace the Duke, at least in the eyes of the public, who would learn about the events of the wedding-night from the irresponsible gossip of the servants.

"Francesco's liaison with the Princess' sister became more and more intimate during this period of mourning, and at the time the Prince and Princess showed a great attachment to him. The Prince had long been acquainted with Francesco's secret, and soon he was no longer able to withstand the pressure brought to bear on him by the Princess and her sister, and consented to Francesco's secret marriage to the Duchess: Francesco was to attain high military rank in the service of a distant court, and the official announcement of the marriage would then follow: the Prince's influence in that court would enable him to bring this about.

"The day of the wedding arrived. The Prince, his consort, and two close friends (one of them was my pre-

decessor) were the only ones to be allowed to attend the
ceremony in the little chapel in the palace. A page who
had been initiated into the secret guarded the door.

"The couple stood before the altar; the Prince's confessor, an old and venerable priest, held a silent celebration,
and then began the liturgy. Suddenly Francesco went pale
and with glassy eyes staring at the pillar by the high altar,
he cried in a hollow voice:

'What do you want with me?'

"Leaning against the pillar stood the painter, a purple
cloak thrown over his shoulders, fixing Francesco with his
black, sunken eyes. The Princess was near to fainting;
everybody trembled with fear, and only the priest remained
calm. Turning to Francesco, he said:

'Why are you afraid of this man if your conscience is
clear?'

"Francesco rose swiftly from his knees and rushed at the
painter with a small knife in his hand, but before he reached
him he fell unconscious to the floor with a dull cry, and the
painter vanished behind the pillar. The people present
awoke from their stupefaction and hastened to the aid of
Francesco, who lay as if dead; in order to avoid arousing
attention, the two friends carried him to the Prince's rooms.
When he regained consciousness, he demanded vehemently
to be taken to his own room, and refused to answer any of
the Prince's questions about the mysterious happenings in
the chapel. The next morning Francesco had fled from the
town with the valuables which he had received as marks
of favour from the court and the Prince.

"The Prince left no stone unturned in his attempts to
solve the mystery of where the painter could have come
from. The chapel only had two entrances, one of which
led from the inner rooms of the palace to the recesses at
the side of the high altar, and the other from the broad main
passage into the nave. The page had guarded this latter

entrance so that no inquisitive person should come near;
the other entrance was shut. It therefore remained incomprehensible how the painter could have appeared in the
chapel and then vanish again. As Francesco lost consciousness he had retained his convulsive grasp on the knife
which he had drawn against the painter, and the page—
the same one who had disrobed the Duke on that tragic
wedding-night, and who this time had guarded the chapel-
door—maintained that it was the same knife that had been
found lying at the Duke's side, being immediately recognis-
able by its shining silver handle.

"Not long after these mysterious events came news of the
Duchess: on the same day that Francesco's wedding was
to have taken place, she had given birth to a son and died
soon afterwards. The Prince mourned her loss, even though
the terrible happenings of the wedding-night laid suspicions
—probably unjustly—at her door. The son was brought up
in a distant land under the name of Count Victor. The
Princess' sister, her peace of mind shattered by all the
horrible events that had forced themselves upon her, went
into a nunnery; she is, as you know, abbess of the Cistercian
convent in . . .

"There was an incident that took place not long ago in
the palace of Baron F. which has a strange bearing on these
happenings at our court, and split both the Baron's family
and ours. The abbess, touched by the distress of a pious
woman who was returning with her little child from a
pilgrimage to the Holy Linden and had sought shelter in
the convent, had ———."

The physician's story was interrupted at this point by
the arrival of a visitor, and I was able to conceal the storm
that raged in my breast. All was now plain to me: Francesco
was my father, and it was he who had murdered the Duke
with the same knife with which I had stabbed Hermogenes.

I determined to leave for Italy in a few days and thus

escape at last from the society into which I had been thrust by a malevolent power. The same evening I appeared at court. There was a great deal of talk about a beautiful lady who had just arrived to be maid of honour in the Princess' entourage and would make her first appearance that evening.

The folding-doors opened and the Princess entered, together with her new companion. *It was Aurelia.*

PART TWO

I—THE TURNING-POINT

W here is the man who has not felt in his breast the wonderful mystery of love? Whoever you may be who come to read these pages—call to mind that noontide of supreme happiness, behold once more that image of angelic beauty, the spirit of love itself, as she came to meet you; it was through her, through her alone, that you seemed assured of your own higher existence. Do you recall how the bubbling springs, the rustling bushes, the caressing evening breezes told so clearly of her love? Can you still picture the flowers that turned their gentle, shining eyes upon you, bringing kisses and words of endearment from her? And she came, yielding to you utterly. You embraced her with burning desire, and thought to rise above the pettiness of earth in the flame of your fervent longing. But the miracle did not happen; you were forced back to earth just as you were about to soar with her to the distant promised land. You had lost her even before you had dared to hope; the voices, the beautiful sounds had all died away, and only the despairing lamentation of the lonely soul was heard in the cruel wilderness.

Gentle reader, if you have ever been crushed under this unutterable sorrow, then tune your heart to the inconsolable grief of this greying monk who, meditating in his gloomy cell on the former glories of his love, bathes his hard bed in bloody tears, and in the silence of the night sends his

165

12

groans of agony echoing down the dark passages of the monastery. But you who are of my spiritual kin—you, too, must believe that the supreme rapture of love, the fulfilment of the miracle, is manifested in death. For this is the message of the mysterious prophetic voices from that primeval age which cannot be conceived in human terms; and as in the ritual mysteries of Antiquity which the children of nature celebrated, so for us, too, is death the hallowed feast of love.

A shaft of lightning pierced my breast; I caught my breath, my pulse throbbed and my heart quivered as if it would burst. I must go to her, clasp her to my heart in the savage frenzy of love!—Why, O unhappy woman, do you oppose the power that binds you to me with iron fetters? Are you not mine—mine for ever? Yet I restrained my passion better than I had done when I first saw Aurelia in the Baron's palace. All eyes were meanwhile turned upon her, and I managed to move in this circle of insignificant people without attracting particular attention or being spoken to, which I would have found unbearable since I only had eyes—ears—thoughts—for her.

Let it not be said that a simple robe is the best adornment for a beautiful girl, for a woman's clothes exercise a magical power over us which we cannot easily resist. It seems to lie in the depths of a woman's nature that when she is arrayed in all her finery, her beauty will glitter with yet greater brilliance, just as flowers are only revealed in their perfection when they break out into a myriad radiant colours. When you first set eyes on your beloved thus adorned, did not a mysterious thrill run through you? She seemed a stranger to you, but even this gave her a special allure. And what rapture, what inexpressible desires welled up within you when you took her hand in yours?

Never before had I seen her in anything but a simple morning-gown; today she appeared, as the custom of the court required, in all her splendour. How lovely she was! What inexpressible rapture, what bliss swept over me at the sight of her! But then the spirit of evil rose within me, lifting its voice to which I lent willing ear: 'Do you not see, Medardus,' it whispered, 'that you are the master of fate, and that destiny, which is in your power, is only drawing together the threads that you have woven?'

There were at the court women who were regarded as the perfection of beauty, but in the presence of Aurelia's grace and charm they seemed pale and insignificant. The most listless courtiers were roused to enthusiasm, and even elderly gentlemen who were engaged in the usual court chatter broke off abruptly; it was amusing to see how they strained to appear on their best behaviour in her presence. She blushed as she gracefully received their addresses of admiration with down-cast eyes, but as the Prince began to gather the older men around him, and some of the handsome young men approached her with deference and exchanged a few friendly words with her, she became more cheerful and at her ease. A major from the bodyguard, whom I knew to be a particular favourite of the ladies, succeeded in attracting her attention, and soon they were engaged in animated conversation. I was standing quite close to her, yet she did not seem to notice me; I wanted to go to her, but I felt as though I were chained to the spot. As I looked closely at the major again, it suddenly seemed as though he were Count Victor. I laughed aloud in scorn:

"Cursed man! Did you lie so soft in the Devil's Gorge that you now lust after the monk's paramour?"

I do not know whether I actually spoke these words but I heard myself laugh. I gave a start as if waking out of a deep dream, when the old seneschal, quietly touching my hand, asked:

"What are you so happy about, Herr Leonard?"

An icy tremor went through me. Were not those the

words of pious Brother Cyrillus, who had put the same
question to me when he noticed my guilty smile during
the ceremony of my investiture? I hardly managed to
stammer a few incoherent words. I could feel that Aurelia
was no longer near me but I did not dare look up; instead
I rushed out of the brightly-lit room. There must have
been something terrible about my appearance, for I noticed
that everybody avoided me in fear.

I kept away from the court, since it seemed impossible
for me to see her again without running the risk of betraying
my deepest secret. I roamed in solitude through field and
forest, seeing and thinking only of her. More and more I
became convinced that an inscrutable destiny had knit
together my fate and hers, and that what had sometimes
appeared to me as a sinful crime was only the fulfilment of
an irrevocable decree. Bolstering up my courage in this
way, I laughed at the danger that might threaten me if
Aurelia were to recognise me as Hermogenes' murderer.
How pitiful those young men appeared to me who in their
delusion were courting the favour of the one who was so
utterly and completely mine that even her faintest breath
seemed determined by her existence in me! These counts,
these barons, these gentlemen-in-waiting, these officers in
their bright cloaks, their shining gold, their glittering
medals—what are they but helpless, gaudily-painted insects
to be crushed under my heel if they become troublesome
to me? I will walk among them in my monastic habit with
Aurelia, adorned as a bride, in my arms, and that haughty,
detestable abbess shall herself prepare the wedding-bed for
the victorious monk whom she despises. My mind full of
such thoughts, I often called Aurelia's name aloud, laughing
and crying like a madman. But the storm soon subsided;
I became calmer and was able to ponder on how best to
approach her.

One day I was walking through the park, considering

whether it was advisable to attend the reception which the Prince had announced for that evening, when someone tapped me on the shoulder. I turned round and came face to face with the physician.

"Allow me to feel your pulse," he said, looking me straight in the face and making to take hold of my arm.

"What does this mean?" I asked, startled.

"Nothing important," he replied; "there is supposed to be some strange, secret madness lurking about which attacks people unawares like a brigand and deals them a blow that makes them cry out, even if their cry sometimes sounds like senseless laughter. On the other hand, the whole thing may be nothing but fancy, and the mad devil nothing but a high temperature. Permit me therefore to feel your pulse, my friend."

"I assure you that I do not understand a single word you are saying," I retorted, but the physician had already taken my arm and was feeling my pulse, looking up at the sky as he did so: one—two—three . . . I could make nothing of his enigmatic remarks and pressed him to tell me what was in his mind.

"Do you not know, my dear Herr Leonard," he said, "that you left the whole court in a state of bewilderment and alarm the other day? The mistress of the robes has been suffering ever since from spasms, and the president of the consistory has had to miss the most important sessions because you were pleased to tread on his gouty feet in your haste, so that he now sits in his armchair, roaring at the pains that shoot through him. This happened, it is said, when you seemed to have a sudden attack of madness and rushed out of the room, after having laughed out loud, for no apparent reason, in such a way that everyone shuddered and felt their hair stand on end."

At that moment I thought of the seneschal and said that I remembered having imagined that I had laughed aloud, but my laughter could not have had such an extraordinary effect, since the seneschal had asked me quite quietly what I was so happy about. "Ah," replied the physician, "that does not mean anything, for the seneschal is a *homo impavidus* who would not be worried even by the Devil himself. He remained in his unruffled *dolcezza,* but the president of the consistory actually believed that the Devil leered out of your face, my good friend; and our beautiful Aurelia was so horror-stricken that all the efforts of the guests to calm her were of no avail and she soon had to retire, to the despair of all the gentlemen whose red-hot ardour was sending clouds of smoke out of their honourable toupees. In the instant, dear Herr Leonard, that you laughed so charmingly, Aurelia is said to have cried in a shrill, heart-rending voice: 'Hermogenes!' Now what can that mean? But perhaps *you* can tell me. You are a merry, wise, likeable man, Herr Leonard, and I am not sorry that I confided to you the remarkable story of Francesco, for you must find it most instructive."

The whole time he was speaking, the physician kept firm hold of my arm and looked straight into my eyes. Drawing my arm rather roughly away, I said:

"I do not know how to interpret your strange remarks, Sir, but I must confess that when I saw Aurelia beset by all those dandies whose burning passion, as you wittily observe, was sending clouds of smoke out of their honourable toupees, my heart was rent by a bitter memory of the past, and in my scorn for the foolish infatuation of those fops, I could not help laughing out loud. I regret that I unwittingly caused such a disturbance, and I will do penance by staying away from the court for a while. I hope that the Princess and Aurelia will forgive me."

"Ah, my dear Herr Leonard," replied the physician, "one sometimes has strange attacks which are easy to resist if only one is of a pure heart."

"Who can boast of that here on earth?" I muttered dully.

The physician's expression and tone of voice suddenly changed.

"You appear to be really ill after all," he said gently and seriously. "You look pale and distraught. Your eyes are sunken and burning with a strange red glow, your pulse beats feverishly, you stammer . . . Shall I prescribe something for you?"

"Poison!" I said, almost inaudibly.

"Oho!" cried the physician. "Is that the way things are with you? Well, well; instead of poison, the dismal remedy of an entertaining society. But it may be that . . . yet strangely enough . . . maybe . . ."

"I would be grateful, Sir," I cried angrily, "if you would stop tormenting me with your incoherent ramblings and tell me outright—"

"One moment," interrupted the physician. "The most unusual mistakes may occur, Herr Leonard. I am virtually certain that on an impression of the moment an hypothesis has been built which might fall to pieces in a few moments. But here comes the Princess with Aurelia. Take advantage of this chance meeting to apologise for your conduct. After all, you only laughed, if in a rather peculiar way; and who can help it if nervous people are frightened on such occasions? Adieu!"

He skipped away in his usual agile fashion. The Princess and Aurelia were coming down the avenue. I trembled and summoned all my strength. In view of the physician's enigmatic remarks, I felt that I had to assert myself without delay, and I approached the ladies boldly. When Aurelia caught sight of me she gave a cry and fell to the ground as if dead; I wanted to go to her, but the Princess waved me away in abhorrence, shouting for help. Lashed by furies and demons I rushed through the park. I locked myself in

the house and threw myself on my bed, grinding my teeth
in rage and desperation.

*   *   *   *

Evening came and darkness fell. I heard the door of the
house open; voices were whispering and murmuring below,
and there came sounds of people groping and stumbling
up the stairs. Finally there was a knock at the door and
I was ordered to open in the name of the law. Without
any clear awareness of what peril I might be in, I felt lost.
I thought of escaping and wrenched open the window. I
saw armed guards mounted in front of the house, one of
whom noticed me at once.

"Where are you going?" he shouted up at me.

At that moment my bedroom door was broken down
and several men entered; by the light of a lantern which
one of them was carrying I recognised them as soldiers.
I was shown the warrant for my arrest; any resistance
would have been foolish. I was pushed into the coach which
was standing in front of the house, and when I arrived
at what appeared to be my destination and asked where I
was, I received the answer:

"At the prison in the upper castle."

This I knew to be the place where dangerous criminals
were locked up during their trial.

After a while a bed was brought, and the jailer asked me
whether there was anything further I required for my
comfort; I said that there was not, and at last I was left
to myself. The footsteps echoing down the long passage,
and the opening and shutting of many doors, made me
realise that I was in one of the deepest dungeons of the
castle. In some unaccountable way I had managed to
remain calm during the whole of the journey to the castle,
and all the impressions that I had received passed before

my eyes in dull, lifeless colours as if I were in a kind of daze. I did not sleep but fell into a state of unconsciousness which paralysed my thoughts and my imagination. When I awoke next morning I could only gradually remember what had happened and where I had been taken.

The arched, cell-like room where I lay would have hardly seemed like a prison had not the tiny window been barred and placed so high that I could not even reach it with outstretched hand, still less look out. Only a few reluctant rays of sunshine crept in. I was taken with a desire to explore my surroundings, and pushing my bed against the wall, I stood the table on it. Just as I was about to climb up, the jailer entered and seemed astounded at my behaviour. He asked me what I was doing, and I replied that I only wanted to look out. Without a word he removed the table, the bed and the chair, and locked me in again. Less than an hour later he reappeared, accompanied by two other men, and led me up and down many flights of stairs and through long passages until at last I entered a small room where the judge was awaiting me. At his side sat a young man to whom he dictated in a loud voice all that I said in answer to the questions put to me. No doubt it was to my former position at court and the general esteem which I had so long enjoyed, that I owed the courtesy with which I was treated, though I was also convinced that my arrest was due to suspicions which rested mainly on Aurelia's forebodings.

The judge ordered me to give a full account of my previous life and circumstances. I requested him to tell me first the reason for my sudden arrest; he answered that I would be tried in due course for the crime with which I was being charged, but that at present it was merely a question of obtaining a full account of my career up to the time of my arrival in the town; he also had to remind me that the court would not lack ways and means of verify-

ing even the minutest detail I gave, and that I should
therefore keep strictly to the truth. This warning, which
the judge, a small, lean man with carroty hair, delivered
in a hoarse, ludicrously croaking voice, and with his grey
eyes staring at me, fell on fertile soil, for I now remembered
that in my story I would have to take up the thread that
I had laid down when I first gave my name and place of
birth. It was probably also advisable to avoid anything
out-of-the-ordinary and to put my career into an everyday
context which would yet be remote and vague, so that the
investigations would have to be protracted. At that moment
the memory of a young Pole came into my mind who had
studied with me in the seminary at B., and I decided to
adopt his humble circumstances for my purpose. Thus
prepared, I started my story:—

"It may well be that I am accused of a serious crime, but
I have been living here in the sight of the Prince and the
whole town, and during my stay there has been no offence
which I could be taken to have committed or in which I
could have been implicated. It must therefore be a stranger
who is accusing me of some misdeed that belongs to an
earlier period, and since I feel entirely free from guilt,
this suspicion has perhaps been aroused by some unfortunate resemblance between me and someone else. Thus I
find it all the more painful that, simply because of empty
suspicions and preconceived notions, I have been locked
up in prison like a common criminal. Why am I not confronted with my irresponsible, even malignant accuser? He
will certainly turn out to be a foolish fellow who—"

"Gently, gently," croaked the judge; "control yourself,
for you might otherwise cause offence to certain esteemed
persons. The stranger who has recognised you, Herr
Leonard—or Herr—(he bit his lip quickly), is neither
irresponsible nor foolish, but . . . well, let that be. Furthermore we have reliable information from . . ."

He named the district where the estates of Baron F. lay, and the whole matter became plain to me. Aurelia had evidently recognised me as the monk who had murdered her brother. But this monk was Medardus, the famous preacher from the Capuchin monastery in B.; Reinhold had recognised him as such, and he had in fact proved himself to be such. The abbess knew that Francesco was the father of this Medardus, and my resemblance to him, which had so disturbed the Princess from the beginning, must have brought to virtual certainty the suspicions which she and the abbess had probably disclosed to each other in their letters. It was also possible that information had been gathered from the monastery at B. itself, and that my progress had been followed and my identity with this monk Medardus established. All this flashed through my mind and I realised the danger of my position. The judge chattered on, which was to my advantage, for now, after trying vainly for a long time to remember it, I came upon the name of the Polish town which I had told the old lady at court was my birthplace. So hardly had the judge ended his sermon with the curt injunction that I should give an account of my life without further ado, than I began:

"My name is actually Leonard Crczynski, and I am the only son of a nobleman who had sold his estate and was staying in Cviecziczevo."

"Eh? What?" cried the judge, trying in vain to pronounce my name and that of my supposed birthplace. The scribe had not the slightest idea how to write the names, and I had to enter them both myself.

"You will observe, Sir," I went on, "how difficult it is for a German to pronounce my name, which is so rich in consonants; that is why, when I came to Germany, I discarded it and called myself simply by my Christian name, Leonard. As to the rest, no career could be more straight-forward than mine. My father, himself a man of consider-

able culture, approved of my marked predilection for the
sciences and was on the point of sending me to a relative of
his in Cracow, a priest called Stanislav Crczynski, when he
died. Nobody troubled about me, and I sold the small
estate, incurred a few debts and then did in fact go to
Cracow, taking with me my father's fortune, and studied
there for several years under my relative's supervision. I
then went to Danzig and Königsberg. Finally I felt an
irresistible urge to travel to Italy; I had hoped to be able to
manage this on the remainder of my small fortune and then
to find a post at a university, but I would have run into
serious difficulties had I not won appreciable sums at the
Prince's faro-table and thus been enabled to stay here at my
leisure before continuing my journey to Italy. There has
been nothing in my life worth telling of. I ought perhaps to
add that it would have been easy for me to prove the truth of
my statements if I had not by a most unfortunate chance
lost my dispatch-case, which contained my credentials, my
itinerary and various other papers."

The judge gave a start, looked at me sharply and asked
almost mockingly what this chance might be that made me
unable to prove my identity.

"Several months ago," I replied, "I was coming over the
mountains on my way here. The pleasantness of the season
and the romantic charm of the scenery made me decide
to travel on foot. One day I was sitting wearily in a small
village inn; I had ordered some refreshment and taken a
sheet of paper from my dispatch-case in order to sketch
something that had just come into my mind. The case
was lying on the table in front of me. Shortly afterwards a
cavalry officer came in who attracted my attention by his
remarkable clothes and unkempt appearance. He ordered
a drink and sat down opposite me, eyeing me in a sinister
fashion. His presence made me uneasy, and I went outside.
After a while he came out as well, paid the landlord and,

bidding me a hasty good-day, galloped off. I was about to leave myself when I remembered the case which I had left lying on the table; I went back, and found it where I had left it. Not until the next day, when I took it out, did I discover that it was not mine at all, but probably the stranger's, who had in turn taken mine by mistake. The only things I found were a few unintelligible jottings and several letters addressed to a Count Victor. You will still find this case and its contents among my possessions. In my own case, as I have said, were my credentials, my itinerary and—it has just occurred to me—my birth-certificate; all this I lost as a result of that mistake."

The judge asked me to give a complete description of the stranger I had mentioned, and I took the opportunity to paint a remarkably skilful composite picture built out of the figure of Count Victor and my own appearance at the time of my escape from Baron F.'s palace. The judge inquired after the most minute details of this episode, and by giving satisfactory answers to all his questions, I rounded off the impression in my own mind so that I really believed in it myself and thus ran no risk of becoming entangled in contradictions. Moreover it had been a most propitious idea that, when justifying my possession of those letters addressed to Count Victor, which were still in the dispatch-case, I had contrived to introduce a fictitious character who could in future represent either the escaped Medardus or Count Victor, whichever the situation required. It also occurred to me that there might be letters among Euphemia's papers which shed light on Victor's plan to appear at court as a monk, and this might obscure and confuse afresh the real circumstances of the matter. My imagination went on working while the judge put his questions, and more and more ways of safeguarding myself against detection unfolded themselves so that I now felt prepared for even the worst eventuality.

Since there appeared to have been enough discussion of my general career, I now expected the judge to concentrate more on the crime for which I was under suspicion, but it was not so: on the contrary, he asked me why I had wanted to escape from the prison. I assured him that this had not been my intention, though the testimony of the jailer, who had caught me in the act of climbing up to the window, seemed to speak against me. The judge threatened to have me put in irons if I tried it again, and I was led back to the dungeon. My bed had been taken away and a palliasse laid on the floor; the table was screwed down, and instead of the chair I found a very low bench.

Three days went by and nobody came for me. I saw only the sullen face of an old servant who brought me my food and lit the lamp in the evening. A sense of apathy crept over me; I became indifferent to everything, and even the vision of Aurelia had faded. Then my spirit began to shake off its lethargy, only to fall deeper into the clutches of the morbid mood produced by the loneliness and mustiness of the dungeon. I could not sleep. Contorted faces leered at me from the strange shadows which the dull, flickering flame of the lamp cast on the walls and ceiling; I blew out the lamp and buried my head in the palliasse, but in the darkness the dull moaning of the prisoners and the rattle of chains echoed even more gruesomely through the horrible silence of the night. Sometimes I seemed to hear the dying groans of Euphemia and Hermogenes, and I cried aloud:

"Am I responsible for your destruction? Did you not surrender yourselves to my avenging arm, you impious wretches?"

A deep, long drawn-out sigh sounded through the vaults, and I shrieked in savage desperation:

"It is you, Hermogenes! Revenge is near! There is no escape!"

On about the ninth night I was lying stretched out on the cold floor of the prison, half senseless with fear and terror. Then I heard a soft knocking beneath me. I listened; the knocking continued and a weird, unearthly laughter sounded from below the floor. I sprang up and threw myself on to my palliasse, but the knocking went on, interspersed with laughs and groans. Then a voice stammered softly, so softly, but in hoarse, terrifying tones: "Me-dar-dus! Me-dar-dus!" in endless repetition. An icy shudder went through my body. Summoning up courage, I cried:

"Who is there? Who is there?"

The laughter became louder and the groaning and wailing and knocking went on: "Me-dar-dus! Me-dar-dus!"

I forced myself up from my bed and shouted into the murky darkness:

"You who are playing ghostly tricks on me, come out into the open and let me see you, or else stop your fearful noise!"

But the knocking grew louder right under my feet, and the voice stammered:

"Hee, hee, hee! Hee, hee, hee! Lit-tle Bro-ther! Little Bro-ther Me-dar-dus! I . . . am . . . am . . . here! O-pen . . . the . . . the . . . door! Let . . . us . . . go . . . in-to . . . the . . . woods!"

The voice now sounded familiar to me; I had heard it somewhere before but not, I thought, so disjointed and stuttering. To my horror I almost seemed to recognise it as my own voice, and as if wanting to see whether it really was so, I imitated the stammer:

"Me-dar-dus! Me-dar-dus!"

The laughter broke out anew but this time angry and scornful:

"Bro-ther! Bro-ther! Do . . . you . . . you . . . know . . .

me? O-pen . . . the . . . door! Let . . . us . . . go . . . go . . .
in-to . . . the . . . the . . . woods!"

"Poor demented fool!" came a dull voice from within
me. "I cannot open the door and go with you into the
lovely woods and the fresh spring breeze which is blowing
outside. I am locked in this musty dungeon, just as you
are."

There was a moan of grief and agony, and the knocking
became gradually softer until it finally died away.

Dawn broke through the window, the locks rattled and
the jailer, whom I had not seen for a long time, entered.

"A great deal of noise and loud talking was heard coming
from your cell last night. How do you account for it?"

"I am in the habit of talking loudly in my sleep," I
replied as calmly as I could, "and if I were also to talk to
myself when I am awake, I presume that this would be
allowed."

"I take it that you know," continued the jailer, "that
any attempt to escape or any intercourse with fellow-
prisoners will be severely punished."

I protested that such was far from being my intention.
A few hours later I was led up to the courtroom. The judge,
not the one who had first interrogated me, but another,
youngish man who I realised at a glance was far superior
to the former in ability and perception, came up to me in a
friendly manner and asked me to sit down. I can still see
him vividly in my mind: he was rather stout for his age,
almost bald, and wore glasses; his whole attitude was one
of such kindness and amiability that I felt that only the
most hardened criminal could possibly resist him. He asked
his questions in an off-hand, almost conversational tone, but
they were well pondered and so precisely formulated that
only definite answers could follow.

"First of all," he began, "I must ask you whether all the
statements you have made about your career are really

well-founded or whether, on reflection, you have recalled further facts which you desire to bring forward."

"I have told you all that I can about my simple life."

"Have you ever moved in the company of priests—or monks?"

"Yes, in Cracow, Danzig, Frauenberg and Königsberg; in this last-named town I knew the lay-brothers who served as deacons and chaplains."

"You did not mention before that you had been in Frauenburg."

"Because I did not consider it worth while mentioning a short stay of, I believe, eight days there, on my way from Danzig to Königsberg."

"You were born in Cviecziczevo, I gather."

The judge put this question suddenly in Polish, with a genuine Polish accent. For the moment I was taken aback, but recovering myself and summoning what little Polish I had learned from my friend Crczynski in the seminary, I replied:

"On my father's small estate near Cviecziczevo."

"What was this estate called?"

"Crczinievo, the family estate."

"For a born Pole you do not speak Polish particularly well—in fact, with a marked German accent. How is that?"

"I have spoken nothing but German for many years. Even in Cracow I mixed to a large extent with Germans, who wanted to learn Polish from me; I may have unconsciously assumed their accent, in the way that one easily adopts a local dialect and forgets one's own superior pronunciation."

The judge looked at me. The shadow of a smile flitted across his lips; then he turned to the clerk and dictated something to him in a quiet voice. I distinctly caught the words 'obviously embarrassed' and was about to enlarge on the subject of my bad Polish when he asked:

13

"Have you ever been to B.?"

"Never."

"The journey from Königsberg may have led you through it."

"I took a different route."

"Have you ever met a monk from the Capuchin monastery in B.?"

"No."

The judge rang a bell. An usher appeared and the judge gave him an order in a low voice. Soon the door opened, and to my horror and dismay I saw Father Cyrillus enter. "Do you know this man?" asked the judge.

"No, I have never seen him before."

Cyrillus fastened his gaze on me and came nearer. He clasped his hands together and cried in a loud voice, tears pouring from his eyes:

"Medardus, Brother Medardus! For the Saviour's sake, in what state do I find you, revelling in iniquity? Brother Medardus, search your heart—confess, repent! God's mercy is everlasting."

The judge did not seem satisfied with what Cyrillus had said, and intervened:

"Do you recognise this man as the monk Medardus from the Capuchin monastery in B.?"

"As Christ may lead me to eternal bliss," answered Cyrillus, "I cannot but believe that, even though he is dressed as a man of the world, he is that Medardus who was a novice under my care and was ordained in the monastery at B. But Medardus has on the left side of his neck a red mark in the shape of a cross, and if this man—"

"You observe," interrupted the judge, turning to me, "that you are taken to be Medardus the Capuchin from the monastery at B. . . . and that this Medardus is charged with grave crimes. If you are not this monk, it will be easy for you to prove it, for the fact that he has an unusual mark on his neck—which you, if your statements are correct, cannot have—offers you the perfect opportunity to establish your innocence. Show me your neck!"

"That is not necessary," I replied coolly. "By some strange fate I seem to bear the closest possible resemblance to this suspected monk, for I even have such a mark on the left side of my neck."

This was in fact so, for that wound in my neck which had been caused by the abbess' crucifix had left a cruciform scar which time had not been able to heal.

"Show me your neck!" repeated the judge.

I did so, and Cyrillus cried:

"By the Holy Virgin! It is! It is the red mark! Medardus! O Brother Medardus, have you completely renounced eternal salvation?"

Weeping, he sank into a chair.

"What is your answer to this venerable priest's allegation?" asked the judge.

In a flash all my faint-heartedness vanished, and Satan himself whispered to me: 'What can these weaklings do to you—you, who are so strong in mind and spirit? Shall not Aurelia be yours?' In wild defiance I burst out:

"This monk, lying there weakly in his chair, is a stupid, feeble-minded old man whose crazed imagination makes him take me for some renegade Capuchin from his monastery to whom I may perhaps bear some slight resemblance."

Up to now the judge had remained calm and composed, without varying his expression or his voice, but at this a grave, ominous look came into his eyes, and he regarded me severely; even his glistening spectacles inspired me with a feeling of terror, and I was unable to speak any further. I shook my fist in fury and cried:

"Aurelia!"

"What's that? What do you mean by that name?" asked the judge sharply.

"A mysterious fate is leading me to an ignominious death," I said nervelessly, "but I am innocent, I am indeed innocent. Set me free . . . have pity . . . I feel the grip of madness upon me . . . set me free . . ."

The judge, who had now become calmer again, dictated to the clerk a great deal which I did not understand; finally he read out to me an account of the entire proceedings, in which all his questions and my answers were recorded, including the incident with Cyrillus. He made me sign my name and then asked me to write something in Polish and in German. I did so. He took the sheet of German and handed it to Father Cyrillus, who had now recovered, and asked:

"Does this handwriting resemble that of your Brother, Cyrillus?"

"It is his writing exactly, down to the smallest detail," answered Cyrillus, turning to me again. He was about to go on but at a glance from the judge he stopped. The judge studied closely the sheet on which I had written some Polish; then he rose, came close to me and said in a grave, imperious voice:

"You are not a Pole. This writing is inaccurate, full of grammatical and orthographical errors. No native Pole would write like this, even if he were far less educated than you are."

"I was born in Cviecziczevo, therefore I am a Pole. But even supposing that I were not, and that mysterious circumstances were compelling me to withhold my true name and rank, that would not make me Medardus the Capuchin, who, as I apparently must believe, escaped from the monastery at B."

"O Brother Medardus!" Cyrillus broke in. "Did not our venerable prior Leonardus send you to Rome, trusting in your constancy and devotion? In the name of Christ, do not continue to disavow in this profane manner the holy estate from which you have fled!"

"Please do not interrupt us," said the judge, and turning to me, went on:

"I must impress upon you that the trustworthy evidence of this priest arouses the gravest suspicion that you really are that Medardus whom people take you to be. Furthermore I will not conceal from you that you will be confronted with several persons who have recognised you beyond all doubt as that monk, and one of them you will greatly fear, if these assumptions are correct. Even among your own possessions certain things have been found which confirm this suspicion. Finally the information we required about your supposed family circumstances will shortly arrive from the law-courts in Posen. I tell you all this more candidly than my office demands in order that you may convince yourself how far I am from plotting some stratagem to force the truth from you. Prepare yourself as you wish; if you really are Medardus, the accused, then, believe me, the judge's eye will soon see through even the cleverest disguise; then, too, you will yourself know exactly what crimes you are accused of. If, on the other hand, you are Leonard von Crczynski, as you claim, and if it is through a strange whim of nature that you have come to resemble Medardus, even to the extent of individual marks, then you will easily find means of proving it. You seemed at first to be in a highly distraught condition, and it was in fact for that reason that I broke off the interrogation, but I also wanted to give you ample time for meditation. After what has happened today, you can scarcely lack material for it."

"So you consider my statement completely false, and see in me the monk Medardus?" I asked.

He replied, with a slight bow:

"Adieu, Herr von Crczynski!" and ordered me to be taken back to the dungeon.

The judge's words had pierced me like burning daggers. My whole story seemed shallow and absurd. It was only too clear that the person with whom I was to be confronted, and whom I was supposed to fear so greatly, must be Aurelia. I wondered what possessions of mine could have aroused suspicion; then my heart dropped as I remembered that I still had a ring with Euphemia's name on it, and that Victor's knapsack, which I had taken with me on my flight, was still tied with my Capuchin cord. I felt that everything was lost, and in despair I rushed to and fro in the dungeon. Then a voice seemed to whisper in my ear: "You fool, why are you so faint-hearted? Do you not remember Victor?" I cried aloud:

"Ha, ha! The game is won, not lost!"

My thoughts were in a whirl. Some time earlier I had remembered that there must be something among Euphemia's papers which would point to Victor's appearance in the palace disguised as a monk. Relying on this, I would pretend in some way that I had met Victor, or even the monk Medardus I was taken to be; I would relate, as if from hearsay, that adventure in the castle which had ended so tragically, and skilfully and innocuously weave into it my own self and my resemblance to both of them. The minutest detail had to be well pondered, and I therefore decided to make a record of the romantic story by which I would clear myself. I was granted the writing materials that I requested in order to set down certain facts of my life which I had hitherto withheld.

I worked well into the night. As I wrote, my imagination was kindled; everything took on the shape of a polished work of art, and more and more closely-woven became the tissue of lies with which I hoped to veil the truth from the judge's gaze.

The castle clock had struck twelve, when the knocking that had disturbed me the night before was heard again,

at first faintly in the distance. I tried not to heed it, but
the regular blows grew louder and louder and the laughing
and groaning started. Striking the table with my fist, I
shouted: "Be quiet down there!" hoping thereby to bolster
up my courage. But the shrill laughter rang through the
arches and the voice stuttered:

"Lit-tle Bro-ther! Lit-tle Bro-ther! Co-ming up . . . up!
O-pen! O-pen!"

There were sounds of scratching, rattling and scraping,
while the laughing and moaning still went on. The noise
became louder; now and again there were dull thuds as of
heavy stones falling. I was standing with the lamp in my
hand. Something moved under my feet. Stepping aside,
I saw that on the spot where I had been standing one of
the flagstones was crumbling away. I took hold of it, and
lifted it out completely with the greatest ease. A faint ray
of light shone up through the hole, and a naked arm with a
shining knife in its hand stretched out towards me. Horror-
struck, I shrank back. The voice came from below:

"Bro-ther Me-dar-dus is . . . is . . . here! Up!—Take!—
In-to . . . the . . . the . . . woods!"

Thoughts of rescue and escape flashed through my mind.
Taking hold of myself, I seized the knife, which the hand
readily let me have, and started scraping away the mortar
between the flagstones. The man below pushed vigorously.
Four or five stones had been cast on one side when suddenly
a naked figure thrust itself waist-high out of the hole and
stared at me like a gruesome spectre, leering and cackling
like a madman. The full light of the lamp fell on his face
and I recognised—*myself*.

I fell into a faint and was awakened by a sharp pain
in my arms. All was bright around me. The jailer was
standing in front of me with his blinding lamp, and the
sound of rattling chains and hammering rang through the
cell. I was being clamped in irons. Besides the manacles

on my hands and feet, I was fettered to the wall by means
of a chain secured to a ring round my body.

"I don't think he'll contemplate breaking out now," said
the jailer.

"What did the fellow actually do?" asked one of the
smithies.

"What?" replied the jailer. "You don't know? The
whole town's full of it. He is a cursed Capuchin who has
committed three murders; it has all come out. In a few
days' time we shall be having a grand gala—that's when
the wheels will turn!"

I lapsed once again into unconsciousness and heard no
more.

Painfully I recovered from my daze. It was still dark,
but at last a few faint gleams of light crept into the low
cell, barely six feet high, into which I had been put. I
was thirsty and took hold of the water-jug that was standing
beside me; I felt something cold and clammy in my hand
and saw an ugly, repulsive toad hop sluggishly away. I
dropped the jug in disgust.

"Aurelia!" I cried in unutterable misery. "Was this the
object of my pitiful lying and deceitfulness before the judge,
this the object of all the Devil's cunning trickery—just to
be able to grudge a few more hours to a torn and shattered
life? What do you want, you madman? To possess Aurelia,
who could only become yours by an outrageous act of
violence? For however much you lie to the world about
your guilt, she will only see in you her brother's murderer.
Miserable fool, where are your high-flown plans now, your
faith in the supernatural power with which you thought
you could direct the movements of fate according to your
whim and fancy? You will perish in shame and wretchedness, even if the arm of justice spares you."

With these loud lamentations I threw myself on the
straw. In that instant I felt something pressing against my

breast: it seemed to be some hard object in the breast-pocket of my coat. I felt in the pocket and drew out a small knife. The whole time that I had been in the dungeon I had not had a knife with me; it must therefore be the one that my ghostly double had handed up to me. Painfully I stood up and held the knife to the light; my eyes fell on the shining silver handle. O inscrutable fate! *It was the knife with which I had murdered Hermogenes.* Suddenly a beam of light shone through my heart, bringing comfort and relief to my misery: the inexplicable way in which I had received the knife was an intimation from the higher power how I was to atone for my misdeeds and reconcile myself with Aurelia in death. My love for her now glowed through my body with a pure, heavenly lustre, and all sinful desire had departed from me. I seemed to see her again as on that day in the confessional: "I do indeed love you, Medardus, but you did not understand me. My love is death!" I heard her voice whispering above my head, and I resolved to confess openly to the judge the story of my erring ways and then surrender myself to death.

The jailer entered, bringing me better food than I had hitherto received and also a bottle of wine.

"By order of the Prince," he said, laying the table which the servant had brought in and unlocking the chain that secured me to the wall. I asked him to tell the judge that I wished to be interrogated again because I had much to reveal that was pressing heavily on my conscience. He promised to convey the message, but I waited in vain to be summoned. Nobody appeared until, when it was already quite dark, the servant came in to light the lamp that hung from the ceiling. I was calmer in my mind than before but felt completely exhausted and soon sank into a deep sleep. I imagined that I was being led into a long, gloomy vaulted chamber in which I saw a row of priests clothed in black gowns, sitting on tall chairs along the wall. In front of them, at a table covered with a crimson cloth, sat the judge, at his side a Dominican friar in the habit of his order.

'Wicked, obdurate monk,' said the judge, in a solemn tone, 'you are now in the hands of the ecclesiastical court, for it is of no avail that you have denied your name and your estate. Franciscus, known as Medardus, speak. Of what crimes are you accused?'

I wanted to confess openly all my sins and misdeeds, but to my horror what I said was quite different from what I intended to say; instead of a solemn confession, I lost myself in senseless, incoherent ramblings. The Dominican, towering up before me and fixing me with his blazing eyes, said:

'On the rack with you, stubborn, unrepentent monk!'

The strange figures rose on every side, pointing their long arms at me and shouting in hoarse, gruesome unison:

'On the rack with him!'

I pulled out my knife and made to plunge it into my heart, but something made my arm move higher and strike my neck; the blade splintered against the mark of the cross and I was left unscathed. The hangman's servants seized me and cast me into a deep, subterranean cave; the Dominican and the judge climbed down after me. Again the latter ordered me to confess. Again I strained every nerve, but my thoughts and words were madly at variance with each other: full of remorse, crushed under the burden of shame, I confessed everything in my mind, but confused, meaningless, ridiculous were the words that came from my mouth. At a sign from the Dominican the servants stripped me naked and tied my arms together behind my back. As I was drawn up I felt my extended limbs cracking and crumbling; I gave a wild cry of agony, and woke up.

The pain in my hands and feet continued; it came from the heavy chains that I was wearing. But I also felt something pressing on my eyes so that I could not open them.

At last a weight seemed to be lifted from my forehead, and I sat up quickly. A Dominican friar was standing at my bedside. My dream was coming true.

An icy shudder ran down my spine. The monk stood like a statue, looking at me unwaveringly with black, sunken eyes, his arms folded. I recognised the mysterious painter, and fell back half-fainting on to my bed. Or was it perhaps only an illusion brought about by my feverish dream? I pulled myself together and sat up, but he was still standing there impassively. I cried out in desperation:

"O terrible man, away with you! But no, you are no man, you are Satan himself, and you have come to plunge me into eternal perdition. Away with you, accursed wretch!"

"Poor, undiscerning fool. I am not he who seeks to bind you in chains or turn you away from the holy work to which you have been called. Medardus, you poor, blind fool, it was I who appeared to you whenever you balanced recklessly above the open grave of damnation. I warned you, but you did not heed me. Arise. Come closer to me."

All this the monk spoke in tones of deep lamentation; his gaze had become kind and tender, and a feeling of deep sorrow came over me. The painter whom I had always dreaded was now standing before me, comforting me in my distress. I got up from my bed and approached him; I touched his robe and fell instinctively at his feet. He laid his hand upon my head as if in blessing. Wonderful visions appeared to me, and I felt as though I were in the forest by the Holy Linden.

"O mysterious figure!" I cried. "Was it you the whole time? On that unhappy morning in the Capuchin church? In the city? And now?"

"I was always near you to save you from shame and destruction," said the painter, "but your heart was hardened against me. You must achieve your own salvation through the work to which you have been called."

"Alas!" I cried. "Why did you not restrain my arm when I—"

"I was not permitted to," he broke in; "do not ask further. It is foolhardy to try to forestall what the power of Heaven has ordained. Medardus, you will arrive at your goal—tomorrow!"

I trembled, for I believed I understood him: he knew and approved of my intention to kill myself. As he moved softly towards the door of the cell, I cried:

"When shall I see you again?"

Turning towards me, he said in a majestic voice that thundered through the arches:

"When you reach your goal!"

"You mean tomorrow?"

The door closed quietly, and he vanished.

At daybreak the jailer entered with his servants, who removed the manacles from my sore hands and feet; apparently I was soon to be taken before the court. Brooding over the thought of my impending death, I walked slowly up to the courtroom.

The judge came quickly towards me. My features must have presented a grim and distorted appearance, for as soon as he saw me, the happy smile that had been on his face turned to an expression of profound pity. He took hold of my hands and led me gently to a chair. Then looking me straight in the face, he said slowly and deliberately:

"Herr von Crczynski, I have cheering news for you. You are free! The trial has been quashed by order of the Prince. You have been mistaken for somebody else, and the reason for the error is your astonishing resemblance to this other person. Your innocence has been clearly established. You are free!"

Everything began to go round and round in my head; a

hundred judges beamed brightly through the mist, while all else was hidden in thick darkness. Then I felt my forehead being bathed, and I recovered from my swoon. The judge read me a short report which stated that he had informed me of the quashing of the trial and effected my release from prison. I signed the document in silence, unable to utter a word. As the judge looked at me with a kindness that deeply moved me, I felt that, since I was now held to be innocent, I ought openly to confess all the atrocities which I had committed and then stab myself with the knife. I was about to speak, but the judge seemed to want me to move away, and I went towards the door. He followed me and said softly:

"I am now no longer speaking as a judge. From the first moment I set eyes on you I was extremely interested in your case; much as appearances were against you—and you must yourself admit that they were—I still hoped that you were not the homicidal monk you were taken to be. I can now tell you confidentially that you are not a Pole, that you were not born in Cviecziczevo, and that your name is not Leonard von Crczynski."

Steadfastly and with composure I replied:

"No."

"And you are not a priest?" went on the judge, lowering his eyes in order to spare me his inquisitorial gaze.

Emotion welled up within me.

"Listen to my—" I began.

"Say no more," he interrupted; "what I believed at the beginning, and still believe, has been confirmed. I see that inscrutable circumstances prevail in this affair, and that you are implicated with certain persons of the court in a mysterious caprice of fate. It is no longer my business to inquire into the matter, and I would consider it unseemly to induce you to tell me any more about yourself. Nevertheless, how would it be if you were to leave this town, and tear yourself away from everything that threatens your peace of mind? After what has happened it surely cannot do you any good to stay here."

As soon as the judge said this, all the sinister shadows that had gathered above my head seemed to fly away. Life had been regained, and the joy of living surged through my veins. The thought of Aurelia came to me again—and was I now to go away from this place—from her?

"And leave *her*?" I said with a sigh.

The judge looked at me in astonishment and then said swiftly:

"Ah, now I begin to see. May Heaven grant, Herr Leonard, that an evil foreboding which has just entered my mind be not fulfilled."

Everything was transformed. Gone was all thought of repentance, and with almost wanton arrogance I asked the judge in a tone of feigned calmness:

"So you still consider me guilty?"

"Permit me, Sir," returned the judge gravely, "to keep my convictions, which only appear to be based on a vivid impression, to myself. It has been established in the most satisfactory manner that you cannot be the monk Medardus, since this Medardus is here and has been recognised by Father Cyrillus, who was misled by your resemblance to him. In fact, he does not even deny that he is the Capuchin. Thus everything has happened that could possibly happen to clear your suspicion, and I cannot but believe all the more that you feel entirely free from guilt."

At that moment an usher called the judge away, and the conversation was broken off just as it was beginning to become embarrassing to me.

I returned to my room and found everything as I had left it. My papers had earlier been confiscated and now lay in a sealed envelope on my desk; the only things missing were Victor's dispatch-case, Euphemia's ring and the Capuchin cord—the suspicions I had had were evidently correct.

After a while one of the Prince's servants appeared and handed me a note from his master, together with a gold box set with precious stones. 'You have been shamefully treated, Herr von Crczynski,' I read, 'but the fault lies neither with me nor with my courts of justice. You bear an incredible resemblance to a certain evil man, but everything has now been settled in your favour. I am sending you this as a token of goodwill and hope to see you very shortly.'

The Prince's graciousness was as immaterial to me as his gift. As a result of my harsh imprisonment my mind had become dead; I felt that I needed to be restored in body, and I was therefore pleased when the physician came to see me. After the medical question had been settled, the physician said:

"Is it not a strange whim of fate that at the very moment when they felt certain that you were the odious monk who had wrought such destruction in the Baron's palace, the monk himself should appear and clear you of all incrimination?"

"I must confess that I am not conversant with the circumstances that brought about my release; the judge simply told me that Medardus the Capuchin, for whom they had been searching, and for whom they had taken me, had given himself up."

"He did not give himself up; he was brought here in a cart, tied hand and foot, and strangely enough, at the very same time as you arrived here. But it has just occurred to me that when I was describing the remarkable events that took place at our court some time ago, I was interrupted at the point of telling you about the dangerous Medardus, Francesco's son, and his outrages in the palace of Baron F. Let me resume where I left off.

"As you know, the sister of our Princess is abbess of the Cistercian convent at B. She once graciously gave shelter to a poor woman who was returning with her child from a pilgrimage to the Holy Linden."

"The woman was Francesco's widow, and the child was that Medardus."

"Quite right—but how do you know?"

"The course of Medardus' life was made known to me in a mysterious way. I am fully cognisant of what happened up to the time when he fled from Baron F.'s castle."

"But how? Who told you?"

"It was revealed to me in a dream."

"Are you joking?"

"Not in the slightest. I feel as if I had heard in a dream the story of an unfortunate wretch who, the sport of sinister forces, was hurled to and fro and driven from crime to crime. On my journey here the coachman lost his way in . . . Forest; I came to the gamekeeper's house, and there—"

"Ah, I understand. There you found the monk."

"I did, but he was insane."

"He does not seem so now. And in his sane moments he confided everything to you?"

"Not exactly. One night, not knowing of my arrival in the house, he came into my room. My remarkable resemblance to him caused him great terror; he took me for his double who had appeared in order to proclaim his death. He stammered and stuttered confessions, but tired as I was after my journey, I fell asleep; he seemed to be talking on, calmly and composedly, and even now I do not really know when and how the dream started. I think he declared that it was not he who had murdered Euphemia and Hermogenes, but Count Victor."

"Odd, extremely odd. But why did you withhold all this from the judge?"

"How could I expect him to attach any importance to

a story which could only have sounded fantastic to him?
Is an enlightened court of justice allowed to believe in the
miraculous?"

"But at least you ought to have guessed that you were
being mistaken for the mad monk, and to have pointed
him out."

"Admittedly, and in fact, on that occasion when a stupid
old man (Cyrillus, I think his name was) declared that I was
definitely his fellow-monk. But it did not occur to me that
the mad monk was actually that Medardus, or that the
crime he confessed to me could be the issue at this trial.
Yet the gamekeeper said that the monk had never told
him his name. How, then, was it discovered?"

"Quite easily. As you know, the monk had been staying
at the gamekeeper's for some time. He seemed cured, but
his delirium broke out afresh with such dreadful consequences that the gamekeeper found himself compelled to
bring him here and have him locked up in the asylum. Day
and night he sat there motionless as a statue, staring in
front of him: he said nothing, and since he would not move
his hands, he had to be fed. Attempts to rouse him from
his coma proved fruitless, and to resort to the most stringent
measures would have been to run the risk of causing a
further outbreak of madness.

"A few days ago the gamekeeper's eldest son came to the
town and went to the asylum to see the monk. Profoundly
moved by the unhappy creature's condition, he came out
of the asylum just as Father Cyrillus, of the Capuchin
monastery in B., was passing by. He spoke to him and asked
him to visit the hapless brother who was imprisoned there,
as some words of comfort from a priest of his own order
might have a salutary effect. When Cyrillus saw the monk,
he recoiled in horror and cried:

'By the Holy Virgin! Medardus, wretched Medardus!'

"A new light seemed to come into the monk's staring

14

eyes; he stood up, then fell lifeless to the floor with a dull cry.

"Accompanied by the others who had witnessed the scene, Cyrillus went at once to the commissioner of police and informed him of everything. The judge who had been briefed to interrogate you went with Cyrillus to the asylum, where he found the monk exhausted but free from all madness. He confessed to being the monk Medardus from the Capuchin monastery at B. Cyrillus admitted that he had been deceived by your extraordinary resemblance to Medardus, and said that he now observed that Herr Leonard's speech, gait, expression and bearing were quite different from those of the monk whom he saw before him. The significant mark of the cross on the left side of the neck, about which there was so much fuss at your trial, was also discovered. The monk was then asked about the happenings in Baron F.'s palace.

'I am a wicked murderer!' he said weakly, almost inaudibly; 'I deeply repent what I have done. Alas, I allowed myself to be robbed of my true self and of my immortal soul. Have pity on me. I will confess everything —everything!'

"When he heard of this, the Prince immediately gave order for your trial to be broken off and for you to be released from custody. That is the story of how you were set free. The monk has now been taken to the dungeons."

"And has confessed to everything? Did he murder Euphemia and Hermogenes? What about Count Victor?"

"As far as I know, the monk's trial only opened today, but as concerns Count Victor, it seems as though all connection with the events at our own court will have to remain obscure and unexplained."

"I cannot see why the incidents that occurred at Baron F.'s palace should have anything to do with the catastrophe at your own court."

"I was thinking rather of the characters involved than the event itself."

"I do not follow you."

"Do you recall my account of that tragedy which nearly cost the Prince his life?"

"Certainly."

"Did you not realise that Francesco cherished an adulterous love for the Italian Princess? That it was he who crept into the bridal chamber before the Duke and stabbed him? Victor was the fruit of this horrible outrage. Both he and Medardus are sons of the one father! Victor has vanished without trace and all investigations have been unavailing."

"The monk hurled him into the Devil's Gorge! A curse on the murderer!"

In the moment I uttered this passionate exclamation the knocking of that ghostly monster in the dungeon became faintly audible. Vainly I tried to suppress the shudder that ran through me. The physician seemed as unobservant of the knocking as of my inner agitation and went on:

"What? Did the monk confess to you that Victor fell by his hand as well?"

"Yes! At least, I conclude that that is the case, when I relate his incoherent mutterings to Victor's disappearance. A curse on the murderer!"

The knocking and groaning grew louder. A piping laugh went through the room which sounded like: 'Me-dar-dus! Me-dar-dus!—Help!' Without noticing anything, the physician continued:

"There appears to be a strange secret about Francesco's origin; he is very probably related to the Prince's house. This much, however, is certain: that Euphemia—"

With a terrifying crash the door was torn off its hinges, and a shrill laugh rang through the room.

"Ha, ha! Ha, ha! Little Brother!" I screamed deliriously. "Here—quickly, if you want to fight with me. It is the owl's wedding-day; let us climb on to the roof and fight with each other, and the one who pushes the other over will become king and be able to drink blood!"

The physician took hold of my arms and cried:

"What's that? What's that? You are ill, dangerously ill. To bed with you at once!"

But I still stared at the open door, expecting my hideous double to appear. I saw nothing, and soon recovered from the wild terror that had seized me with its icy claws. The physician insisted that I was more ill than I wanted to believe, and attributed everything to the dungeon and to the nervous emotions aroused by the trial. I needed his attention, but my rapid recovery was furthered less by his medical skill than by the fact that the knocking was no longer audible, and that my fearful double seemed to have departed.

* * * *

One morning, as the spring sunshine was sending its golden rays through my window and the scent of sweet flowers was wafted in from the garden, I was filled with an irresistible desire to leave my room, and heedless of the physician's orders, I went down into the park. The trees and bushes sighed gently, greeting the man who had been rescued from the throes of death. I drew a deep breath, as if I had just woken from a long dream; indeed, my whole life seemed like a dream, and as I wandered down a shady avenue of dark plane-trees, I imagined that I was again in the garden of the monastery at B. . . Rising above the distant thickets stood the tall cross at which I used to pray for strength to overcome temptation; I felt as if I should cast myself down before it and atone for the wicked thoughts that Satan had dangled before me. With my hands clasped and held high, I strode on towards it. The wind rose, and I seemed to hear the brethren chanting, but it was only the strange voices of the forest, carried by the wind as it rippled through the trees. I was almost exhausted and had to hold fast to a tree to prevent myself from falling. Summoning all my strength, I stumbled on but was only able to reach the bed of moss in front of the bushes; an overpowering weakness came over me, and I sank to the ground like a feeble old man, moaning dismally.

There was a rustle close by and—Aurelia stood before me! Through her sorrowful tears shone a ray of passionate longing as on that day when she had come to me in the confessional.

"Can you ever forgive me?" she murmured.

I threw myself at her feet in rapture:

"O Aurelia! I would endure torture for your sake—even death!"

I felt myself gently lifted up. Aurelia sank into my arms, and I covered her with burning kisses. Startled by a noise close at hand, she freed herself at last from my embrace.

"All my hopes and longings are now fulfilled," she whispered.

At that moment I saw the Princess coming up the avenue. Moving away into the bushes, I became aware to my astonishment that what I had taken to be a cross was nothing but a black, withered tree-trunk.

My weariness had vanished. Aurelia's kisses sent a new fire surging through me, and I felt as though the sacred mystery of love, the secret of life itself, had been revealed to me in all its glory. This was the culmination of my life; from now on it would follow a downward path, that the destiny decreed by the powers above might be fulfilled.

When I sat down to record what happened after Aurelia had seen me again, the whole period seemed shrouded in a heavenly dream. I once entreated you, gentle reader, whoever you may be who come to read these pages, to recall the high noontide of your own life in order that you might share the sufferings of this repentant monk, now old and grey, and join in his lamentations. I now beseech you once more to call that moment to mind, for then I need not describe to you how Aurelia's love transfigured me and everything around me, how I saw and grasped with renewed strength this life within life, how I was inspired with a feeling of heavenly bliss. No morbid thought could enter my mind, for Aurelia's love had freed me from sin, and in some strange way I even began to believe that it was not I who had murdered Euphemia and Hermogenes, but the mad monk I had met in the gamekeeper's house. All that I had confessed to the physician seemed not a lie but the true course of an enigmatic story which even I could not explain. The Prince welcomed me like a friend given up as lost and found again, and this set the pattern which everyone followed; only the Princess, even more gracious than before, was still austere and reserved.

Aurelia surrendered herself to me in utter innocence. She did not feel her love as a crime to be hidden from the world, and still less was I able to conceal the emotion for which alone I was living. Everybody knew of our relationship but nobody spoke about it, for the look in the Prince's eyes showed that he would, if not encourage, at least tacitly permit our love. Thus I was able to see Aurelia whenever I wished, sometimes even without anyone else being present. I clasped her to my breast; she returned my kisses passionately, but feeling how she trembled with the coyness of virginity, I could not give way to my sinful lust, and every wicked thought perished in a shiver that ran through my body. She seemed to fear no danger, and there was indeed none, for often when she was sitting alone beside me, her divine charms shining more brightly than ever, she looked at me with such indescribable gentleness and purity that it seemed as though even here on earth Heaven were granting the penitent sinner to draw nigh to the saint.

For she was not Aurelia but Saint Rosalia. I fell at her
feet, crying:

"O pious saint, surely my heart may not be stirred by
an earthly love for you?"

Stretching out her hand to me, she said in a sweet, gentle
voice:

"I am not a saint, for all my piousness. And I love you
dearly."

For several days I did not see her, as she was staying with
the Princess in a country residence not far distant. I could
not stand her absence any longer and rushed to the place.
Arriving late in the evening, I met a chambermaid in the
garden who pointed out Aurelia's room to me. As I opened
the door softly and went in, a breath of warm air perfumed
with the wonderful scent of flowers dazed me, and strange
memories stirred in my mind: was this not Aurelia's room
in the Baron's palace where I . . .

As soon as this thought struck me, a dark figure seemed
to appear, and a cry of 'Hermogenes!' went through my
heart. In terror I rushed forwards, pushing open the door
to the bed-chamber, which was ajar. Aurelia, her back
towards me, was kneeling in front of a tabouret, on which
lay an open book. I looked instinctively behind me. I saw
nothing, and cried in a surge of ecstasy:

"Aurelia! O Aurelia!"

She turned round quickly, but before she could rise I
was kneeling beside her, holding her in my arms.

"Leonard! My beloved!" she whispered.

An uncontrollable desire was seething within me. She
lay powerless in my embrace; her hair hung in luxuriant
tresses over my shoulders and her bosom heaved. She gave
a gentle sigh. Savagely I clasped her to me; her eyes
burned with a strange glow, and she returned my fierce
kisses with even greater ardour. There was a noise as of
the beating of wings, and a piercing scream, like that of a

man mortally wounded, rent the air.

"Hermogenes!" shrieked Aurelia, and fell unconscious from my arms.

I rushed out of the room. In the corridor I met the Princess returning from a walk. Looking at me haughtily, she said:

"I am shocked to find you here, Herr Leonard!"

Overcoming my confusion, I replied, in a tone almost too aggressive to be courteous, that one often struggles unavailingly against sudden impulses, and that what appears improper may often turn out to be quite the opposite.

As I hastened through the dark streets, someone seemed to be running behind me and whispering: 'I . . . I . . . am . . . am . . . still . . . with . . . with . . . you, lit-tle . . . Bro-ther . . . Me-dar-dus!'

Looking round, I realised that it was only the spectre of my double haunting my imagination, but I could not rid myself of it. I even came to feel that I must talk to it and tell it that I had again behaved very stupidly in allowing myself to be frightened by the mad Hermogenes; Saint Rosalia was to be mine, mine alone, for that was why I was a monk and had received holy orders.

My double cackled and groaned as before and stuttered: 'Quick! Quick!'

'Be patient,' I said, 'be patient, my friend. Everything will turn out all right. I did not strike Hermogenes properly. He has the same cursed crucifix on his neck as we have, but my deft little knife still has a sharp point.'

'He, he, he! Strike well! Strike well!' came a whisper, borne on the rustling breeze which wafted towards me from the glowing eastern sky.

Just after I had returned to my room, I was summoned to the Prince. He came towards me kindly.

"Herr Leonard," he began, "you have gained my very real affection, and I should not like to lose you. I want to see you happy. Besides that, you are due the utmost compensation for what you have suffered. Do you know, Herr Leonard, who was responsible for your arrest?"

"I do not, Sir."

"Baroness Aurelia!—You are astounded? Yes, Herr Leonard, it was Baroness Aurelia who (he laughed out loud) took you for a Capuchin! Well, if you really are a Capuchin, then you are the most likeable one I ever met! Tell me frankly, are you really something of a priest?"

"Gracious Sir, I do not know what evil destiny it is that is always seeking to turn me into that monk who . . ."

"Let us forget the subject. I am not an inquisitor—although it would be a calamity if you were bound by a religious vow. But to business! Do you not wish to avenge yourself for the injustice that Baroness Aurelia has wrought upon you?"

"Who could harbour such a thought against that sweet child?"

"You love Aurelia?"

He looked at me intently. I said nothing, laying my hand on my breast. The Prince went on:

"I know. You have loved her from the moment she first came into the hall with the Princess. She returns your love with an ardour of which I would never have thought her capable. She lives only for you; the Princess has told me everything. Will you believe me when I tell you that after your arrest Aurelia fell into a mood of grief and despair which brought her near to death? At that time she still took you for her brother's murderer, and her sorrow was thus all the more inexplicable to us. She already loved you then. Now, Herr Leonard—or rather, Herr von Crczynski —you are a nobleman. I will establish you at court in a manner acceptable to you. You shall marry Aurelia. In a few days we will celebrate the betrothal, and I myself will give the bride away."

I stood there dumbfounded, torn by conflicting emotions.
"Adieu, Herr Leonard!" said the prince, and left the
room, giving me a friendly wave.

Aurelia my wife, the consort of a murderous monk?
Never! That was not what the powers of destiny desired,
whatever be inflicted on the poor creature—such was the
thought that rose within me. I knew that I must make an
instant decision, but in vain I brooded on how to part
from Aurelia without causing myself too great sorrow. The
thought of not seeing her again was beyond endurance, but
that she was to become my wife filled me with aversion. I
felt all too clearly that if the guilty monk were to stand
before the altar of the Lord, playing his evil game with
holy vows, the figure of the mysterious painter would
appear, not comforting me as in the prison but threatening
terrible vengeance, and plunge me into destruction. But
then I heard another voice inside me: 'Aurelia shall be
yours! Impotent fool, how can you change what providence
has decreed?' And then the first voice came again:
'Humble yourself in the dust! What outrage are you con-
templating, miserable sinner? Never can she be yours. It
is Saint Rosalia herself whom you are striving to enfold
in your lustful embrace!'
Tossed to and fro in this cruel conflict, I could see no
escape from the ruin that faced me on all sides. Gone was
that mood of exaltation which made my whole life seem
like a dream; I saw myself as a murderer and a common
libertine. All that I had told the judge and the physician
was nothing but foolish, clumsy lies: there had been no
inner voice speaking to me, as I had tried to persuade
myself.
Sunk in thought, I wandered down the street. The
rattling of a coach and the shout of the driver roused me,
and I jumped quickly to one side. The Princess' carriage

rolled by and the physician leaned out of the window, waving genially to me. I followed him to his house. He jumped out of the carriage and, taking me to his room, said:

"I have just come from Aurelia, and there is a great deal to tell you.—Well, now, you violent, hasty fellow! What have you been doing? You suddenly appear before Aurelia like a ghost, and as a result the poor, nervous girl is taken ill."

I blenched, and the physician was not slow to notice it.

"Still," he continued, "the matter is not serious. She is on her feet again and tomorrow she will return with the Princess to the palace. She talked a great deal about you and yearns passionately to see you again and crave your pardon, for she is sure she must have appeared naïve and foolish to you."

When I recalled what had happened in the country residence, I did not know what to make of Aurelia's attitude.

The physician made it clear that he was fully conversant with the Prince's plans for my future, and by his infectious vivacity and blitheness he soon succeeded in driving me out of my melancholy mood. He described again how he had found Aurelia lying on the couch like a child unable to recover from a deep dream, and how she had told him of her sad visions. He repeated her story, imitating her timorous voice and the sighs with which she interspersed her words, and by his caricature of her lamentations and his witty shafts of irony he painted a delightful picture of the scene. The effect was heightened by his portrayal of the haughty Princess, which delighted me immensely.

"When you came to this town," he said finally, "did you ever imagine that so many remarkable things would happen to you? First the incredible misunderstanding which delivered you into the hands of the criminal court, and then the truly enviable happiness which your friend the Prince has prepared for you."

"I must confess that I was deeply touched by the kindness with which the Prince welcomed me at the outset, yet I feel that the added esteem now accorded to me by him and by everybody at court is really due to the injustice I have suffered."

"Not so much to that as to another, more trivial circumstance which you can probably guess."

"Far from it."

"Admittedly we still call you simply Herr Leonard, but everyone knows now that you are a nobleman, since the information received from Posen has confirmed your statements."

"Yet how can that have any effect on the Prince or on the respect I enjoy at court? When the Prince first met me and invited me to join his circle, I protested that I was of humble origin, but he said that my knowledge ennobled me and made me fit to appear in his company."

"That is really what he thinks, toying in his fickle way with science and art. You will have noticed at court many scholars and artists of humble birth, but the sensitive among them, those who do not share his facile nature and are constitutionally unable to assume an attitude of detached irony which would set them above the whole situation, are only rarely seen. Despite a sincere desire to appear unprejudiced, there seems ingrained in the nobleman's attitude to the commoner a certain condescension, a tolerance of what in fact is felt to be unseemly. This is unbearable to any man who feels, with justifiable pride, that in high society it is often he who has to be condescending and submit to what is intellectually vulgar and in poor taste.

"You, Herr Leonard, are yourself a nobleman, yet, as I hear, also cultured in mind and spirit. That is probably why you are the first nobleman in whom, even in the company of other noblemen at court, I have never detected anything 'noble' in the derogatory sense. You may think that, as a commoner, I am merely expressing a prejudice, or that something has happened to me personally to arouse such an attitude. But it is not so. I happen to belong to one of the classes which, exceptionally, are not only tolerated but actually sought after. Physicians and father-confessors are rulers, masters of body and soul, and thus automatically members of high society. For may not indigestion and eternal damnation incommode even the most noble of courtiers a little? As far as confessors are concerned, however, this is only true of Catholics. Protestant pastors, at least in country districts, are only domestic staff who, having tickled their employers' consciences, retire to the lower end of the table and share in all humility in the eating and drinking. It is hard to throw off a prejudice, but the good will is usually lacking as well, for many noblemen must feel that it is only to their rank that they owe their position in life, since nothing else they possess could possibly entitle them to it.

"In this age when intellectual values are assuming more and more importance, ancestral and family pride has become a quaint, almost ludicrous phenomenon. Starting in the days of chivalry and with the profession of arms, a class arose whose sole task was to defend the other classes, and the subordinate relationship of protected to protector followed naturally. Let the scholar be proud of his learning, the artist of his art, the craftsman and the merchant of their trades, says the knight; but if you, having no experience of fighting, are confronted by a savage enemy whom you cannot overcome, then it is I who protect you with my sword, and what to me is a sport and a pleasure saves both your life and your possessions.

"But the use of brute force is fast diminishing, and the power of the mind is asserting itself in every realm. It is becoming clear that a strong arm, a breastplate and a powerfully-wielded sword cannot conquer what the mind is seeking; even war and military training are giving way before it. Each person is thrown back on to his own resources and forced to justify himself in the eyes of the world by his own intellectual achievement, whatever superficial brilliance may attend his position in the state. Ancestral pride, derived from chivalry, reflects a fundamentally opposite ideal, namely, my ancestors were heroes, therefore I, too, am a hero. The farther back one takes this, the better, for if one knows when one's grandfather developed his heroic qualities and had the rank of knight conferred upon him, one loses one's faith in it, as well as in all miracles which are too close to us. Everything depends on heroism and physical strength again. Strong, healthy parents generally produce children of similar stock as themselves, and adventurousness and courage are handed down in the same way. The prime need in the age of chivalry was therefore to preserve the purity of the knightly class; it was the duty of a woman of noble blood to bear a knight whom the townsfolk would beg for protection from other knights.

"Where the power of the mind is concerned, things are not like this. Wise fathers often produce stupid sons, and because our age ascribes a nobility of intellect to those who have a nobility of lineage, it is probably more worrying to be descended from Leibnitz than from Amadis of Gaul or some ancient knight of the Round Table. The age is moving irrevocably forwards, and the situation of our noble classes is rapidly deteriorating. This may well explain their tactless behaviour towards highly-cultured commoners; a mixture of appreciative respect and intolerable condescension, the product of a deep despair that the triviality of their past glory will be exposed to the knowing gaze of the wise, and their insufficiencies held up to ridicule. We may thank God that many noblemen and their ladies now realise the spirit of the age and are striving towards that higher mode of life which nurtures wisdom and art—the twin powers which shall destroy the medieval monster for ever."

The physician's remarks had led on to unfamiliar ground. It had never occurred to me to meditate on the nobleman and his relationship to the commoner. The physician probably had no idea that I had originally belonged to the second class—that which, in his view, was untouched by the haughtiness of the nobleman. Had I not been reverend confessor to the foremost families in B.? As I pondered further I realised how once again I had woven my own destiny, in that my nobility came from the name Cviecziczevo which I had given that old lady at court, and that in this way the Prince had come upon the idea of marrying me to Aurelia.

The Princess had returned, and I hurried to Aurelia. She received me with sweet coyness. I took her in my arms and really believed at that moment that she would become mine. She was softer, more yielding than ever. Tears shone in her eyes, and her voice was like the sorrowful plea of a fretful child who has done wrong but whose bad temper has now passed. I thought of my visit to the country residence and insisted on learning all that had happened, adjuring her to confide to me what had so frightened her. She said nothing and lowered her gaze, but as the thought of my hideous double took hold of me, I cried:

"Aurelia! In the name of all the saints, what was the terrible figure you saw behind us?"

She stared at me, her eyes wide open. Suddenly she sprang up as if to run away, and covering her face with her hands, she sobbed:

"No, no! It is not he!"

Gently I took her in my arms, and she sank down, exhausted.

"It is not who?" I asked violently, sensing the thoughts

that might come into her mind.

"Oh, my friend, my beloved," she said in low, sad tones, "would you not take me for a mad dreamer if I were to tell you of everything that disturbs the happiness and purity of my love? My life is beset by a horrible nightmare. Its terrible visions were thrust between us when I saw you for the first time, and it brushed me with its icy wings when you suddenly entered my room in the country residence. As you are kneeling beside me now, so a wicked monk once knelt, that he might use the holy moment of prayer for his foul deed. As he slunk round me like a wild beast stalking its prey, he became my brother's murderer. And you—your features—your voice—oh, do not make me say more!"

She leaned back; as she rested on a corner of the couch, her head supported against her hand, the youthful curves of her body lay voluptuously before me. I stood before her and my sensual gaze revelled in her charms, but a diabolical scorn fought against my lust, crying: 'O unhappy woman, sold to the Devil—have you really escaped from the monk who sought in prayer to tempt you? Now you are his betrothed!'

In that instant the love which had seared through me when I saw her again in the park after my escape from death, had vanished, and I became filled with the idea that her downfall might form the brilliant climax to my life.

She was called away to the Princess. It became clear to me that her life bore a secret relationship to my own, but I could find no way of learning what it was as long as, despite my pleading, she would not explain further those unconnected remarks she had made. Chance, however, was to reveal what Aurelia sought to withhold.

One day I was in the office of the superintendent of the household, one of whose duties was to despatch private letters of the Prince and the courtiers. He happened to be out of the room, when Aurelia's maid entered, carrying a thick envelope which she placed on top of the others already lying on the table. A quick glance told me that the address—that of the abbess, the Princess' sister—was in Aurelia's handwriting. The thought flashed through me that the letter might contain the answers to all my questions, and before the superintendent returned I took it away with me.

You, O monk, or you, O reader, who are caught in the snares of the world, if you seek a lesson or warning from my life, then read the pages which I now append. Read this pure, devout girl's confessions, which are bathed in the bitter tears of a despairing, repentant sinner. May the spirit of piety be kindled within you, to light your path and comfort you in the hour of temptation.

AURELIA TO THE ABBESS OF THE CISTERCIAN CONVENT
AT . . .

My dear, good Mother—

How can I find words to tell you that I am happy and that the menacing figure that came into my life like a terrible ghost, striking at all my hopes and joys, has at last been banished by the divine magic of love? Now I realise with deep sorrow that I should have opened my heart to you in holy confession when you recalled the memory of my unhappy brother—and of my father, who died of grief—and comforted me in my distress. But only now can I reveal the terrible secret hidden in my breast. It is as though some evil power had held before my eyes a vision of supreme happiness which proved to be a horrible nightmare; I was to be tossed to and fro by the raging sea before plunging to my doom. But miraculously Heaven came to my aid at the moment

15

when my misery was at its most profound. To tell you
the whole story I must go back to my childhood, for it
was then that the seed was planted which multiplied so
perniciously through the years.

Once, when I was only three or four years old, I was
playing with Hermogenes in the castle garden. We were
picking flowers, and Hermogenes, who was not normally
disposed to such things, consented to plait garlands so
that I could adorn myself with them.

'Let us now go and see mother,' I said, when I had
completely covered myself with flowers. But Hermogenes
sprang up hastily and cried:

'Let us rather stay here, for mother is in the Blue
Room with the Devil.'

I did not know what he meant, but I felt afraid and
began to cry.

'Stupid girl, what are you crying for?' exclaimed
Hermogenes. 'Mother talks to the Devil every day. He
does her no harm.'

I was afraid of Hermogenes because he glowered so
threatingly and spoke so roughly: at other times he
would say nothing for hours on end. Mother was very
ill at that time, and often seized with terrible fits which
brought her near to death.

Then Hermogenes and I were taken away. I never
ceased to lament, but he only muttered sullenly:

'It is the Devil who has done this to her!'

And so in my naïveté I conceived the notion that my
mother had an alliance with some demon—for such was
my idea of the Devil.

One day when I had been left alone, an uneasy feeling
came over me as I realised that I was in the same Blue
Room where Hermogenes had said that mother talked
to the Devil. I was unable to flee for fright. Then the
door opened and my mother entered, as pale as death.

She crept along the bare wall and cried in dull tones:
'Francesco! Francesco!'

There was a whirring sound behind the wall; it parted
in two, and a life-size portrait of a handsome man
magnificently dressed in a purple cloak became visible.
The face and form of this man made an indescribable
impression on me, and I shouted for joy. Looking round,
my mother noticed me and exclaimed:

'What do you want here, Aurelia? Who brought you
here?'

She was usually so kind and gentle but now she was
angrier than I had ever seen her before. I thought it
was all my fault and stammered through my tears:

'Oh, mother, they left me here by myself; I did not
want to stay here.'

But when I saw that the picture had vanished, I cried:

'Oh, the beautiful picture! Where is the beautiful
picture?'

My mother lifted me up and, kissing me, said:

'You are my dear, good child, but nobody is allowed
to see the picture, and now it has gone for ever.'

I did not tell anyone what had happened, but once I
could not help saying to Hermogenes:

'Hermogenes, mother does not speak to the Devil but
to a handsome man, though he is only a picture. He
springs out of the wall when mother calls him.'

Hermogenes stared in front of him and muttered:

'It does not matter what the Devil looks like, says the
reverend father, for he still cannot harm mother.'

I shuddered and implored him not to talk any more
about the Devil.

We went to the city and I forgot about the picture;
even our return to the country after my mother's death
did not revive its memory. The wing of the castle which
contained the Blue Room remained uninhabited; they

were my mother's rooms, which my father could not enter without arousing the most poignant memories, but when repairs were being carried out to the building, the rooms finally had to be opened up. I went into the Blue Room while the workmen were engaged in pulling up the floorboards. As one of them lifted a panel in the middle of the room, there was a whirring sound behind the wall; it opened to reveal the portrait of the unknown man. Under the floor they found a spring; when it was pressed, it set a machine in motion which slid open one of the wall-panels. Then that vivid recollection of my childhood days came back to me. I wept bitterly but could not avert my gaze from the wonderful figure whose shining eyes were fixed upon me. My father had probably been told of what was happening, for he came into the room while I was still standing in front of the picture. As soon as he caught sight of it, he stopped dead and murmured:

'Francesco! Francesco!'

Then he turned swiftly to the workmen and ordered them in a loud voice to tear the picture from the wall, roll it up and hand it over to Reinhold.

I felt as though I should never again see that handsome man who, in his resplendent robe, appeared to me like a great prince from the world of the spirits, yet a strange reluctance restrained me from asking my father not to destroy the painting. After a few days, however, I completely forgot that this scene had made such an impression on me.

I was now fourteen years old and still a wild, reckless creature, forming a sharp contrast to the solemn, serious Hermogenes; my father often said that Hermogenes seemed more like a quiet girl and I like an unbridled youth. This was soon to change. Hermogenes began to develop a passion for military affairs; he lived only for fighting, and as war was soon expected to break out, he begged his father to let him go on active service. At the same time I fell into a strange frame of mind which affected my whole life; an unaccountable sickness seemed to issue from my soul and spread relentlessly over my whole existence; tears sprang to my eyes at the slightest provocation, and a strange yearning grew in me to the point of physical pain, causing my limbs to shake convulsively. My father noticed my condition, attributed it to over-excited nerves and sought the assistance of the doctor, who prescribed various remedies, none of which had any effect. I do not know how it happened, but suddenly the picture of that unknown man seemed to be standing in front of me, its pitying gaze turned upon me. 'Alas! Must I die? What is it that torments me?' I cried. 'You love me,' answered the vision in my dream; 'that is your torment. But can you break the vows which bind the man of God?' To my amazement I now perceived that he was wearing the habit of a Capuchin friar. I forced my scattered senses together. I was convinced that the monk had only been a mock creature of my imagination, yet I felt that somehow the mystery of love had been revealed to me. Yes, I loved this man with all the newly-awakened strength, all the fervent passion of which a young heart is capable.

It appeared to have been in these dreamlike moments when I thought I saw the unknown man, that my malady had reached its height, for my neurotic condition rapidly improved, and it was only my vision of that picture, my fantastic love for a creature who existed merely in my imagination, that made me appear like a dreamer. I was numb to the outside world. In company I sat silent and motionless, absorbed in my ideal, and through not paying attention to the conversation, I often gave wrong answers, so that people probably took me for a simpleton.

In my brother's room I once saw a new book lying on

the table, and opened it. It was a novel called *The Monk,**
translated from the English. A shudder went through me
at the thought that my unknown lover was a monk;
never had I suspected that it could be sinful to love a
priest. I felt that the book might help me in my per-
plexity, and taking it up, I began to read. The incredible
story carried me away, but when the first murder had
been committed, and when the wicked monk's crimes
became more and more atrocious and he finally made an
alliance with the powers of darkness, I was seized with
terror and recalled the words of Hermogenes: 'Mother
is talking to the Devil.' Now I believed that my unknown
lover, like the monk in the novel, had sold himself to
the Devil and intended to lead me into wickedness, yet
I could not withstand the love that burned within me.
I knew now that there was such a thing as guilty love,
and my abhorrence of it struggled against the emotion
that filled my breast. This struggle brought about a state
of nervous tension in me, and whenever a man stood near
me, I was gripped by a feeling that he was the monk who
sought my downfall.

Reinhold returned from his journey and told many
stories about a Capuchin called Medardus, who was
famous far and wide as a preacher, and whom he had
himself heard in B. I thought of the monk in the novel,
and suddenly felt a mysterious foreboding that the vision
which I loved and feared might be that Medardus. I
could not bear the thought, and I became more and more
distracted as I fought to control myself. I was drifting
in a sea of dreams and visions, but in vain I tried to
banish the image of the monk from my mind; unhappy
child that I was, I could not resist my sinful love for the
man of God.

*The story by Matthew Gregorory ('Monk') Lewis, published in 1796,
which had made a deep impression on Hoffmann (Transl).

Once a priest arrived who used to visit my father from time to time. He embarked on a long account of the manifold temptations of the Devil and described the wretched state of the young soul which only offered weak resistance to the invasion of evil. My father interposed certain remarks as if he were talking about me.

'Only boundless trust,' concluded the priest, 'only unwavering confidence, not so much in one's friends as in religion and her servants, can bring redemption.'

This unforgettable conversation made me decide to seek the comfort of the Church and unburden my heart in holy confession. As we were living in the town, I resolved to go early next morning to the monastery chapel, which was close at hand. It was a terrible night of torture that I had to endure: horrible, wanton visions I had never seen or imagined before fluttered around me, and then the monk suddenly appeared in their midst, offering me the arm of salvation and saying:

'Tell me that you love me, and I will free you from all your suffering.'

And I could not but cry involuntarily:

'Yes, Medardus, I love you!'

The demons vanished. At last I rose, dressed myself and went into the chapel.

Dawn's bright rays were shining through the stained-glass windows, and a lay-brother was sweeping the aisles. Close to the side door by which I had entered stood an altar dedicated to Saint Rosalia; I said a brief prayer before it and moved towards the confessional, where I saw a monk sitting. It was Medardus! Seized with mad fear and love, I felt that only unflinching courage could save me. I confessed to him my sinful love for a priest—I even went further!

'It is you, Medardus, for whom I cherish this ineffable love!' These were the last words I was able to utter, but the solace of religion, like balsam from Heaven, poured from the lips of the monk who no longer seemed to be Medardus. Soon afterwards an aged pilgrim took my arm and led me slowly down the aisle to the main door. He spoke blessed words of comfort to me, but I must have dropped off to sleep, like a child rocked by sweet, gentle sounds. When I awoke, I was lying fully-dressed on the couch in my room. A voice exclaimed:

'Praised be God and the saints! The crisis is over.'

It was the doctor speaking to my father. I was told that they had found me that morning in a coma and feared that I had had a stroke.

You can see, my dear, pious Mother, that my confession before Medardus was only a lurid dream provoked by my neurotic condition, and Saint Rosalia, to whom I often prayed and whose image I invoked in my dreams, allowed everything to appear to me in this way so that I might be rescued from the snare which the Devil had laid for me. My insane love for that phantom in monastic habit had vanished. I recovered completely and entered into life again with a new serenity and cheerfulness.

But this wicked monk was destined to bring me once more near to death, for I immediately recognised that that Medardus who had appeared at our palace was the same monk before whom I had confessed in my dream. 'He is the Devil with whom mother used to talk. Beware! He will lie in wait for you!' Thus spoke the voice of the unhappy Hermogenes. But I did not heed his warning. From the first moment the monk turned his lustful, gleaming eyes upon me and invoked Saint Rosalia with feigned rapture, I found him horrible and repulsive. All the terrible events that happened after that, my dear Mother, you already know.

But I must also confess to you that the presence of the

monk was the more dangerous in that it stirred within
me the same emotion as had the first thought of sin when
I had fought against the temptations of evil. There were
moments when, in my blindness, I believed the monk's
hypocritical preaching, when it even seemed as though
a divine spark had kindled in me a pure, celestial love.
But then, even in prayer, the fire of hell would begin to
smoulder within him. I prayed to the Gods, and they
sent my brother to watch over me like a guardian angel.

Imagine, then, my horror when here, shortly after my
first appearance at court, a man approached me whom
I thought I recognised at the first glance as Medardus,
although he was dressed as a layman. I fainted at his
approach, and when I recovered to find myself in the
arms of the Princess, I cried:

'It is he, it is he—my brother's murderer!'

'Yes, it is he,' said the Princess, 'the hooded monk
Medardus who escaped from the monastery. His
striking resemblance to his father, Francesco . . .'

O come to my aid, ye Heavens! As I write this name,
cold shudders run down my spine. That picture of my
mother's was Francesco, and the vision of the monk that
tormented me had exactly the same features. And I
recognised him as the figure in the wonderful dream of
my confession. Medardus is Francesco's son, Franz,
whom you, Reverend Mother, brought up so devoutly,
and who has fallen into sin and shame. What connection
was there between my mother and Francesco, that she
preserved his portrait in such secrecy and seemed to
surrender herself to the memory of former bliss whenever
she looked at it? How did Hermogenes come to see in
this picture the Devil, and how did it become the
foundation of my strange aberrations? I am filled with
fear and misgiving. O almighty Saviour, have I now
eluded the clutches of the demon that bewitched me?

But I can write no more. I feel as if I were set in the midst of darkness, with no star of hope to shed its friendly light upon my path.

(A few days later)

No menacing clouds of doubt shall cast their shadow over the days of bright sunshine that have now been vouchsafed to me! The venerable Father Cyrillus has, I know, already informed you of the sad course taken by the proceedings against Leonard which the authorities had instigated as a result of my rashness. That the real Medardus was caught; that his madness, which may have been sham, soon completely disappeared; that he confessed to his crimes; that he is awaiting his punishment—but enough, for the shameful fate of the murderer who was so dear to you as a child would wound your heart too deeply.

This remarkable affair was the only subject of conversation at court. Leonard was taken to be a wily and hardened criminal, because he had denied everything, but their words pierced me to the quick, for a mysterious voice kept saying to me: 'He is innocent, and his innocence shines forth as clear as the day.' I felt a profound sympathy for him and had to admit to myself that the very thought of him aroused emotions which were only too plain—yes, I cherished an inexpressible love for him while he yet appeared to the world as a foul assassin. But he is innocent. He loves me, and soon he will be mine, mine alone. The childhood vision which an evil power maliciously tried to destroy is coming to life in all its glory.

O give us your blessing, Reverend Mother! Would that your happy child could weep in your arms in heavenly joy and delight! Leonard closely resembles that Francesco, although he seems taller; at the same time he is sharply distinguished from Francesco and from the monk Medardus by features peculiar to his race (you know that he is a Pole). It was utterly ridiculous for me to mistake even for a moment the handsome, gifted Leonard for a renegade monk. But the impression left by those gruesome scenes in our palace is still so vivid that often, when Leonard comes to me unexpectedly and looks at me with his flashing eyes, which are so much like those of Medardus, a feeling of dread comes over me, and I am in danger of offending my lover by my childish behaviour. I feel as if only through the nuptial blessing will these shadowy figures be banished which still cast their evil influence over my life. Pray earnestly for me and my beloved, dear Reverend Mother. It is the Prince's wish that the wedding shall take place soon; I will write to tell you the actual day, so that you may remember your child in her most solemn, most blissful hour . . .

Again and again I read Aurelia's letter. The spirit of Heaven seemed to shine forth from it, lighting up the sinful darkness in my soul. I was filled with awe at the sight of her and no longer dared to caress her passionately as before. She could not but notice the change in me, and I confessed that I had stolen her letter, excusing myself by appealing to an unaccountable urge which I had not been able to resist: I made out that some invisible power must have desired me to learn of that vision in the confessional in order to show that it had ordained our union.

"O pious child of Heaven," I said, "I, too, once had a beautiful dream in which you confessed your love to me, but I was an unhappy monk, crushed by a cruel fate and tormented by the pains of hell. I loved you beyond measure, but my love was execrable sin, a double sin, for I was a monk and you were Saint Rosalia."

Aurelia gave a frightened start.

"Oh, Leonard, say no more!" she cried. "There is an unfathomable mystery running through our lives. Let us not touch the veil that hides it, for who knows what dreadful things it conceals? Let us remain valiant and cling to each other in constant love; thus shall we overcome the powers of darkness which threaten us. It was inevitable that you should read my letter. I should have disclosed everything to you, for there must be no secret between us. Yet I feel that you are struggling against ominous forces which used to torment you, and which some groundless fear is causing you to suppress. Be honest, Leonard! Oh, how a frank confession would ease your heart and make our love shine yet more brightly!"

Aurelia's words made me painfully aware that the spirit of dishonesty still dwelt within me and that only a few moments ago I had wickedly deceived her. This feeling grew stronger and stronger, compelling me to confess everything and yet still keep her love.

"O my divine Aurelia, you rescued me—"

At that moment the Princess entered, and the sight of her filled me with diabolical scorn. She would now have to submit to me, and I confronted her boldly as Aurelia's betrothed. For only when I was alone with Aurelia was I free from evil thoughts and inspired with joy and felicity, and only now did I realise how passionately I longed to be wedded to her.

One night my mother appeared to me in a dream. Tears streamed from her eyes, falling like glistening, silver stars and forming a halo round my head, only to be scattered suddenly by a horrible black hand.

"I bore you free from all blemish," she said gently. "Is your strength now broken, that you can no longer resist the temptations of Satan? Now for the first time I can see into your soul, for my earthly burden has been lifted from me. Rise, Franciscus! I will deck you with flowers and ribbons, for it is Saint Bernard's Day. Be kind and good, as you were in your childhood."

I felt moved to sing the praises of Saint Bernard, as I had done in my youth, but a roaring noise turned my hymn into a savage howl, drawing black veils between me and the image of my mother.

Several days after this vision I met the judge in the street.

He approached me in a friendly manner and said:

"Have you heard that the case of Medardus the Capuchin has been reopened? His sentence—probably of death—had already been drawn up when he began to show fresh signs of madness. The court had received the news of his mother's death, and when I told him of it, he gave a wild laugh and cried in a voice that would have struck terror into the most resolute heart:

'Ha, ha, ha! The Duchess (he named the wife of our Prince's murdered brother) died long ago!'

"He has now had a fresh medical examination, and it is suspected that his madness is sham."

I asked the day and hour of my mother's death. She had died at the same moment as she had appeared to me in my dream. As if probing my innermost thoughts she had become the mediator between me and the pure, divine Aurelia, for only now did I perceive that Aurelia was to me as a patron saint, and that her love would always be with me to protect me. My dark secret had now become a mysterious power transmitted by the inscrutable forces of destiny.

The day arrived which the Prince had fixed for the wedding. As I entered Aurelia's room, she came towards me, bathed in sweet, angelic beauty; she was dressed in white and adorned with fragrant roses. Her robe and her coiffure seemed strangely reminiscent of an earlier age—then I recalled with a shudder the picture above the altar at which we were to be married: it portrayed the martyr-

dom of Saint Rosalia, and Aurelia was dressed in exactly
the same way as she. Looking at me with eyes which shone
with a radiance matched only by the stars in the firmament,
Aurelia gave me her hand. I drew her to my breast, and a
kiss of purest rapture sent through my veins the feeling
that only through her could my soul be redeemed.

One of the Prince's servants announced that the company
was ready to receive us. Aurelia quickly drew on her gloves,
and I took her arm. Then the chambermaid suddenly
noticed that Aurelia's hair had become disarranged, and
hastened away to fetch some hair-pins. The delay seemed
to disturb her. As we waited by the door, there was a
dull rumbling in the street outside, raucous voices shouted
and the noise was heard of a heavy cart rattling slowly by.
I hurried to the window. In front of the palace stood an
open cart driven by the hangman's servant. Sitting backwards in it was the monk, in front of whom stood a Capuchin
praying aloud with him. The monk was disfigured by a
deathly pallor and an unkempt beard, but the features of
my gruesome double were only too plain. Crowds were
thronging round the cart, and as it moved off he turned his
terrible eyes upon me, laughing and howling:

"Bridegroom! Bridegroom! Come on to the roof! Up
there we will fight with each other, and the one who pushes
the other over will become king, and be able to drink
blood!"

"Horrible wretch!" I screamed. "What do you want
with me?"

Aurelia flung her arms round me and tore me away from
the window, crying:

"O Holy Virgin! They are leading Medardus, my
brother's murderer, to his death! Leonard! Oh, Leonard!"

The demons of hell raged within me, and I seized her in
fury.

"Ha, ha, ha! Mad, foolish woman! I—I am Medardus!

It is I who am your lover, your betrothed—I who am your brother's murderer! You, who are the bride of a monk, will you snivel and whine so that destruction will fall on your bridegroom's head? Ho, ho, ho! I am king and shall drink your blood!"

I let her fall to the floor, drew out my knife and stabbed at her. A fountain of blood gushed over my hand. I rushed down the staircase and fought my way through the crowd to the cart. Seizing the monk, I tore him from his seat. I felt myself gripped from behind, and stabbed about me with my knife. Wrenching myself free, I jumped away but the mob came after me. I felt a wound in my side, but with my knife in my right hand, and dealing powerful blows with my left, I fought my way to the nearby wall of the park and vaulted over it with a tremendous leap.

"Murderer! Murderer! Stop!" shouted the voices behind me. I heard them preparing to burst open the gate to the park. I rushed on without stopping. I came to the broad moat which separated the park from the forest, cleared it with a mighty jump, and ran on and on through the forest until I sank down exhausted under a tree.

When I recovered my senses, it was already dark. My only thought was to flee like a hunted beast. I got up but hardly had I moved away when a man sprang out of the bushes and jumped on to my back, clinging to my neck. In vain I tried to shake him off. I threw myself on the ground, jammed my back against the trees, but all to no avail. He cackled and laughed mockingly. Then the moon broke brightly through the black pine-trees, and the pallid, hideous face of the monk, the supposed Medardus, my double, stared at me with its glassy eyes as it had done in the cart.

"Hee, hee, hee! Hee, hee, hee! Little Brother! I . . . am . . . al-ways . . . with . . . you, will . . . not . . . not . . . leave . . . you. Can-not . . . run . . . like . . . like . . . you.

Must . . . must . . . carry . . . me. Have . . . come . . . from
. . . the . . . the . . . gal-lows. Want-ed . . . to . . . to . . .
break . . . me . . . on . . . on . . . the . . . wheel. Hee, hee!''

The horrible spectre laughed and howled. With the
strength of wild terror I leapt up like a tiger in the strangle-
hold of a python, crashing against trees and rocks so as,
if not to kill him, at least to wound him so severely that he
would be forced to let me go. But he laughed all the more
hysterically, and I was the one who received the wounds. I
tried to free his hands which were locked together under my
chin, but he threatened to choke me.

At last, after a fit of frenzy, he suddenly jumped off.
I had only run a few yards when he jumped on to me again,
cackling and laughing, and stuttering those terrible words.
Again that struggle in wild rage—again free—again in the
grip of the hideous monster.

I cannot say how long I fled through the dark forest,
pursued by my double. It seemed an eternity before I ate
or drank anything. Of one vivid moment, however, I still
have a clear impression: I had just succeeded in throwing
him off, when a bright light shone through the forest and
I heard a monastery bell tolling matins.

"I have murdered Aurelia!" At this thought the icy
arms of death closed around me, and I sank unconscious
to the ground.

II — ATONEMENT

A gentle warmth spread through my body and I felt a
strange tingling in my veins. Feeling turned to thought,
but my character seemed split into a thousand parts; each
part was independent and had its own consciousness, and
in vain did the head command the limbs, which, like faith-
less vassals, would not obey its authority. The thoughts in
these separate parts now started to revolve like points of
light, faster and faster, forming a fiery circle which became
smaller as the speed increased, until it finally appeared like
a stationary ball of fire, its burning rays shining from the
flickering flames. 'Those are my limbs dancing; I am
waking up.' Such was my first clear thought, but a sudden
pain shot through me at that moment and the chiming of
bells sounded in my ears.

"Flee! Flee!" I cried aloud. I could now open my eyes.
The bells continued to ring. At first I thought I was still
in the forest, and was amazed when I looked at myself
and the objects around me. Dressed in the habit of a
Capuchin, I was lying stretched out on a comfortable
mattress in a lofty room; the only other items of furniture
were a few cane-chairs, a small table and a simple bed.
I realised that my unconsciousness must have lasted some
time and that in some way or other I had been brought to
a monastery which offered hospitality to the sick; perhaps
my clothes were torn and I had been given this habit for

the time being. I appeared at least to be out of all danger.

These thoughts reassured me completely and I decided to await what would happen, since I could assume that someone would soon visit me. I felt utterly exhausted but quite free from pain. A few moments after I had regained full consciousness I heard footsteps in the long passage. The door opened and two men entered, one a layman, the other in the habit of one of the Orders of Hospitallers. They approached me without speaking. The layman looked at me intently and appeared greatly surprised.

"I have now recovered, Sir," I began in a tired voice. "Heaven be praised for having restored me to life. But where am I? How did I get here?"

Without replying, he turned to the priest and said in Italian:

"This is indeed amazing. He looks completely different; his voice, though toneless, is quite clear. He must have had a stroke."

"There seems to be no longer any doubt about his recovery," rejoined the priest.

"That depends on how he reacts in the next few days," said the other. "Do you know enough German to be able to speak to him?"

"Alas, no," answered the priest.

"I can speak Italian," I interposed. "Tell me where I am and how I got here."

The layman, who I now saw was a doctor, seemed agreeably surprised at this.

"Ah, that's good," he exclaimed. "You are in a place, reverend Sir, where all possible attention will be given to your well-being. Three months ago you were brought here in a highly critical condition, but by our care and solicitude you appear to have been set on the road to recovery. If we have the good fortune to heal you completely, you will eventually be able to proceed on your way, for I hear that you are making for Rome."

"Did I then come to you in the clothes which I am now wearing?" I inquired.

"Certainly," replied the doctor. "But do not worry yourself or ask questions; you shall learn everything in due course. Here you will be cared for with the utmost kindness."

He felt my pulse. In the meantime the priest had fetched a cup, which he offered me.

"Drink this," said the doctor, "and tell me what you think it is."

"It is a highly nourishing broth," I said, after I had tasted it.

The doctor smiled in satisfaction and said to the priest: "Excellent! Excellent!"

They left my room. I now believed that my assumption was correct: I was in a hospital. After three days of nutritious foods and strong tonics I was able to get up. The priest opened the window, and warm, glorious air such as I had never before breathed flowed into the room. There was a garden surrounding the building; strange, wonderful trees were in blossom and luxuriant vines clung to the walls. Above all I could not tear my eyes from the fragrant, deep-blue sky, which seemed like something from a distant world of magic.

"But where am I?" I cried in delight. "Have the saints deemed me worthy to dwell in such a celestial country?"

The priest smiled comfortingly and said:

"You are in Italy, Brother, in Italy!"

My astonishment grew and grew, and I insisted that he should tell me in what circumstances I had come to the hospital. He referred me to the doctor, who eventually told me that three months earlier a queer man had brought me there and asked for me to be given asylum; I was, as I had guessed, in a hospital administered by the Hospitallers.

As I grew stronger, the doctor and the priest both entered into lengthy conversations with me and gave me ample opportunity to talk; my extensive knowledge of the most varied subjects enabled me to do so with great ease, and the doctor urged me to write certain things down, reading them afterwards in my presence and appearing highly satisfied. Yet it often struck me as peculiar that, instead of actually praising what I had written, he used to say:

"Well, well—that's fine—I was not mistaken—remarkable, remarkable!"

At certain hours I was now allowed to go down into the garden, where I sometimes saw pallid, emaciated, gruesomely distorted figures being led around by the brethren. Once when I was on the point of going back to the house, I came across a tall, thin man in a strange cloak the colour of ochre. He was being led by two priests, one on either side, and after every step he gave a grotesque little jump, whistling as he did so. I stopped in bewilderment, but the priest who was with me drew me swiftly away, and said:

"Come, Brother Medardus. Such things are not good for you."

"How do you know my name?" I cried.

The vehemence of the exclamation seemed to unsettle him.

"Why should we not know your name?" he replied. "The man who brought you here stated it specifically, and you are entered in the register as Medardus, Brother from the Capuchin monastery at B."

The blood drained from my cheeks. Yet whoever this unknown man was who had brought me there, even supposing he were initiated into my terrible secret, he could not have had evil designs upon me.

One day I was lying by the open window, drinking deeply of the glorious air. Suddenly I caught sight of a small, skinny figure with a pointed hat and a shabby, faded cloak, hopping and skipping, rather than walking, up the main drive leading to the hospital. When he saw me, he waved his hat in the air and blew me a kiss. There was something familiar about the man but I could not distinguish his features clearly, and he disappeared behind the trees before I could discern who he was.

After a while there was a knock at my door. I opened it and found the same figure as I had seen in the garden.

"Schönfeld!" I cried in amazement. "How in Heaven's name did you get here?" For it was that strange little barber who had rescued me in the city.

"Oh, dear! Oh, dear!" he sighed, pulling a tearful face in his droll fashion. "How else should I have got here, reverend Sir, but by being driven by the evil fate that pursues every genius? I had to flee because of a murder—"

"Because of a murder?" I interrupted violently.

"Because of a murder," he repeated; "in a fit of rage I slew the left side-whiskers of the youngest city councillor and inflicted severe wounds on the right-hand ones as well."

"Kindly cease your jesting," I interrupted again, "and be sober for once. Either talk sensibly or leave me alone."

"Ah, my dear Brother Medardus," he said with sudden earnestness, "now that you have recovered, you want to send me away, but you had to endure my presence when you were sick and when I was your room-mate and slept in that bed."

"What's that?" I cried, taken aback, "How did you arrive at the name of Medardus?"

"Would you be kind enough to look in the right-hand corner of your habit?" he said with a smile.

I did so and saw with fright that the name Medardus had been sewn into it; moreover as I examined the habit more closely, I found unmistabable indications that it was the one I had hidden in a hollow tree on my flight from Baron F.'s palace. Schönfeld observed my agitation, and

smiled queerly. Putting his index-finger to his nose and
standing on tiptoe, he looked me in the eye. I remained
silent. Then he said softly and deliberately:

"Your Grace is clearly surprised at the fine robe he has
been given, yet it appears to suit you admirably, far better,
in fact, than that nut-brown costume with cheap cloth
buttons which my sober Damon put on you. It was I,
I, the misunderstood, the spurned Pietro Belcampo who
covered your nakedness with this dress. Brother Medardus,
you were not in a particularly elegant state when I found
you. Your coat—or spencer—or tail-coat—consisted simply
of your own skin, and as to a respectable coiffure, it just
did not exist, since by dabbling in my Art you had created
your own Caracalla with the ten-toothed comb that grows
on your hands."

"Stop this folly, Schönfeld!" I cried indignantly.

"Here in Italy my name is Pietro Belcampo," he interrupted, highly incensed; "yes, Pietro Belcampo. And
whether you know it or not, Medardus, I myself am the
Folly that is always pursuing you in order to assist your
power of reason. And whether you realise it or not, you
will only find salvation in Folly, for your much-vaunted
reason is an utterly worthless thing and cannot sustain itself;
it stumbles backwards and forwards like a frail child and
has to enter into a partnership with Folly, which then helps
it along because it knows how to find the right way home—
to the madhouse. And that is where we have both arrived,
my dear Brother Medardus, which is as it should be."

I shivered and thought of the figures I had seen, of the
skipping man in the cloak of yellow ochre, and could not
doubt that Schönfeld, crazy as he was, was telling the
truth.

"Folly, my dear Brother Medardus," he went on, raising
his voice and gesticulating wildly, "appears on earth as
the true Queen of the Spirits. Reason is nothing but an

inefficient *chargé d'affaires* who never troubles about what
goes on outside his sphere and makes the troops drill on
the barrack-square out of boredom; as a result, they are
incapable of firing a single decent shot when the enemy
attacks. But Folly, the true Queen, enters in triumph with
trumpets and drums, followed by jubilant crowds. The
serfs rise from the corners to which Reason had banished
them, and will no longer stand up and sit down at the
chamberlain's behest. Looking down his list, this worthy
says: 'Look, Folly has knocked my best pupils off their
balance; in fact, they have all become unbalanced. That's
a play on words, Brother Medardus; and a play on words
is a hot curling-iron in the hand of Folly, which uses it
to shape its thoughts.

"I beseech you once more," I cried, "to stop this senseless
chatter, if you can, and tell me how you came here and
what you know about me and about the habit I am
wearing."

As I said this, I took hold of him and pushed him into a
chair. He seemed to ponder my words, casting his eyes
down and breathing deeply. Then he said in a faint,
toneless voice:

"Twice I have saved your life. It was I who assisted
your escape from the city, and it was I again who brought
you here."

"But where did you find me?" I cried, letting him go.
He jumped up at once and shouted, his eyes gleaming:

"Brother Medardus, had I not carried you away on my
shoulders, small and puny as I am, you would now be lying
on the wheel, your limbs torn and mangled."

Trembling, I sank weakly into a chair. The door opened
and the priest who tended me entered hastily.

"How did you get in here? Who allowed you to enter
this room?" he shouted at Belcampo. Tears came into the
little man's eyes and he said, imploringly:

"O reverend Sir, I could no longer resist the urge to speak to the friend whom I had plucked from the jaws of death!"

I pulled myself together.

"Tell me, my dear Brother," I said to the priest, "did this man really bring me here?"

He hesitated.

"Now I understand where I am," I continued, "and I can believe that I was in the most terrible state imaginable. But you can see that I have completely recovered, and may now be allowed to learn all that has hitherto been deliberately withheld from me."

"It is as you have heard," answered the priest. "Some three or four months ago this man brought you to our asylum. He had found you, he said, lying apparently dead about four miles from here in the forest which separates our territory from . . . ; he recognised you as the Capuchin Medardus from the monastery at B., whom he had known before, and who, on his journey to Rome, had once passed through the place where he used to live. You were in a state of complete apathy: you walked when you were led; you stood still when you were left alone; you sat or lay down when you were shown how. Food and drink had to be fed to you. You uttered only dull, unintelligible noises, and your eyes stared unseeingly. But Belcampo did not leave your side. After four weeks you were seized by a terrible frenzy, and it became necessary to take you to one of the cells kept apart for such cases. You were like a wild beast, but I do not want to describe your condition any further for fear lest the memory be too painful to you. Four weeks later your apathy set in again and then turned to a coma, from which you have now awakened."

During the priest's story Schönfeld had sat down and cupped his chin in his hand, as if sunk in deep meditation. Then he said:

"I know only too well that at times I am a crazy fool, but the atmosphere here in the madhouse, harmful to sane people, has had a beneficial effect on me. I am beginning to take stock of myself, and that is not a bad sign. If I only exist by virtue of my own consciousness, then it is simply a matter of letting this consciousness remove the harlequin's dress from what is conscious, and I shall be able to present myself as a respectable gentleman. But is not a barber of genius inevitably a clown right from the beginning? Clowning is a protection against madness, and I can assure you, reverend Sir, that even by north-north-west I can clearly distinguish a church spire from a lamp-post."

"If this really is the case," I said, "then you can prove it by telling me calmly how you found me and brought me here."

"I will," returned Schönfeld, "in spite of the long face that the priest here is pulling.

"By the morning after the night when you escaped, the mysterious painter had also vanished, together with his collection of paintings. Great as was the excitement that this aroused, it was soon overshadowed by fresh incidents. Only when the news arrived of the murder in Baron F.'s palace, and warrants were issued for the arrest of the monk Medardus from the Capuchin monastery in B., did people remember that the painter had related the whole story in the club and had recognised you as Brother Medardus. The landlord of the inn where you had stayed confirmed that it was I who had assisted your escape. Suspicion fastened on me, and I was almost thrown into prison. I had no difficulty in deciding to flee from the miserable life that had long been oppressive to me, and I determined to go to Italy. On my way there I saw you in the town where the residence of Prince . . . lies. There was talk of your marriage to Aurelia, and of the execution of the monk Medardus. I too saw this monk. — Hm. — Still, be that as it may, I considered *you* to be the real Medardus. I tried to confront you, but you did not see me, and I left the town and went my way.

"Once, on a long journey, as I was preparing at first light to set out through the murky forest, there was a rustling in the thicket and a man leapt past me. His hair and beard were dishevelled and there was a wild, haggard look in his eyes, but he was wearing elegant clothes. The next moment he had vanished from sight. I had only gone a few steps further when I saw to my horror a naked figure prostrate before me on the ground. My first thought was that a murder had been committed, and that the man I had seen was the murderer. Bending down, I recognised the figure as you. You were still breathing, and close beside you lay the habit which you are now wearing. With great difficulty I put it on you and dragged you away.

"At last you awoke from your unconsciousness but you remained in the condition which the reverend gentleman here has already described. It cost me no little effort to carry you, and not until evening did I reach an inn in the middle of the forest. I left you in your torpid state lying on the grass and went in to fetch food and drink. Inside there were some dragoons who, according to the landlord's wife, had traced as far as the border a monk who had escaped in some unaccountable way just at the moment when he was to have been executed for serious crimes committed in . . . It was a mystery to me how you got out of the town and into the forest, but the conviction that you were in fact the Medardus who was being searched for, made me take the utmost care to extricate you from the peril in which you appeared to be.

"By various subterfuges I got you over the border and finally brought you to this asylum, into which we were both taken, since I declared that I would not be parted from you.

Here you were safe, for under no circumstances would a sick man be handed over to a foreign country for trial. There was nothing very impressive about your five senses while I was living here with you and caring for you, nor could I find much praise for your physical condition; your head drooped limply on your breast, and when anyone tried to make you stand erect, you wobbled about like a badly-made skittle. Your speech, too, was most pitiful; you became confoundedly monosyllabic and said, in your more enlightened moments: 'Hoo, hoo!' and 'Me-me-', which did not give a particularly clear picture of your thoughts and desires—in fact, I began to think that these had both deserted you and were wandering about on their own. At last you became extremely high-spirited, jumping into the air, shouting with delight, and ripping off your habit so as to be free from all restrictions. As to your appetite—"

"Stop, Schönfeld!" I interrupted the horrible little clown. "I have already been told of the dreadful condition in which I was found. Praised be the grace and eternal forbearance of the Lord, praised be the intercession of the saints and the blest, that I am now saved!"

"Now what is the good of that, reverend Sir?" he continued. "I mean, of that peculiar mental function known as awareness? It is nothing but the miserable activity of some pettifogging toll-keeper, or customs-officer, or assistant chief controller, who sets up a poky little office in his mind and says, whenever any goods are to be sent out: 'Oh, no! Export prohibited. They must remain here.' The finest jewels are buried in the ground like worthless seeds, and the most that comes up is beetroot, from which, with practice, a quarter of an ounce of foul-tasting sugar can be squeezed by applying a pressure of a thousand tons. Well, well, well. And yet this pitiful exportation is supposed to lay the foundation for trade with the heavenly city, where all is magnificence and splendour.

In Heaven's name, Sir! I would throw all my precious powder *à la Maréchal, à la Pompadour* and *à la reine de Golconde* into the deepest part of the river if only, even as a middleman, I could come by a speck of dust from yonder with which to powder the wigs of learned professors and their colleagues—after having powdered my own. But what am I saying?—If, instead of giving you that flea-coloured coat, my Damon could have equipped you, O most venerable of monks, with a satin robe like that in which the proud and prosperous citizens of the Holy City pay their visits to the privy, then, indeed, everything would have turned out differently. As it was, the world took you for a miserable *adscriptus glebae,* and the Devil for your *cousin germain.*"

Schönfeld had stood up and was walking, or rather skipping, from one corner of the room to the other, gesticulating wildly and pulling bizarre faces. Taking him by both hands, I said:

"Do you really want to make your home here and take my place? Are you incapable of dropping your clowning for more than a moment?"

He grinned and said:

"Is everything I say when the spirit moves me really so stupid?"

"That is just the unfortunate part about it," I replied. "There is often a profound meaning underlying your drolleries, but you deck out everything with such lurid images that a genuine thought portrayed in natural colours appears ridiculous, like a robe draped with motley rags. You are like a drunkard who cannot walk straight but staggers from side to side; your sense of direction is crooked."

"What is direction, reverend Capuchin?" he said softly, still with that bitter-sweet smile on his lips. "Direction presupposes a goal from which we take our bearings. Are you certain of your goal, dear Brother? Do you not fear that you may sometimes have over-indulged your taste for alcoholic liquor in the inn, so that, like a steeplejack who feels dizzy, you see two goals without knowing which is the right one?—You must attribute it to my profession, dear friar, that I possess such a sense of the frivolous; it is a kind of seasoning, like Spanish pepper with cauliflower, and without it a tonsorial artist is a pitiful creature, too stupid to use the prerogative which is his to enjoy."

The priest had been attentively regarding now me, now the grimacing Schönfeld, but since we spoke in German he could not understand a word. He now interrupted our conversation:

"You will forgive me, gentlemen, if my duty requires me to bring to an end a discussion which cannot possibly be of benefit to either of you. My Brother, you are still too weak to talk at such length about things which probably arouse painful memories of your former life. You will eventually be able to learn everything piece by piece from your friend, for when you have completely recovered and leave our asylum, he will no doubt accompany you into the world. Besides this (he turned to Schönfeld) you speak in a fashion which is calculated to conjure up the most vivid impressions in the listener's mind. In Germany you are probably considered mad, and even here you would pass for an excellent buffoon. You could make your fortune on the stage."

Schönfeld stared at the priest, stood on tiptoe, clapped his hands above his head and cried in Italian:

"O voice of the spirits! O voice of destiny! You have spoken to me through the mouth of this priest. Belcampo, Belcampo, such was your ignorance of your true vocation. The matter is settled!"

With this he sprang out of the room. The next morning he came to me, ready to depart.

"You are now entirely restored to health, my dear Brother Medardus," he said, "and no longer need my

assistance. I shall go where my inner voice directs. Farewell.
But permit me for the last time to demonstrate to you my
Art, though it now appears to me as a contemptible trade."

He drew out his knife, scissors and comb, and with a host
of grimaces and farcical remarks he trimmed my tonsure
and beard. In spite of his loyalty to me I had begun to find
him weird and uncanny, and I was glad when he had gone.

By means of strong tonics the doctor had almost fully
restored me to health; my colour had become fresher, and
I regained my strength by going for longer and longer
walks. I was certain that I would be able to stand a journey
on foot, and I left the asylum—a place of refuge for the sick
in mind but ghostly and frightening to the healthy. I had
been credited with the intention of making a pilgrimage to
Rome; I now decided really to do so, and strode out along
the road which I had been told led in that direction.

*   *   *   *

Although my mind was completely healed, I was
conscious of a strange numbness which spread a thick mist
over every image that arose in my memory, turning it into
a colourless grey. Having thus no clear recollection of the
past, I was completely absorbed in the cares of the moment.
I gazed into the distance, searching for the next place where
I could beg food or a night's lodging, and was sincerely
grateful when devout souls filled my bag and flask in
response to the mechanical prayers which I babbled—for
even my mentality had sunk to that of a common mendicant.

At last, a few hours' journey from Rome, I came to the
great Capuchin monastery which stands alone, surrounded
only by a few outhouses. As a monk I would certainly be
admitted, and I intended to enjoy a long rest there in
absolute comfort. I pretended that since the time when
my monastery in Germany had been dissolved, I had been
on extensive pilgrimages and now wished to enter another

monastery of my order. I was received with the generosity
and kindness characteristic of Italian monks, and the prior
declared that, in so far as the fulfilment of a vow did not
compel me to continue my pilgrimage, I could stay there
as long as I pleased, since I was from a foreign country.

It was time for vespers, and the monks were assembling
in the chancel. The magnificent sweep of the nave took
my breath away, but my earth-bound spirit could no longer
leap for joy as it had done when, as a child, I saw the chapel
of the Holy Linden. After I had said my prayer at the high
altar I walked down the side-aisles, regarding the altar-
pieces, which portrayed, as was customary, the martyrdom
of the saint to whom the altar was dedicated. Finally I came
to a side-chapel where the altar was illuminated by the
fiery rays of the sun which broke through the stained-glass
windows. I mounted the steps to look at the painting.
Saint Rosalia—the fateful picture in my monastery—O
God!—*It was Aurelia*! My whole life, my countless crimes
and misdeeds, the murder of Hermogenes and Aurelia—
everything just one single, terrible thought that seared my
mind like a red-hot blade. I cast myself down, tearing my
habit in a frenzy of despair, my cries echoing through the
chapel:

"I am cursed! I am cursed! No grace, no comfort on
earth or in Heaven! O wicked sinner that I am, condemned
to eternal damnation!"

I felt myself being lifted up. The monks had gathered
in the chapel, and in front of me stood the prior, a tall,
venerable old man. Looking at me gravely, yet with
infinite kindness, he took hold of my hands. It was as if a
saint, touched with divine pity, were holding the wayward
soul aloft above the sea of flames into which it would have
fallen.

"You are sick, Brother," he said. "We will take you
into the monastery, where you will be able to recover."

I kissed his hands and his robe, unable to speak. I was taken to the refectory, and at a sign from the prior the monks withdrew.

"My Brother," he began, "sin appears to lie heavily upon you, for only the most profound, most harrowing repentance for some terrible transgression could lead to such conduct. Yet the forbearance of the Lord is great, strong and mighty is the intercession of the saints. Have courage; confess to me, and through your atonement you will receive the consolation of the Church."

At that moment it seemed to me as though the prior were that old pilgrim from the Holy Linden, as though he were the only person in the whole world to whom I could reveal the wickedness of my life.

I was still unable to speak a word and threw myself at the old man's feet.

"I am going into the monastery chapel," he said solemnly, and left me alone.

I took hold of myself and hastened after him. He was sitting in the confessional, and I did all that the spirit commanded: I confessed everything, everything. Terrible was the penance the prior laid upon me. Banished from the church, excluded like a leper from the gatherings of the brethren, I lay in the vaults of the monastery, ekeing out a pitiable existence on tasteless herbs boiled in water, whipping and torturing myself with instruments devised by the most subtle cruelty, and raising my voice in self-accusation, in contrite prayer for my redemption from hell, whose flames were already glowing within me. But when the blood poured from a hundred wounds, when pain raged in the poisonous bites of a hundred scorpions, until my strength finally gave way and I was enveloped in the guardian arms of sleep, like a child powerless to resist— then wicked visions came to me in my dreams, subjecting me to further torment. My whole life took on a horrible

shape. I saw Euphemia approaching me in voluptuous
beauty, and cried out:

'What do you want with me, O wicked woman? Hell
has no power over me!'

She flung open her robe, and I shuddered with terror;
her body had shrivelled to a skeleton, and innumerable
serpents were writhing inside it, stretching out their heads
and their burning red tongues towards me.

'Leave me alone!' I screamed. 'Your serpents are
striking at my wounded breast and feeding on my heart's
blood. But I shall die, I shall die! Death will deliver me
from your vengeance!'

The figure shrieked:

'My serpents will feed on your heart's blood, but you will
not feel it, for that is not your torment: your torment is the
thought of sin, which is everlasting!'

Hermogenes, covered in blood, rose up, but Euphemia
fled from him, and he glided past, pointing to the wound
in the shape of a cross on his neck. I wanted to pray. There
was a confused rustling and whispering; people I had
known before appeared, madly distorted; heads crawled
about with grasshoppers' legs growing out of their ears, and
leering at me obscenely; strange birds, ravens with human
heads, were beating their wings overhead. I saw the choirmaster from B. and his sister, who was wildly dancing a
waltz while her brother accompanied her by playing on his
breast, which had become a fiddle. Belcampo, with the
ugly face of a lizard, was sitting on a horrible dragon;
he made a rush at me as if to comb my beard with a red-hot
iron comb, but he did not reach me. The chaos became
madder and madder, the figures more and more weird,
from the smallest ant dancing with human feet to the
elongated skeleton of a horse with glittering eyes, its skin
a saddle-cloth on which was sitting a knight with a shining
owl's-head; his armour was a mug with the bottom knocked

17

out, his helmet a funnel turned upside down. The jests of hell were being played on earth. I heard myself laughing, but my laughter sent an even fiercer pain through my body and my wounds bled the more profusely. Then the rabble dispersed and the figure of a woman appeared. She came nearer. It was Aurelia!

'I am alive, and yours alone!' she said.

Foul thoughts welled up inside me. In lustful frenzy I threw my arms round her. My weakness had fled, but there was a burning pain against my breast, coarse bristles plucked at my eyes, and Satan screeched with delight:

'Now you are mine alone!'

With a cry of horror I awoke, and soon the blood was gushing forth under the lashes of the knotted cord with which I chastised myself in my wretchedness.

At last the period was over which the prior had laid down for the severest part of my atonement, and I emerged from the vaults to undertake my further devotions in the monastery itself, but in a special cell set apart from the brethren. Then, as my penance became progressively lighter, I was allowed to enter the chapel and join the other monks. But this final penance, which consisted only of the usual daily chastisement, did not satisfy me. I steadfastly refused any better food and for whole days I lay prostrate on the cold marble floor in front of the picture of Saint Rosalia. I tormented myself cruelly in my lonely cell, thinking by physical pain to deaden the agony in my mind. But in vain. Again and again the figures appeared, evoked by my thoughts; I was in the clutches of Satan himself, who mockingly tempted and tortured me.

The severity of my penance, and the unprecedented way in which I performed it, attracted the attention of the monks. They regarded me with fear and awe, and I even heard them whisper to each other:

"He is a saint!"

This struck terror into my heart, for I recalled that dreadful moment in the Capuchin church at B. when in my mad presumptuousness I had shouted at the painter who was staring at me: "I am Saint Anthony!"

Eventually the final period of my penance also came to an end, without my having ceased to torment myself, in spite of the fact that my constitution seemed broken under the suffering. My eyes were dull, my bleeding body like a skeleton, and after I had lain for hours on the ground I was unable to get up without assistance. The prior sent for me.

"Do you feel, my Brother," he said, "that your soul has been unburdened through your severe penance? Have you received the consolation of Heaven?"

"No, reverend Father!" I answered, in deep despair.

"By imposing on you the strictest possible penance, my Brother," he went on, "as you had confessed to me a series of terrible deeds, I satisfied the rules of the Church, which require that the evil-doer who is not reached by the arm of justice, and who penitently confesses his crimes to the servant of the Lord, shall also give public testimony of the genuineness of his repentance. He shall turn his spirit heavenwards and yet chastise the flesh, so that earthly pain may redeem the evil pleasure which his transgressions brought him. Nevertheless I believe, and many teachers agree with me, that the most terrible agony endured by the repentant sinner does not lighten the burden of his sins one iota as long as he puts his entire confidence in the value of such penance and so deems himself worthy of the grace of the Everlasting Father. It is not given to human reason to examine how the Lord weighs our deeds. Lost is the man who, even if he is really free from wickedness, arrogantly believes that he can storm the citadel of Heaven with his ostentatious piety; and lost is that penitent sinner who, by thinking that his transgression has been obliterated by his devotions, reveals that his inner repentance is not genuine.

"You, Brother Medardus, do not feel comfort: that proves the truth of your repentance. Desist now from all chastisement; I desire it so. Take richer sustenance and do not continue to eschew the company of the brethren. Learn also that I am more intimately acquainted with the mysterious convolutions of your life than you are yourself. A destiny which you could not elude gave Satan power over you, and by your crimes you merely became his tool. But do not deceive yourself that for that reason you appear less sinful in the eyes of the Lord, for you were given the strength to resist Satan boldly and conquer him. Is there a human heart where evil does not rage, opposing the good? Without this struggle there would be no virtue, for virtue is only the victory of the good principle over the bad, just as sin is the result of the opposite.

"Learn, then, that there is one crime of which you accuse yourself which you have committed only in your imagination. Aurelia lives! In your delirium you stabbed yourself, and it was the blood from your own wound that gushed over your hand."

I fell to my knees, raising my hands in prayer, and tears sprang to my eyes.

"Learn further," continued the prior, "that the mysterious painter of whom you spoke in your confession has visited our monastery from time to time for as long as I can remember, and may perhaps come again in the near future. He placed in my custody a book containing, besides a number of sketches, a story to which he added a few lines each time he came. He did not forbid me to show it to anybody, and I will entrust it to you all the more readily since it is my most holy duty to do so. You will learn of the relationship between the various strange destinies which plunged you at one moment into a higher realm of

miraculous visions and at the next into the most commonplace of worlds. It is said that the miraculous has vanished
from the earth, but I do not believe it. The miracles are
still there, for even if we are no longer willing to call by
that name the most wonderful aspects of our daily life,
because we have managed to deduce from a succession of
events a law of cyclic recurrence, nevertheless there often
passes through that cycle a phenomenon which puts all
our wisdom to shame, and which, in our stupid obstinacy,
we refuse to believe because we are unable to comprehend
it.

"I count that painter among the extraordinary phenomena which makes a mockery of any such laboriously
deduced law, and I doubt whether his physical presence
is what we call real. It is at least certain that nobody has
ever observed him performing the normal functions of life.
Nor did I ever see him write or sketch, in spite of the fact
that each time after he had stayed with us there were more
pages to the book than before. It is also remarkable that
all the confused scribblings which it contains only seemed
to me to be fanciful sketches and did not become intelligible
until you, my dear Brother Medardus, had made your
confession to me. I must not express any further opinion
on what I believe about this painter; you will guess it for
yourself, or maybe the secret will reveal itself to you of its
own accord. Go—fortify yourself. If you feel restored in
spirit, as I trust in a few days you will, you shall receive
from me this remarkable book."

I did as the prior wished. I ate with the brethren, ceased
my chastisings, and confined myself to fervent prayers at
the altars of the saints. Even though the wound in my heart
continued to bleed, and even though there was no lessening
of the pain that racked me, yet the terrible visions had
departed. Often when I was lying sleepless on my hard
bed, angels' wings seemed to flutter above my head, and I

saw bending over me the sweet countenance of the living
Aurelia, her eyes filled with tears of divine pity. She
stretched out her hand above me as if in protection; my
eyelids closed, and a soft, refreshing slumber renewed my
strength.

When the prior observed that my mind had regained
some of its vitality, he gave me the painter's book, exhorting
me to read it closely in my cell. I opened it, and my eyes
fell at once on various sketches for the frescoes in the Holy
Linden. This did not cause me the slightest surprise, for
there was no enigma in this book for me; I had known
for a long time what it contained. The barely legible
writing in brightly-coloured ink on the final pages described
all my dreams and forebodings, but with such clear,
sharply-defined outlines as I could never have achieved.

Editor's Note

Without going further into what he found in the painter's
book, Brother Medardus proceeds to describe how he bade
farewell to the generous brethren and to the prior who was
admitted to his secret; how he made his pilgrimage to
Rome, praying before the altars in Saint Peter's, in Saint
Sebastian and Saint Laurence, San Giovanni a Laterano,
Santa Maria Maggiore and so on; how he even attracted
the notice of the Pope himself, and finally acquired an odour
of sanctity which, since he had now come to feel intensely
that he was nothing but a repentant sinner, forced him to
leave Rome. But without reading what the painter had
written, you and I, gentle reader, would know far too little
to be able to draw together even loosely the tangled threads
of Medardus' story. To change the metaphor, we would
be unable to find the central point from which the bright
rays of light emanated.

The Capuchin's manuscript was wrapped in old, faded parchment covered in a minute and most unusual handwriting which aroused my considerable curiosity. With great difficulty I succeeded in deciphering it, and eventually realised, to my amazement, that it was the story told in the painter's book which Medardus had spoken of. It was written in medieval Italian, almost in the style of a chronicle, full of aphorisms. In German it sounds strangely dead and dull, but I must give a translation of it in order to make Medardus' story intelligible. Before I do so, however, I must regretfully record the following facts.

The family from which the oft-mentioned Francesco was descended still lives in Italy, and the descendants of the Prince in whose town Medardus resided are also still alive; it was therefore impossible to use real names, and there is nobody more awkward and clumsy in the whole world than he who places this book in your hands, gentle reader, when he has to invent false names where real ones—beautiful and romantic-sounding ones—already exist, as was the case here. Your editor thought he could easily avoid the difficulty by saying simply "the Prince", "the Baron" and so forth, but now that the old painter has clarified these involved and mysterious family relationships, I realise that I would not be able to make myself satisfactorily understood with such general appellations; I would have to supplement the painter's chronicle with all kinds of explanations and instructions, as though one were to decorate and distort a simple chorale with ornate figurations.

Let me speak personally as the editor and beg you, gentle reader, to note the following points before you read on: Camillo, Prince of P., is the ancestor of the family from which Francesco, Medardus' father, is descended; Theodore, Prince of W., is the father of Prince Alexander of W., at whose court Medardus resided, and his brother Albert, Prince of W., married the Italian Princess Giacinta

B. Baron F.'s family in the mountains is already known to
you, and it is only necessary for me to add that Baroness F.
is Italian, being the daughter of Count Pietro S., a son of
Count Filippo S. As long as you retain these few Christian
names and initials in your mind, dear reader, everything
will become clear.

Here now, instead of the continuation of the story, is
what the painter had written.

. . . And so it came to pass that the republic of Genoa,
hard pressed by Algerian corsairs, appealed to the great
naval hero Camillo, Prince of P., to raid the audacious
buccaneers with four fully-manned galleons. Camillo,
always thirsting after adventure and glory, at once wrote
to his eldest son Francesco, commanding him to govern
the land in his absence. Francesco was studying painting
at the academy of Leonardo da Vinci, and the spirit of
art had taken such complete hold of him that he could think
of nothing else. Thus he valued art above material gain
and honour, and all other human activities simply appeared
to him as pitiful strivings after empty vanity. He could
not leave his art or his master, who was now of advancing
years, and he wrote back to his father that he knew how to
wield the brush but not the sceptre, and that he wished
to remain with Leonardo. The proud Prince Camillo was
most irate, and sent out trusted servants to bring his son
back, but Francesco persisted in his refusal to return,
declaring that he considered a Prince surrounded by the
splendour of his kingdom to be but a miserable creature
in comparison with a fine painter, and that great deeds
of battle were a mere cruel, mundane sport, whilst a
painter's creations were the pure reflection of a celestial
spirit. Camillo was filled with wrath and swore to disown
Francesco and transfer the succession to his younger son
Zenobio. Francesco was greatly pleased at this, and even

signed a document solemnly revoking his succession to the
Prince's throne in favour of his younger brother.

And so it came about that the old Prince Camillo lost
his life in a hard, bloody battle against the Algerians.
Zenobio became ruler, whilst Francesco, renouncing his
name and rank, became a painter, and eked out a scanty
existence on the small yearly allowance which his brother
granted him. Francesco had always been a proud,
exuberant youth; Leonardo was the only one who could
curb his wildness, and when he had given up his noble rank,
he became Leonardo's devout and faithful son, helping
him to complete many a large and important work. By
rising to his master's eminence he became famous throughout the land, and was frequently commissioned to paint
altar-pieces in churches and monasteries. Old Leonardo
advised and assisted him loyally, until at last he died, at
a great age.

Then like a fire that has been smouldering for a long time,
pride and wantonness broke out again in the young
Francesco. He considered himself the greatest painter of
his time, and coupling his artistic perfection with his rank,
he called himself the "noble painter". He spoke disdain-
fully of old Leonardo, and departing from the pure, simple
manner, he created a new style, which, through its volup-
tuousness of form and magnificence of colour, dazzled the
multitude, whose exaggerated eulogies made him all the
more vain and arrogant. In Rome he fell into the company
of wild, abandoned young men, and as he always wanted
to be in the forefront of events, he soon became the boldest
sailor on the sea of vice. Utterly corrupted by the false,
hollow glory of paganism, these men, with Francesco at
their head, formed a secret society in which, blaspheming
against Christianity, they imitated the rites of the ancient
Greeks and celebrated impious, sacrilegious feasts with
brazen wenches. There were painters and, even more,

sculptors among them who were completely absorbed in
the art of Antiquity and scorned all that modern artists,
inspired by Christianity, had conceived and executed in its
glory. Francesco painted untiringly the figures of false
heathen gods, and nobody was able to portray as realistically
as he the sensuous beauty of the female form, for he drew
the erotic quality from living models and his formal values
from the marble busts of Antiquity. Instead of seeking
inspiration in a spirit of reverence from the glorious
paintings by the devout old masters which hung in churches
and monasteries, he modelled his figures on false heathen
gods, being obsessed above all with a famous portrait of
Venus which he perpetually held in his imagination.

On one occasion the allowance granted to him by
Zenobio was later in arriving than usual, and Francesco,
whose riotous living quickly disposed of everything he
earned, found himself in serious financial trouble. He then
remembered that some long time ago a Capuchin monastery
had commissioned him to paint a picture of Saint Rosalia
for a high price, and for the sake of the money he now
resolved to undertake the work on which, because of his
detestation of all Christian saints, he had hitherto not
wanted to embark. He intended to portray Saint Rosalia
in the nude, with features like those of that Venus. The
first sketch was successful beyond all expectations, and his
wanton companions praised his wicked idea of painting a
heathen idol instead of a Christian saint for the monks to
hang in their church.

But as Francesco began to paint, everything took on an
entirely different shape from that which he intended, and
a mightier power overwhelmed the spirit of base falsehood
which had formerly ruled him. Gradually the face of a
heavenly angel emerged from the mists, but as if from fear
of harming the saint and incurring the punishment of the
Lord, he did not dare to complete her face, but draped

round her naked body demure and graceful robes—a crimson gown and an azure cloak. In their letter to Francesco the monks had simply referred to a picture of Saint Rosalia, without specifying whether he should take for his subject some memorable story from her life, and he had therefore painted nothing but the figure of the saint in the centre of his canvas. Now he felt moved to surround her with all sorts of creatures which united in a mysterious way to portray her martyrdom. He was completely absorbed in his picture: it was as though it had become a powerful spirit which was holding him in its arms, high above the wicked life which he had hitherto been living. Yet he was still unable to complete her face, and this tormented him day and night. He no longer thought of the portrait of Venus; instead, he seemed to see old Leonardo watching him sorrowfully and to hear him lament: 'Would that I could help you, but I cannot, for you must first renounce all evil desires and seek in humility and penitence the intercession of the saint against whom you have so wantonly sinned.'

The men whom he had so long avoided visited him in his studio, and found him lying stretched out on his bed like a sick man. When he told them that, as if an evil demon had broken his strength, he was unable to finish the picture of Saint Rosalia, they all laughed and cried:

"Come, come, brother. How is it that you have suddenly been taken so sick? Let us offer an oblation of wine to Aesculapius and the good Hygieia, that your sickness may be healed!"

Syracusan wine was brought and the men filled their glasses. Then standing in front of the unfinished picture, they offered libations to the heathen gods. They began to carouse heartily, but when they brought wine to Francesco, he would not drink, nor would he have any part in their revels, despite the toast which they drank to Venus. One of them said:

"This foolish painter really does seem to be ill, both in mind and body. I must fetch a doctor."

Throwing his cloak over his shoulder and buckling on his rapier, he went out of the room. A few moments later he returned and said:

"Well, here we are. I am the doctor; I will soon cure this invalid."

Trying to copy the gait and bearing of an aged physician, he tottered around with bent knees, wrinkling and puckering his youthful features in such a weird fashion that he looked like an ugly old man. The others roared with laughter and shouted:

"Ha, ha! Look at the learned faces the doctor is pulling!"

The doctor approached the sick Francesco and said scornfully in a raucous voice:

"Oh you poor fellow! Now I suppose I must get you out of this miserable condition. Oh, you unhappy fellow, how pale and ill you look! Venus won't think much of you in this state! Maybe Donna Rosalia will take care of you if you have sinned. Oh, feeble fellow, take a sip of my miraculous medicine! Since you want to depict the saints, my potion will certainly fortify you, for it is wine from Saint Anthony's cellar!"

The "doctor" produced a bottle from under his cloak and opened it. A strange scent filled the room, overcoming the men so that they sank into their chairs and closed their eyes as if in sleep. But Francesco, enraged at being despised as an impotent fool, tore the bottle from the doctor's hands and drank deeply from it.

"May it bring you health!" laughed the doctor, who had now resumed his youthful expression and his vigorous gait. He roused the others from their stupour, and they reeled down the stairs with him.

As Mount Vesuvius roars and sends forth its destructive flames, so streams of fire shot through Francesco's soul. All the pagan subjects he had ever painted appeared as living forms before his eyes, and he cried out fiercely: "You too must come, my beloved goddess. You too must live and be mine, or I shall deliver myself up to the gods of the underworld."

Then he saw Venus standing close to the picture, beckoning gently to him. Leaping from his bed, he began to paint the head of Saint Rosalia, for he now felt able to portray faithfully the enchanting features of his Venus. It was as though his will could no longer command his hand, for the brush continually slipped away from the clouds enveloping the saint's head, and painted involuntarily the heads of the barbaric figures which surrounded her. But her celestial countenance emerged more and more plainly, and suddenly she looked at him with such dazzling eyes that he fell to the ground as if struck by lightning. When he had recovered his senses, he sat up painfully, but dared not turn his eyes towards the picture. He crept with bowed head to the table, where the doctor's bottle was still standing, and took a deep draught. His strength immediately returned, and he looked across at the painting. It stood before him, finished but for the final stroke. Yet it was not the face of Saint Rosalia but his beloved Venus, looking at him with eyes full of voluptuous passion. In that instant Francesco became inflamed with wild, sensual lust; he screamed out in a frenzy, recalling the story of the sculptor Pygmalion and praying to Venus, as that King of Cyprus had done, to breathe life into his painting. Soon he felt as if the picture were beginning to move, but as he was about to take it in his arms, he saw that it was still only lifeless canvas. Tearing his hair, he behaved like one possessed of the Devil.

For two days and nights his hysteria continued. On the

third day, while he was standing before the picture, motionless as a statue, the door of his room opened and he heard a rustling sound behind him as of a woman's dress. Turning round, he saw alive before him, in all her loveliness, the woman of his picture. Speechless, he fell at her feet, raising his hands to her in worship. The woman lifted him up, a gentle smile on her lips, and told him that, when she had been a little girl and he a student at Leonardo's academy, she had often seen him and cherished even then an all-consuming love for him; she had left her parents and relatives and come to Rome to look for him, for an inner voice had told her that he loved her too, and that he had painted her portrait out of desire and longing for her. Francesco realised that he was under the spell of a mysterious spiritual relationship to this woman, and that this relationship had caused his passionate love and the wonderful picture to merge into one. Fervently he embraced her, and wanted to take her to the church so that the priest might unite them at once in the holy bonds of matrimony. But at this she appeared shocked and said:

"My beloved Francesco, are you not a noble artist who will not allow himself to be bound by the shackles of the Christian Church? Have you not devoted yourself body and soul to the freshness and joyfulness of Antiquity and its hedonist gods? What has our union to do with melancholy priests who spend their lives wailing disconsolately in gloomy chapels? Let us feast our love in happiness and joy."

Francesco was entranced by her words, and the same evening, in the company of those degenerate men he called his friends, he celebrated his marriage to her according to heathen rites. She had brought with her a box full of jewels and money, and Francesco, revelling in sinful pleasures and completely renouncing his art, lived with her for many years.

She became pregnant, and the wondrousness of her beauty became even more dazzling. She was the living image of Venus, and Francesco could hardly endure the luscious joys which his life brought him. One night he was wakened by a low, frightened moan. Jumping up in fear and shining the light towards his wife, he saw that she had borne him a son. The servants hastened to fetch the doctor and the midwife. Francesco took the child from its mother's bosom, but in the same instant she gave a terrible scream and writhed convulsively as if powerful hands had seized her. The midwife arrived, followed by the doctor, but as they turned to help her, they recoiled in horror, for she was dead. Her neck and breast were disfigured by dark, ugly patches, and instead of her young and beautiful features they found themselves looking at a wrinkled, hideously distorted face with large, protruding eyes. The women screamed in terror, and the neighbours, hearing the noise, rushed in, for there had been all manner of strange rumours about the unknown woman right from the beginning. Everybody had abhorred the lascivious life that she had led with Francesco, and the point had been reached at which her sinful cohabitation was about to be denounced to the ecclesiastical authorities. Now, as they looked at her body, gruesomely disfigured by death, it was plain to all of them that she had been in alliance with the Devil, who had finally claimed her; her beauty had been but a deceitful illusion produced by cursed witchcraft. All those who had come into the room fled in fright, and nobody would touch the body. Francesco now realised with whom he had been associating, and a terrible fear took hold of him. His manifold crimes passed through his mind, and divine justice began to be meted out even on earth, for the flames of hell had already begun to consume his soul.

The next day an official from the ecclesiastical court arrived with the bailiffs to arrest Francesco. But his courage and pride returned, and seizing his rapier he fought his way through them and escaped. Some distance from Rome he found a cave in which, completely exhausted as he was, he hid himself. Without being aware of it, he had wrapped his new-born child in his cloak and carried it off with him. In his fury he was on the point of dashing it against the rocks, but as he held it aloft it gave out pitiful, pleading tones which filled him with compassion, and he laid it on a bed of soft moss and fed it drop by drop with the juice of an orange. He spent many weeks in the cave like a penitent hermit, turning aside from his evil ways and praying to the saints; above all he implored Saint Rosalia, whom he had so vilely offended, to intercede for him before the throne of the Lord.

One evening Francesco was kneeling in prayer in the wilderness, his eyes turned towards the western sun, which was plunging into the fiery waves of the sea. As the glow faded in the grey evening mists, he became conscious of a bright, rose-coloured shimmer in the air above him, which began to take on human shape. He saw Saint Rosalia, surrounded by angels. There was a soft rustling, and he heard the words:

'O Lord, forgive the man who in his weakness could not resist the temptation of the Devil.'

Shafts of light shone through the rosy lustre, and the muffled boom of thunder rolled through the vaults of Heaven:

'Who has sinned like this man? He shall find no grace, no rest in the grave so long as his stem continues to multiply in sin and wickedness!'

Francesco grovelled in the dust and knew that judgment had been passed on him. Forgetting his little son, he fled from the cave and lived in wretchedness and misery, since he was no longer able to paint. Sometimes he felt as though he should paint wonderful pictures to the glory of the Church, and he planned great works which were to portray the legends of the Virgin and Saint Rosalia. Yet how could he even start to work when he had no money to buy canvas or paint, and only dragged out a painful existence on the meagre alms thrown to him at church doors?

So it came about that, as he was sitting in a church, staring at the bare walls and designing paintings in his imagination, two veiled women came up to him, one of whom said in a sweet, angelic voice:

"In distant Prussia, at the place where the angels of the Lord have set the image of the Virgin Mary upon a linden-tree, there is a church which is as yet unadorned with paintings. Go there; let your art be your holy devotion, and your stricken soul shall receive eternal comfort."

As Francesco turned to look up at the women, they faded into the soft sunlight, and a scent of lilies and roses filled the church. He now knew who the women were, and resolved to start on his pilgrimage the next morning. The same evening one of Zenobio's servants, who had been searching for him everywhere, came to him, paid him two years' allowance and invited him to his master's court. Francesco kept only a small sum for himself and, distributing the rest to the poor, set out for Prussia.

His road led him through Rome, and shortly before he came to the city, he passed the Capuchin monastery for which he had painted the picture of Saint Rosalia. He saw the picture, which had been incorporated into the altar-piece, but on closer inspection he discovered that it was only a copy of his painting; the monks, he was informed, had not wanted to keep the original because of the strange rumours about the painter from whose posthumous possessions they had received it; after having commissioned a copy of it, they had sold the original to the Capuchin monastery in B. . .

18

After a wearisome pilgrimage he arrived at the monastery
of the Holy Linden and fulfilled the command he had
received from the Virgin Mary. So gloriously did he
decorate the church that he felt the spirit of grace beginning
to work within him, and his soul came to know the bliss of
divine comfort.

It so happened that, while Count Filippo S. was out
hunting in a wild, desolate district, he was overtaken by a
severe storm. The wind howled through the ravines and
the rain poured down in torrents, as if another Flood were
about to destroy man and beast. He found a cave and
managed to pull himself and his horse into it. Black clouds
covered the sky, and it was so dark that he could not make
out what was stirring and rustling close by him. Fearing
there might be a wild beast hiding there, he drew his sword
to protect himself against any attack. When the storm had
passed, however, and rays of sunlight broke into the cave,
he saw to his amazement that a tiny naked boy was lying
beside him on a bed of leaves, looking at him with bright,
sparkling eyes. Close by the child was an ivory goblet in
which the Count found a few drops of sweet-smelling wine,
which the child drank avidly. The Count sounded his horn.
Gradually his retinue, which had scattered hither and
thither, assembled and, at his command, waited to see
whether the person who had laid the child in the cave
would return to take it away. As night began to fall, he
said:

"I cannot leave this little boy alone and helpless. I will
take him with me, and have it made known that I have done
so, in order that his parents, or whoever laid him in the
cave, may come and claim him from me."

Weeks, months, years went by and nobody came. The
Count had the foundling christened Francesco. As the boy
grew up, he became both in mind and body a wonderful

youth, so that the Count loved him as his own son, and being himself childless, he thought to leave him his entire wealth.

When Francesco was twenty-five years old, Count Filippo was smitten with a foolish infatuation for a beautiful but poor girl and married her, although she was very young and he well on in years. Francesco was soon seized by a sinful desire to possess the Countess, and in spite of the fact that she was most upright and virtuous, and did not want to break her vow of allegiance to the Count, he finally succeeded in ensnaring her so that she yielded to his wanton lust. The two children, Count Pietro and Countess Angiola, whom old Filippo embraced in the rapture of fatherhood, were the fruits of this sin, which remained for ever hidden both from him and the world.

Driven by an urge within me, I went to my brother Zenobio and said:

"I have renounced the throne, and even if you die before me, childless, I wish to remain a poor painter and spend my life in quiet devotion, practising my art. Nevertheless, our realm shall not fall into the hands of a foreign state. That Francesco whom Count Filippo brought up is my son. It was I who, after my hectic escape, left him in the cave where the Count found him. The ivory goblet that was lying at his side is engraved with our crest. An even more convincing proof is the boy's appearance, which shows beyond doubt that he is descended from our house. Receive the boy as your son, Brother Zenobio, and let him be your successor."

Zenobio's qualms as to whether Francesco had been born in lawful wedlock were dispelled by a certificate of adoption sanctioned by the Pope, which I obtained. Thus ended my son's sinful, adulterous life. Soon a legitimate son was born to him, whom he called Paolo Francesco.

My guilty stem has guiltily multiplied, yet can my son's repentance not atone for these crimes? He stood before me as before the Lord's judgment-seat, for I could see deep into his soul. That which was hidden from the world I learned from the spirit which raised me above the turmoil of life, that I might scan its depths from on high and yet not fall headlong to my doom.

Francesco's departure meant death for the Countess, for only now did she awaken to the wickedness of her sin, and she was unable to endure the struggle between her love for the malefactor and her repentance for her transgression. When Count Filippo was ninety years old he died, a doting old man. His supposed son Pietro moved with his sister Angiola to the court of Francesco, who had succeeded Zenobio.

Paolo Francesco's betrothal to Vittoria, Princess of M., was celebrated with great jubilation, but when Pietro saw the Princess in all her loveliness, he was inflamed with love and, heedless of the danger, courted her favour. His intentions, however, passed unnoticed by Paolo Francesco, since the latter was in love with Pietro's sister, who coldly rejected all his advances.

Vittoria retired from the court, pretending that she had a holy vow to fulfil in quiet solitude before her wedding. She did not return for a year. The wedding was arranged, and immediately afterwards Pietro was to return with his sister Angiola to his own town. The flame of Paolo Francesco's love had been fanned more and more by Angiola's adamant refusals, and his passion now degenerated into animal lust, which he was only able to curb by thoughts of gratification. And so, before he went into the bridal chamber on his wedding day, Paolo Francesco treacherously assaulted Angiola in her bedchamber, and while she was still unconscious—for she had been given opiates at the wedding feast

—satisfied his lust. Angiola almost died as a result of this outrage, and Paolo Francesco, tortured by pangs of conscience, confessed what he had done. In a fit of rage Pietro was on the point of striking the perfidious traitor to the ground, but his arm dropped back, paralysed, as he remembered that his revenge had preceded Paolo Francesco's deed; for little Giacinta, Duchess of B . . ., whom everybody took to be the daughter of Vittoria's sister, was the fruit of the secret liaison that Pietro had carried on with Paolo Francesco's betrothed.

Pietro went with Angiola to Germany, where she bore a son called Franz, whom she brought up with great care. The innocent girl reconciled herself at last to the thought of Paolo Francesco's terrible deed, and her charm and beauty began to blossom again. Prince Theodor of W. fell deeply in love with her, and she responded to his affection from the depths of her heart. In a short time she became his wife and bore him two sons, whilst at the same time Count Pietro married a German lady, by whom he had a daughter.

The conscience of the pious Angiolo was pure, yet whenever the horrible memory of Paolo Francesco's deed came back to her, she fell to brooding that her sin, albeit committed in innocence, could not be forgiven, and would be avenged on her and on her descendents. Even confession and complete absolution could not set her mind at rest. Then, like an inspiration from Heaven, it suddenly dawned on her that she should confess everything to her husband, and although she probably did not foresee what a struggle it would be for her to make this confession, she swore a solemn oath to take this bold step, and kept it. Prince Theodor learned of the atrocity with horror, and it seemed as though his rage might even be vented on the innocent Princess. She therefore went away for some months to a distant palace, during which time the Prince fought to overcome the bitter feelings which assailed him. Finally, not only did he return to the Princess and offer her the hand of reconciliation, but also, unbeknown to her, provided for Franz's education.

After the death of the Prince and his consort, Count Pietro and the young Prince Alexander of W. were the only ones who knew the secret of Franz's birth. None of the painter's descendents bore such a striking resemblance. either in mind or body, to that Francesco whom Count Filippo had brought up, as this Franz. He was a wonderful youth, inspired by a divine power, swift and fiery both in thought and deed. May the sin of his father and of his father's father not fall upon him, and may he overcome the evil temptations of the Devil!

Before Prince Theodor died, his two sons, Alexander and Johann, travelled to Italy. In Rome they parted company, not so much from open disagreement as because of their different inclinations and ambitions. Alexander came to Paolo Francesco's court, and fell so deeply in love with Paolo's youngest daughter (the child of Paolo and Vittoria) that he wished to marry her. With an abhorrence which he could not comprehend, however, his father rejected the proposal, and so only after his father's death was Alexander able to marry her.

On his way home Duke Johann had met his brother Franz, and found such pleasure in his company, without suspecting their kinship, that soon he could not leave him. The reason why the Duke, instead of returning home, went back to his brother's palace in Italy, was Franz. It was the will of an inscrutable providence that both Johann and Franz should set eyes on Giacinta, the daughter of Vittoria and Pietro, and be consumed with a violent passion for her. The seeds of wickedness were sown—and who can withstand the powers of darkness?

The sins of my youth were indeed terrible, but I have

been saved from perdition by the intercession of the Blessed
Virgin and Saint Rosalia, and been permitted to suffer the
torments of damnation here on earth until my sinful line
shall have perished for ever. As I summon my thoughts,
so I am oppressed by the burden of earthly things; as I
sense the mysterious power of the future, so I am dazzled
by the false brilliance of life in the present, and my eye
cannot follow the fleeting visions, cannot recognise their
real forms. Often I catch a glimpse of the thread in which
the forces of evil, fighting against my soul's salvation, seek
to enmesh me, and in my foolishness I try to seize and break
it. But I must endure my fate, and through constant
penance bear steadfastly the suffering laid upon me that I
might atone for my sins. I have driven the Count and
Franz away from Giacinta, but Satan is planning Franz's
ineluctable downfall.

Franz, accompanied by Duke Johann, arrived at the
palace where Count Pietro was staying with his consort
and his daughter Aurelia, who had just celebrated her
fifteenth birthday. As Paolo Francesco had been smitten
with wild desire when he saw Angiola, so the fire of forbidden lust smouldered in his son's heart when he set eyes
on the sweet child Aurelia. By all manner of diabolical
ruses he so managed to seduce the chaste, immature girl
that she surrendered her entire soul to him and had sinned
before ever the thought of sin had entered her mind. When
his deed could no longer be kept secret, Franz threw himself
at her mother's feet and confessed everything. Count
Pietro, though he was himself beset with sin and crime,
would have killed both Franz and Aurelia had he known.
The Countess punished Franz by forbidding him ever to
come near her daughter or herself again, under pain of
disclosing his evil deed to Pietro. She succeeded in keeping
her daughter away from the Count, and in a distant land
Aurelia gave birth to a daughter.

But Franz could not forget Aurelia, and learning where she was, he hastened to her, and rushed into her room just as the Countess, left alone by the servants, was sitting at her daughter's bedside nursing the tiny child on her lap. Horror-stricken at the unexpected sight of the villain, the Countess rose and commanded him to leave the room.

"Away with you, or you shall die! Count Pietro knows of your outrage!" she cried, and forced him out of the door. A fit of savage rage came over Franz. He snatched the child from her arms, struck her a heavy blow so that she fell over backwards, and rushed away. When Aurelia recovered, she found her mother dead; in falling she had struck her head against the edge of an iron chest.

Franz's intention was to kill the child. He wrapped it in shawls, ran down the stairs in the evening gloom, and was about to rush out of the house, when he heard a dull moaning that seemed to come from a room on the ground-floor. Instinctively he stopped and listened, then crept closer. At that moment a woman whom he recognised as Baroness S.'s nurse, in whose house he was living, came out of the room, weeping sorrowfully. He asked why she was crying.

"Alas," wailed the woman, "a terrible tragedy has befallen me! As little Euphemia was sitting on my lap, laughing and playing, her head suddenly fell back and now she is dead. There are blue marks on her forehead, and I shall be accused of having dropped her."

Franz went quickly into the room, and as his eyes fell on the dead child, he realised that providence desired his child to live, for it bore an extraordinary resemblance to the dead Euphemia. The nurse, perhaps not so blameless as she pretended, and bribed by Franz's handsome gift, was content with the exchange. He wrapped the dead child in the shawls and threw it into the river. Aurelia's child was brought up as Euphemia, the daughter of Baroness S., and the world remained unaware of the secret. She could not be received into the bosom of the Church through the sacrament of baptism, for the child through whose death her own life had been preserved was already baptised. After many years Aurelia married Baron F., to whom she bore two children, Hermogenes and Aurelia.

The eternal power of Heaven had permitted me to accompany the Duke and Francesco (as he was known in Italian) to the town where his brother, the Prince, resided. With my strong arm I wanted to hold Francesco fast as he tottered on the edge of the abyss. O foolish thought! I was myself but a poor sinner who had not yet found grace before the throne of the Almighty. Francesco murdered his brother, after ravishing Giacinta. Francesco's son is the ill-fated boy whom the Prince brought up under the name of Count Victor. Francesco, the murderer, wanted to marry the pious sister of the Princess, but I was able to prevent this monstrous crime at the very moment when it was being perpetrated in the house of God.

Franz, who had fled, tortured by the thought of his unforgivable sin, was only brought to repentance by the state of profound misery to which he had been brought. Weighed down by sickness and sorrow, he came to the house of a villager, who received him kindly. The villager's daughter, a quiet, pious maiden, fell deeply in love with the stranger and nursed him tenderly. And so it came about that, when Franz had recovered his health, he returned the maiden's love, and they were united in wedlock. By his skill and knowledge Franz succeeded in augmenting the not inconsiderable wealth he had inherited from his father, and came to enjoy great earthly prosperity.

But vain and insecure is the happiness of the sinner who is not reconciled with God. Franz fell again into abject

poverty, and in his dejection he felt both mind and body
being eaten away by a morbid suffering. His life became
one continuous act of penance. At last Heaven sent him a
ray of comfort: he was to make a pilgrimage to the Holy
Linden, where the Lord would show mercy on him through
the birth of a son.

In the forest that surrounds the monastery of the Holy
Linden I came upon the troubled mother weeping over the
fatherless new-born child, and soothed her with words of
sympathy. O how wonderful is the grace which the Lord
bestows on the child born within the sanctuary of the blest!
For the Child Jesus himself will appear to him and kindle
the spark of love in his heart.

The mother had her baby baptised Franz, after his father.
Will it be you, Franciscus, who, born on consecrated ground,
will atone for your father's guilt by a life of piety and bring
him peace in his grave? 'Let the boy devote himself utterly
to the things of Heaven, far from the world and its seductive
pleasures. Let him become a priest.'

Such were the words that the man of God spoke to the
mother in exhortation. This must surely have been the
prophecy of that grace which now shines upon me in its
brightness. I see this youth engaged in a mortal struggle
against the sinister power which attacks him. He falls,
but a celestial figure raises the crown of victory above his
head—it is Saint Rosalia herself who has saved him!

As long as the everlasting power of Heaven is with me, I
will be at hand to protect the boy, the youth, the man, with
all the strength at my command. He will be . . .

EDITOR's NOTE

At this point, gentle reader, the old painter's faded
writing becomes so indistinct that it is quite impossible to
decipher anything further. Let us therefore return to the
manuscript of the extraordinary Capuchin friar.

III—RETURN TO THE MONASTERY

My sanctity had been noised abroad in such a manner that people stopped me in the streets of Rome, beseeching me with bowed head and humble mien to give them my blessing. Whether or not attention had been aroused by the strictness of my devotions, it was clear that my strange appearance would soon become a legend to the impressionable and excitable inhabitants of the city, and that, without my suspecting it in the least, they might already have made me the hero of some religious tale. I was often disturbed in my meditations by awestruck sighs and the murmur of soft prayers as I lay on the altar-steps, and I became aware of devout souls kneeling all around me, apparently imploring my intercession. As in the Capuchin monastery, I heard behind me exclamations of "*Il Santo!*", and shafts of pain shot through my heart.

I was about to leave Rome when I was frightened to learn from the prior of the monastery in which I was staying that the Pope had summoned me to appear before him. I was filled with a foreboding that the powers of evil were seeking anew to bind me in their wicked chains, but I plucked up courage and went to the Vatican at the appointed hour.

The Pope, a fine figure still in the prime of life, received me sitting in a richly-decorated chair. Two handsome boys in ecclesiastical robes were serving him with iced water and cooling the air with fans of herons' feathers. I approached him humbly and made the customary reverence. He looked at me intently, but there was kindness in his expression, and instead of the grave severity which, from having seen him at a distance, I had imagined characterised his attitude, there was a gentle smile on his face. He asked me where I came from, what had brought me to Rome, in fact, the most general questions about my personal life. Then rising to his feet, he said:

"I have summoned you because I have heard stories of your rare piety. Why, Friar Medardus, do you perform your devotions publicly in the most frequented churches? If you think to create thereby the impression of being a saint, so that you may be worshipped by the fanatical mob, then search your heart to see what leads you to act thus. If you do not stand undefiled before the Lord and before me, his appointed Regent, you will swiftly come to a shameful end."

The Pope spoke these words in a stern voice, his eyes flashing. For the first time in what seemed an eternity I no longer felt guilty of the sin of which I was accused; not only did I retain my composure but also, sustained by the thought that my atonement had sprung from a feeling of true contrition, I was able to reply, in a spirit of exaltation:

"O most holy Regent of the Almighty, you have power to see into my heart, and will know how I am oppressed by the burden of my sins. But you will also admit the truth of my repentance. I am far from all vile hypocrisy, far from all false ambition to deceive the people. Grant, O most holy Sir, that this penitent monk may reveal to you the course of his sinful life and the acts of profound devotion which he has already undertaken."

As briefly as I could I told the whole story of my life, without, however, mentioning any names. The Pope became more and more attentive. He sat down in his chair, resting his head in his hands, his eyes fixed on the ground. Suddenly he stood up. Folding his hands and putting his right foot forward as if to approach me, he gazed at me unwaveringly. When I had finished, he sat down again.

"Your story, Friar Medardus," he said, "is the most remarkable I have ever heard. Do you believe in the open, visible intervention of an evil demon which the Church calls the Devil?"

Before I could reply, he went on:

"Do you believe that it was the wine you stole from among the relics which drove you to these crimes?"

"Like water teeming with foul odours it gave strength to the seed of evil latent within me, so that it multiplied beyond all knowledge."

The Pope was silent for a few moments. Then he continued with a serious expression:

"What if Nature were to follow in the realm of the spirit the physical law by which an organism can only reproduce its own kind; if propensity and desire, like the in-dwelling power which makes the leaves green, were to be handed down from father to son, obliterating free will? There are whole families of robbers and murderers. This would then be the original sin, an eternal, ineradicable curse on a guilty house, for which no sacrifice could atone."

"But if he who is born a sinner cannot but sin again by virtue of his heritage, then there can be no sin," I interposed.

"Indeed there can," he replied. "The spirit of God has created a giant, capable of subduing the wild beast within us. This giant is called Self-Knowledge and from its struggle with the beast emerges Freedom of the Spirit. The giant's victory is virtue, the beast's victory, Sin."

He paused. Then his countenance brightened, and he added gently:

"Do you think, Friar Medardus, that it is meet for the Regent of the Almighty to argue thus about sin and virtue?"

"Gracious Father," I replied, "you have deemed your servant worthy to listen to your profound philosophy, and it is indeed becoming that you should speak of that struggle which you have long since brought to a triumphant conclusion."

"You have a high opinion of me, Brother Medardus," said the Pope. "Or is it that you look upon my tiara as the laurel wreath which proclaims me as a hero and conquerer of the world?"

"It must be a glorious feeling to be a ruler of men," I said. "From that position of eminence all things must appear in a new perspective, and a more coherent pattern of life revealed. Such an exalted station brings with it that blessed gift of a true prince—the power to see things as a whole."

"You mean," rejoined the Pope, "that even rulers whose will and reason are weak possess a certain shrewdness which passes for wisdom and impresses the multitude. But what is the relevance of this?"

"I wanted first to speak of the blessings of the princes whose kingdom is of this world," I said, "and then of the celestial blessings of the Regent of the Almighty. In a mysterious way the spirit of the Lord shines upon the cardinals in the conclave. The mind that yearns after revelation and gives itself over to devout meditation in a lonely cell, is inspired by a ray from Heaven, and a single name rings out from every mouth, like a hymn of praise. The decrees of God are only understood in earthly terms, and thus, most gracious Sir, your triple crown, which symbolises the profound mystery of your Lord, the Lord of all worlds, is in fact the laurel which proclaims you hero and victor. Your kingdom is not of this world, yet you are called to rule over all nations, gathering the members of the invisible Church under the Lord's banner. The worldly kingdom assigned to you is your throne which shines in celestial glory."

"You claim, Brother Medardus," interrupted the Pope, "that I have cause to be content with the throne assigned to me. My Rome is indeed decked out in regal splendour—this you will have observed already if you have not completely averted your gaze from the things of earth. Yet I do not believe you. You are an excellent orator, and your words have impressed me. I can see that we shall get to know each other better. Remain here in Rome; in a few days you may become prior, and later I might even choose you as my confessor. Go. Behave less extravagantly in church, for you will certainly not rise to the eminence of a saint—the calendar is already full. Go!"

The Pope's final words surprised me as much as his whole demeanour, which was entirely different from the impression that I had formerly held of the supreme head of the Christian faith. I had no doubt that he regarded everything I had said about the divine nature of his calling as vain and artful flattery; he proceeded from the idea that I wanted to raise myself to the status of a saint, and that since, for a variety of reasons, he was forced to bar my progress towards this end, I was now intent on acquiring prestige and influence in some other way. For reasons unknown to me he was not prepared to enter into a discussion of this either.

So forgetting that, before the Pope had summoned me to him, I had firmly intended to leave Rome, I resolved to continue my devotions. Yet I felt too agitated to be able to devote myself entirely to the things of heaven as I had done hitherto. Even in prayer I could not help thinking of my former life. The vision of my sins had faded, and in my mind's eye I saw nothing but a brilliant career, started as a Prince's favourite, continued as the Pope's confessor, and culminating in some position of undreamt-of eminence. Thus of my own accord, and not because the Pope had so ordained, I ceased my devotions and spent my time strolling through the streets of Rome.

One day, as I was crossing the Piazza di Spagna, I saw a
crowd gathering round a puppet show. I heard Pulcinello's
comical laugh and the guffaws of the onlookers. The first
act was over and the second about to begin. The little
curtain rose, revealing young David with his sling and his
sack full of pebbles; amidst bizarre gesticulations he undertook to slay the uncouth giant Goliath and save Israel.
There was a deep roar and Goliath, with a huge head,
appeared. To my amazement I immediately recognised
the head as belonging to the mad Belcampo. He had
fastened to it a little body with miniature arms and legs,
concealing his own arms and shoulders behind a cloth
arranged to resemble the broad folds of Goliath's cloak.
Making the oddest grimaces and grotesquely shaking his
dwarf-like body, Goliath made a haughty speech which
David interrupted from time to time with his titters. The
crowd roared with laughter, and I too, fascinated by this
new, fantastic guise of Belcampo's, was so carried away
that I burst out laughing with a childlike delight which had
long been denied me. How often, alas, had my laughter
been but the agonised convulsion of a deep, heart-rending
torment!

The fight with the giant was preceded by a long disputa-
tion in which David proved in the most ingenious and
learned manner why he was bound to slay his terrible
opponent. Belcampo made the muscles of his face twitch
like flashes of lightning: Goliath's toy arms struck out at
the diminutive David, but ducking skilfully, he bobbed up
again in all sorts of places, sometimes even in one of the
folds of the giant's cloak. At last he launched the stone
at Goliath's head. The giant sank to the ground, and the
curtain fell.

I was still laughing heartily at Belcampo's strange talent
when someone tapped me lightly on the shoulder. An
abbot was standing beside me.

"I am glad to see, Brother," he remarked, "that you have not lost your delight in the pleasures of earth, for having witnessed your remarkable acts of penance, I would scarcely have thought it possible that you could laugh at such clowning."

His words made me feel that I ought to be ashamed of my merriment, and almost instinctively I replied:

"You may believe me, Brother, when I say that a man who has once swum with the tide of life will never lack the strength to pull away from the current and set his own bold course."

The moment I said this, I regretted it. Fixing his glittering eyes on me, the abbott said:

"A most striking metaphor. Now, I believe, I understand you completely, and I admire you from the bottom of my heart."

"But how, Sir, can a poor penitent monk arouse your admiration?"

"Excellent, reverend Sir! You are resuming your former rôle. Are you a favourite of the Pope?"

"The Regent of the Almighty has been gracious enough to give me audience, and I revere him in a manner befitting his dignity."

"And as his worthy servant, you will do your duty. But the present Regent, believe me, is a paragon of virtue compared with Alexander the Sixth, and you may have miscalculated. However, go on playing your rôle—what starts happily is soon played out. Farewell, reverend Sir.

Laughing mockingly, he left me, and I stood there, rooted to the spot. If I took his last words in conjunction with my own remarks about the Pope, I would have to realise that this dignitary was far from being the conqueror of the flesh which I had taken him to be; I would also face the terrible knowledge that to those aware of the true situation, if not

19

to others also, my penance must have appeared as a hypocritical endeavour to obtain a position of importance for
myself. I returned sorrowfully to my monastery and prayed
fervently in the deserted chapel. Then the scales fell from
my eyes, and I saw that it had been both an attempt by
the power of darkness to lead me again into temptation,
and at the same time a punishment ordained by Heaven.
My only salvation lay in flight, and I resolved to set out
next day at dawn.

Darkness had almost fallen when the house-bell rang
loudly. A moment later the porter entered my cell and
announced that an oddly-dressed man was urgently asking
to speak to me. I went to the parlour, and there was
Belcampo. Capering towards me, he gripped both my arms
and drew me swiftly into a corner.

"Medardus," he said hurriedly, in a low voice, "whatever
means you adopt to bring about your ruin, folly will pursue
you on the wings of the west wind, or the south wind,
or the south-west wind, or some other wind, and pluck you
from the abyss, even if there is only a corner of your robe
sticking out. Oh, Medardus, feel what friendship is, feel
what love can do, believe in David and Jonathan, dearest
Capuchin!"

"I admired your performance as Goliath," I interrupted,
"but tell me your business quickly. What brings you here?"

"What brings me?" said Belcampo. "Mad love for a
Capuchin monk to whose hair I once attended, who cast
golden ducats about him, who associated with horrid
spectres, who, having committed a modest murder, intended
to marry the loveliest girl in the world in noble, or rather,
ignoble fashion."

"Stop, you horrible clown!" I cried. "I have paid
dearly for the things with which you wantonly reproach
me."

"So the spot is still sensitive, Sir, where the enemy

inflicted his deep wounds?" he went on. "Well, well; in that case I will be kind and gentle, like a good child. I will control myself and no longer leap about, either physically or intellectually. I will merely tell you, beloved Capuchin, that my fond affection for you is largely the result of your sublime pranks. Since it is of great benefit that this mad principle should continue to live and flourish on earth as long as possible, I have rescued you from every mortal danger into which your temerity has led you. While I was playing Goliath I overheard a conversation that concerns you. The Pope intends to make you prior of the Capuchin monastery here and to choose you as his confessor. Flee from Rome, for there are daggers lying in wait for you; I know the assassin who has been hired to dispatch you to the next world. You are a thorn in the flesh of the Dominican, the Pope's present confessor, and his associates. You must leave at once."

I was so thunderstruck at this news that I scarcely noticed that Belcampo, embracing me again and again, and making his usual weird grimaces and leaps, had at last taken his departure.

It must have been past midnight when I heard the outer gate of the monastery open and a carriage rumble across the cobbles. After a while I heard footsteps in the passage, and there was a knock at the door of my cell. I opened it, and the Father Guardian entered, followed by a heavily-masked man carrying a torch.

"Brother Medardus," said the Father Guardian, "a man lying in the throes of death has expressed the wish to receive at your hands the last sacraments and words of comfort. Act according to your office and follow this man, who will take you where you are needed."

A cold shiver ran through me at the thought that I was to be taken into the presence of death, but I could not

refuse, and followed the masked man. Opening the door
of the carriage, he made me get in. Inside I found two
men, who made room for me between them. I asked where
I was being taken and who it was who desired to receive
the last sacrament from me, but there was no reply. The
carriage rolled on through the streets, and by the sound of
the wheels I would have guessed that we were already outside the city, but soon I heard it drive through a gate and
then down cobbled streets again. At last it stopped. My
hands were quickly tied together and a thick hood was put
over my face.

"No harm will come to you," said a rough voice, "but
you must remain silent about everything you see and hear,
or you will instantly be put to death."

I was lifted out of the carriage. There was a rattling of
locks, and a gate creaked open on its ponderous, unwieldy
hinges. I was led through long corridors and finally down
flights of stairs, deeper and deeper. The echo of our footsteps told me that we were now in the vaults; their purpose
was betrayed by the overbearing stench of corpses. At last
we stopped. My hands were released and the hood removed
from my head. I was in a spacious vault dimly lit by a lamp
hanging from the ceiling. At my side stood a figure in a
black mask—presumably the same man who had brought
me here—and all around the room Dominican friars were
sitting on low benches. The gruesome dream that I had
had in the dungeon came to my mind; I was convinced
that I was going to die a terrible death, yet I remained
calm and prayed fervently, not for deliverance, but for a
blissful end.

There was an ominous silence for a few moments. Then
one of the friars approached me and said in a toneless
voice:

"We have passed judgment on a monk of your order,
Medardus, and the sentence is now to be carried out. From

you, a holy man, he is awaiting absolution from his sins. Do according to your office."

The masked man took me by the arm and led me on through a narrow passage into a small vault. Lying on a palliasse in the corner was a pale, wasted skeleton of a man clothed in rags. The masked man put down his lamp on a stone table in the middle of the room and went out. I moved nearer to the prisoner. With a great effort he turned his head towards me. I stood petrified: for I recognised the features of the venerable Brother Cyrillus. A smile of divine contentment crossed his face.

"So the servants of Hell who live here did not deceive me," he said in a lifeless voice. "From them I learned that you, my dear Brother Medardus, were in Rome, and as I so greatly longed to see you again because I had done you such a grave injustice, they promised to bring you to me in my hour of death. That hour is now come, and they have kept their word."

I knelt at the side of the pious old man and implored him to tell me how he had come to be imprisoned and condemned to death.

"My dear Brother Medardus," said Cyrillus, "not until I have confessed with a contrite heart how sinfully my error led me to treat you, and not until you have reconciled me with God, can I tell you of my misery, my earthly downfall. You know that I, and with me our whole monastery, took you for a wicked sinner; you had, as we believed, brought infamous crimes upon your head, and we expelled you from our community. Yet it was but a single fateful moment when the Devil threw the noose round your neck and dragged you from that hallowed place into the iniquitous life of the world. Feigning your name, your dress, your person, a diabolical imposter perpetrated those outrages which almost brought upon you the shameful death of a murderer. The Lord miraculously revealed that although you had wickedly transgressed by intending to break your vow, you were innocent of those terrible deeds. Return to our monastery. Leonardus and the brethren will receive you with joy and affection—you whom they believed lost. Oh, Medardus . . ."

Overcome by weakness he fell into a deep swoon. I fought against the agitation aroused in me by his words, which seemed to presage some new miracle, and thought only of him and the salvation of his soul. Having no other resources, I sought to bring him back to life by slowly stroking his head and breast with my right hand, in the manner customary in monasteries for rousing the sick from unconsciousness. He recovered, and made his confession— he, the pious soul, to me, the sinner. But as I absolved him from his transgressions, the most serious of which consisted merely of doubts which had entered his mind from time to time, I felt as if the spirit of Heaven were being kindled within me and as if I were the unworthy instrument through which the Almighty spoke in human terms to the human being not yet freed from his earthly shackles. Lifting his gaze to Heaven, Cyrillus said:

"O Brother Medardus, how your words have refreshed me! I shall now advance cheerfully to meet the doom that these cursed villains have prepared for me. I shall die a victim of the evil and treachery which surrounds the throne of him who wears the triple crown."

I heard dull footsteps approaching. Keys rattled in the lock of the door. Forcing himself together, Cyrillus gripped my hand and whispered in my ear:

"Return to our monastery. Leonardus has been informed of everything, and knows how I shall die. Enjoin him to keep silent about my death; weary old man that I am, death would have soon overtaken me in any case. Farewell, my Brother. Pray for the salvation of my soul. I shall be with you and the brethren when you sing my requiem in the

monastery. Promise me that you will say nothing about
what you have seen and heard, for you will only bring
about your own destruction and involve our monastery
in endless disputes."

I did as he wished. Masked men entered and lifted him
from his bed. He was too exhausted to walk, and they
dragged him along the passage to the vault in which I had
been before. They beckoned to me, and I followed them.
The Dominican friars gathered in a closed circle round the
old man; he was made to kneel down on a little heap of
earth that had been set in the centre of the circle, and a
crucifix was put into his hands. I, too, joined the circle,
since I considered it my duty to do so, and prayed aloud.
One of the Dominicans took me by the arm and drew me
aside. At that moment I caught sight of a masked man who
had entered the circle from behind. A sword flashed in his
hand, and Cyrillus' blood-stained head came to rest at my
feet. I swooned.

When I regained consciousness, I was in a small, cell-like
chamber. A Dominican came up to me and said with a
spiteful grin:

"You looked extremely scared, Brother, yet you ought
really to have been delighted, for you have witnessed an
excellent martyrdom with your own eyes. I presume that
that is what we must call it when a brother from your
monastery meets his well-merited end, since you are one
and all supposed to be saints."

"We are not saints," I said, "but an innocent person
has never yet been murdered in our monastery. Release
me; I have gladly carried out my duty. The spirit of this
transfigured soul will be near me if I fall into the hands of
evil murderers."

"I have not the slightest doubt," returned the Dominican,
"that the late Brother Cyrillus will be able to assist you in
such a contingency, but pray do not call his execution a

murder, dear Brother. Cyrillus had sinned gravely against the Regent of the Almighty, and it was he who ordered his death. But he must have confessed everything to you, so it is pointless to discuss the matter. Drink this instead, to fortify your nerves; you look pale and distraught."

He handed me a crystal goblet in which sparkled a crimson wine with a powerful aroma. I cannot describe the feeling that shot through me as I lifted the goblet to my lips, but there was no doubt that it was the same wine that Euphemia had poured out for me on that terrible night. Instinctively, with no clear thought as to what I was doing, I poured the wine into the left sleeve of my habit, holding my hand in front of my eyes as if dazzled by the lamp.

"May it bring you health!" cried the Dominican, pushing me quickly out of the door. I was thrust into the carriage, which to my surprise I found empty, and driven away.

The shocks of the night, the mental strain, my profound grief at the fate of the unhappy Cyrillus—everything combined to produce in me a state of numbness, so that I allowed myself to be pulled out of the carriage without resisting and deposited with no great gentleness on the ground.

Dawn broke, and I found myself lying outside the monastery gate. Getting to my feet, I pulled the bell. The gatekeeper was frightened by my pale, haggard appearance and must have reported to the prior the state in which I had returned, for immediately after matins the latter came into my cell, a look of concern on his face. To his questions I only replied vaguely that the death of the man whom I had been called to absolve had been too gruesome not to leave its mark upon me. But soon the raging pain in my left arm became so fierce that I could not go on talking, and I cried out in anguish. The doctor came. He tore away the sleeve which was clinging to my skin, and found the whole arm mangled and eaten away.

"They gave me wine to drink but I poured it into my sleeve," I groaned, weak with the agony.

"There was corrosive poison in it!" said the doctor, hastening to apply palliatives, which eased the pain after a while. Through the doctor's skill and the prior's care and attention it was possible to save my arm, which they had first feared would have to be amputated, but the skin was shrivelled to the bone, and all its power of movement had gone.

"Now I understand all too clearly the significance of that event which has deprived you of your arm," said the prior. "Brother Cyrillus disappeared mysteriously from our monastery and from Rome, and you too, Brother Medardus, will vanish in the same way if you do not leave the city at once. There were various suspicious enquiries about you while you were sick, and it was only due to my watchfulness and the unity of the pious brethren here that the murderers did not pursue you right into your cell. You certainly appear to be a remarkable man, followed everywhere by a strange fate. Unwittingly you have aroused far too much attention during your short stay in Rome for certain persons not to wish you out of the way. Return to your own monastery. Peace be with you."

I realised that my life was in constant peril as long as I stayed in Rome, but to the torturing memory of my misdeeds, which the strictest penance had not been able to erase, was now added the physical torment of my withered arm, and I set little store by a pain-stricken existence whose wearisome yoke could be lifted from my shoulders by a swift death. I accustomed myself more and more to the thought of a violent death, even coming to see in it a glorious martyrdom earned by the strictness of my atonement. I pictured myself walking out of the monastery gate; a dark figure emerged from the shadows and stabbed me with a dagger. Crowds collected round the blood-stained body. 'Medardus, the devout, penitent Medardus has been assassinated!'—so the shouts rang through the streets, while the people thronged closer and closer, uttering cries of lamentation; women knelt to bandage with white cloths the wound from which the blood was pouring. One of them caught sight of the cross on my neck and cried: 'He is a martyr, a saint! Behold the mark of the Lord which he bears upon his neck!' They all fell on their knees. Happy the man who can touch the saint's body, or even his robe! A bier is brought, the body laid upon it, wreathed in flowers, and amidst loud chanting and praying the youths bear it in triumphal procession to Saint Peter's!

Thus I conceived in my imagination a vivid picture of my glorification here on earth, without suspecting that the spirit of sinful pride was seeking afresh to entice me.

At last my strong constitution enabled me to bear the terrible pain and resist the effect of the deadly potion. The doctor predicted my early recovery, and only in the moments of delirium which I suffered before falling asleep did I experience feverish attacks, which made me break out in a cold sweat. It was at times such as these that I was obsessed with the vision of my martyrdom, and imagined myself stabbed to the heart. Yet instead of seeing myself lying prostrate in the Piazza di Spagna, surrounded by a crowd of people who saw me as a saint, I was lying alone in the garden of the monastery at B. Instead of blood, a repulsive, colourless fluid poured from the gaping wound, and a voice said: 'Is that the blood of a martyr? Let me purify this foul water and colour it, so that the fire which has conquered light may crown the hero!' It was I who spoke these words, but with the feeling that I had parted company with my dead self came the realisation that I was the disembodied spirit of my personality, appearing as a red glow in the sky. I soared upwards to the glittering mountain-peaks and sought to enter my castle-home, but lightning rent the vault of heaven, and I fell back. 'It is I,' said my Spirit, 'who colour your flowers, your blood. Flowers and blood are the jewels which I am preparing for your wedding.' As I fell, I caught sight of the body, foul water flowing from the wound in its breast. My breath tried to change the water into blood but it could not; the body arose, fixed me with its terrible hollow eyes and screamed: 'Blind, foolish Spirit! There is no conflict between light and fire, for light is the ordeal by fire and will be accomplished through the blood which you are seeking to poison!' The body fell back. All the flowers in that place hung their withered heads—men threw themselves on to the ground, their faces like pale ghosts—a mighty lament arose: 'O Lord, is the burden of our sins so heavy that thou grantest our adversary power to destroy our sacrifice?' Louder and louder grew the sounds of lamentation, like the roaring waves of the sea; the Spirit was about to splinter into a thousand pieces—and I was torn from my dream as though by a thunderbolt. The monastery clock was striking twelve, and a dazzling light was shining into my cell from the chapel-windows. I heard a voice within me: 'The dead have risen from their graves and are worshipping the Lord.' I began to pray.

There was a tap at the door, and I assumed that one of the monks had come to see me. But a moment later I was horrified to hear the fearful laughing and tittering of my ghostly double:

"Little Brother . . . Little Brother . . . I am back again . . . The wound is bleeding . . . bleeding . . . red . . . red . . . Come with me, little Brother Medardus . . . come with me!"

I tried to jump up from my bed but fear had paralysed my limbs, and any movement I tried to make sent a searing pain through my muscles. Only the Spirit remained, praying that I might be delivered from the powers of Hell.

And as I heard my prayer subdue the knocking and the laughing of my terrible double, there arose a strange humming sound, as if swarms of poisonous insects had been stirred by the south wind and were attacking the flowering grain; the humming turned into the lamentation of the crowd, and my soul knew that this was the prophetic dream which was to soothe and heal my bleeding wound.

At that moment the glow of the evening sun broke through the dark mists, revealing the figure of Christ. A single drop of blood glistened in each of his wounds. The grace of the Lord was restored to the earth, and the mourning of the people was turned into a paean of joy. But the colourless blood continued to flow from Medardus' wound, and he prayed fervently: 'Am I to be the only man on earth to suffer the torments of eternal damnation?' The bushes parted, and a rose appeared, turning on Medardus a soft, angelic smile and surrounding him with the delicate scent of spring breezes. 'It is not the fire that has conquered, for there is no conflict between light and fire. Fire is the Word, which transfigures the sinful.' These words seemed to come from the rose itself—and the rose now bore the gentle countenance of a woman. Shrouded in a white robe, roses twined in her dark hair, she moved towards me.

"Aurelia!" I screamed, waking from my dream. The scent of roses filled the cell and I seemed to see her before me, looking gravely into my eyes. Then her features vanished into the rays of morning light which were shining through the window.

Now I knew the temptation of the Devil and my own sinful weakness, and hurrying down to the chapel, I prayed devoutly at the altar of Saint Rosalia. No chastisement, no penance in the manner proper to monastic ritual. And by the time the midday sun stood high in the heavens, I was already several hours' journey away from Rome. Not only Cyrillus' exhortation but also an irresistible longing to see my own country again drove me back along the same path which I had followed to Rome. In my desire to escape from my calling I had unconsciously taken the most direct road to the goal set before me by Prior Leonardus.

I avoided the town in which the Prince's court lay, not because I was afraid of being recognised and handed over to the authorities again, but because not without evoking painful memories could I have appeared again in the place where I had betrayed my religious calling and made bold to seek after worldly pleasures. Even stronger was the fear that, despite the new strength that had entered me through my prolonged penance and my reformed life, I would be powerless to overcome that sinister power whose attacks I had so often suffered. Could I bear to see Aurelia again in all her charm and beauty without surrendering to the spirit of evil? Often I saw her before my eyes, but when feelings stirred within me which I knew to be sinful, I crushed them with the entire force of my will. I saw the reality of my atonement in my consciousness of the contrition which bade me evade these attacks, and in the reassuring conviction that at least the diabolical spirit of pride, the presumptuousness which had led me to vie with the powers of darkness, had departed.

Soon I was in the mountains. One morning a palace loomed out of the mist in the valley below. As I came nearer to it, I knew that I was on the estate of Baron F., but the grounds were completely neglected, the avenues overgrown and covered with weeds. Cows were grazing in the long grass on what used to be the beautiful lawn; many of the windows were broken, and the drive leading to the front entrance had gone to rack and ruin. There was not a soul to be seen. In eerie solitude I stood there, speechless. A faint groan came from a shrubbery which was still in tolerable condition, and I perceived a white-haired old man sitting there who, though I was near enough to him, did not appear to have seen me. As I went nearer I heard him say:

"Dead—those whom I loved are all dead! Oh, Aurelia, you too, the last of them all, are dead to this world!"

I recognised old Reinhold, and stood rooted to the spot.

"Aurelia dead? No, no, you are wrong, old friend. The Almighty saved her from the murderer's knife!"

Reinhold gave a start and cried:

"Who's there? Who's there? Leopold! Leopold!"

A boy ran up. When he saw me he bowed deeply and said:

"Laudetur Jesus Christus!"

"In omnia saecula saeculorum," I responded.

The old man rose to his feet and cried in agitation:

"Who's there? Who's there?"

I now saw that he was blind.

"A priest is here," said the boy, "a brother of the Capuchin order."

The old man seemed terror-stricken and screamed:

"Take me away, boy, take me away! Into the house and lock the doors! Tell Peter to keep guard—away, away!"

Summoning his remaining strength he made to flee from me as from a beast of prey. The boy stared at me, awestruck, but the old man, instead of allowing himself to be led, pulled him away, and soon they disappeared through the door, which I heard being bolted behind them.

Hastily I left the scene of my most evil crimes, which this incident had brought back to me more vividly than ever. Soon I found myself surrounded by thick bushes, and I sat down wearily on a mossy bank at the foot of a tree; not far away was a small mound on which stood a cross.

When I awoke from the sleep of utter exhaustion into which I had fallen, an old peasant was sitting beside me. As soon as he saw that I was awake, he doffed his cap courteously and said in a good-humoured tone:

"You must have come a long way, reverend Sir, and been extremely tired, for otherwise you would never have fallen into such a deep sleep at this fearful spot. But maybe you do not know the circumstances relating to this place?"

I answered that, as a foreign pilgrim who had stopped here on his way from Rome, I had not the slightest idea what had happened.

"You and the brethren of your order are closely implicated in it," said the peasant, "and I must admit that when I saw you sleeping so peacefully, I sat down here in order to protect you from any possible danger.

"Several years ago a Capuchin monk was said to have been murdered here; it is at least certain that at that time a Capuchin was passing through our village, and having spent the night there, wandered off into the mountains. The same day my neighbour was walking along the valley path at the bottom of the Devil's Gorge, when suddenly he heard in the distance a scream which echoed strangely down the valley. He even claims to have seen a figure hurtle from the mountain peak into the abyss, but this strikes me as very unlikely. At any rate, all of us in the village, without knowing why, thought that the Capuchin might have fallen over the precipice, and several of us climbed down, as far as was possible without risking our lives, in order at least to recover the body of the unfortunate man. However, we could not find anything, and laughed heartily at our neighbour when he declared that, as he was returning home along the valley path one moonlit night, he had seen to his horror a naked man climb out of the Devil's Gorge.

"All this was pure imagination, but we learned later that, for some unknown reason, the Capuchin had been murdered here by a nobleman and his body flung into the valley. I am convinced that the murder was committed at this very

spot. Listen, reverend Sir. Once I was sitting here, deep
in thought, when my gaze lighted on that hollow tree beside
you. Suddenly I imagined I saw a piece of dark-brown
cloth hanging out of a crack. Jumping up, I went over to
the tree and pulled out a brand-new Capuchin habit; there
was blood on one of the sleeves, and the name Medardus
was sewn into a corner. Poor as I am, I thought I would
be performing a service if I were to sell the habit and, with
the money I obtained, have masses read for the poor priest
who had been murdered without being able to prepare
himself for death.

"So I took the habit to the town, but no dealer would
buy it, nor was there a Capuchin monastery nearby to
which I could take it. At last a man came along, a gamekeeper or a forester, to judge from his clothes—who said
that he needed just such a habit, and paid me handsomely
for it. I had the priest read a mass, and since it was
impossible to put up a cross in the Devil's Gorge, I erected
one here as a memorial to the friar's ignominious death.
But the late lamented gentleman must have considerably
overstepped his proper bounds, for his ghost is still said to
haunt the countryside. So the mass could not have done
much good. I beseech you, reverend Sir, to read a mass
for the soul of your fellow-brother Medardus. Give me
your promise."

"You are mistaken, my good friend," I said; "Brother
Medardus, who passed through your village some years ago
on his way to Italy, was not murdered. He does not need
to have masses read for his soul, for he is alive, and can
still work for his own salvation. I myself am that Medardus!"

As I said this, I opened my habit and showed him the
name Medardus embroidered in the corner. Immediately
he saw the name, he blenched, and stared at me, horror-
stricken. Then he jumped up and rushed off into the forest,
screaming at the top of his voice. He evidently took me to

be the ghost of the murdered Medardus, and it would have been pointless to try and convince him of his delusion.

The remoteness and silence of this spot, broken only by the dull roar of the nearby mountain torrent, could not but arouse a feeling of eerieness, and the thought of my hideous double came back to me. Stricken with the same terror that had seized the peasant, I felt myself tremble, as though the spectre were about to step out of the bushes. Pulling myself together, I walked on, and only when this fearful thought had passed did it occur to me that I had now learnt how the mad monk had come into possession of the habit which he had discarded during his flight, and which I recognised beyond all doubt as my own: the gamekeeper at whose house he had stayed and whom he had asked to procure a new habit, had bought it from the peasant in the town. I was deeply disturbed by the way in which that terrible incident at the Devil's Gorge had been perversely misconstrued, for I realised that all the circumstances pointed towards a tragic confusion between Victor and myself. The experience which the peasant's frightened neighbour had had, seemed to me to be very important, and I confidently anticipated some clearer explanation, without having any idea as to when or how it would be forthcoming.

At last, after many weeks of ceaseless wandering, I arrived home. My heart beat faster as I saw the towers of the Cistercian convent rise up before me. I entered the village, and came to the open square in front of the convent chapel. From afar came the sound of men's voices chanting a hymn; a cross appeared, and behind it a procession of monks, walking two by two. I recognised my fellow-brethren! At their head walked old Leonardus, led by a young brother whom I did not know. Without noticing me, they filed through the open gate and into the convent. Soon the Dominicans and Franciscans from B . . . also arrived in procession, and closed coaches drove into the courtyard

20

bringing the nuns of the Order of Saint Clare.

It was evident that some special event was being celebrated. I entered the open chapel, and found everything
being swept and cleaned with great thoroughness. The high
altar and side altars were being hung with garlands, and one
of the vergers talked a great deal about the fresh roses that
had to be brought early next morning, because the abbess
had expressly ordered the high altar to be decorated with
roses.

I was now resolved to join the brethren, and after I had
fortified my spirit with fervent prayer I went into the
convent and asked to see the prior. I was led into a chamber
where Leonardus was sitting, surrounded by the brethren.
Tears choked my words, and I fell at his feet, overwhelmed
with grief and repentance.

"Medardus!" he cried. A murmur ran through the
assembled brethren:

"Brother Medardus has returned to us at last!"

They lifted me up and embraced me, exclaiming:

"Praised be the powers of Heaven for having rescued you
from the evil clutches of the world! But tell us what
happened, Brother!"

The prior rose, and beckoned me to follow him into the
chamber which he occupied whenever he visited the
convent.

"Medardus," he began, "you have wantonly broken your
vow. By shamefully running away instead of fulfilling your
commission, you have most basely betrayed our monastery.
If I were to follow the strict monastic law, I would imprison
you for life."

"Pass judgment on me as the law demands, reverend
Father," I answered. "I would be happy to cast off the
burden of this cruel cheerless life, for I know that not even
the severity of the penance to which I subjected myself
could afford me consolation here on earth."

"Have courage," said Leonardus." I have spoken to you as your prior; let me now speak to you as a father and friend. By a miracle you were saved from the death that threatened you in Rome, but Cyrillus was sacrificed—"

"So you know?" I cried in astonishment.

"Everything," he replied. "I know that you were at his side in his last moments and that they intended to poison you with the wine. Despite their watchfulness you must have found an opportunity to pour it all away, for had you drunk even a single drop you would have been dead within ten minutes."

"But look at this!" I cried. I lifted the sleeve of my habit and showed him my arm eaten away to the bone, telling him how I had suspected their evil intent and had poured the wine into my sleeve. He recoiled at the terrible sight and murmured:

"You have indeed atoned for your transgressions. But as for good Cyrillus . . ."

I told the prior that I was still unaware of the real reason for poor Cyrillus' secret execution. He said:

"Maybe you would have suffered that fate too if, like Cyrillus, you had declared yourself to be an envoy of our monastery. As you know, this monastery has a right to certain revenues which Cardinal X. illegally appropriated. The Cardinal unexpectedly struck up a friendship with the Pope's confessor, to whom he had previously been ill-disposed, in order to gain in the person of the Dominican a powerful ally to pit against Cyrillus. This cunning monk soon discovered how Cyrillus' downfall could be brought about. He took him to see the Pope, and gave such a glowing account of his character that the Pope came to regard him as an exceptional person and received him into the priests of his entourage.

"It was not long before Cyrillus realised that the kingdom of the Regent of the Almighty was all too much of this world, whose pleasures he sought and found; and that he was the tool of a clique of hypocrites who, despite his strength of will, bent him to their purpose by the most wicked means and tossed him to and fro between Heaven and Hell. The pious Cyrillus, as one might expect, was highly incensed at this and felt called upon to pierce the Pope's conscience with his burning words, that he might turn his thoughts from the things of earth. The Pope was greatly moved by Cyrillus' eloquence, and the Dominican skilfully exploited this so as to lead up to the final blow that would destroy Cyrillus. He even told the Pope that there was a conspiracy afoot to represent him in the eyes of the Church as unworthy of the triple crown, and that it was the business of Cyrillus to induce him to undertake some public penance, which would serve as the signal for the revolt that was being hatched by the cardinals. The Pope was now easily able to detect the ulterior motive behind our brother's exhortations, and began to hate him, although he still tolerated his company in order to avoid any untoward suspicion. The next time Cyrillus found an opportunity to speak to the Pope alone, he said outright that a man who had not completely renounced the pleasures of the flesh and was not leading a true, holy life, was unfit to be the servant of the Lord, and that he was a source of ignominy and shame to the Church, which would have to take steps to remove him from her midst.

"A few days later, and just at a time when Cyrillus had been seen coming out of the Pope's inner chamber, it was found that the iced water which the Pope used to drink was poisoned. You do not need me to assure you that Cyrillus was innocent, for you know him. But the Pope was convinced of his guilt and commanded that he be secretly executed by the Dominicans.

"You had attracted great attention in Rome. By the way in which you had expressed your opinions to him, and particularly by the story of your life, the Pope felt that there was some kind of spiritual bond between himself and you. With your aid he thought to rise to a position from which he could fortify himself with infamous sophistries about religion and virtue, so as, if I may put it so, to plunge the more readily into sin. Your devotions appeared to him just calculated hypocrisy—a means to your ulterior end. He admired you and basked in your praises. Thus before the Dominican suspected anything, your star rose in the firmament, and you became more dangerous to this faction than Cyrillus could have ever been.

"As you observe, Medardus, I am fully cognisant of your activities in Rome and know every single word that you spoke to the Pope. There is nothing mysterious in this, for there is a friend of our monastery always near his Holiness, and he has told me everything. Even when you thought you were alone with the Pope, he was at hand to listen.

When you undertook your severe acts of penance in the Capuchin monastery—whose prior is a close relative of mine—I believed your repentance to be sincere. It may well have been so, but in Rome the evil spirit of pride, to which you had already succumbed when you were here with us, took hold of you again. Why did you accuse yourself before the Pope of crimes which you had never committed? Were you ever at Baron F.'s palace?"

"O reverend father," I cried in anguish, "that was the scene of my most shameful deed. Heaven has decreed that as long as I live I shall never be cleansed from this sin. Am I but a wicked hypocrite to you, too, reverend father?"

"As I see and speak to you now," said the prior, "I am indeed almost persuaded that, after your acts of penance, you were no longer capable of lying, but at the same time I am perplexed by a mystery which I still cannot solve.

"Soon after your flight from the Prince's court—Heaven

would not endure the crime you were about to commit, and spared the pious Aurelia—soon after your flight, as I say, and after the monk had miraculously escaped whom even Cyrillus had taken to be you, it became known that it was not you but Count Victor, disguised as a Capuchin, who had been in the Baron's palace. Certain letters of Euphemia's had already indicated this, but it was assumed that she, too, had been deceived, since Reinhold maintained that he knew you far too well to be mistaken, however close the similarity. It remained incomprehensible how Euphemia could have been misled.

"Then, to our surprise, the Count's groom came forward and told how his master, who for months had been living as a hermit in the mountains, had suddenly confronted him near the so-called Devil's Gorge, disguised as a Capuchin. Although he did not know how the Count had come by the habit, he had been in no way surprised at this disguise, since he had known of the Count's plan to enter the palace in a monk's habit, wear it for a year, and thereby, presumably, carry out certain secret plans. He had his suspicions as to how the Count had obtained the habit, for his master had said the previous day that he had seen a Capuchin friar in the village, and hoped to get hold of his robe by hook or by crook. He, the groom, had not seen the monk, but he had heard him scream, and shortly afterwards there had been talk in the village of a Capuchin who had been murdered. He had known his master too well and spoken to him too often during his flight from the palace for there to be any possibility of a mistake.

"The groom's account weakened Reinhold's case, and the only mystery that remained was Victor's complete disappearance. The Princess put forward the idea that the man who had called himself Herr von Crczynski from Cviecziczevo might in fact have been Count Victor. She based her opinion on his striking resemblance to Francesco

—whose guilt nobody doubted any longer—and on the emotions aroused in her whenever she set eyes on him. Many others supported her, and claimed that they had always detected a marked nobility of bearing in this adventurer who had been ridiculously mistaken for a monk in disguise. The gamekeeper's story about the mad monk who had been living in the woods and eventually been received into his house, could now be brought into line with Victor's crime, provided certain particulars were accepted as true. A friar from Medardus' monastery had definitely recognised the delirious monk as Medardus; Victor had hurled him over the precipice, but by some miracle he had survived; after having recovered from his daze, he had managed, despite the deep gash in his head, to crawl out of the gorge, but pain, hunger and thirst drove him out of his mind; in this condition he roamed about in the mountains, perhaps receiving from time to time some scraps of food and a few old rags from peasants who took pity on him, until he came into the vicinity of the old gamekeeper's house. But two points remain unsolved: firstly, how was Medardus able to cover such a distance through the mountains without being stopped; and secondly, how, in moments of what even physicians acknowledged to be the most composed and perfect sanity, could he confess to crimes which he had never committed?

"Those who accepted the plausibility of this theory observed that nothing at all was known of the fate of Medardus after he had escaped from the Devil's Gorge, so that his madness might only have broken out at the time when his pilgrimage led him into the forest; and as concerned his confession of the crimes with which he had been charged, that simply indicated that he had never been fully cured, and that even in moments of apparent sanity he was still mad; the thought that he really had committed these crimes had become an obsession.

"When asked for his views, the judge, by whose wisdom everyone set great store, stated that the man claiming to be Herr von Crczynski was neither a Pole nor a Count, and certainly not Count Victor, though, on the other hand, he was by no means innocent; the monk was still insane and not responsible for his actions, so that the authorities could only keep him in prison as a precautionary measure. It was impossible to tell the Prince of this verdict, for it was he alone, enraged by the evil deeds committed at the Baron's palace, who had set aside the court's proposal that the monk should be held in prison, and had ordered him to be put to death. But just as everything in this short, unhappy life, whether event or action, at first appears so important and then rapidly loses its lustre, so the happenings at the Prince's court, and above all at the palace, which had caused alarm and horror at the time, now sank to the level of cheap gossip.

"The idea that Aurelia's betrothed had been Count Victor recalled memories of the Italian Princess. Those who had not heard the story before, learned it from the others, who now felt no longer compelled to withhold it, and everyone who had seen Medardus found it perfectly natural that his features should be identical with those of Count Victor, since they were sons of the same father. The physician was sure that this was the situation, and said to the Prince: 'Let us rejoice, Sir, that both these unpleasant characters have now gone, and leave the matter there.' The Prince eagerly agreed, for he was well aware that Medardus and his double had led him to make one error after another. 'The affair will remain a mystery,' he said, 'so let us not try to draw aside the veil which some strange fate has mercifully cast over it.' As for Aurelia—"

"O tell me, reverend Father," I interrupted eagerly, "what happened to Aurelia?"

"Brother Medardus," said the prior, smiling gently, "is

that pernicious flame in your heart still not quenched? Does it still flare up at the slightest provocation? Are you still not free from those sinful urges to which you once yielded? And yet you expect me to believe that you have truly repented, that the spirit of deceit has utterly departed from you? No, Medardus—I would only accept the sincerity of your repentance if you had really committed the crimes of which you accuse yourself. Only then could I believe that they had so shattered your mind that, heedless of what I had told you of outward and inward penitence, you had turned, as a shipwrecked sailor grasps at any floating spar, to false, illusory forms of penance; these made you appear, not just to a despised Pope but to every truly pious man, like a cheap trickster. Was your devotion, your exaltation pure whenever your mind turned to Aurelia?"

I cast my eyes down in shame.

"You are honest, Medardus," continued the prior. "Your silence is eloquent. I was convinced beyond doubt that it was you who acted the rôle of a Polish nobleman and wanted to marry Aurelia. I followed your progress closely: a strange fellow who calls himself Pietro Belcampo, the Tonsorial Artist, whom you last saw in Rome, brought me reports. I was sure that you had callously murdered Hermogenes and Euphemia, and was horrified at the thought that you were about to enfold Aurelia in your wicked embrace. I could have brought about your destruction, but far from feeling called to play the part of an avenger, I left you and your fate in the hands of the Almighty. You were miraculously saved, and this convinced me of itself that your earthly downfall had not yet been ordained. Let me now tell you what extraordinary circumstances later led me to believe that it actually was Count Victor who had appeared as a Capuchin in Baron F.'s palace.

"Not long ago Brother Sebastian, the gate-keeper, was

awakened by the sound of sobbing and groaning, as of a man in the throes of death. Dawn had already broken, so he got out of bed and opened the gates. Lying on the ground outside was a man, half-frozen with cold, who managed with great difficulty to mutter that he was Medardus, the monk who had fled from our monastery. Greatly frightened, Sebastian came and told me what had happened, and together with the brethren I went down and brought the exhausted man into the refectory. In spite of his hideously distorted features we thought we recognised him, and several of the brethren were of the opinion that it was only the different clothes that gave him such an unusual appearance. He still had his beard and tonsure, but he was dressed in lay clothes which, though ragged and dirty, still revealed their original elegance. He was wearing silk stockings, and on one of his shoes was a gold buckle; a satin waistcoat, ———"

"——— a chestnut-coloured cloak of fine cloth," I interrupted, "an embroidered shirt, and a plain gold ring on his finger."

"Quite right," replied Leonardus in astonishment. "But how ———"

"They were the clothes I wore on that fateful wedding-day! My double pursued me into the forest and, while I was lying there unconscious, stripped me and dressed me in the habit he was wearing. It was this horrible figure who, pretending to be me, was found by Brother Sebastian at the monastery gate."

I urged the prior to go on with his story, and as he spoke, the truth behind the mysterious events that had happened gradually dawned on me.

"It was not long," he continued, "before the man began to show unmistakable signs of madness, and although, as I have said, his features bore the closest possible resemblance to yours, and although he cried incessantly: 'I am

Medardus, the fugitive; I want to do penance in this monastery!'—everybody soon realised that it was merely an obsession on his part. We dressed him in a Capuchin habit, took him into the chapel and told him to perform the usual devotions, but when he tried to do so we saw at once that he could never have been in a monastery before. Thus I could not escape the thought: what if this were the monk who had escaped from the Prince's palace—what if this were Victor? I knew the story the mad monk had told the gamekeeper, but when I considered all the circumstances—the way the Devil's elixir had been discovered, the vision in the dungeon, in fact, the whole of the monk's sojourn in the monastery—I still suspected that the whole affair might be a psychological freak produced by a diseased mind. The remarkable thing from this point of view is that in his hysteria the monk always screamed that he was a Count and a ruler.

"I decided to hand him over to the mental asylum at St Getreu,* for I hoped that, if it were possible at all to restore him to health, the director of this asylum, a highly-gifted doctor with an extensive knowledge of all mental abnormalities, would be able to do so. But matters were not to reach this point. The third night I was aroused by the bell which, as you know, is tolled whenever my attendance is required in the sick-room. I went in, and was told that the stranger had urgently asked to see me; his delirium appeared to have completely left him, and he probably wanted to make confession, for he was so weak that he was unlikely to last the night.

" 'Forgive me, reverend Sir,' he said, after I had spoken words of consolation to him, 'for having presumed to deceive you. I am not the monk Medardus who fled from your monastery—it is Count Victor that you see before you.

---

*A famous institution near Bamberg which Hoffmann frequently visited (Transl.)

I am a nobleman, and I advise you to remember this, for my wrath might otherwise descend upon you.'

" 'Whether you are a nobleman or not,' I replied, 'makes no difference within these walls, or in your present condition. It would be better for you to turn from the things of earth and humbly await what the Almighty has in store for you.'

"He stared at me with glassy eyes and seemed about to lose consciousness; recovering himself, he said:

" 'I feel that I am about to die. But first I must relieve my heart of its burden. You wield great power over me, for however much you try to disguise yourself, I can see that you are Saint Anthony, and you know best what destruction your elixirs have wrought. I had great plans in my mind when I decided to present myself as a priest, wearing a long beard and a brown habit. But when I searched my heart, it seemed that my secret thoughts were emerging in human shape as horrible forms of my own self. With savage force this second self flung me into the raging torrent at the bottom of the abyss. The Princess lifted me in her arms and washed my wounds, and soon my pain had gone. I had indeed become a monk but my second self proved stronger and drove me to murder not only the Princess who had saved me and whom I dearly loved, but also her brother. I was thrown into the dungeon, but you yourself know, Saint Anthony, how I drank your accursed potion and how you spirited me away. The gamekeeper in the forest treated me badly although he knew of my noble birth; my second self appeared in the house, accused me of all manner of abominable deeds, and, because hitherto we had done everything together, wanted to continue our association. So we stayed together, but shortly after we had escaped, we quarrelled. The puny self of my body preyed more and more on the self of my mind; I threw it to the ground, gave it a savage beating and took its clothes.'

"The unhappy creature had started intelligibly enough but he quickly lost himself in a maze of senseless, hysterical chatter. An hour later, just as the bell was tolling for matins, he gave a harrowing cry and collapsed, apparently dead. I had him taken to the mortuary, and instructed that he be buried in the consecrated ground of our garden. But imagine our amazement and horror when, shortly afterwards, we found that the body we had intended to lay in its coffin had vanished without trace. All inquiries proved in vain, and I had to abandon the hope of ever learning more about the enigmatic sequence of events which linked your fate with that of the Count. Yet when I compared the happenings in the palace with the monk's delirious ramblings, I could hardly doubt that he was Count Victor. As the groom had hinted, Victor had killed a Capuchin who was travelling through the mountains on a pilgrimage, and stolen the friar's habit in order to carry out his plan in the palace. Though he had probably not intended it so, his outrage had ended with the murder of Euphemia and Hermogenes. Perhaps he was already insane, as Reinhold suggested, or maybe he was driven out of his mind by pangs of conscience during his flight. The fact that he had killed the monk and was wearing his habit had brought about this obsession that he himself was a monk, and that his personality had split into two mutually antagonistic parts. If this were so, then only the period between his flight from the palace and his arrival at the gamekeeper's house would still remain obscure; and it is inexplicable how the story of his stay in the monastery and his rescue from the dungeon could have formed in his mind. There can be little doubt that there were external forces at work as well, but it is highly remarkable that this story should be a complete, if somewhat perverted account of your own life. There is, however, still a discrepancy between the time when, according to the gamekeeper, the monk arrived at his house, and the date when Reinhold says that Victor fled from the palace. For if we are to believe the gamekeeper, the mad Victor must have been seen in the forest immediately after his arrival at the palace.

"Stop, reverend Father!" I broke in agitatedly. "May I perish in misery and despair and forfeit all claim to forgiveness, if I do not disclose to you in utter contrition all that happened to me after I left the monastery!"

The prior's astonishment grew and grew as I told him the whole story of my life. When I had finished, he said:

"I cannot but believe you, Brother Medardus, for I heard the note of true repentance in your voice. Victor must have been saved from the abyss into which you hurled him, and it must have been he whom the gamekeeper received into his house. He pursued you as your double and died here in the monastery. He was the mere plaything of that sinister force which intervened in your life, distracting your gaze from your true goal. O Brother Medardus, the Devil walks the earth unceasingly, offering his elixirs to men. Who has not at some time or other delighted in his potions? It is the will of Heaven that man shall know the evil consequences of a moment of folly, that through this knowledge his resistance may be strengthened. For God has ordained that, as the pattern of life in nature is conditioned by the force of poison, so the principle of moral goodness presupposes the test of evil. I can speak to you in this way, Medardus, because I know that you understand me. Go now, and join the brethren."

At that moment the agonising pain of love and yearning shot through me, and I cried:

"Aurelia! Oh, Aurelia!"

The prior rose and said gravely:

"You have doubtless observed that the convent is being decorated for a great celebration. Tomorrow Aurelia is to take the veil and receive the name of Rosalia."

Speechless I stood there before him, rooted to the spot.

"Go and join the brethren!" he cried, almost in anger; and in a daze I went down to the refectory, where I found the monks assembled. Once more they besieged me with questions about my life, but I was unable to speak. All the visions of the past grew dim, and only the image of Aurelia shone before my eyes. Under the pretext of making my devotions I left the brethren and went to the chapel, which stood at the far end of the long garden. I tried to pray, but the slightest sound tore me from my meditation. Thinking I heard voices, I went out of the chapel and saw, not far from me, two nuns walking slowly past, and between them a novice. It was Aurelia. She passed by and was lost to sight behind the bushes. The whole day, the whole night—nothing but the thought of her.

At daybreak the convent bells proclaimed the celebration of Aurelia's investiture, and the brethren gathered in a large chamber. The abbess entered, accompanied by two sisters. I cannot express the feeling that came over me as I saw her again; she had loved my father so dearly, and now, although he had wantonly flaunted the union that would have brought him earthly joy and bliss, she was bestowing on his son the affection that had destroyed her happiness. She had tried to bring me up in virtue and piety, but I had heaped crime upon crime, like my father, frustrating her devout hope of finding consolation for the depravity of the father in the virtuousness of the son. I listened with bowed head as she briefly announced once more to the assembled priests that Aurelia was about to take the veil, exhorting them to pray earnestly for her at the moment she took the vow, lest Satan should torment her with doubts.

"The trials which this maiden has had to undergo," she said, "were severe. The Fiend tried to entice her, employing all his cunning to confound her thoughts so that she would

be unwittingly drawn into sin, and then, when she awoke
from her dream, be plunged into shame and despair. But
the power of the Almighty protected her, and if Satan were
still to attempt to approach her with evil intent, her victory
would be all the more glorious. Pray, my brethren, not that
the bride of Christ shall remain steadfast—for her mind is
already devoted to the things of Heaven—but that no
earthly evil shall disturb this holy service of dedication. For
an uncontrollable fear has entered my heart."

It was clear that the abbess regarded me, and me alone,
as the tempter, and that she related my arrival to Aurelia's
investiture, perhaps even expected me to perpetrate some
outrage.

She did not deign to look at me. Deeply hurt, I felt a
scornful hatred rising inside me, the same feeling that I had
had when I saw the Princess in the palace, and instead of
casting myself at her feet I wanted to confront her boldly
and say:

' Were you always such an exalted person? Have you
never known the pleasures of the flesh? When you saw my
father, did sinful thoughts never enter your mind? Even
when you bore the crook in procession and were adorned
with the infula, did his image not stir physical passions
within you in unguarded moments? What was your feeling,
O haughty woman, when you clasped to your breast the
son of your sinful lover, and uttered his name in such tones
of anguish? Have you never struggled against the powers
of darkness?"

The sudden change in my thoughts, the transformation
of the penitent sinner into the man who, having won his
battle, proudly enters a new life, must have shown itself on
my face, for the brother standing next to me said:

"What is the matter, Medardus? Why are you looking
with such hatred at the saintly abbess?"

I gave a short, contemptuous laugh and replied under my breath:

"Perhaps she is a saintly abbess, for she was always so austere that the affairs of earth never seemed to touch her. But to me she seems like a heathen priestess, preparing to draw her knife and perform the human sacrifice."

I do not know what caused me to say these words, for they were not in my train of thought, but they brought with them a confusion of lurid images which seemed to merge in the distance into a single terrible vision. Was Aurelia to leave the world for ever, to bind herself, as I had done, by a vow which I now saw as nothing but a product of religious mania? As when, in the power of Satan, I had sought by sin and crime to grasp the highest offerings of life, I now planned that Aurelia and I would be united, if only through sharing for a single instant the greatest rapture that life on earth has to give, and then perish as creatures who had surrendered to the powers of Hell—for at that moment the thought of murder shot through my mind. O blind, wicked sinner that I was! I could not see that in the moment I took the abbess' words to be directed at myself, I was exposed to the severest trial of all, and that Satan himself had again taken hold of me, enticing me to commit the most heinous atrocity which I had ever contemplated.

The brother to whom I had spoken gave me a frightened look.

"In the name of Jesus, what are you saying?" he cried.

I looked across towards the abbess, who was preparing to leave the chamber. Her gaze fell on me, and a deathly pallor came into her cheeks. Her body swayed, and the nuns had to support her. I seemed to hear her whisper:

"O all ye saints—my foreboding!"

Soon after Prior Leonardus was summoned to her.

The bells were now ringing again, and mingled with the

21

chimes came the deep tones of the organ and the sound of
the sisters chanting. The prior returned to the chamber.
The brethren of the various orders assembled and moved
in procession to the church, which was almost as crowded
as on Saint Bernard's Day. The high altar was decked with
fragrant roses; on one side stood raised seats for the priests,
and opposite was a platform on which sat the musicians.
The bishop himself conducted the ceremony.

Leonardus called me to sit at his side, and I observed
that he was watching me closely. My slightest movement
attracted his attention, and he made me pray ceaselessly
from my breviary. The nuns of Saint Clare gathered
before the altar in a close group, surrounded by a low rail.

The moment arrived. Leading Aurelia, the Cistercian
nuns appeared from within the convent and passed through
the gate behind the altar. As soon as the congregation saw
her, a whisper spread through the church; the organ ceased,
and the simple, deeply-moving chant of the nuns was heard.
I had still not looked up. Gripped by a terrible fear, I
shuddered convulsively, and my breviary fell to the floor.
I bent down to pick it up, but a sudden dizziness came over
me, and I would have fallen had not Leonardus taken hold
of me.

"What is the matter, Medardus?" he said, softly. "You
appear strangely moved. Resist the evil demon that assails
you."

Summoning all my strength, I looked up and saw Aurelia
kneeling before the altar. Her grace and beauty were more
dazzling than ever. She was wearing the same robe as on
that day we were to have been joined in wedlock, and roses
and myrtle were entwined in her hair. Her cheeks were
flushed, and from her heavenward gaze shone an expression
of pure, celestial joy. How could the moment when I first
set eyes on her, the moment when I saw her again at the
Prince's court, compare with this? My burning passion

raged as never before. 'O God, O all ye Saints, let me not
go mad—save me from this agony! Let me not go mad, for
I shall commit a terrible crime and deliver my soul to
eternal damnation!' Such was my silent prayer, for I knew
that the spirit of evil was gradually gaining hold on me.
I felt as though Aurelia were implicated in the crime which
I alone had committed, as though she must feel her sacred
vow before the altar of the Lord to be nothing but the
solemn oath which would bind her to me and make her
mine. I saw her, not as the bride of Christ, but as the
sinful lover of a monk who had broken faith with God, and
I was consumed with a violent desire to seize her in my
lustful embrace and then send her to her death. More and
more violent became the onslaughts of the evil spirit, and I
was on the point of screaming:

"Stop, blind fools! It is not a pure virgin that you are
making the bride of Heaven, but a monk's lover!"

I fumbled in my habit for my knife, intending to hurl
myself into the midst of the nuns and tear her away from
them.

But she was already beginning to repeat the vow. As
she spoke, a soft, warm glow seemed to break through the
dark, wind-swept clouds, and rays of light shone into my
heart; with every word I gained fresh strength and finally
emerged victorious from the struggle. All menacing
thoughts of sin, all traces of earthly lust had vanished.
Aurelia was the holy bride of Heaven whose prayer had
saved me from everlasting perdition. Her vow was my
salvation, my hope, and a feeling of divine serenity filled
my soul.

Leonardus, whom I did not notice again till now, seemed
to sense my change of heart, and said gently:

"You have overcome the enemy, my son! For this was
the final trial that Heaven had prepared for you."

The vow had been pronounced. While the sisters of

Saint Clare sang an antiphon, Aurelia was to receive her robe. The garlands of myrtle and roses had been taken from her hair, but as one of the nuns was about to cut the flowing tresses, there was a disturbance at the back of the chapel. I saw people being thrust aside and thrown to the ground. The tumult came closer, and suddenly a half-naked man burst savagely through the crowd, knocking down everybody around him with his clenched fists. There was a wild, hysterical look in his eyes, and a tattered Capuchin habit hung over his body. *It was my double.*

I was seized with a sense of impending tragedy, but just as I was on the point of jumping down to confront him, he sprang on to the rail in front of the altar. The nuns fled, screaming; the abbess held Aurelia tightly in her arms.

"Ha, ha!" screeched the madman. "Are you trying to rob me of my Princess? Ha, ha, ha! She is my bride! She is my bride!"

He seized Aurelia. Brandishing a knife aloft in his hand, he plunged it into her breast up to the hilt, and the blood gushed forth.

"Hurrah! Hurrah!" he shouted. "Now she is mine! Now I have won my Princess!"

He leapt down behind the altar, tore through the gate and into the cloisters. The nuns screamed in terror.

"Murder! Murder in the house of the Lord!" cried the people, surging forwards towards the high altar.

"Guard all the doors of the convent so that the assassin cannot escape!" shouted Leonardus.

The crowd rushed out. Those of the monks who were strong enough grabbed the processional banners that were leaning in the corner and pursued the monster through the cloisters.

Everything had happened in the space of a moment. I knelt at Aurelia's side. The nuns had bandaged the wound with white cloths as best they could and were now attending to the abbess, who had fainted. I heard a familiar voice behind me:

"Sancta Rosalia, ora pro nobis!"

All those who were still in the chapel cried out:

"A miracle! A miracle! She is a martyr! Sancta Rosalia, ora pro nobis!"

I looked up. The old painter was standing beside me, grave and gentle, as when he had appeared to me in the dungeon. I felt no earthly sorrow at Aurelia's death, no fear at the painter's sudden appearance, for my soul now knew how the mysterious bonds would be broken which other-worldly forces had joined.

"A miracle! A miracle!" came the cries of the people. "Do you see the old man in the purple cloak? He stepped out of the picture above the altar! We saw it with our own eyes!"

They all fell on their knees, and the confusion of the tumult gave way to the sound of weeping and sobbing and the murmur of prayers being offered. The abbess awoke from her swoon and said, in heartrending tones:

"O Aurelia, my child, my daughter! Almighty God, so hast Thou ordained!"

A litter was brought, with pillows and blankets. As she was lifted on to it Aurelia gave a deep sigh and opened her eyes. The painter, who was standing behind her, laid his hand on her head. His countenance was as of a great saint, and everybody, even the abbess, seemed filled with a sense of awe and wonder.

I was kneeling close to the litter. As Aurelia's gaze fell upon me, a feeling of unbearable grief came over me, and I uttered a dull groan. In a soft voice she said:

"Why do you mourn? The Almighty has deemed me worthy to say farewell to the world in the very instant when I see through the vanity of all earthly pleasure, and when my breast is filled with a longing for the kingdom of joy and felicity."

I rose and stood close by the litter.

"Aurelia, O blessed virgin! Look down on me for one brief moment from your celestial heights and release me from the torment of doubt which besets my soul. Aurelia! Do you despise this sinner who came into your life like Satan himself? Severe was the penance imposed upon me, yet I know that all the penance in the world cannot lessen the enormity of my crimes. Aurelia! Are you reconciled to me in death?"

As if brushed by the wings of an angel, she smiled and closed her eyes. I prayed fervently:

"O Saviour of the world, O Blessed Virgin! I am now alone, condemned to irrevocable despair. O save me from the agonies of Hell!"

Aurelia opened her eyes again and said:

"Medardus, you surrendered to the powers of darkness, but did not I also sin, in that I thought to achieve earthly happiness through my guilty love? It was ordained by God that we should redeem the sins of our forbears, and we were thus united in that love which rules above the stars and has nothing in common with earthly love. Yet the Devil, in his treachery, concealed from us the deeper meaning of our love and tempted us to interpret the Sacred after the manner of the Profane. Was it not I who first declared my love to you in the confessional? Did I not kindle in your mind the deadly flame of lust instead of the sacred thought of eternal love? And did I not cause you to seek to quench this fire in a torrent of sin and crime? Have courage, Medardus! The madman whom the Devil induced to believe that he was you, and that he had to complete what you had begun, was an instrument in the hand of the Lord, that His will might be done. Have courage, Medardus. Soon . . . soon . . ."

She fainted. While she was talking she had closed her eyes, and it was only with difficulty that she managed to speak. But death could not yet claim her.

"Did she make confession to you, reverend Sir?" asked the nuns inquisitively.

"It was not I who comforted her," I answered, "but she who filled my soul with divine consolation."

"Be of good cheer, Medardus, for your hour of trial is almost over, when I, too, shall share your happiness."

It was the painter who uttered these words. I approached him and said:

"Then do not leave me, O wonderful man!"

I wanted to go on speaking, but my senses were dazed, and I fell into a semi-coma from which I was awakened by the sound of shouting. The painter had gone; peasants, citizens of the town and soldiers had forced their way into the chapel, and demanded to be allowed to search the whole convent for the assassin, who must still be somewhere inside. The abbess, rightly fearing that some impropriety might be committed, refused, but despite the dignity of her demeanour she was unable to calm the inflamed passions of the crowd. They accused her of shielding the murderer because he was a monk, and at any moment it seemed as though they would storm the convent. Then Leonardus mounted the pulpit, and after a few outspoken words on the subject of the desecration of holy places, he told the assembled throng that the assassin was not a monk at all but a madman who had been given refuge in the monastery: he had appeared to have died, and had been taken, dressed in the habit of the order, to the mortuary, but he had not been dead at all, and had escaped. Leonardus added that, if the man were still in the convent, the precautions that had already been taken would make it impossible for him to escape. The crowd calmed down, asking only that Aurelia be borne in solemn procession across the courtyard and thence into the convent, instead of being taken simply through the cloisters. Their wish was granted.

With bowed heads the nuns raised the litter, which had been hung with garlands of roses. Aurelia, too, was adorned with roses and myrtle as before. Four nuns bore a canopy above the stretcher, and behind them walked the abbess, supported by two sisters; then came the rest of the nuns with the sisters of Saint Clare, followed by the brethren of the various orders, and finally the people. The procession moved through the chapel. One of the sisters had made her way to the chancel, and as the column reached the centre of the church, the deep, awe-inspiring tones of the organ reverberated through the arches.

But once more Aurelia raised herself slowly, and stretched out her hands to Heaven in prayer. The people fell on their knees, crying:

"Sancta Rosalia, ora pro nobis!"

And so was fulfilled what in my sinful ignorance and wickedness I had defiantly declared when I saw Aurelia for the first time.

As the nuns set the litter down in the lower chamber of the convent, surrounded by sisters and brethren praying fervently, Aurelia gave a deep sigh and fell into the arms of the abbess, who was kneeling beside her. She was dead.

The crowd would not move away from the convent gate, and when the bells proclaimed that she had departed this life, they burst into cries of lamentation. Many vowed to stay in the village until the funeral rites had been performed, and to observe a strict fast during that time.

The news of the terrible murder, and of the martyrdom of the bride of Heaven, quickly spread. Her funeral, which took place four days later, assumed the character of a feast which celebrates the transfiguration of a saint, and, as normally happened only on Saint Bernard's Day, people lay on the green in front of the convent the whole of the preceding day, waiting for the event. But instead of the usual hustle and bustle there came only the sound of

subdued murmurs and sighs of mourning. The story of
the monstrous crime before the altar of the Lord was passed
from mouth to mouth, and the only time a voice was raised
aloud was to utter a curse upon the assassin, who had
vanished without trace.

These four days, which I spent mostly alone in the chapel
in the garden, had a profounder influence on the salvation
of my soul than the whole of my long penance in the
Capuchin monastery near Rome. Aurelia's dying words
had uncovered the secret of my sins, and I realised that
despite the power of virtue and piety with which I had been
endued, I was as a wretched coward when confronted by
Satan, who was intent on fostering my sinful lineage. The
seed of evil had still been small at the time when I saw the
choirmaster's sister and when wanton pride had only just
begun to stir within me, but then Satan had put that
accursed elixir into my hands; I had not heeded the
warnings of the mysterious painter or the prior or the abbess,
and when Aurelia came to me in the confessional, I delivered
myself body and soul into the hands of evil. How, held in
the Devil's mocking clutches, could I have recognised the
bond which the Almighty had forged between us as a
symbol of eternal love? Satan had fettered me to a monster
whose body I was to inhabit with my mind and whose spirit
was to enter my own spirit. His death, which may have
been a mere trick on the part of the Devil, I had to attribute
to myself, and this introduced me to the idea of murder.
Thus the monk, himself a child of sin, became the evil
principle which plunged me into the most abominable
crimes and inflicted on me the most hideous tortures. Up
to the time that Aurelia pronounced the vow, my heart
had not been free from sin and the foe still had power over
me, bringing with it the certain knowledge that her death
was the promise of my salvation.

As the choir sang the words 'confutatis maledictis

flammis acribus addictis' in the solemn requiem, I felt myself tremble, but at 'Voca me cum benedictis' I seemed to see Aurelia standing before me in heavenly brightness. She looked down upon me then turned her head heavenwards, her halo glittering, to pray for my soul's salvation: 'Oro supplex et acclinis cor contritum quasi cinis'.

I sank to the ground, but how different were my innermost feelings, my humble entreaties, from that passion of self-mortification, those cruel, savage acts of penance which I had performed in the Capuchin monastery. Only now was my mind capable of distinguishing the true from the false, and with this knowledge I could repel any new attack by the enemy. It was not Aurelia's death itself but the terrible form that it had taken which had pierced my heart; yet I now knew that through the grace of the Eternal Father she had triumphed in the supreme test.

The martyrdom of the bride of Christ, pure and redeemed. Was she then to be lost to me? Nay, for as she left this vale of sorrows, she had kindled the eternal love that now glowed within me. I now know that her death was the consummation of that love which, as she had told me, rules above the stars and has nothing in common with the things of earth. Such thoughts as these lifted me above my earthly self, and these days in the convent were truly the most blissful of my whole life.

Leonardus intended to return to the town with the brethren after the interment, which took place the following morning, but just as the procession was about to leave, the abbess summoned me to her room. She was in a state of great emotion, and her eyes were filled with tears.

"Now I know everything, Medardus, my son—everything! Yes, I call you again my son, for you have overcome all the trials and temptations that befell you in your misery. O Medardus, only she, she who can intercede for us at the throne of God, is free from sin. Did not I myself stand on the edge of the abyss when, thinking only of the pleasures of the flesh, I was about to surrender my life to a murderer? Medardus, my son, I have wept sinful tears in my lonely cell as I recalled the memory of your father. Go now. The fear that, adding to my own guilt, I had brought you up as the wickedest of all sinners, has now left my soul for ever."

Leonardus, who must have disclosed to the abbess all the facts about my life which she had not before known, showed me by his attitude that he, too, had forgiven me and committed me to the grace of the Lord. The monastery was the same as it had always been, and I took my place among the brethren as before.

One day Leonardus said to me:

"Brother Medardus, I wish to impose on you what will doubtless seem like a new penance."

I asked humbly what it was. He replied:

"You are to write the story of your life. Do not omit a single incident, however trivial, that happened to you, particularly during your chequered career in the world. Your imagination will recapture all the gruesome, ludicrous, horrible, comical aspects of that life; it may even be that you will see Aurelia, not as Rosalia, the martyred nun, but as something else. Yet if the spirit of evil has really departed from you, and if you have turned away from the temptations of the world, you will rise above these things, and no trace of them will remain."

I did as the prior bade me, and it was as he had said. For as I wrote, my heart was rent by grief and ecstasy, fear and joy, horror and delight.

You who come to read these pages will recall how I spoke of the bright noontide of love, when my vision of Aurelia became real. The joys of earth spell the destruction of man, stupid and wanton as he is, but there is something higher than this. When all thoughts of sinful desire have vanished, and when your beloved kindles in your heart the celestial blessings that are shed on man below—*this* is the high noon-tide of love. And it was this knowledge that fortified me when the memory of those glorious moments which the world had given me drew bitter tears from my eyes and opened the wounds that had long been closed. I know that even in death Satan may still have power to torment this wicked sinner, but resolutely, yea, with fervent longing, I await the moment which shall take me from the earth, for it will be the moment when everything is fulfilled which Aurelia—Saint Rosalia herself—vouchsafed when she died.

Pray for me in my hour of death, O Blessed Virgin, lest the powers of Hell, to whom I have so often succumbed, overwhelm me and hurl me into the pit of everlasting damnation.

APPENDIX

by

Father Spiridion
Librarian of the Capuchin Monastery in B...

During the night of the third of September, 17— there were a number of extraordinary happenings in our monastery. Around midnight I heard a strange laughing and cackling, interspersed with hollow groans, coming from the cell next to mine, which was that of Brother Medardus. I seemed to hear a horrible voice saying:

"Come with me, Brother Medardus, and we will go and look for your betrothed."

I got up, and was about to go to Brother Medardus' cell when I was seized with fear and began to tremble feverishly. Instead of going to Medardus' cell I hurried to Prior Leonardus, and having finally succeeded in waking him, told him what I had heard. He was greatly frightened and, jumping up, told me to fetch some candles, and we would then go to Brother Medardus.

I did as he said and lit the candles at the altar of the Virgin Mary in the passage. We ascended the stairs. But however attentively we listened, we could not hear the terrible voice any more. Instead we caught a faint sound of pealing bells, and a scent of roses seemed to fill the air. We went nearer. The door of the cell opened, and a tall, mysterious figure with a thick white beard came out, wearing a purple-coloured cloak. I felt greatly afraid, for I knew that the man must be a ghost, since the monastery gates were locked and no stranger could enter. Leonardus, however, faced him boldly, though without speaking.

"The hour of fulfilment is not far hence," said the figure in a deep, solemn voice, and vanished down the dark passage. My fear became even greater, and I almost allowed the candle to drop from my nerveless hand.

The prior, who in his sanctity and strength of faith set little store by ghosts, took me by the arm and said:

"Let us now go into Brother Medardus' cell."

We did so. He was lying on his bed, dying. Death had sealed his lips, and he could only utter feeble groans. Leonardus stayed by him while I awakened the brethren, pulling the bell with all my might and shouting:

"Wake up, wake up! Brother Medardus is dying!"

They all rose hastily, and lighting their candles, followed me to the cell. A feeling of deep sadness filled our hearts. We carried him on a litter into the chapel and laid him before the high altar. Then to our amazement he gained strength and began to speak, so that after having heard his confession and pronounced the absolution of his sins, Leonardus himself was able to administer extreme unction.

While Leonardus remained below and talked to Brother Medardus, we went into the chancel and sang the customary offices for the soul of our dying brother. The following day, the fifth of September, 17—, as the monastery clock was chiming twelve noon, he passed away in the prior's arms. We noticed that it was the same day and hour as Sister Rosalia had been horribly murdered a year ago, just after she had taken the vow.

There was another strange occurrence during the requiem. A strong scent of roses gradually spread through the church, and we saw that a bouquet of beautiful roses, which were very rare at this time of year, had been attached to the portrait of Saint Rosalia. (This wonderful picture is said to have been painted long ago by a mysterious Italian painter; our monastery had bought it for a considerable sum from the Capuchin monastery near Rome, whilst they had only kept a copy of it). The gatekeeper said that a ragged, poverty-stricken beggar had climbed up without our noticing it and tied the flowers to the portrait.

This beggar appeared during the interment and mingled with the brethren. We wanted to send him away, but Prior Leonardus, having regarded him keenly, bade us allow him to remain. He was received into the monastery as a lay-brother, and we called him Brother Peter, because his name had been Peter Schönfeld. We did not grudge him this proud name, for he was of an exceptionally quiet and kindly disposition. He spoke very rarely, but sometimes he laughed in a quaint way which greatly delighted us. The prior once told us that the irony of fate had turned Peter into a buffoon, and that through his constant buffoonery he had lost his reason. None of us understood what the learned Leonardus meant by this, but we realised that he must have known Brother Peter for a long time.

And so, *ad majorem dei gloriam,* I have now added to these pages, which, I am told, contain the story of Brother Medardus' life (for I have not read them myself), an exact and careful account of the circumstances of his death. May his soul be granted rest and peace. And may God raise him again from the dead and receive him into the company of the blest—for he died a truly pious man.

PRINCIPAL DATES IN THE LIFE OF E. T. A. HOFFMANN

1776   Ernst Theodor Wilhelm Hoffmann born on January 24 in Königsberg.

1792   Matriculation at the University of Königsberg as a student of law.

1795   Entry into the Prussian Civil Service.

1799   *Scherz, List und Rache*, a *Singspiel* on the morality by Goethe.

1800   Appointment to the Law Courts in Posen. During the succeeding six years he also held legal positions in Plozk and Warsaw.

1802   Marriage to nineteen-year-old Michalina Rohrer, daughter of a Polish local government official in Plozk.

1808–13   Kapellmeister and theatrical producer in Bamberg. These years mark the emotional climax of his life—his love for Julia Marc, the thirteen-year-old daughter of a patrician Jewish family in Bamberg, who inspired the heroines of many of his works, among them Aurelia in *Die Elixiere des Teufels*—and the emergence of his characteristic literary gifts. At this time also he changed his third name from Wilhelm to Amadeus in reverence for Mozart.

1813   Bankruptcy of the Bamberg theatre. Appointment as music director to the operatic company of Joseph Seconda in Dresden and Leipzig.
Beethovens Instrumentalmusik (essay).
Der goldene Topf (allegorical tale).

1814   Hoffmann's final break with the life of a professional musician and return to Prussian government service as a deputy judge at the *Kammergericht* in Berlin, a post he retained until his death. Completion of the opera *Undine*, with libretto by Fouqué.

1814–15   Publication of Hoffmann's first collection of essays, sketches and short stories: *Fantasiestücke in Callots Manier* (containing *Ritter Gluck*, *Don Juan* and two books of *Kreisleriana*). Composition of *Die Elixiere des Teufels*, published the following year.

1816   *Nachtstücke I* (a collection of short stories, including *Der Sandmann*).

1817   *Nachtstücke II* (including *Das Majorat*).

1819   Volumes I and II of *Die Erzählungen der Serapionsbrüder*, containing thirteen tales, among them *Nussknacker und Mausekönig* and *Die Bergwerke zu Falun*. Part One of the unfinished novel *Kater Murr*.

1820   Volumes III and IV of *Die Serapionsbrüder*, including *Das Fräulein von Scudéri*, *Die Brautwahl* and fourteen other items.

1821   Part Two of *Kater Murr*; the projected third part was never started.

1822   Onset of the paralysis which eventually spread over his whole body. June 25: Death of Hoffmann from *tabes dorsalis*.